Fruitfulness

Fruitfulness

Émile Zola

MINT EDITIONS

Fruitfulness was first published in 1899.

This edition published by Mint Editions 2021.

ISBN 9781513281056 | E-ISBN 9781513286075

Published by Mint Editions®

**MINT
EDITIONS**
minteditionbooks.com

Publishing Director: Jennifer Newens
Design & Production: Rachel Lopez Metzger
Project Manager: Micaela Clark
Translated by Ernest Alfred Vizetelly
Typesetting: Westchester Publishing Services

Contents

I

That morning, in the little pavilion of Chantebled, on the verge of the woods, where they had now been installed for nearly a month, Mathieu was making all haste in order that he might catch the seven-o'clock train which every day conveyed him from Janville to Paris. It was already half-past six, and there were fully two thousand paces from the pavilion to Janville. Afterwards came a railway journey of three-quarters of an hour, and another journey of at least equal duration through Paris, from the Northern Railway terminus to the Boulevard de Grenelle. He seldom reached his office at the factory before half-past eight o'clock.

He had just kissed the children. Fortunately they were asleep; otherwise they would have linked their arms about his neck, laughed and kissed him, being ever unwilling to let him go. And as he hastily returned to the principal bedroom, he found his wife, Marianne, in bed there, but awake and sitting up. She had risen a moment before in order to pull back a curtain, and all the glow of that radiant May morning swept in, throwing a flood of gay sunshine over the fresh and healthy beauty of her four-and-twenty years. He, who was three years the elder, positively adored her.

"You know, my darling," said he, "I must make haste, for I fear I may miss the train—and so manage as well as you can. You still have thirty sous left, haven't you?"

She began to laugh, looking charming with her bare arms and her loose-flowing dark hair. The ever-recurring pecuniary worries of the household left her brave and joyous. Yet she had been married at seventeen, her husband at twenty, and they already had to provide for four children.

"Oh! we shall be all right," said she. "It's the end of the month to-day, and you'll receive your money to-night. I'll settle our little debts at Janville to-morrow. There are only the Lepailleurs, who worry me with their bill for milk and eggs, for they always look as if they fancied one meant to rob them. But with thirty sous, my dear! why, we shall have quite a high time of it!"

She was still laughing as she held out her firm white arms for the customary morning good-by.

"Run off, since you are in a hurry. I will go to meet you at the little bridge to-night."

"No, no, I insist on your going to bed! You know very well that even if I catch the quarter-to-eleven-o'clock train, I cannot reach Janville before half-past eleven. Ah! what a day I have before me! I had to promise the Moranges that I would take dejeuner with them; and this evening Beauchene is entertaining a customer—a business dinner, which I'm obliged to attend. So go to bed, and have a good sleep while you are waiting for me."

She gently nodded, but would give no positive promise. "Don't forget to call on the landlord," she added, "to tell him that the rain comes into the children's bedroom. It's not right that we should be soaked here as if we were on the high-way, even if those millionaires, the Seguins du Hordel, do let us have this place for merely six hundred francs a year."

"Ah, yes! I should have forgotten that. I will call on them, I promise you."

Then Mathieu took her in his arms, and there was no ending to their leave-taking. He still lingered. She had begun to laugh again, while giving him many a kiss in return for his own. There was all the love of bounding health between them, the joy that springs from the most perfect union, as when man and wife are but one both in flesh and in soul.

"Run off, run off, darling! Remember to tell Constance that, before she goes into the country, she ought to run down here some Sunday with Maurice."

"Yes, yes, I will tell her—till to-night, darling."

But he came back once more, caught her in a tight embrace, and pressed to her lips a long, loving kiss, which she returned with her whole heart. And then he hurried away.

He usually took an omnibus on his arrival at the Northern Railway terminus. But on the days when only thirty sous remained at home he bravely went through Paris on foot. It was, too, a very fine walk by way of the Rue la Fayette, the Opera-house, the Boulevards, the Rue Royale, and then, after the Place de la Concorde, the Cours la Reine, the Alma bridge, and the Quai d'Orsay.

Beauchene's works were at the very end of the Quai d'Orsay, between the Rue de la Federation and the Boulevard de Grenelle. There was hereabouts a large square plot, at one end of which, facing the quay, stood a handsome private house of brickwork with white stone dressings, that had been erected by Leon Beauchene, father of

ÉMILE ZOLA

Alexandre, the present master of the works. From the balconies one could perceive the houses which were perched aloft in the midst of greenery on the height of Passy, beyond the Seine; whilst on the right arose the campanile of the Trocadero palace. On one side, skirting the Rue de la Federation, one could still see a garden and a little house, which had been the modest dwelling of Leon Beauchene in the heroic days of desperate toil when he had laid the foundations of his fortune. Then the factory buildings and sheds, quite a mass of grayish structures, overtopped by two huge chimneys, occupied both the back part of the ground and that which fringed the Boulevard de Grenelle, the latter being shut off by long windowless walls. This important and well-known establishment manufactured chiefly agricultural appliances, from the most powerful machines to those ingenious and delicate implements on which particular care must be bestowed if perfection is to be attained. In addition to the hundreds of men who worked there daily, there were some fifty women, burnishers and polishers.

The entry to the workshops and offices was in the Rue de la Federation, through a large carriage way, whence one perceived the far-spreading yard, with its paving stones invariably black and often streaked by rivulets of steaming water. Dense smoke arose from the high chimneys, strident jets of steam emerged from the roof, whilst a low rumbling and a shaking of the ground betokened the activity within, the ceaseless bustle of labor.

It was thirty-five minutes past eight by the big clock of the central building when Mathieu crossed the yard towards the office which he occupied as chief designer. For eight years he had been employed at the works where, after a brilliant and special course of study, he had made his beginning as assistant draughtsman when but nineteen years old, receiving at that time a salary of one hundred francs a month. His father, Pierre Froment,* had four sons by Marie his wife—Jean the eldest, then Mathieu, Marc, and Luc—and while leaving them free to choose a particular career he had striven to give each of them some manual calling. Leon Beauchene, the founder of the works, had been dead a year, and his son Alexandre had succeeded him and married Constance Meunier, daughter of a very wealthy wall-paper manufacturer of the Marais, at the time when Mathieu entered the establishment, the master of which was scarcely five years older than himself. It was there that Mathieu had

---

* Of *Lourdes*, *Rome*, and *Paris*.

become acquainted with a poor cousin of Alexandre's, Marianne, then sixteen years old, whom he had married during the following year.

Marianne, when only twelve, had become dependent upon her uncle, Leon Beauchene. After all sorts of mishaps a brother of the latter, one Felix Beauchene, a man of adventurous mind but a blunderhead, had gone to Algeria with his wife and daughter, there to woo fortune afresh; and the farm he had established was indeed prospering when, during a sudden revival of Arab brigandage, both he and his wife were murdered and their home was destroyed. Thus the only place of refuge for the little girl, who had escaped miraculously, was the home of her uncle, who showed her great kindness during the two years of life that remained to him. With her, however, were Alexandre, whose companionship was rather dull, and his younger sister, Seraphine, a big, vicious, and flighty girl of eighteen, who, as it happened, soon left the house amid a frightful scandal—an elopement with a certain Baron Lowicz, a genuine baron, but a swindler and forger, to whom it became necessary to marry her. She then received a dowry of 300,000 francs. Alexandre, after his father's death, made a money match with Constance, who brought him half a million francs, and Marianne then found herself still more a stranger, still more isolated beside her new cousin, a thin, dry, authoritative woman, who ruled the home with absolute sway. Mathieu was there, however, and a few months sufficed: fine, powerful, and healthy love sprang up between the young people; there was no lightning flash such as throws the passion-swayed into each other's arms, but esteem, tenderness, faith, and that mutual conviction of happiness in reciprocal bestowal which tends to indissoluble marriage. And they were delighted at marrying penniless, at bringing one another but their full hearts forever and forever. The only change in Mathieu's circumstances was an increase of salary to two hundred francs a month. True, his new cousin by marriage just vaguely hinted at a possible partnership, but that would not be till some very much later date.

As it happened Mathieu Froment gradually became indispensable at the works. The young master, Alexandre Beauchene, passed through an anxious crisis. The dowry which his father had been forced to draw from his coffers in order to get Seraphine married, and other large expenses which had been occasioned by the girl's rebellious and perverse conduct, had left but little working capital in the business. Then, too, on the morrow of Leon Beauchene's death it was found that, with the carelessness often evinced in such matters, he had neglected to leave a will; so that Seraphine eagerly opposed her brother's interests, demanding her personal share of the inheritance, and even suggesting the sale of the works. The property had narrowly escaped being cut up, annihilated. And Alexandre Beauchene still shivered with terror and anger at the recollection of that time, amidst all his delight at having at last rid himself of his sister by paying her in money the liberally estimated value of her share. It was in order to fill up the void thus created in his finances that he had espoused the half-million represented by Constance—an ugly creature, as he himself bitterly acknowledged, coarse male as he was. Truth to tell, she was so thin, so scraggy, that before consenting to make her his wife he had often called her "that bag of bones." But, on the other hand, thanks to his marriage with her, all his losses were made good in five or six years' time; the business of the works even doubled, and great prosperity set in. And Mathieu, having become a most active and necessary coadjutor, ended by taking the post of chief designer, at a salary of four thousand two hundred francs per annum.

Morange, the chief accountant, whose office was near Mathieu's, thrust his head through the doorway as soon as he heard the young man installing himself at his drawing-table. "I say, my dear Froment," he exclaimed, "don't forget that you are to take dejeuner with us."

"Yes, yes, my good Morange, it's understood. I will look in for you at twelve o'clock."

Then Mathieu very carefully scrutinized a wash drawing of a very simple but powerful steam thresher, an invention of his own, on which he had been working for some time past, and which a big landowner of Beauce, M. Firon-Badinier, was to examine during the afternoon.

The door of the master's private room was suddenly thrown wide open and Beauchene appeared—tall, with a ruddy face, a narrow brow, and big brown, protruding eyes. He had a rather large nose, thick lips, and a full black beard, on which he bestowed great care, as he likewise did on his hair, which was carefully combed over his head in order to conceal the serious baldness that was already coming upon him, although he was scarcely two-and-thirty. Frock-coated the first thing in the morning, he was already smoking a big cigar; and his loud voice, his peals of gayety, his bustling ways, all betokened an egotist and good liver still in his prime, a man for whom money—capital increased and increased by the labor of others—was the one only sovereign power.

"Ah! ah! it's ready, is it not?" said he; "Monsieur Firon-Badinier has again written me that he will be here at three o'clock. And you know that I'm going to take you to the restaurant with him this evening; for one can never induce those fellows to give orders unless one plies them with good wine. It annoys Constance to have it done here; and, besides, I prefer to entertain those people in town. You warned Marianne, eh?"

"Certainly. She knows that I shall return by the quarter-to-eleven-o'clock train."

Beauchene had sunk upon a chair: "Ah! my dear fellow, I'm worn out," he continued; "I dined in town last night; I got to bed only at one o'clock. And there was a terrible lot of work waiting for me this morning. One positively needs to be made of iron."

Until a short time before he had shown himself a prodigious worker, endowed with really marvellous energy and strength. Moreover, he had given proof of unfailing business instinct with regard to many profitable undertakings. Invariably the first to appear at the works, he looked after everything, foresaw everything, filling the place with his bustling zeal, and doubling his output year by year. Recently, however, fatigue had been gaining ground on him. He had always sought plenty of amusement, even amid the hard-working life he led. But nowadays certain "sprees," as he called them, left him fairly exhausted.

He gazed at Mathieu: "You seem fit enough, you do!" he said. "How is it that you manage never to look tired?"

As a matter of fact, the young man who stood there erect before his drawing-table seemed possessed of the sturdy health of a young oak tree. Tall and slender, he had the broad, lofty, tower-like brow of the Froments. He wore his thick hair cut quite short, and his beard, which curled slightly, in a point. But the chief expression of his face rested in his eyes, which were at once deep and bright, keen and thoughtful, and almost invariably illumined by a smile. They showed him to be at once a man of thought and of action, very simple, very gay, and of a kindly disposition.

"Oh! I," he answered with a laugh, "I behave reasonably."

But Beauchene protested: "No, you don't! The man who already has four children when he is only twenty-seven can't claim to be reasonable. And twins too—your Blaise and your Denis to begin with! And then your boy Ambroise and your little girl Rose. Without counting the other little girl that you lost at her birth. Including her, you would now have had five youngsters, you wretched fellow! No, no, I'm the one who behaves reasonably—I, who have but one child, and, like a prudent, sensible man, desire no others!"

He often made such jesting remarks as these, through which filtered his genuine indignation; for he deemed the young couple to be over-careless of their interests, and declared that the prolificness of his cousin Marianne was quite scandalous.

Accustomed as Mathieu was to these attacks, which left him perfectly serene, he went on laughing, without even giving a reply, when a workman abruptly entered the room—one who was currently called "old Moineaud," though he was scarcely three-and-forty years of age. Short and thick-set, he had a bullet head, a bull's neck, and face and hands scarred and dented by more than a quarter of a century of toil. By calling he was a fitter, and he had come to submit a difficulty which had just arisen in the piecing together of a reaping machine. But, his employer, who was still angrily thinking of over-numerous families, did not give him time to explain his purpose.

"And you, old Moineaud, how many children have you?" he inquired.

"Seven, Monsieur Beauchene," the workman replied, somewhat taken aback. "I've lost three."

"So, including them, you would now have ten? Well, that's a nice state of things! How can you do otherwise than starve?"

Moineaud began to laugh like the gay thriftless Paris workman that he was. The little ones? Well, they grew up without his even noticing it, and, indeed, he was really fond of them, so long as they remained at home. And, besides, they worked as they grew older, and brought a little money in. However, he preferred to answer his employer with a jest which set them all laughing.

After he had explained the difficulty with the reaper, the others followed him to examine the work for themselves. They were already turning into a passage, when Beauchene, seeing the door of the women's workshop open, determined to pass that way, so that he might give his customary look around. It was a long, spacious place, where the polishers, in smocks of black serge, sat in double rows polishing and grinding their pieces at little work-boards. Nearly all of them were young, a few were pretty, but most had low and common faces. An animal odor and a stench of rancid oil pervaded the place.

The regulations required perfect silence there during work. Yet all the girls were gossiping. As soon, however, as the master's approach was signalled the chatter abruptly ceased. There was but one girl who, having her head turned, and thus seeing nothing of Beauchene, went on furiously abusing a companion, with whom she had previously started a dispute. She and the other were sisters, and, as it happened, daughters of old Moineaud. Euphrasie, the younger one, she who was shouting, was a skinny creature of seventeen, light-haired, with a long, lean, pointed face, uncomely and malignant; whereas the elder, Norine, barely nineteen, was a pretty girl, a blonde like her sister, but having a milky skin, and withal plump and sturdy, showing real shoulders, arms, and hips, and one of those bright sunshiny faces, with wild hair and black eyes, all the freshness of the Parisian hussy, aglow with the fleeting charm of youth.

Norine was ever quarrelling with Euphrasie, and was pleased to have her caught in a misdeed; so she allowed her to rattle on. And it thereupon became necessary for Beauchene to intervene. He habitually evinced great severity in the women's workshop, for he had hitherto held the view that an employer who jested with his workgirls was a lost man. Thus, in spite of the low character of which he was said to give proof in his walks abroad, there had as yet never been the faintest suggestion of scandal in connection with him and the women in his employ.

"Well, now, Mademoiselle Euphrasie!" he exclaimed; "do you intend to be quiet? This is quite improper. You are fined twenty sous, and if I hear you again you will be locked out for a week."

The girl had turned round in consternation. Then, stifling her rage, she cast a terrible glance at her sister, thinking that she might at least have warned her. But the other, with the discreet air of a pretty wench conscious of her attractiveness, continued smiling, looking her employer full in the face, as if certain that she had nothing to fear from him. Their eyes met, and for a couple of seconds their glances mingled. Then he, with flushed cheeks and an angry air, resumed, addressing one and all: "As soon as the superintendent turns her back you chatter away like so many magpies. Just be careful, or you will have to deal with me!"

Moineaud, the father, had witnessed the scene unmoved, as if the two girls—she whom the master had scolded, and she who slyly gazed at him—were not his own daughters. And now the round was resumed and the three men quitted the women's workshop amidst profound silence, which only the whir of the little grinders disturbed.

When the fitting difficulty had been overcome downstairs and Moineaud had received his orders, Beauchene returned to his residence accompanied by Mathieu, who wished to convey Marianne's invitation to Constance. A gallery connected the black factory buildings with the luxurious private house on the quay. And they found Constance in a little drawing-room hung with yellow satin, a room to which she was very partial. She was seated near a sofa, on which lay little Maurice, her fondly prized and only child, who had just completed his seventh year.

"Is he ill?" inquired Mathieu.

The child seemed sturdily built, and he greatly resembled his father, though he had a more massive jaw. But he was pale and there was a faint ring round his heavy eyelids. His mother, that "bag of bones," a little dark woman, yellow and withered at six-and-twenty, looked at him with an expression of egotistical pride.

"Oh, no! he's never ill," she answered. "Only he has been complaining of his legs. And so I made him lie down, and I wrote last night to ask Dr. Boutan to call this morning."

"Pooh!" exclaimed Beauchene with a hearty laugh, "women are all the same! A child who is as strong as a Turk! I should just like anybody to tell me that he isn't strong."

Precisely at that moment in walked Dr. Boutan, a short, stout man of forty, with very keen eyes set in a clean-shaven, heavy, but extremely good-natured face. He at once examined the child, felt and sounded him; then with his kindly yet serious air he said: "No, no, there's nothing. It is the mere effect of growth. The lad has become rather pale through spending the winter in Paris, but a few months in the open air, in the country, will set him right again."

"I told you so!" cried Beauchene.

Constance had kept her son's little hand in her own. He had again stretched himself out and closed his eyes in a weary way, whilst she, in her happiness, continued smiling. Whenever she chose she could appear quite pleasant-looking, however unprepossessing might be her features. The doctor had seated himself, for he was fond of lingering and chatting in the houses of friends. A general practitioner, and one who more particularly tended the ailments of women and children, he was naturally a confessor, knew all sorts of secrets, and was quite at home in family circles. It was he who had attended Constance at the birth of that much-spoiled only son, and Marianne at the advent of the four children she already had.

Mathieu had remained standing, awaiting an opportunity to deliver his invitation. "Well," said he, "if you are soon leaving for the country, you must come one Sunday to Janville. My wife would be so delighted to see you there, to show you our encampment."

Then he jested respecting the bareness of the lonely pavilion which they occupied, recounting that as yet they possessed only a dozen plates and five egg-cups. But Beauchene knew the pavilion, for he went shooting in the neighborhood every winter, having a share in the tenancy of some extensive woods, the shooting-rights over which had been parcelled out by the owner.

"Seguin," said he, "is a friend of mine. I have lunched at your pavilion. It's a perfect hovel!"

Then Constance, contemptuous at the idea of such poverty, recalled what Madame Seguin—to whom she referred as Valentine—had told her of the dilapidated condition of the old shooting-box. But the doctor, after listening with a smile, broke in:

"Mme. Seguin is a patient of mine. At the time when her last child was born I advised her to stay at that pavilion. The atmosphere is wholesome, and children ought to spring up there like couch-grass."

Thereupon, with a sonorous laugh, Beauchene began to jest in his habitual way, remarking that if the doctor were correct there would probably be no end to Mathieu's progeny, numerous as it already was. But this elicited an angry protest from Constance, who on the subject of children held the same views as her husband himself professed in his more serious moments.

Mathieu thoroughly understood what they both meant. They regarded him and his wife with derisive pity, tinged with anger.

The advent of the young couple's last child, little Rose, had already increased their expenses to such a point that they had been obliged to seek refuge in the country, in a mere pauper's hovel. And yet, in spite of Beauchene's sneers and Constance's angry remarks, Mathieu outwardly remained very calm. Constance and Marianne had never been able to agree; they differed too much in all respects; and for his part he laughed off every attack, unwilling as he was to let anger master him, lest a rupture should ensue.

But Beauchene waxed passionate on the subject. That question of the birth-rate and the present-day falling off in population was one which he thought he had completely mastered, and on which he held forth at length authoritatively. He began by challenging the impartiality of Boutan, whom he knew to be a fervent partisan of large families. He made merry with him, declaring that no medical man could possibly have a disinterested opinion on the subject. Then he brought out all that he vaguely knew of Malthusianism, the geometrical increase of births, and the arithmetical increase of food-substances, the earth becoming so populous as to be reduced to a state of famine within two centuries. It was the poor's own fault, said he, if they led a life of starvation; they had only to limit themselves to as many children as they could provide for. The rich were falsely accused of social wrong-doing; they were by no means responsible for poverty. Indeed, they were the only reasonable people; they alone, by limiting their families, acted as good citizens should act. And he became quite triumphant, repeating that he knew of no cause for self-reproach, and that his ever-growing fortune left him with an easy conscience. It was so much the worse for the poor, if they were bent on remaining poor. In vain did the doctor urge that the Malthusian theories were shattered, that the calculations had been based on a possible, not a real, increase of population; in vain too did he prove that the present-day economic crisis, the evil distribution of wealth under the capitalist system, was the one hateful cause of poverty, and that whenever labor should be justly apportioned among one and all the fruitful earth would easily provide sustenance for happy men ten times more numerous than they are now. The other refused to listen to anything, took refuge in his egotism, declared that all those matters were no concern of his, that he felt no remorse at being rich, and that those who wished to become rich had, in the main, simply to do as he had done.

"Then, logically, this is the end of France, eh?" Boutan remarked maliciously. "The number of births ever increases in Germany, Russia, and elsewhere, while it decreases in a terrible way among us. Numerically the rank we occupy in Europe is already very inferior to what it formerly was; and yet number means power more than ever nowadays. It has been calculated that an average of four children per family is necessary in order that population may increase and the strength of a nation be maintained. You have but one child; you are a bad patriot."

At this Beauchene flew into a tantrum, quite beside himself, and gasped: "I a bad patriot! I, who kill myself with hard work! I, who even export French machinery! . . . Yes, certainly I see families, acquaintances around me who may well allow themselves four children; and I grant that they deserve censure when they have no families. But as for me, my dear doctor, it is impossible. You know very well that in my position I absolutely can't."

Then, for the hundredth time, he gave his reasons, relating how the works had narrowly escaped being cut into pieces, annihilated, simply because he had unfortunately been burdened with a sister. Seraphine had behaved abominably. There had been first her dowry; next her demands for the division of the property on their father's death; and the works had been saved only by means of a large pecuniary sacrifice which had long crippled their prosperity. And people imagined that he would be as imprudent as his father! Why, if Maurice should have a brother or a sister, he might hereafter find himself in the same dire embarrassment, in which the family property might already have been destroyed. No, no! He would not expose the boy to the necessity of dividing the inheritance in accordance with badly framed laws. He was resolved that Maurice should be the sole master of the fortune which he himself had derived from his father, and which he would transmit to his heir increased tenfold. For his son he dreamt of supreme wealth, a colossal fortune, such as nowadays alone ensures power.

Mathieu, refraining from any intervention, listened and remained grave; for this question of the birth-rate seemed to him a frightful one, the foremost of all questions, deciding the destiny of mankind and the world. There has never been any progress but such as has been determined by increase of births. If nations have accomplished evolutions, if civilization has advanced, it is because the nations have multiplied and subsequently spread through all the countries of the earth. And will not to-morrow's evolution, the advent of truth and justice, be brought about by the constant onslaught of the greater number, the revolutionary fruitfulness of the toilers and the poor?

It is quite true that Mathieu did not plainly say all these things to himself; indeed, he felt slightly ashamed of the four children that he already had, and was disturbed by the counsels of prudence addressed to him by the Beauchenes. But within him there struggled his faith in life, his belief that the greatest possible sum of life must bring about the greatest sum of happiness.

At last, wishing to change the subject, he bethought himself of Marianne's commission, and at the first favorable opportunity exclaimed: "Well, we shall rely on you, Marianne and I, for Sunday after next, at Janville."

But there was still no answer, for just then a servant came to say that a woman with an infant in her arms desired to see Madame. And Beauchene, having recognized the wife of Moineaud, the fitter, bade her come in. Boutan, who had now risen, was prompted by curiosity to remain a little longer.

La Moineaude, short and fat like her husband, was a woman of about forty, worn out before her time, with ashen face, pale eyes, thin faded hair, and a weak mouth which already lacked many teeth. A large family had been too much for her; and, moreover, she took no care of herself.

"Well, my good woman," Constance inquired, "what do you wish with me?"

But La Moineaude remained quite scared by the sight of all those people whom she had not expected to find there. She said nothing. She had hoped to speak to the lady privately.

"Is this your last-born?" Beauchene asked her as he looked at the pale, puny child on her arm.

"Yes, monsieur, it's my little Alfred; he's ten months old and I've had to wean him, for I couldn't feed him any longer. I had nine others before this one, but three are dead. My eldest son, Eugene, is a soldier in Tonquin. You have my two big girls, Euphrasie and Norine, at the works. And I have three left at home—Victor, who is now fifteen, then Cecile and Irma, who are ten and seven. After Irma I thought I had done with children for good, and I was well pleased. But, you see, this urchin came! And I, forty too—it's not just! The good Lord must surely have abandoned us."

Then Dr. Boutan began to question her. He avoided looking at the Beauchenes, but there was a malicious twinkle in his little eyes, and it was evident that he took pleasure in recapitulating the employer's arguments against excessive prolificness. He pretended to get angry and to reproach the Moineauds for their ten wretched children—the boys fated to become food for powder, the girls always liable to misfortune. And he gave the woman to understand that it was her own fault if she was in distress; for people with a tribe of children about them could never become rich. And the poor creature sadly answered that he was quite right, but that no idea of becoming rich could ever have entered their heads. Moineaud knew well enough that he would never be a cabinet minister, and so it was all the same to them how many children they might have on their hands. Indeed, a number proved a help when the youngsters grew old enough to go out to work.

Beauchene had become silent and slowly paced the room. A slight chill, a feeling of uneasiness was springing up, and so Constance made haste to inquire: "Well, my good woman, what is it I can do for you?"

"*Mon Dieu*, madame, it worries me; it's something which Moineaud didn't dare to ask of Monsieur Beauchene. For my part I hoped to find you alone and beg you to intercede for us. The fact is we should be very, very grateful if our little Victor could only be taken on at the works."

"But he is only fifteen," exclaimed Beauchene. "You must wait till he's sixteen. The law is strict."

"No doubt. Only one might perhaps just tell a little fib. It would be rendering us such a service—"

"No, it is impossible."

Big tears welled into La Moineaude's eyes. And Mathieu, who had listened with passionate interest, felt quite upset. Ah! that wretched toil-doomed flesh that hastened to offer itself without waiting until it was even ripe for work! Ah! the laborer who is prepared to lie, whom hunger sets against the very law designed for his own protection!

When La Moineaude had gone off in despair the doctor continued speaking of juvenile and female labor. As soon as a woman first finds herself a mother she can no longer continue toiling at a factory. Her lying-in and the nursing of her babe force her to remain at home, or else grievous infirmities may ensue for her and her offspring. As for the child, it becomes anemic, sometimes crippled; besides, it helps to keep wages down by being taken to work at a low scale of remuneration. Then the doctor went on to speak of the prolificness of wretchedness, the swarming of the lower classes. Was not the most hateful natality of all that which meant the endless increase of starvelings and social rebels?

"I perfectly understand you," Beauchene ended by saying, without any show of anger, as he abruptly brought his perambulations to an end. "You want to place me in contradiction with myself, and make me confess that I accept Moineaud's seven children and need them, whereas I, with my fixed determination to rest content with an only son, suppress, as it were, a family in order that I may not have to subdivide my estate. France, 'the country of only sons,' as folks say nowadays—that's it, eh? But, my dear fellow, the question is so intricate, and at bottom I am altogether in the right!"

Then he wished to explain things, and clapped his hand to his breast, exclaiming that he was a liberal, a democrat, ready to demand all really progressive measures. He willingly recognized that children were necessary, that the army required soldiers, and the factories workmen. Only he also invoked the prudential duties of the higher classes, and reasoned after the fashion of a man of wealth, a conservative clinging to the fortune he has acquired.

Mathieu meanwhile ended by understanding the brutal truth: Capital is compelled to favor the multiplication of lives foredoomed to wretchedness; in spite of everything it must stimulate the prolificness of the wage-earning classes, in order that its profits may continue. The law is that there must always be an excess of children in order that there may be enough cheap workers. Then also speculation on the wages' ratio wrests all nobility from labor, which is regarded as the worst misfortune a man can be condemned to, when in reality it is the most precious of boons. Such, then, is the cancer preying upon mankind. In countries of political equality and economical inequality the capitalist regime, the faulty distribution of wealth, at once restrains and precipitates the birth-rate by perpetually increasing the wrongful apportionment of means. On one side are the rich folk with "only" sons, who continually increase their fortunes; on the other, the poor folk, who, by reason of their unrestrained prolificness, see the little they possess crumble yet more and more. If labor be honored to-morrow, if a just apportionment of wealth be arrived at, equilibrium will be restored. Otherwise social revolution lies at the end of the road.

But Beauchene, in his triumphant manner, tried to show that he possessed great breadth of mind; he admitted the disquieting strides of a decrease of population, and denounced the causes of it—alcoholism, militarism, excessive mortality among infants, and other numerous matters. Then he indicated remedies; first, reductions in taxation, fiscal means in which he had little faith; then freedom to will one's estate as one pleased, which seemed to him more efficacious; a change, too, in the marriage laws, without forgetting the granting of affiliation rights.

However, Boutan ended by interrupting him. "All the legislative measures in the world will do nothing," said the doctor. "Manners and customs, our notions of what is moral and what is not, our very conceptions of the beautiful in life—all must be changed. If France is becoming depopulated, it is because she so chooses. It is simply necessary then for her to choose so no longer. But what a task—a whole world to create anew!"

At this Mathieu raised a superb cry: "Well! we'll create it. I've begun well enough, surely!"

But Constance, after laughing in a constrained way, in her turn thought it as well to change the subject. And so she at last replied to his invitation, saying that she would do her best to go to Janville, though she feared she might not be able to dispose of a Sunday to do so.

Dr. Boutan then took his leave, and was escorted to the door by Beauchene, who still went on jesting, like a man well pleased with life, one who was satisfied with himself and others, and who felt certain of being able to arrange things as might best suit his pleasure and his interests.

An hour later, a few minutes after midday, as Mathieu, who had been delayed in the works, went up to the offices to fetch Morange as he had promised to do, it occurred to him to take a short cut through the women's workshop. And there, in that spacious gallery, already deserted and silent, he came upon an unexpected scene which utterly amazed him. On some pretext or other Norine had lingered there the last, and Beauchene was with her, clasping her around the waist whilst he eagerly pressed his lips to hers. But all at once they caught sight of Mathieu and remained thunderstruck. And he, for his part, fled precipitately, deeply annoyed at having been a surprised witness to such a secret.

II

M orange, the chief accountant at Beauchene's works, was a man of thirty-eight, bald and already gray-headed, but with a superb dark, fan-shaped beard, of which he was very proud. His full limpid eyes, straight nose, and well-shaped if somewhat large mouth had in his younger days given him the reputation of being a handsome fellow. He still took great care of himself, invariably wore a tall silk hat, and preserved the correct appearance of a very painstaking and well-bred clerk.

"You don't know our new flat yet, do you?" he asked Mathieu as he led him away. "Oh! it's perfect, as you will see. A bedroom for us and another for Reine. And it is so close to the works too. I get there in four minutes, watch in hand."

He, Morange, was the son of a petty commercial clerk who had died on his stool after forty years of cloistral office-life. And he had married a clerk's daughter, one Valerie Duchemin, the eldest of four girls whose parents' home had been turned into a perfect hell, full of shameful wretchedness and unacknowledgable poverty, through this abominable incumbrance. Valerie, who was good-looking and ambitious, was lucky enough, however, to marry that handsome, honest, and hard-working fellow, Morange, although she was quite without a dowry; and, this accomplished, she indulged in the dream of climbing a little higher up the social ladder, and freeing herself from the loathsome world of petty clerkdom by making the son whom she hoped to have either an advocate or a doctor. Unfortunately the much-desired child proved to be a girl; and Valerie trembled, fearful of finding herself at last with four daughters on her hands, just as her mother had. Her dream thereupon changed, and she resolved to incite her husband onward to the highest posts, so that she might ultimately give her daughter a large dowry, and by this means gain that admittance to superior spheres which she so eagerly desired. Her husband, who was weak and extremely fond of her, ended by sharing her ambition, ever revolving schemes of pride and conquest for her benefit. But he had now been eight years at the Beauchene works, and he still earned but five thousand francs a year. This drove him and his wife to despair. Assuredly it was not at Beauchene's that he would ever make his fortune.

"You see!" he exclaimed, after going a couple of hundred yards with Mathieu along the Boulevard de Grenelle, "it is that new house yonder at the street corner. It has a stylish appearance, eh?"

Mathieu then perceived a lofty modern pile, ornamented with balconies and sculpture work, which looked quite out of place among the poor little houses predominating in the district.

"Why, it is a palace!" he exclaimed, in order to please Morange, who thereupon drew himself up quite proudly.

"You will see the staircase, my dear fellow! Our place, you know, is on the fifth floor. But that is of no consequence with such a staircase, so easy, so soft, that one climbs it almost without knowing."

Thereupon Morange showed his guest into the vestibule as if he were ushering him into a temple. The stucco walls gleamed brightly; there was a carpet on the stairs, and colored glass in the windows. And when, on reaching the fifth story, the cashier opened the door with his latchkey, he repeated, with an air of delight: "You will see, you will see!"

Valerie and Reine must have been on the watch, for they hastened forward. At thirty-two Valerie was still young and charming. She was a pleasant-looking brunette, with a round smiling face in a setting of superb hair. She had a full, round bust, and admirable shoulders, of which her husband felt quite proud whenever she showed herself in a low-necked dress. Reine, at this time twelve years old, was the very portrait of her mother, showing much the same smiling, if rather longer, face under similar black tresses.

"Ah! it is very kind of you to accept our invitation," said Valerie gayly as she pressed both Mathieu's hands. "What a pity that Madame Froment could not come with you! Reine, why don't you relieve the gentleman of his hat?"

Then she immediately continued: "We have a nice light anteroom, you see. Would you like to glance over our flat while the eggs are being boiled? That will always be one thing done, and you will then at least know where you are lunching."

All this was said in such an agreeable way, and Morange on his side smiled so good-naturedly, that Mathieu willingly lent himself to this innocent display of vanity. First came the parlor, the corner room, the walls of which were covered with pearl-gray paper with a design of golden flowers, while the furniture consisted of some of those white lacquered Louis XVI pieces which makers turn out by the gross. The rosewood piano showed like a big black blot amidst all the rest. Then, overlooking the Boulevard de Grenelle, came Reine's bedroom, pale blue, with furniture of polished pine. Her parents' room, a very small apartment, was at the other end of the flat, separated from the parlor by the dining-room.

The hangings adorning it were yellow; and a bedstead, a washstand, and a wardrobe, all of thuya, had been crowded into it. Finally the classic "old carved oak" triumphed in the dining-room, where a heavily gilded hanging lamp flashed like fire above the table, dazzling in its whiteness.

"Why, it's delightful," Mathieu, repeated, by way of politeness; "why, it's a real gem of a place."

In their excitement, father, mother, and daughter never ceased leading him hither and thither, explaining matters to him and making him feel the things. He was most struck, by the circumstance that the place recalled something he had seen before; he seemed to be familiar with the arrangement of the drawing-room, and with the way in which the nicknacks in the bedchamber were set out. And all at once he remembered. Influenced by envy and covert admiration, the Moranges, despite themselves, no doubt, had tried to copy the Beauchenes. Always short of money as they were, they could only and by dint of great sacrifices indulge in a species of make-believe luxury. Nevertheless they were proud of it, and, by imitating the envied higher class from afar, they imagined that they drew nearer to it.

"And then," Morange exclaimed, as he opened the dining-room window, "there is also this."

Outside, a balcony ran along the house-front, and at that height the view was really a very fine one, similar to that obtained from the Beauchene mansion but more extensive, the Seine showing in the distance, and the heights of Passy rising above the nearer and lower house-roofs.

Valerie also called attention to the prospect. "It is magnificent, is it not?" said she; "far better than the few trees that one can see from the quay."

The servant was now bringing the boiled eggs and they took their seats at table, while Morange victoriously explained that the place altogether cost him sixteen hundred francs a year. It was cheap indeed, though the amount was a heavy charge on Morange's slender income. Mathieu now began to understand that he had been invited more particularly to admire the new flat, and these worthy people seemed so delighted to triumph over it before him that he took the matter gayly and without thought of spite. There was no calculating ambition in his nature; he envied nothing of the luxury he brushed against in other people's homes, and he was quite satisfied with the snug modest life he led with Marianne and his children. Thus he simply felt surprised at finding the Moranges so desirous of cutting a figure and making money, and looked at them with a somewhat sad smile.

Valerie was wearing a pretty gown of foulard with a pattern of little yellow flowers, while her daughter, Reine, whom she liked to deck out coquettishly, had a frock of blue linen stuff. There was rather too much luxury about the meal also. Soles followed the eggs, and then came cutlets, and afterwards asparagus.

The conversation began with some mention of Janville.

"And so your children are in good health? Oh! they are very fine children indeed. And you really like the country? How funny! I think I should feel dreadfully bored there, for there is too great a lack of amusements. Why, yes, we shall be delighted to go to see you there, since Madame Froment is kind enough to invite us."

Then, as was bound to happen, the talk turned on the Beauchenes. This was a subject which haunted the Moranges, who lived in perpetual admiration of the Beauchenes, though at times they covertly criticised them. Valerie was very proud of being privileged to attend Constance's Saturday "at-homes," and of having been twice invited to dinner by her during the previous winter. She on her side now had a day of her own, Tuesday, and she even gave little private parties, and half ruined herself in providing refreshments at them. As for her acquaintances, she spoke with profound respect of Mme. Seguin du Hordel and that lady's magnificent mansion in the Avenue d'Antin, for Constance had obligingly obtained her an invitation to a ball there. But she was particularly vain of the friendship of Beauchene's sister, Seraphine, whom she invariably called "Madame la Baronne de Lowicz."

"The Baroness came to my at-home one afternoon," she said. "She is so very good-natured and so gay! You knew her formerly, did you not? After her marriage, eh? when she became reconciled to her brother and their wretched disputes about money matters were over. By the way, she has no great liking for Madame Beauchene, as you must know."

Then she again reverted to the manufacturer's wife, declared that little Maurice, however sturdy he might look, was simply puffed out with bad flesh; and she remarked that it would be a terrible blow for the parents if they should lose that only son. The subject of children was thus started, and when Mathieu, laughing, observed that they, the Moranges, had but one child, the cashier protested that it was unfair to compare him with M. Beauchene, who was such a wealthy man. Valerie, for her part, pictured the position of her parents, afflicted with four daughters, who had been obliged to wait months and months for boots and frocks and hats, and had grown up anyhow, in perpetual terror lest they should never find husbands. A family was all very well, but when it happened to consist of daughters the situation became terrible for people of limited means; for if daughters were to be launched properly into life they must have dowries.

"Besides," said she, "I am very ambitious for my husband, and I am convinced that he may rise to a very high position if he will only listen to me. But he must not be saddled with a lot of incumbrances. As things stand, I trust that we may be able to get rich and give Reine a suitable dowry."

Morange, quite moved by this little speech, caught hold of his wife's hand and kissed it. Weak and good-natured as he was, Valerie was really the one with will. It was she who had instilled some ambition into him, and he esteemed her the more for it.

"My wife is a thoroughly good woman, you know, my dear Froment," said he. "She has a good head as well as a good heart."

Then, while Valerie recapitulated her dream of wealth, the splendid flat she would have, the receptions she would hold, and the two months which, like the Beauchenes, she would spend at the seaside every summer, Mathieu looked at her and her husband and pondered their position. Their case was very different from that of old Moineaud, who knew that he would never be a cabinet minister. Morange possibly dreamt that his wife would indeed make him a minister some day. Every petty bourgeois in a democratic community has a chance of rising and wishes to do so. Indeed, there is a universal, ferocious rush, each seeking to push the others aside so that he may the more speedily climb a rung of the social ladder. This general ascent, this phenomenon akin to capillarity, is possible only in a country where political equality and economic inequality prevail; for each has the same right to fortune and has but to conquer it. There is, however, a struggle of the vilest egotism, if one wishes to taste the pleasures of the highly placed, pleasures which are displayed to the gaze of all and are eagerly coveted by nearly everybody in the lower spheres. Under a democratic constitution a nation cannot live happily if its manners and customs are not simple, and if the conditions of life are not virtually equal for one and all. Under other circumstances than these the liberal professions prove all-devouring: there is a rush for public functions; manual toil is regarded with contempt; luxury increases and becomes necessary; and wealth and power are furiously appropriated by assault in order that one may greedily taste the voluptuousness of enjoyment. And in such a state of affairs, children, as Valerie put it, were incumbrances, whereas one needed to be free, absolutely unburdened, if one wished to climb over all one's competitors.

Mathieu also thought of that law of imitation which impels even the least fortunate to impoverish themselves by striving to copy the happy ones of the world. How great the distress which really lurks beneath that envied luxury that is copied at such great cost! All sorts of useless needs are created, and production is turned aside from the strictly necessary. One can no longer express hardship by saying that people lack bread; what they lack in the majority of cases is the superfluous, which they are unable to renounce without imagining that they have gone to the dogs and are in danger of starvation.

At dessert, when the servant was no longer present, Morange, excited by his good meal, became expansive. Glancing at his wife he winked towards their guest, saying:

"Come, he's a safe friend; one may tell him everything."

And when Valerie had consented with a smile and a nod, he went on: "Well, this is the matter, my dear fellow: it is possible that I may soon leave the works. Oh! it's not decided, but I'm thinking of it. Yes, I've been thinking of it for some months past; for, when all is said, to earn five thousand francs a year, after eight years' zeal, and to think that one will never earn much more, is enough to make one despair of life."

"It's monstrous," the young woman interrupted: "it is like breaking one's head intentionally against a wall."

"Well, in such circumstances, my dear friend, the best course is to look out for something elsewhere, is it not? Do you remember Michaud, whom I had under my orders at the works some six years ago? A very intelligent fellow he was. Well, scarcely six years have elapsed since he left us to go to the Credit National, and what do you think he is now earning there? Twelve thousand francs—you hear me—twelve thousand francs!"

The last words rang out like a trumpet-call. The Moranges' eyes dilated with ecstasy. Even the little girl became very red.

"Last March," continued Morange, "I happened to meet Michaud, who told me all that, and showed himself very amiable. He offered to take me with him and help me on in my turn. Only there's some risk to run. He explained to me that I must at first accept three thousand six hundred, so as to rise gradually to a very big figure. But three thousand six hundred! How can one live on that in the meantime, especially now that this flat has increased our expenses?"

At this Valerie broke in impetuously: "'Nothing venture, nothing have!' That's what I keep on repeating to him. Of course I am in favor of prudence; I would never let him do anything rash which might compromise his future. But, at the same time, he can't moulder away in a situation unworthy of him."

"And so you have made up your minds?" asked Mathieu.

"Well, my wife has calculated everything," Morange replied; "and, yes, we have made up our minds, provided, of course, that nothing unforeseen occurs. Besides, it is only in October that any situation will be open at the Credit National. But, I say, my dear friend, keep the matter entirely to yourself, for we don't want to quarrel with the Beauchenes just now."

Then he looked at his watch, for, like a good clerk, he was very punctual, and did not wish to be late at the office. The servant was hurried, the coffee was served, and they were drinking it, boiling hot as it was, when the arrival of a visitor upset the little household and caused everything to be forgotten.

"Oh!" exclaimed Valerie, as she hastily rose, flushed with pride, "Madame la Baronne de Lowicz!"

Seraphine, at this time nine-and-twenty, was red-haired, tall and elegant, with magnificent shoulders which were known to all Paris. Her red lips were wreathed in a triumphant smile, and a voluptuous flame ever shone in her large brown eyes flecked with gold.

"Pray don't disturb yourselves, my friends," said she. "Your servant wanted to show me into the drawing-room, but I insisted on coming in here, because it is rather a pressing matter. I have come to fetch your charming little Reine to take her to a matinee at the Circus."

A fresh explosion of delight ensued. The child remained speechless with joy, whilst the mother exulted and rattled on: "Oh! Madame la Baronne, you are really too kind! You are spoiling the child. But the fact is that she isn't dressed, and you will have to wait a moment. Come, child, make haste, I will help you—ten minutes, you understand—I won't keep you waiting a moment longer."

Seraphine remained alone with the two men. She had made a gesture of surprise on perceiving Mathieu, whose hand, like an old friend, she now shook.

"And you, are you quite well?" she asked.

"Quite well," he answered; and as she sat down near him he instinctively pushed his chair back. He did not seem at all pleased at having met her.

He had been on familiar terms with her during his earlier days at the Beauchene works. She was a frantic pleasure-lover, and destitute of both conscience and moral principles. Her conduct had given rise to scandal even before her extraordinary elopement with Baron de Lowicz, that needy adventurer with a face like an archangel's and the soul of a swindler. The result of the union was a stillborn child. Then Seraphine, who was extremely egotistical and avaricious, quarrelled with her husband and drove him away. He repaired to Berlin, and was killed there in a brawl at a gambling den. Delighted at being rid of him, Seraphine made every use of her liberty as a young widow. She figured at every fete, took part in every kind of amusement, and many scandalous stories were told of her; but she contrived to keep up appearances and was thus still received everywhere.

"You are living in the country, are you not?" she asked again, turning towards Mathieu.

"Yes, we have been there for three weeks past."

"Constance told me of it. I met her the other day at Madame Seguin's. We are on the best terms possible, you know, now that I give my brother good advice."

In point of fact her sister-in-law, Constance, hated her, but with her usual boldness she treated the matter as a joke.

"We talked about Dr. Gaude," she resumed; "I fancied that she wanted to ask for his address; but she did not dare."

"Dr. Gaude!" interrupted Morange. "Ah! yes, a friend of my wife's spoke to her about him. He's a wonderfully clever man, it appears. Some of his operations are like miracles."

Then he went on talking of Dr. Gaude's clinic at the Hopital Marbeuf, a clinic whither society folks hastened to see operations performed, just as they might go to a theatre. The doctor, who was fond of money, and who bled his wealthy lady patients in more senses than one, was likewise partial to glory and proud of accomplishing the most dangerous experiments on the unhappy creatures who fell into his hands. The newspapers were always talking about him, his cures were constantly puffed and advertised by way of inducing fine ladies to trust themselves to his skill. And he certainly accomplished wonders, cutting and carving his patients in the quietest, most unconcerned way possible, with never a scruple, never a doubt as to whether what he did was strictly right or not.

Seraphine had begun to laugh, showing her white wolfish teeth between her blood-red lips, when she noticed the horrified expression which had appeared on Mathieu's face since Gaude had been spoken of. "Ah!" said she; "there's a man, now, who in nowise resembles your squeamish Dr. Boutan, who is always prattling about the birth-rate. I can't understand why Constance keeps to that old-fashioned booby, holding the views she does. She is quite right, you know, in her opinions. I fully share them."

Morange laughed complaisantly. He wished to show her that his opinions were the same. However, as Valerie did not return with Reine, he grew impatient, and asked permission to go and see what they were about. Perhaps he himself might be able to help in getting the child ready.

As soon as Seraphine was alone with Mathieu she turned her big, ardent, gold-flecked eyes upon him. She no longer laughed with the same laugh as a moment previously; an expression of voluptuous irony appeared on her bold bad face. After a spell of silence she inquired, "And is my good cousin Marianne quite well?"

"Quite well," replied Mathieu.

"And the children are still growing?"

"Yes, still growing."

"So you are happy, like a good paterfamilias, in your little nook?"

"Perfectly happy."

Again she lapsed into silence, but she did not cease to look at him, more provoking, more radiant than ever, with the charm of a young sorceress whose eyes burn and poison men's hearts. And at last she slowly resumed: "And so it is all over between us?"

He made a gesture in token of assent. There had long since been a passing fancy between them. He had been nineteen at the time, and she two-and-twenty. He had then but just entered life, and she was already married. But a few months later he had fallen in love with Marianne, and had then entirely freed himself from her.

"All over—really?" she again inquired, smiling but aggressive.

She was looking very beautiful and bold, seeking to tempt him and carry him off from that silly little cousin of hers, whose tears would simply have made her laugh. And as Mathieu did not this time give her any answer, even by a wave of the hand, she went on: "I prefer that: don't reply: don't say that it is all over. You might make a mistake, you know."

For a moment Mathieu's eyes flashed, then he closed them in order that he might no longer see Seraphine, who was leaning towards him. It seemed as if all the past were coming back. She almost pressed her lips to his as she whispered that she still loved him; and when he drew back, full of mingled emotion and annoyance, she raised her little hand to his mouth as if she feared that he was again going to say no.

"Be quiet," said she; "they are coming."

The Moranges were now indeed returning with Reine, whose hair had been curled. The child looked quite delicious in her frock of rose silk decked with white lace, and her large hat trimmed with some of the dress material. Her gay round face showed with flowery delicacy under the rose silk.

"Oh, what a love!" exclaimed Seraphine by way of pleasing the parents. "Somebody will be stealing her from me, you know."

Then it occurred to her to kiss the child in passionate fashion, feigning the emotion of a woman who regrets that she is childless. "Yes; indeed one regrets it very much when one sees such a treasure as this sweet girl of yours. Ah! if one could only be sure that God would give one such a charming child—well, at all events, I shall steal her from you; you need not expect me to bring her back again."

The enraptured Moranges laughed delightedly. And Mathieu, who knew her well, listened in stupefaction. How many times during their short and passionate attachment had she not inveighed against children! In her estimation maternity poisoned love, aged woman, and made a horror of her in the eyes of man.

The Moranges accompanied her and Reine to the landing. And they could not find words warm enough to express their happiness at seeing such coveted wealth and luxury come to seek their daughter. When the door of the flat was closed Valerie darted on to the balcony, exclaiming, "Let us see them drive off."

Morange, who no longer gave a thought to the office, took up a position near her, and called Mathieu and compelled him likewise to lean over and look down. A well-appointed victoria was waiting below with a superb-looking coachman motionless on the box-seat. This sight put a finishing touch to the excitement of the Moranges. When Seraphine had installed the little girl beside her, they laughed aloud.

"How pretty she looks! How happy she must feel!"

Reine must have been conscious that they were looking at her, for she raised her head, smiled and bowed. And Seraphine did the same, while the horse broke into a trot and turned the corner of the avenue. Then came a final explosion—

"Look at her!" repeated Valerie; "she is so candid! At twelve years old she is still as innocent as a child in her cradle. You know that I trust her to nobody. Wouldn't one think her a little duchess who has always had a carriage of her own?"

Then Morange reverted to his dream of fortune. "Well," said he, "I hope that she *will* have a carriage when we marry her off. Just let me get into the Credit National and you will see all your desires fulfilled."

And turning towards Mathieu he added, "There are three of us, and, as I have said before, that is quite enough for a man to provide for, especially as money is so hard to earn."

III

At the works during the afternoon Mathieu, who wished to be free earlier than usual in order that, before dining in town, he might call upon his landlord, in accordance with his promise to Marianne, found himself so busy that he scarcely caught sight of Beauchene. This was a relief, for the secret which he had discovered by chance annoyed him, and he feared lest he might cause his employer embarrassment. But the latter, when they exchanged a few passing words, did not seem to remember even that there was any cause for shame on his part. He had never before shown himself more active, more devoted to business. The fatigue he had felt in the morning had passed away, and he talked and laughed like one who finds life very pleasant, and has no fear whatever of hard work.

As a rule Mathieu left at six o'clock; but that day he went into Morange's office at half-past five to receive his month's salary. This rightly amounted to three hundred and fifty francs; but as five hundred had been advanced to him in January, which he paid back by instalments of fifty, he now received only fifteen louis, and these he pocketed with such an air of satisfaction that the accountant commented on it.

"Well," said the young fellow, "the money's welcome, for I left my wife with just thirty sous this morning."

It was already more than six o'clock when he found himself outside the superb house which the Seguin du Hordel family occupied in the Avenue d'Antin. Seguin's grandfather had been a mere tiller of the soil at Janville. Later on, his father, as a contractor for the army, had made a considerable fortune. And he, son of a parvenu, led the life of a rich, elegant idler. He was a member of the leading clubs, and, while passionately fond of horses, affected also a taste for art and literature, going for fashion's sake to extreme opinions. He had proudly married an almost portionless girl of a very ancient aristocratic race, the last of the Vaugelades, whose blood was poor and whose mind was narrow. Her mother, an ardent Catholic, had only succeeded in making of her one who, while following religious practices, was eager for the joys of the world. Seguin, since his marriage, had likewise practised religion, because it was fashionable to do so. His peasant grandfather had had ten children; his father, the army contractor, had been content with six; and he himself had two, a boy and a girl, and deemed even that number more than was right.

One part of Seguin's fortune consisted of an estate of some twelve hundred acres—woods and heaths—above Janville, which his father had purchased with some of his large gains after retiring from business. The old man's long-caressed dream had been to return in triumph to his native village, whence he had started quite poor, and he was on the point of there building himself a princely residence in the midst of a vast park when death snatched him away. Almost the whole of this estate had come to Seguin in his share of the paternal inheritance, and he had turned the shooting rights to some account by dividing them into shares of five hundred francs value, which his friends eagerly purchased. The income derived from this source was, however, but a meagre one. Apart from the woods there was only uncultivated land on the estate, marshes, patches of sand, and fields of stones; and for centuries past the opinion of the district had been that no agriculturist could ever turn the expanse to good account. The defunct army contractor alone had been able to picture there a romantic park, such as he had dreamt of creating around his regal abode. It was he, by the way, who had obtained an authorization to add to the name of Seguin that of Du Hordel—taken from a ruined tower called the Hordel which stood on the estate.

It was through Beauchene, one of the shareholders of the shooting rights, that Mathieu had made Seguin's acquaintance, and had discovered the old hunting-box, the lonely, quiet pavilion, which had pleased him so much that he had rented it. Valentine, who good-naturedly treated Marianne as a poor friend, had even been amiable enough to visit her there, and had declared the situation of the place to be quite poetical, laughing the while over her previous ignorance of it like one who had known nothing of her property. In reality she herself would not have lived there for an hour. Her husband had launched her into the feverish life of literary, artistic, and social Paris, hurrying her to gatherings, studios, exhibitions, theatres, and other pleasure resorts— all those brasier-like places where weak heads and wavering hearts are lost. He himself, amid all his passion for show, felt bored to death everywhere, and was at ease only among his horses; and this despite his pretensions with respect to advanced literature and philosophy, his collections of curios, such as the bourgeois of to-day does not yet understand, his furniture, his pottery, his pewter-work, and particularly his bookbindings, of which he was very proud. And he was turning his wife into a copy of himself, perverting her by his extravagant opinions and his promiscuous friendships, so that the little devotee who had been confided to his keeping was now on the high road to every kind of folly. She still went to mass and partook of the holy communion; but she was each day growing more and more familiar with wrong-doing. A disaster must surely be at the end of it all, particularly as he foolishly behaved to her in a rough, jeering way, which greatly hurt her feelings, and led her to dream of being loved with gentleness.

When Mathieu entered the house, which displayed eight lofty windows on each of the stories of its ornate Renaissance facade, he laughed lightly as he thought: "These folks don't have to wait for a monthly pittance of three hundred francs, with just thirty sous in hand."

The hall was extremely rich, all bronze and marble. On the right hand were the dining-room and two drawing-rooms; on the left a billiard-room, a smoking-room, and a winter garden. On the first floor, in front of the broad staircase, was Seguin's so-called "cabinet," a vast apartment, sixteen feet high, forty feet long, and six-and-twenty feet wide, which occupied all the central part of the house; while the husband's bed and dressing rooms were on the right, and those of the wife and children on the left hand. Up above, on the second floor, two complete suites of rooms were kept in reserve for the time when the children should have grown up.

A footman, who knew Mathieu, at once took him upstairs to the cabinet and begged him to wait there, while Monsieur finished dressing. For a moment the visitor fancied himself alone and glanced round the spacious room, feeling interested in its adornments, the lofty windows of old stained glass, the hangings of old Genoese velvet and brocaded silk, the oak bookcases showing the highly ornamented backs of the volumes they contained; the tables laden with bibelots, bronzes, marbles, goldsmith's work, glass work, and the famous collection of modern pewter-work. Then Eastern carpets were spread out upon all sides; there were low seats and couches for every mood of idleness, and cosy nooks in which one could hide oneself behind fringes of lofty plants.

"Oh! so it's you, Monsieur Froment," suddenly exclaimed somebody in the direction of the table allotted to the pewter curios. And thereupon a tall young man of thirty, whom a screen had hitherto hidden from Mathieu's view, came forward with outstretched hand.

"Ah!" said Mathieu, after a moment's hesitation, "Monsieur Charles Santerre."

This was but their second meeting. They had found themselves together once before in that same room. Charles Santerre, already

ÉMILE ZOLA

famous as a novelist, a young master popular in Parisian drawing-rooms, had a fine brow, caressing brown eyes, and a large red mouth which his moustache and beard, cut in the Assyrian style and carefully curled, helped to conceal. He had made his way, thanks to women, whose society he sought under pretext of studying them, but whom he was resolved to use as instruments of fortune. As a matter of calculation and principle he had remained a bachelor and generally installed himself in the nests of others. In literature feminine frailty was his stock subject he had made it his specialty to depict scenes of guilty love amid elegant, refined surroundings. At first he had no illusions as to the literary value of his works; he had simply chosen, in a deliberate way, what he deemed to be a pleasant and lucrative trade. But, duped by his successes, he had allowed pride to persuade him that he was really a writer. And nowadays he posed as the painter of an expiring society, professing the greatest pessimism, and basing a new religion on the annihilation of human passion, which annihilation would insure the final happiness of the world.

"Seguin will be here in a moment," he resumed in an amiable way. "It occurred to me to take him and his wife to dine at a restaurant this evening, before going to a certain first performance where there will probably be some fisticuffs and a rumpus to-night."

Mathieu then for the first time noticed that Santerre was in evening dress. They continued chatting for a moment, and the novelist called attention to a new pewter treasure among Seguin's collection. It represented a long, thin woman, stretched full-length, with her hair streaming around her. She seemed to be sobbing as she lay there, and Santerre declared the conception to be a masterpiece. The figure symbolized the end of woman, reduced to despair and solitude when man should finally have made up his mind to have nothing further to do with her. It was the novelist who, in literary and artistic matters, helped on the insanity which was gradually springing up in the Seguins' home.

However, Seguin himself now made his appearance. He was of the same age as Santerre, but was taller and slimmer, with fair hair, an aquiline nose, gray eyes, and thin lips shaded by a slight moustache. He also was in evening dress.

"Ah! well, my dear fellow," said he with the slight lisp which he affected, "Valentine is determined to put on a new gown. So we must be patient; we shall have an hour to wait."

Then, on catching sight of Mathieu, he began to apologize, evincing much politeness and striving to accentuate his air of frigid distinction. When the young man, whom he called his amiable tenant, had acquainted him with the motive of his visit—the leak in the zinc roof of the little pavilion at Janville—he at once consented to let the local plumber do any necessary soldering. But when, after fresh explanations, he understood that the roofing was so worn and damaged that it required to be changed entirely, he suddenly departed from his lofty affability and began to protest, declaring that he could not possibly expend in such repairs a sum which would exceed the whole annual rental of six hundred francs.

"Some soldering," he repeated; "some soldering; it's understood. I will write to the plumber." And wishing to change the subject he added: "Oh! wait a moment, Monsieur Froment. You are a man of taste, I know, and I want to show you a marvel."

He really had some esteem for Mathieu, for he knew that the young fellow possessed a quick appreciative mind. Mathieu began to smile, outwardly yielding to this attempt to create a diversion, but determined at heart that he would not leave the place until he had obtained the promise of a new roof. He took hold of a book, clad in a marvellous binding, which Seguin had fetched from a bookcase and tendered with religious care. On the cover of soft snow-white leather was incrusted a long silver lily, intersected by a tuft of big violet thistles. The title of the work, "Beauty Imperishable," was engraved up above, as in a corner of the sky.

"Ah! what a delightful conception, what delightful coloring!" declared Mathieu, who was really charmed. "Some bindings nowadays are perfect gems." Then he noticed the title: "Why, it's Monsieur Santerre's last novel!" said he.

Seguin smiled and glanced at the writer, who had drawn near. And when he saw him examining the book and looking quite moved by the compliment paid to it, he exclaimed: "My dear fellow, the binder brought it here this morning, and I was awaiting an opportunity to surprise you with it. It is the pearl of my collection! What do you think of the idea—that lily which symbolizes triumphant purity, and those thistles, the plants which spring up among ruins, and which symbolize the sterility of the world, at last deserted, again won over to the only perfect felicity? All your work lies in those symbols, you know."

"Yes, yes. But you spoil me; you will end by making me proud."

Mathieu had read Santerre's novel, having borrowed a copy of it from Mme. Beauchene, in order that his wife might see it, since it was a book that everybody was talking of. And the perusal of it had exasperated him. Forsaking the customary bachelor's flat where in previous works he had been so fond of laying scenes of debauchery, Santerre had this time tried to rise to the level of pure art and lyrical symbolism. The story he told was one of a certain Countess Anne-Marie, who, to escape a rough-mannered husband of extreme masculinity, had sought a refuge in Brittany in the company of a young painter endowed with divine inspiration, one Norbert, who had undertaken to decorate a convent chapel with paintings that depicted his various visions. And for thirty years he went on painting there, ever in colloquy with the angels, and ever having Anne-Marie beside him. And during those thirty years of love the Countess's beauty remained unimpaired; she was as young and as fresh at the finish as at the outset; whereas certain secondary personages, introduced into the story, wives and mothers of a neighboring little town, sank into physical and mental decay, and monstrous decrepitude. Mathieu considered the author's theory that all physical beauty and moral nobility belonged to virgins only, to be thoroughly imbecile, and he could not restrain himself from hinting his disapproval of it.

Both Santerre and Seguin, however, hotly opposed him, and quite a discussion ensued. First Santerre took up the matter from a religious standpoint. Said he, the words of the Old Testament, "Increase and multiply," were not to be found in the New Testament, which was the true basis of the Christian religion. The first Christians, he declared, had held marriage in horror, and with them the Holy Virgin had become the ideal of womanhood. Seguin thereupon nodded approval and proceeded to give his opinions on feminine beauty. But these were hardly to the taste of Mathieu, who promptly pointed out that the conception of beauty had often varied.

"To-day," said he, "you conceive beauty to consist in a long, slim, attenuated, almost angular figure; but at the time of the Renaissance the type of the beautiful was very different. Take Rubens, take Titian, take even Raffaelle, and you will see that their women were of robust build. Even their Virgin Marys have a motherly air. To my thinking, moreover, if we reverted to some such natural type of beauty, if women were not encouraged by fashion to compress and attenuate their figures so that their very nature, their very organism is changed, there would perhaps be some hope of coping with the evil of depopulation which is talked about so much nowadays."

The others looked at him and smiled with an air of compassionate superiority. "Depopulation an evil!" exclaimed Seguin; "can you, my dear sir, intelligent as you are, still believe in that hackneyed old story? Come, reflect and reason a little."

Then Santerre chimed in, and they went on talking one after the other and at times both together. Schopenhauer and Hartmann and Nietzsche were passed in review, and they claimed Malthus as one of themselves. But all this literary pessimism did not trouble Mathieu. He, with his belief in fruitfulness, remained convinced that the nation which no longer had faith in life must be dangerously ill. True, there were hours when he doubted the expediency of numerous families and asked himself if ten thousand happy people were not preferable to a hundred thousand unhappy ones; in which connection political and economic conditions had to be taken into account. But when all was said, he remained almost convinced that the Malthusian hypotheses would prove as false in the future as they had proved false in the past.

"Moreover," said he, "even if the world should become densely populated, even if food supplies, such as we know them, should fall short, chemistry would extract other means of subsistence from inorganic matter. And, besides, all such eventualities are so far away that it is impossible to make any calculation on a basis of scientific certainty. In France, too, instead of contributing to any such danger, we are going backward, we are marching towards annihilation. The population of France was once a fourth of the population of Europe, but now it is only one-eighth. In a century or two Paris will be dead, like ancient Athens and ancient Rome, and we shall have fallen to the rank that Greece now occupies. Paris seems determined to die."

But Santerre protested: "No, no; Paris simply wishes to remain stationary, and it wishes this precisely because it is the most intelligent, most highly civilized city in the world. The more nations advance in civilization the smaller becomes their birth-rate. We are simply giving the world an example of high culture, superior intelligence, and other nations will certainly follow that example when in turn they also attain to our state of perfection. There are signs of this already on every side."

"Quite so!" exclaimed Seguin, backing up his friend. "The phenomenon is general; all the nations show the same symptoms, and are decreasing in numbers, or will decrease as soon as they become civilized. Japan is affected already, and the same will be the case with China as soon as Europe forces open the door there."

Mathieu had become grave and attentive since the two society men, seated before him in evening dress, had begun to talk more rationally. The pale, slim, flat virgin, their ideal of feminine beauty, was no longer in question. The history of mankind was passing by. And almost as if communing with himself, he said: "So you do not fear the Yellow Peril, that terrible swarming of Asiatic barbarians who, it was said, would at some fatal moment sweep down on our Europe, ravage it, and people it afresh? In past ages, history always began anew in that fashion, by the sudden shifting of oceans, the invasion of fierce rough races coming to endow weakened nations with new blood. And after each such occurrence civilization flowered afresh, more broadly and freely than ever. How was it that Babylon, Nineveh, and Memphis fell into dust with their populations, who seem to have died on the spot? How is it that Athens and Rome still agonize to-day, unable to spring afresh from their ashes and renew the splendor of their ancient glory? How is it that death has already laid its hand upon Paris, which, whatever her splendor, is but the capital of a France whose virility is weakened? You may argue as you please and say that, like the ancient capitals of the world, Paris is dying of an excess of culture, intelligence, and civilization; it is none the less a fact that she is approaching death, the turn of the tide which will carry splendor and power to some new nation. Your theory of equilibrium is wrong. Nothing can remain stationary; whatever ceases to grow, decreases and disappears. And if Paris is bent on dying, she will die, and the country with her."

"Well, for my part," declared Santerre, resuming the pose of an elegant pessimist, "if she wishes to die, I shan't oppose her. In fact, I'm fully determined to help her."

"It is evident that the really honest, sensible course is to check any increase of population," added Seguin.

But Mathieu, as if he had not heard them, went on: "I know Herbert Spencer's law, and I believe it to be theoretically correct. It is certain that civilization is a check to fruitfulness, so that one may picture a series of social evolutions conducing now to decrease and now to increase of population, the whole ending in final equilibrium, by the very effect of culture's victory when the world shall be entirely populated and civilized. But who can foretell what road will be followed, through what disasters and sufferings one may have to go? More and more nations may disappear, and others may replace them; and how many thousands of years may not be needed before the final adjustment, compounded of truth, justice, and peace, is arrived at? At the thought of this the mind trembles and hesitates, and the heart contracts with a pang."

Deep silence fell while he thus remained disturbed, shaken in his faith in the good powers of life, and at a loss as to who was right—he or those two men so languidly stretched out before him.

But Valentine, Seguin's wife, came in, laughing and making an exhibition of masculine ways, which it had cost her much trouble to acquire.

"Ah! you people; you must not bear me any malice, you know. That girl Celeste takes such a time over everything!"

At five-and-twenty Valentine was short, slight, and still girlish. Fair, with a delicate face, laughing blue eyes, and a pert little nose, she could not claim to be pretty. Still she was charming and droll, and very free and easy in her ways; for not only did her husband take her about with him to all sorts of objectionable places, but she had become quite familiar with the artists and writers who frequented the house. Thus it was only in the presence of something extremely insulting that she again showed herself the last of the Vaugelades, and would all at once draw herself up and display haughty contempt and frigidity.

"Ah! it's you, Monsieur Froment," she said amiably, stepping towards Mathieu and shaking his hand in cavalier fashion. "Is Madame Froment in good health? Are the children flourishing as usual?"

Seguin was examining her dress, a gown of white silk trimmed with unbleached lace, and he suddenly gave way to one of those horribly rude fits which burst forth at times amid all his great affectation of politeness. "What! have you kept us waiting all this time to put that rag on? Well, you never looked a greater fright in your life!"

And she had entered the room convinced that she looked charming! She made an effort to control herself, but her girlish face darkened and assumed an expression of haughty, vindictive revolt. Then she slowly turned her eyes towards the friend who was present, and who was gazing at her with ecstasy, striving to accentuate the slavish submissiveness of his attitude.

"You look delicious!" he murmured; "that gown is a marvel."

Seguin laughed and twitted Santerre on his obsequiousness towards women. Valentine, mollified by the compliment, soon recovered her birdlike gayety, and such free and easy conversation ensued between the

　　　　　　　　　　　　　　　　　　　　　ÉMILE ZOLA

trio that Mathieu felt both stupefied and embarrassed. In fact, he would have gone off at once had it not been for his desire to obtain from his landlord a promise to repair the pavilion properly.

"Wait another moment," Valentine at last said to her husband; "I told Celeste to bring the children, so that we might kiss them before starting."

Mathieu wished to profit by this fresh delay, and sought to renew his request; but Valentine was already rattling on again, talking of dining at the most disreputable restaurant possible, and asking if at the first performance which they were to attend they would see all the horrors which had been hissed at the dress rehearsal the night before. She appeared like a pupil of the two men between whom she stood. She even went further in her opinions than they did, displaying the wildest pessimism, and such extreme views on literature and art that they themselves could not forbear laughing. Wagner was greatly over-estimated, in her opinion; she asked for invertebrate music, the free harmony of the passing wind. As for her moral views, they were enough to make one shudder. She had got past the argumentative amours of Ibsen's idiotic, rebellious heroines, and had now reached the theory of pure intangible beauty. She deemed Santerre's last creation, Anne-Marie, to be far too material and degraded, because in one deplorable passage the author remarked that Norbert's kisses had left their trace on the Countess's brow. Santerre disputed the quotation, whereupon she rushed upon the volume and sought the page to which she had referred.

"But I never degraded her," exclaimed the novelist in despair. "She never has a child."

"Pooh! What of that?" exclaimed Valentine. "If Anne-Marie is to raise our hearts she ought to be like spotless marble, and Norbert's kisses should leave no mark upon her."

But she was interrupted, for Celeste, the maid, a tall dark girl with an equine head, big features, and a pleasant air, now came in with the two children. Gaston was at this time five years old, and Lucie was three. Both were slight and delicate, pale like roses blooming in the shade. Like their mother, they were fair. The lad's hair was inclined to be carroty, while that of the girl suggested the color of oats. And they also had their mother's blue eyes, but their faces were elongated like that of their father. Dressed in white, with their locks curled, arrayed indeed in the most coquettish style, they looked like big fragile dolls.

The parents were touched in their worldly pride at sight of them, and insisted on their playing their parts with due propriety.

"Well, don't you wish anybody good evening?"

The children were not timid; they were already used to society and looked visitors full in the face. If they made little haste, it was because they were naturally indolent and did not care to obey. They at last made up their minds and allowed themselves to be kissed.

"Good evening, good friend Santerre."

Then they hesitated before Mathieu, and their father had to remind them of the gentleman's name, though they had already seen him on two or three occasions.

"Good evening, Monsieur Froment."

Valentine took hold of them, sat them on her lap, and half stifled them with caresses. She seemed to adore them, but as soon as she had sat them down again she forgot all about them.

"So you are going out again, mamma?" asked the little boy.

"Why, yes, my darling. Papas and mammas, you know, have their affairs to see to."

"So we shall have dinner all alone, mamma?"

Valentine did not answer, but turned towards the maid, who was waiting for orders;—

"You are not to leave them for a moment, Celeste—you hear? And, above all things, they are not to go into the kitchen. I can never come home without finding them in the kitchen. It is exasperating. Let them have their dinner at seven, and put them to bed at nine. And see that they go to sleep."

The big girl with the equine head listened with an air of respectful obedience, while her faint smile expressed the cunning of a Norman peasant who had been five years in Paris already and was hardened to service, and well knew what was done with children when the master and mistress were absent.

"Madame," she said in a simple way, "Mademoiselle Lucie is poorly. She has been sick again."

"What? sick again!" cried the father in a fury. "I am always hearing of that! They are always being sick! And it always happens when we are going out! It is very disagreeable, my dear; you might see to it; you ought not to let our children have papier-mache stomachs!"

The mother made an angry gesture, as if to say that she could not help it. As a matter of fact, the children were often poorly. They had

ÉMILE ZOLA

experienced every childish ailment, they were always catching cold or getting feverish. And they preserved the mute, moody, and somewhat anxious demeanor of children who are abandoned to the care of servants.

"Is it true you were poorly, my little Lucie?" asked Valentine, stooping down to the child. "You aren't poorly now, are you? No, no, it's nothing, nothing at all. Kiss me, my pet; bid papa good night very prettily, so that he may not feel worried in leaving you."

She rose up, already tranquillized and gay again; and, noticing that Mathieu was looking at her, she exclaimed:

"Ah! these little folks give one a deal of worry. But one loves them dearly all the same, though, so far as there is happiness in life, it would perhaps be better for them never to have been born. However, my duty to the country is done. Each wife ought to have a boy and a girl as I have."

Thereupon Mathieu, seeing that she was jesting, ventured to say with a laugh:

"Well, that isn't the opinion of your medical man, Dr. Boutan. He declares that to make the country prosperous every married couple ought to have four children."

"Four children! He's mad!" cried Seguin. And again with the greatest freedom of language he brought forward his pet theories. There was a world of meaning in his wife's laughter while Celeste stood there unmoved and the children listened without understanding. But at last Santerre led the Seguins away. It was only in the hall that Mathieu obtained from his landlord a promise that he would write to the plumber at Janville and that the roof of the pavilion should be entirely renovated, since the rain came into the bedrooms.

The Seguins' landau was waiting at the door. When they had got into it with their friend, it occurred to Mathieu to raise his eyes; and at one of the windows he perceived Celeste standing between the two children, intent, no doubt, on assuring herself that Monsieur and Madame were really going. The young man recalled Reine's departure from her parents; but here both Lucie and Gaston remained motionless, gravely mournful, and neither their father nor their mother once thought of looking up at them.

IV

At half-past seven o'clock, when Mathieu arrived at the restaurant on the Place de la Madeleine where he was to meet his employer, he found him already there, drinking a glass of madeira with his customer, M. Firon-Badinier. The dinner was a remarkable one; choice viands and the best wines were served in abundance. But Mathieu was struck less by the appetite which the others displayed than by Beauchene's activity and skill. Glass in hand, never losing a bite, he had already persuaded his customer, by the time the roast arrived, to order not only the new thresher but also a mowing machine. M. Firon-Badinier was to take the train for Evreux at nine-twenty, and when nine o'clock struck, the other, now eager to be rid of him, contrived to pack him off in a cab to the St.-Lazare railway station.

For a moment Beauchene remained standing on the pavement with Mathieu, and took off his hat in order that the mild breezes of that delightful May evening might cool his burning head.

"Well, that's settled," he said with a laugh. "But it wasn't so easily managed. It was the Pommard which induced the beggar to make up his mind. All the same, I was dreadfully afraid he would make me miss my appointment."

These remarks, which escaped him amid his semi-intoxication, led him to more confidential talk. He put on his hat again, lighted a fresh cigar, and took Mathieu's arm. Then they walked on slowly through the passion-stirred throng and the nightly blaze of the Boulevards.

"There's plenty of time," said Beauchene. "I'm not expected till half-past nine, and it's close by. Will you have a cigar? No? You never smoke?"

"Never."

"Well, my dear fellow, it would be ridiculous to feign with you, since you happened to see me this morning. Oh, it's a stupid affair! I'm quite of that opinion; but, then, what would you have?"

Thereupon he launched out into long explanations concerning his marital life and the intrigue which had suddenly sprung up between him and that girl Norine, old Moineaud's daughter. He professed the greatest respect for his wife, but he was nevertheless a loose liver; and Constance was now beginning to resign herself to the inevitable. She closed her eyes when it would have been unpleasant for her to keep them open. She knew very well that it was essential that the business should be kept together and pass intact into the hands of their son Maurice. A tribe of children would have meant the ruin of all their plans.

Mathieu listened at first in great astonishment, and then began to ask questions and raise objections, at most of which Beauchene laughed gayly, like the gross egotist he was. He talked at length with extreme volubility, going into all sorts of details, at times assuming a semi-apologetic manner, but more frequently justifying himself with an air of triumph. And, finally, when they reached the corner of the Rue Caumartin he halted to bid Mathieu good-by. He there had a little bachelor's lodging, which was kept in order by the concierge of the house, who, being very well paid, proved an extremely discreet domestic.

As he hurried off, Mathieu, still standing at the corner of the street, could not help thinking of the scenes which he had witnessed at the Beauchene works that day. He thought of old Moineaud, the fitter, whom he again saw standing silent and unmoved in the women's workroom while his daughter Euphrasie was being soundly rated by Beauchene, and while Norine, the other girl, looked on with a sly laugh. When the toiler's children have grown up and gone to join, the lads the army of slaughter, and the girls the army of vice, the father, degraded by the ills of life, pays little heed to it all. To him it is seemingly a matter of indifference to what disaster the wind may carry the fledgelings who fall from the nest.

It was now half-past nine o'clock, and Mathieu had more than an hour before him to reach the Northern railway station. So he did not hurry, but strolled very leisurely up the Boulevards. He had eaten and drunk far more than usual, and Beauchene's insidious confidential talk, still buzzing in his ears, helped on his intoxication. His hands were hot, and now and again a sudden glow passed over his face. And what a warm evening it was, too, on those Boulevards, blazing with electric lights, fevered by a swarming, jostling throng, amid a ceaseless rumble of cabs and omnibuses! It was all like a stream of ardent life flowing away into the night, and Mathieu allowed himself to be carried on by the torrent, whose hot breath, whose glow of passion, he ever felt sweeping over him.

Then, in a reverie, he pictured the day he had just spent. First he was at the Beauchenes' in the morning, and saw the father and mother standing, like accomplices who fully shared one another's views, beside the sofa on which Maurice, their only son, lay dozing with a pale and waxen face. The works must never be exposed to the danger of being subdivided. Maurice alone must inherit all the millions which the business might yield, so that he might become one of the princes of industry. And therefore the husband hurried off to sin while the wife closed her eyes. In this sense, in defiance of morality and health, did the capitalist bourgeoisie, which had replaced the old nobility, virtually re-establish the law of primogeniture. That law had been abolished at the Revolution for the bourgeoisie's benefit; but now, also for its own purposes, it revived it. Each family must have but one son.

Mathieu had reached this stage in his reflections when his thoughts were diverted by several street hawkers who, in selling the last edition of an evening print, announced a "drawing" of the lottery stock of some enterprise launched by the Credit National. And then he suddenly recalled the Moranges in their dining-room, and heard them recapitulate their dream of making a big fortune as soon as the accountant should have secured a post in one of the big banking establishments, where the principals raise men of value to the highest posts. Those Moranges lived in everlasting dread of seeing their daughter marry a needy petty clerk; succumbing to that irresistible fever which, in a democracy ravaged by political equality and economic inequality, impels every one to climb higher up the social ladder. Envy consumed them at the thought of the luxury of others; they plunged into debt in order that they might imitate from afar the elegance of the upper class, and all their natural honesty and good nature was poisoned by the insanity born of ambitious pride. And here again but one child was permissible, lest they should be embarrassed, delayed, forever impeded in the attainment of the future they coveted.

A crowd of people now barred Mathieu's way, and he perceived that he was near the theatre, where a first performance was taking place that evening. It was a theatre where free farcical pieces were produced, and on its walls were posted huge portraits of its "star," a carroty wench with a long flat figure, destitute of all womanliness, and seemingly symbolical of perversity. Passers-by stopped to gaze at the bills, the vilest remarks were heard, and Mathieu remembered that the Seguins and Santerre were inside the house, laughing at the piece, which was of so filthy a nature that the spectators at the dress rehearsal, though they were by no means over-nice in such matters, had expressed their disgust by almost wrecking the auditorium. And while the Seguins were gloating over this horror, yonder, at their house in the Avenue d'Antin, Celeste had just put the children, Gaston and Lucie, to bed, and had then hastily returned to the kitchen, where a friend, Madame Menoux, who kept a little haberdasher's shop in the neighborhood, awaited her. Gaston, having been given some wine to drink, was already asleep; but Lucie, who again felt sick, lay shivering in her bed, not daring to call Celeste, lest the servant, who did not like to be disturbed, should ill-treat her. And, at two o'clock in the morning, after offering Santerre an oyster supper at a night restaurant, the Seguins would come home, their minds unhinged by the imbecile literature and art to which they had taken for fashion's sake, vitiated yet more by the ignoble performance they had witnessed, and the base society they had elbowed at supper. They seemed to typify vice for vice's sake, elegant vice and pessimism as a principle.

Indeed, when Mathieu tried to sum up his day, he found vice on every side, in each of the spheres with which he had come in contact. And now the examples he had witnessed filled him no longer with mere surprise; they disturbed him, they shook his beliefs, they made him doubt whether his notions of life, duty, and happiness might not after all be inaccurate.

He stopped short and drew a long breath, seeking to drive away his growing intoxication. He had passed the Grand Opera and was reaching the crossway of the Rue Drouot. Perhaps his increase of fever was due to those glowing Boulevards. The private rooms of the restaurants were still ablaze, the cafes threw bright radiance across the road, the pavement was blocked by their tables and chairs and customers. All Paris seemed to have come down thither to enjoy that delightful evening. There was endless elbowing, endless mingling of breath as the swelling crowd sauntered along. Couples lingered before the sparkling displays of jewellers' shops. Middle-class families swept under dazzling arches of electric lamps into cafes concerts, whose huge posters promised the grossest amusements. Hundreds and hundreds of women went by with trailing skirts, and whispered and jested and laughed; while men darted in pursuit, now of a fair chignon, now of a dark one. In the open cabs men and women sat side by side, now husbands and wives long since married, now chance couples who had met but an hour ago. But Mathieu went on again, yielding to the force of the current, carried along like all the others, a prey to the same fever which sprang from the surroundings, from the excitement of the day, from the customs of the age. And he no longer took the Beauchenes, the Moranges, the Seguins as isolated types; it was all Paris that symbolized vice, all Paris that yielded to debauchery and sank into degradation. There were the folks of high culture, the folks suffering from literary neurosis; there were the merchant princes; there were the men of liberal professions, the lawyers, the doctors, the engineers; there were the people of the lower middle-class, the petty tradesmen, the petty clerks; there were even the manual workers, poisoned by the example of the upper spheres—all practising the doctrines of egotism as vanity and the passion for money grew more and more intense. . . No more children! Paris was bent on dying. And Mathieu recalled how Napoleon I, one evening after battle, on beholding a plain strewn with the corpses of his soldiers, had put his trust in Paris to repair the carnage of that day. But times had changed. Paris would no longer supply life, whether it were for slaughter or for toil.

And as Mathieu thought of it all a sudden weakness came upon him. Again he asked himself whether the Beauchenes, the Moranges, the Seguins, and all those thousands and thousands around him were not right, and whether he were not the fool, the dupe, the criminal, with his belief in life ever renascent, ever growing and spreading throughout the world. And before him arose, too, the image of Seraphine, the temptress, opening her perfumed arms to him and carrying him off to the same existence of pleasure and baseness which the others led.

Then he remembered the three hundred francs which he carried in his pocket. Three hundred francs, which must last for a whole month, though out of them he had to pay various little sums that he already owed. The remainder would barely suffice to buy a ribbon for Marianne and jam for the youngsters' bread. And if he set the Moranges on one side, the others, the Beauchenes and the Seguins, were rich. He bitterly recalled their wealth. He pictured the rumbling factory with its black buildings covering a great stretch of ground; he pictured hundreds of workmen ever increasing the fortune of their master, who dwelt in a handsomely appointed pavilion and whose only son was growing up for future sovereignty, under his mother's vigilant eyes. He pictured, too, the Seguins' luxurious mansion in the Avenue d'Antin, the great hall, the magnificent staircase, the vast room above, crowded with marvels; he pictured all the refinement, all the train of wealth, all the tokens of lavish life, the big dowry which would be given to the little girl, the high position which would be purchased for the son. And he, bare and empty-handed, who now possessed nothing, not even a stone at the edge of a field, would doubtless always possess nothing, neither factory buzzing with workmen, nor mansion rearing its proud front aloft. And he was the imprudent one, and the others were the sensible, the wise. What would ever become of himself and his troop of children? Would he not die in some garret? would they not lead lives of abject wretchedness? Ah! it was evident the others were right, the others were sensible. And he felt unhinged, he regarded himself with contempt, like a fool who has allowed himself to be duped.

Then once more the image of Seraphine arose before his eyes, more tempting than ever. A slight quiver came upon him as he beheld the blaze of the Northern railway station and all the feverish traffic around it. Wild fancies surged through his brain. He thought of Beauchene. Why should he not do likewise? He recalled past times, and, yielding to sudden madness, turned his back upon the station and retraced his steps towards the Boulevards. Seraphine, he said to himself, was doubtless waiting for him; she had told him that he would always be welcome. As for his wife, he would tell her he had missed his train.

At last a block in the traffic made him pause, and on raising his eyes he saw that he had reached the Boulevards once more. The crowd still streamed along, but with increased feverishness. Mathieu's temples were beating, and wild words escaped his lips. Why should he not live the same life as the others? He was ready, even eager, to plunge into it. But the block in the traffic continued, he could not cross the road; and while he stood there hesitation and doubt came upon him. He saw in that increasing obstruction a deliberate obstacle to his wild design. And all at once the image of Seraphine faded from before his mind's eye and he beheld another, his wife, his dear wife Marianne, awaiting him, all smiles and trustfulness, in the fresh quietude of the country. Could he deceive her? . . . Then all at once he again rushed off towards the railway station, in fear lest he should lose his train. He was determined that he would listen to no further promptings, that he would cast no further glance upon glowing, dissolute Paris, and he reached the station just in time to climb into a car. The train started and he journeyed on, leaning out of his compartment and offering his face to the cool night breeze in order that it might calm and carry off the evil fever that had possessed him.

The night was moonless, but studded with such pure and such glowing stars that the country could be seen spreading far away beneath a soft bluish radiance. Already at twenty minutes past eleven Marianne found herself on the little bridge crossing the Yeuse, midway between Chantebled, the pavilion where she and her husband lived, and the station of Janville. The children were fast asleep; she had left them in the charge of Zoe, the servant, who sat knitting beside a lamp, the light of which could be seen from afar, showing like a bright spark amid the black line of the woods.

Whenever Mathieu returned home by the seven o'clock train, as was his wont, Marianne came to meet him at the bridge. Occasionally she brought her two eldest boys, the twins, with her, though their little legs moved but slowly on the return journey when, in retracing their steps, a thousand yards or more, they had to climb a rather steep hillside. And that evening, late though the hour was, Marianne had yielded to that pleasant habit of hers, enjoying the delight of thus going forward through the lovely night to meet the man she worshipped. She never went further than the bridge which arched over the narrow river. She seated herself on its broad, low parapet, as on some rustic bench, and thence she overlooked the whole plain as far as the houses of Janville, before which passed the railway line. And from afar she could see her husband approaching along the road which wound between the cornfields.

That evening she took her usual seat under the broad velvety sky spangled with gold. And with a movement which bespoke her solicitude she turned towards the bright little light shining on the verge of the sombre woods, a light telling of the quietude of the room in which it burnt, the servant's tranquil vigil, and the happy slumber of the children in the adjoining chamber. Then Marianne let her gaze wander all around her, over the great estate of Chantebled, belonging to the Seguins. The dilapidated pavilion stood at the extreme edge of the woods whose copses, intersected by patches of heath, spread over a lofty plateau to the distant farms of Mareuil and Lillebonne. But that was not all, for to the west of the plateau lay more than two hundred and fifty acres of land, a marshy expanse where pools stagnated amid brushwood, vast uncultivated tracts, where one went duck-shooting in winter. And there was yet a third part of the estate, acres upon acres of equally sterile soil, all sand and gravel, descending in a gentle slope to the embankment of the railway line. It was indeed a stretch of country lost to culture, where the few good patches of loam remained unproductive, inclosed within the waste land. But the spot had all the beauty and exquisite wildness of solitude, and was one that appealed to healthy minds fond of seeing nature in freedom. And on that lovely night one could nowhere have found more perfect and more balmy quiet.

Marianne, who since coming to the district had already threaded the woodland paths, explored the stretches of brushwood around the meres, and descended the pebbly slopes, let her eyes travel slowly over the expanse, divining spots she had visited and was fond of, though the darkness now prevented her from seeing them. In the depths of the woods an owl raised its soft, regular cry, while from a pond on the right ascended a faint croaking of frogs, so far away that it sounded like the vibration of crystal. And from the other side, the side of Paris, there came a growing rumble which, little by little, rose above all the other sounds of the night. She heard it, and at last lent ear to nothing else. It was the train, for whose familiar roar she waited every evening. As soon as it left Monval station on its way to Janville, it gave token of its coming, but so faintly that only a practised ear could distinguish its rumble amid the other sounds rising from the country side. For her part, she heard it immediately, and thereupon followed it in fancy through every phase of its journey. And never had she been better able to do so than on that splendid night, amid the profound quietude of the earth's slumber. It had left Monval, it was turning beside the brickworks, it was skirting St. George's fields. In another two minutes it would be at Janville. Then all at once its white light shone out beyond the poplar trees of Le Mesnil Rouge, and the panting of the engine grew louder, like that of some giant racer drawing near. On that side the plain spread far away into a dark, unknown region, beneath the star-spangled sky, which on the very horizon showed a ruddy reflection like that of some brasier, the reflection of nocturnal Paris, blazing and smoking in the darkness like a volcano.

Marianne sprang to her feet. The train stopped at Janville, and then its rumble rose again, grew fainter, and died away in the direction of Vieux-Bourg. But she no longer paid attention to it. She now had eyes and ears only for the road which wound like a pale ribbon between the dark patches of corn. Her husband did not take ten minutes to cover the thousand yards and more which separated the station from the little bridge. And, as a rule, she perceived and recognized him far off; but on that particular night, such was the deep silence that she could distinguish his footfall on the echoing road long before his dark, slim figure showed against the pale ground. And he found her there, erect under the stars, smiling and healthy, a picture of all that is good. The milky whiteness of her skin was accentuated by her beautiful black hair, caught up in a huge coil, and her big black eyes, which beamed with all the gentleness of spouse and mother. Her straight brow, her nose, her mouth, her chin so boldly, purely rounded, her cheeks which glowed like savory fruit, her delightful little ears—the whole of her face, full of love and tenderness, bespoke beauty in full health, the gayety which comes from the accomplishment of duty, and the serene conviction that by loving life she would live as she ought to live.

"What! so you've come then!" Mathieu exclaimed, as soon as he was near her. "But I begged you not to come out so late. Are you not afraid at being alone on the roads at this time of night?"

She began to laugh. "Afraid," said she, "when the night is so mild and healthful? Besides, wouldn't you rather have me here to kiss you ten minutes sooner?"

Those simple words brought tears to Mathieu's eyes. All the murkiness, all the shame through which he had passed in Paris horrified him. He tenderly took his wife in his arms, and they exchanged the closest, the most human of kisses amid the quiet of the slumbering fields. After the scorching pavement of Paris, after the eager struggling of the day and the degrading spectacles of the night, how reposeful was that far-spreading silence, that faint bluish radiance, that endless unrolling of plains, steeped in refreshing gloom and dreaming of fructification by the morrow's sun! And what suggestions of health, and rectitude, and felicity rose from productive Nature, who fell asleep beneath the dew of night solely that she might reawaken in triumph, ever and ever rejuvenated by life's torrent, which streams even through the dust of her paths.

Mathieu slowly seated Marianne on the low broad parapet once more. He kept her near his heart; it was a halt full of affection, which neither could forego, in presence of the universal peace that came to them from the stars, and the waters, and the woods, and the endless fields.

"What a splendid night!" murmured Mathieu. "How beautiful and how pleasant to live in it!"

Then, after a moment's rapture, during which they both heard their hearts beating, he began to tell her of his day. She questioned him with loving interest, and he answered, happy at having to tell her no lie.

"No, the Beauchenes cannot come here on Sunday. Constance never cared much for us, as you well know. Their boy Maurice is suffering

　　　　　　　　　　　　　　　　　ÉMILE ZOLA

in the legs; Dr. Boutan was there, and the question of children was discussed again. I will tell you all about that. On the other hand, the Moranges have promised to come. You can't have an idea of the delight and vanity they displayed in showing me their new flat. What with their eagerness to make a big fortune I'm much afraid that those worthy folks will do something very foolish. Oh! I was forgetting. I called on the landlord, and though I had a good deal of difficulty over it, he ended by consenting to have the roof entirely relaid. Ah! what a home, too, those Seguins have! I came away feeling quite scared. But I will tell you all about it by and by with the rest."

Marianne evinced no loquacious curiosity; she quietly awaited his confidences, and showed anxiety only respecting themselves and the children.

"You received your salary, didn't you?" she asked.

"Yes, yes, you need not be afraid about that."

"Oh! I'm not afraid, it's only our little debts which worry me."

Then she asked again: "And did your business dinner go off all right? I was afraid that Beauchene might detain you and make you miss your train."

He replied that everything had gone off properly, but as he spoke he flushed and felt a pang at his heart. To rid himself of his emotion he affected sudden gayety.

"Well, and you, my dear," he asked, "how did you manage with your thirty sous?"

"My thirty sous!" she gayly responded, "why, I was much too rich; we fared like princes, all five of us, and I have six sous left."

Then, in her turn, she gave an account of her day, her daily life, pure as crystal. She recapitulated what she had done, what she had said; she related how the children had behaved, and she entered into the minutest details respecting them and the house. With her, moreover, one day was like another; each morning she set herself to live the same life afresh, with never-failing happiness.

"To-day, though, we had a visit," said she; "Madame Lepailleur, the woman from the mill over yonder, came to tell me that she had some fine chickens for sale. As we owe her twelve francs for eggs and milk, I believe that she simply called to see if I meant to pay her. I told her that I would go to her place to-morrow."

While speaking Marianne had pointed through the gloom towards a big black pile, a little way down the Yeuse. It was an old water-mill which was still worked, and the Lepailleurs had now been installed in it for three generations. The last of them, Francois Lepailleur, who considered himself to be no fool, had come back from his military service with little inclination to work, and an idea that the mill would never enrich him, any more than it had enriched his father and grandfather. It then occurred to him to marry a peasant farmer's daughter, Victoire Cornu, whose dowry consisted of some neighboring fields skirting the Yeuse. And the young couple then lived fairly at their ease, on the produce of those fields and such small quantities of corn as the peasants of the district still brought to be ground at the old mill. If the antiquated and badly repaired mechanism of the mill had been replaced by modern appliances, and if the land, instead of being impoverished by adherence to old-fashioned practices, had fallen into the hands of an intelligent man who believed in progress, there would no doubt have been a fortune in it all. But Lepailleur was not only disgusted with work, he treated the soil with contempt. He indeed typified the peasant who has grown weary of his eternal mistress, the mistress whom his forefathers loved too much. Remembering that, in spite of all their efforts to fertilize the soil, it had never made them rich or happy, he had ended by hating it. All his faith in its powers had departed; he accused it of having lost its fertility, of being used up and decrepit, like some old cow which one sends to the slaughter-house. And, according to him, everything went wrong: the soil simply devoured the seed sown in it, the weather was never such as it should be, the seasons no longer came in their proper order. Briefly, it was all a premeditated disaster brought about by some evil power which had a spite against the peasantry, who were foolish to give their sweat and their blood to such a thankless creature.

"Madame Lepailleur brought her boy with her, a little fellow three years old, called Antonin," resumed Marianne, "and we fell to talking of children together. She quite surprised me. Peasant folks, you know, used to have such large families. But she declared that one child was quite enough. Yet she's only twenty-four, and her husband not yet twenty-seven."

These remarks revived the thoughts which had filled Mathieu's mind all day. For a moment he remained silent. Then he said, "She gave you her reasons, no doubt?"

"Give reasons—she, with her head like a horse's, her long freckled face, pale eyes, and tight, miserly mouth—I think she's simply a fool, ever in admiration before her husband because he fought in Africa and

ÉMILE ZOLA

reads the newspapers. All that I could get out of her was that children cost one a good deal more than they bring in. But the husband, no doubt, has ideas of his own. You have seen him, haven't you? A tall, slim fellow, as carroty and as scraggy as his wife, with an angular face, green eyes, and prominent cheekbones. He looks as though he had never felt in a good humor in his life. And I understand that he is always complaining of his father-in-law, because the other had three daughters and a son. Of course that cut down his wife's dowry; she inherited only a part of her father's property. And, besides, as the trade of a miller never enriched his father, Lepailleur curses his mill from morning till night, and declares that he won't prevent his boy Antonin from going to eat white bread in Paris, if he can find a good berth there when he grows up."

Thus, even among the country folks, Mathieu found a small family the rule. Among the causes were the fear of having to split up an inheritance, the desire to rise in the social system, the disgust of manual toil, and the thirst for the luxuries of town life. Since the soil was becoming bankrupt, why indeed continue tilling it, when one knew that one would never grow rich by doing so? Mathieu was on the point of explaining these things to his wife, but he hesitated, and then simply said: "Lepailleur does wrong to complain; he has two cows and a horse, and when there is urgent work he can take an assistant. We, this morning, had just thirty sous belonging to us, and we own no mill, no scrap of land. For my part I think his mill superb; I envy him every time I cross this bridge. Just fancy! we two being the millers—why, we should be very rich and very happy!"

This made them both laugh, and for another moment they remained seated there, watching the dark massive mill beside the Yeuse. Between the willows and poplars on both banks the little river flowed on peacefully, scarce murmuring as it coursed among the water plants which made it ripple. Then, amid a clump of oaks, appeared the big shed sheltering the wheel, and the other buildings garlanded with ivy, honeysuckle, and creepers, the whole forming a spot of romantic prettiness. And at night, especially when the mill slept, without a light at any of its windows, there was nothing of more dreamy, more gentle charm.

"Why!" remarked Mathieu, lowering his voice, "there is somebody under the willows, beside the water. I heard a slight noise."

"Yes, I know," replied Marianne with tender gayety. "It must be the young couple who settled themselves in the little house yonder a fortnight ago. You know whom I mean—Madame Angelin, that schoolmate of Constance's."

The Angelins, who had become their neighbors, interested the Froments. The wife was of the same age as Marianne, tall, dark, with fine hair and fine eyes, radiant with continual joy, and fond of pleasure. And the husband was of the same age as Mathieu, a handsome fellow, very much in love, with moustaches waving in the wind, and the joyous spirits of a musketeer. They had married with sudden passion for one another, having between them an income of some ten thousand francs a year, which the husband, a fan painter with a pretty talent, might have doubled had it not been for the spirit of amorous idleness into which his marriage had thrown him. And that spring-time they had sought a refuge in that desert of Janville, that they might love freely, passionately, in the midst of nature. They were always to be met, holding each other by the waist, on the secluded paths in the woods; and at night they loved to stroll across the fields, beside the hedges, along the shady banks of the Yeuse, delighted when they could linger till very late near the murmuring water, in the thick shade of the willows.

But there was quite another side to their idyl, and Marianne mentioned it to her husband. She had chatted with Madame Angelin, and it appeared that the latter wished to enjoy life, at all events for the present, and did not desire to be burdened with children. Then Mathieu's worrying thoughts once more came back to him, and again at this fresh example he wondered who was right—he who stood alone in his belief, or all the others.

"Well," he muttered at last, "we all live according to our fancy. But come, my dear, let us go in; we disturb them."

They slowly climbed the narrow road leading to Chantebled, where the lamp shone out like a beacon. When Mathieu had bolted the front door they groped their way upstairs. The ground floor of their little house comprised a dining-room and a drawing-room on the right hand of the hall, and a kitchen and a store place on the left. Upstairs there were four bedrooms. Their scanty furniture seemed quite lost in those big rooms; but, exempt from vanity as they were, they merely laughed at this. By way of luxury they had simply hung some little curtains of red stuff at the windows, and the ruddy reflection from these hangings seemed to them to impart wonderfully rich cheerfulness to their home.

They found Zoe, their peasant servant, asleep over her knitting beside the lamp in their own bedroom, and they had to wake her and send her as quietly as possible to bed. Then Mathieu took up the lamp and entered the children's room to kiss them and make sure that they were comfortable. It was seldom they awoke on these occasions. Having placed the lamp on the mantelshelf, he still stood there looking at the three little beds when Marianne joined him. In the bed against the wall at one end of the room lay Blaise and Denis, the twins, sturdy little fellows six years of age; while in the second bed against the opposite wall was Ambroise, now nearly four and quite a little cherub. And the third bed, a cradle, was occupied by Mademoiselle Rose, fifteen months of age and weaned for three weeks past. She lay there half naked, showing her white flowerlike skin, and her mother had to cover her up with the bedclothes, which she had thrust aside with her self-willed little fists. Meantime the father busied himself with Ambroise's pillow, which had slipped aside. Both husband and wife came and went very gently, and bent again and again over the children's faces to make sure that they were sleeping peacefully. They kissed them and lingered yet a little longer, fancying that they had heard Blaise and Denis stirring. At last the mother took up the lamp and they went off, one after the other, on tiptoe.

When they were in their room again Marianne exclaimed: "I didn't want to worry you while we were out, but Rose made me feel anxious to-day; I did not find her well, and it was only this evening that I felt more at ease about her." Then, seeing that Mathieu started and turned pale, she went on: "Oh! it was nothing. I should not have gone out if I had felt the least fear for her. But with those little folks one is never free from anxiety."

She then began to make her preparations for the night; but Mathieu, instead of imitating her, sat down at the table where the lamp stood, and drew the money paid to him by Morange from his pocket. When he had counted those three hundred francs, those fifteen louis, he said in a bitter, jesting way, "The money hasn't grown on the road. Here it is; you can pay our debts to-morrow."

This remark gave him a fresh idea. Taking his pencil he began to jot down the various amounts they owed on a blank page of his pocket diary. "We say twelve francs to the Lepailleurs for eggs and milk. How much do you owe the butcher?" he asked.

"The butcher," replied Marianne, who had sat down to take off her shoes; "well, say twenty francs."

"And the grocer and the baker?"

"I don't know exactly, but about thirty francs altogether. There is nobody else."

Then Mathieu added up the items: "That makes sixty-two francs," said he. "Take them away from three hundred, and we shall have two hundred and thirty-eight left. Eight francs a day at the utmost. Well, we have a nice month before us, with our four children to feed, particularly if little Rose should fall ill."

The remark surprised his wife, who laughed gayly and confidently, saying: "Why, what is the matter with you to-night, my dear? You seem to be almost in despair, when as a rule you look forward to the morrow as full of promise. You have often said that it was sufficient to love life if one wished to live happily. As for me, you know, with you and the little ones I feel the happiest, richest woman in the world!"

At this Mathieu could restrain himself no longer. He shook his head and mournfully began to recapitulate the day he had just spent. At great length he relieved his long-pent-up feelings. He spoke of their poverty and the prosperity of others. He spoke of the Beauchenes, the Moranges, the Seguins, the Lepailleurs, of all he had seen of them, of all they had said, of all their scarcely disguised contempt for an improvident starveling like himself. He, Mathieu, and she, Marianne, would never have factory, nor mansion, nor mill, nor an income of twelve thousand francs a year; and their increasing penury, as the others said, had been their own work. They had certainly shown themselves imprudent, improvident. And he went on with his recollections, telling Marianne that he feared nothing for himself, but that he did not wish to condemn her and the little ones to want and poverty. She was surprised at first, and by degrees became colder, more constrained, as he told her all that he had upon his mind. Tears slowly welled into her eyes; and at last, however lovingly he spoke, she could no longer restrain herself, but burst into sobs. She did not question what he said, she spoke no words of revolt, but it was evident that her whole being rebelled, and that her heart was sorely grieved.

He started, greatly troubled when he saw her tears. Something akin to her own feelings came upon him. He was terribly distressed, angry with himself. "Do not weep, my darling!" he exclaimed as he pressed her to him: "it was stupid, brutal, and wrong of me to speak to you in that way. Don't distress yourself, I beg you; we'll think it all over and talk about it some other time."

She ceased to weep, but she continued silent, clinging to him, with her head resting on his shoulder. And Mathieu, by the side of that loving, trustful woman, all health and rectitude and purity, felt more and more confused, more and more ashamed of himself, ashamed of having given heed to the base, sordid, calculating principles which others made the basis of their lives. He thought with loathing of the sudden frenzy which had possessed him during the evening in Paris. Some poison must have been instilled into his veins; he could not recognize himself. But honor and rectitude, clear-sightedness and trustfulness in life were fast returning. Through the window, which had remained open, all the sounds of the lovely spring night poured into the room. It was spring, the season of love, and beneath the palpitating stars in the broad heavens, from fields and forests and waters came the murmur of germinating life. And never had Mathieu more fully realized that, whatever loss may result, whatever difficulty may arise, whatever fate may be in store, all the creative powers of the world, whether of the animal order, whether of the order of the plants, for ever and ever wage life's great incessant battle against death. Man alone, dissolute and diseased among all the other denizens of the world, all the healthful forces of nature, seeks death for death's sake, the annihilation of his species. Then Mathieu again caught his wife in a close embrace, printing on her lips a long, ardent kiss.

"Ah! dear heart, forgive me; I doubted both of us. It would be impossible for either of us to sleep unless you forgive me. Well, let the others hold us in derision and contempt if they choose. Let us love and live as nature tells us, for you are right: therein lies true wisdom and true courage."

V

Mathieu rose noiselessly from his little folding iron bedstead beside the large one of mahogany, on which Marianne lay alone. He looked at her, and saw that she was awake and smiling.

"What! you are not asleep?" said he. "I hardly dared to stir for fear of waking you. It is nearly nine o'clock, you know."

It was Sunday morning. January had come round, and they were in Paris. During the first fortnight in December the weather had proved frightful at Chantebled, icy rains being followed by snow and terrible cold. This rigorous temperature, coupled with the circumstance that Marianne was again expecting to become a mother, had finally induced Mathieu to accept Beauchene's amiable offer to place at his disposal the little pavilion in the Rue de la Federation, where the founder of the works had lived before building the superb house on the quay. An old foreman who had occupied this pavilion, which still contained the simple furniture of former days, had lately died. And the young folks, desiring to be near their friend, worthy Dr. Boutan, had lived there for a month now, and did not intend to return to Chantebled until the first fine days in April.

"Wait a moment," resumed Mathieu; "I will let the light in."

He thereupon drew back one of the curtains, and a broad ray of yellow, wintry sunshine illumined the dim room. "Ah! there's the sun! And it's splendid weather—and Sunday too! I shall be able to take you out for a little while with the children this afternoon."

Then Marianne called him to her, and, when he had seated himself on the bed, took hold of his hand and said gayly: "Well, I hadn't been sleeping either for the last twenty minutes; and I didn't move because I wanted you to lie in bed a little late, as it's Sunday. How amusing to think that we were afraid of waking one another when we both had our eyes wide open!"

"Oh!" said he, "I was so happy to think you were sleeping. My one delight on Sundays now is to remain in this room all the morning, and spend the whole day with you and the children." Then he uttered a cry of surprise and remorse: "Why! I haven't kissed you yet."

She had raised herself on her pillows, and he gave her an eager clasp. In the stream of bright sunshine which gilded the bed she herself looked radiant with health and strength and hope. Never had her heavy brown tresses flowed down more abundantly, never had her big eyes smiled with gayer courage. And sturdy and healthful as she was, with her face all kindliness and love, she looked like the very personification of Fruitfulness, the good goddess with dazzling skin and perfect flesh, of sovereign dignity.

They remained for a moment clasped together in the golden sunshine which enveloped them with radiance. Then Mathieu pulled up Marianne's pillows, set the counterpane in order, and forbade her to stir until he had tidied the room. Forthwith he stripped his little bedstead, folded up the sheets, the mattress, and the bedstead itself, over which he slipped a cover. She vainly begged him not to trouble, saying that Zoe, the servant whom they had brought from the country, could very well do all those things. But he persisted, replying that the servant plagued him, and that he preferred to be alone to attend her and do all that there was to do. Then, as he suddenly began to shiver, he remarked that the room was cold, and blamed himself for not having already lighted the fire. Some logs and some small wood were piled in a corner, near the chimney-piece.

"How stupid of me!" he exclaimed; "here am I leaving you to freeze."

Then he knelt down before the fireplace, while she protested: "What an idea! Leave all that, and call Zoe."

"No, no, she doesn't know how to light the fire properly, and besides, it amuses me."

He laughed triumphantly when a bright clear fire began to crackle, filling the room with additional cheerfulness. The place was now a little paradise, said he; but he had scarcely finished washing and dressing when the partition behind the bed was shaken by a vigorous thumping.

"Ah! the rascals," he gayly exclaimed. "They are awake, you see! Oh! well, we may let them come, since to-day is Sunday."

For a few moments there had been a noise as of an aviary in commotion in the adjoining room. Prattling, shrill chirping, and ringing bursts of laughter could be heard. Then came a noise as of pillows and bolsters flying about, while two little fists continued pummelling the partition as if it were a drum.

"Yes, yes," said the mother, smiling and anxious, "answer them; tell them to come. They will be breaking everything if you don't."

Thereupon the father himself struck the wall, at which a victorious outburst, cries of triumphal delight, arose on the other side. And Mathieu scarcely had time to open the door before tramping and scuffling could be heard in the passage. A triumphal entry followed. All four of them wore long nightdresses falling to their little bare feet, and they trotted along and laughed, with their brown hair streaming about, their faces quite pink, and their eyes radiant with candid delight. Ambroise, though he was younger than his brothers, marched first, for he was the boldest and most enterprising. Behind him came the twins, Blaise and Denis, who were less turbulent—the latter especially. He taught the others to read, while Blaise, who was rather shy and timid, remained the dreamer of them all. And each gave a hand to little Mademoiselle Rose, who looked like an angel, pulled now to the right and now to the left amid bursts of laughter, while she contrived to keep herself steadily erect.

"Ah! mamma," cried Ambroise, "it's dreadfully cold, you know; do make me a little room."

Forthwith he bounded into the bed, slipped under the coverlet, and nestled close to his mother, so that only his laughing face and fine curly hair could be seen. But at this the two others raised a shout of war, and rushed forward in their turn upon the besieged citadel.

"Make a little room for us, mamma, make a little room! By your back, mamma! Near your shoulder, mamma!"

Only little Rose remained on the floor, feeling quite vexed and indignant. She had vainly attempted the assault, but had fallen back. "And me, mamma, and me," she pleaded.

It was necessary to help her in her endeavors to hoist herself up with her little hands. Then her mother took her in her arms in order that she might have the best place of all. Mathieu had at first felt somewhat anxious at seeing Marianne thus disturbed, but she laughed and told him not to trouble. And then the picture they all presented as they nestled there was so charming, so full of gayety, that he also smiled.

"It's very nice, it's so warm," said Ambroise, who was fond of taking his ease.

But Denis, the reasonable member of the band, began to explain why it was they had made so much noise "Blaise said that he had seen a spider. And then he felt frightened."

This accusation of cowardice vexed his brother, who replied: "It isn't true. I did see a spider, but I threw my pillow at it to kill it."

"So did I! so did I!" stammered Rose, again laughing wildly. "I threw my pillow like that—houp! houp!"

They all roared and wriggled again, so amusing did it seem to them. The truth was that they had engaged in a pillow fight under pretence of killing a spider, which Blaise alone said that he had seen. This unsupported testimony left the matter rather doubtful. But the whole brood looked so healthful and fresh in the bright sunshine that their father could not resist taking them in his arms, and kissing them here and there, wherever his lips lighted, a final game which sent them into perfect rapture amid a fresh explosion of laughter and shouts.

"Oh! what fun! what fun!"

"All the same," Marianne exclaimed, as she succeeded in freeing herself somewhat from the embraces of the children, "all the same, you know, I want to get up. I mustn't idle, for it does me no good. And besides, you little ones need to be washed and dressed."

They dressed in front of the big blazing fire; and it was nearly ten o'clock when they at last went down into the dining-room, where the earthenware stove was roaring, while the warm breakfast milk steamed upon the table. The ground floor of the pavilion comprised a dining-room and a drawing-room on the right of the hall, and a kitchen and a study on the left. The dining-room, like the principal bedchamber, overlooked the Rue de la Federation, and was filled every morning with cheerfulness by the rising sun.

The children were already at table, with their noses in their cups, when a ring at the street door was heard. And it was Dr. Boutan who came in. His arrival brought a renewal of noisy mirth, for the youngsters were fond of his round, good-natured face. He had attended them all at their births, and treated them like an old friend, with whom familiarity is allowable. And so they were already thrusting back their chairs to dart towards the doctor, when a remark from their mother restrained them.

"Now, please just leave the doctor quiet," said she, adding gayly, "Good morning, doctor. I'm much obliged to you for this bright sunshine, for I'm sure you ordered it so that I might go for a walk this afternoon."

"Why, yes, of course I ordered it—I was passing this way, and thought I would look in to see how you were getting on."

Boutan took a chair and seated himself near the table, while Mathieu explained to him that they had remained late in bed.

"Yes, that is all right, let her rest: but she must also take as much exercise as possible. However, there is no cause to worry. I see that she has a good appetite. When I find my patients at table, I cease to be a doctor, you know, I am simply a friend making a call."

Then he put a few questions, which the children, who were busy breakfasting, did not hear. And afterwards there came a pause in the conversation, which the doctor himself resumed, following, no doubt, some train of thought which he did not explain: "I hear that you are to lunch with the Seguins next Thursday," said he. "Ah! poor little woman! That is a terrible affair of hers."

With a gesture he expressed his feelings concerning the drama that had just upset the Seguins' household. Valentine, like Marianne, was to become a mother. For her part she was in despair at it, and her husband had given way to jealous fury. For a time, amid all their quarrels, they had continued leading their usual life of pleasure, but she now spent her days on a couch, while he neglected her and reverted to a bachelor's life. It was a very painful story, but the doctor was in hopes that Marianne, on the occasion of her visit to the Seguins, might bring some good influence to bear on them.

He rose from his chair and was about to retire, when the attack which had all along threatened him burst forth. The children, unsuspectedly rising from their chairs, had concerted together with a glance, and now they opened their campaign. The worthy doctor all at once found the twins upon his shoulders, while the younger boy clasped him round the waist and the little girl clung to his legs.

"Puff! puff! do the railway train, do the railway train, please do."

They pushed and shook him, amid peal after peal of flute-like laughter, while their father and mother rushed to his assistance, scolding and angry. But he calmed the parents by saying: "Let them be! they are simply wishing me good day. And besides, I must bear with them, you know, since, as our friend Beauchene says, it is a little bit my fault if they are in the world. What charms me with your children is that they enjoy such good health, just like their mother. For the present, at all events, one can ask nothing more of them."

When he had set them down on the floor, and given each a smacking kiss, he took hold of Marianne's hands and said to her that everything was going on beautifully, and that he was very pleased. Then he went off, escorted to the front door by Mathieu, the pair of them jesting and laughing gayly.

Directly after the midday meal Mathieu wished to go out, in order that Marianne might profit by the bright sunshine. The children had been dressed in readiness before sitting down to table, and it was scarcely more than one o'clock when the family turned the corner of the Rue de la Federation and found itself upon the quays.

This portion of Grenelle, lying between the Champ de Mars and the densely populated streets of the centre of the district, has an aspect all its own, characterized by vast bare expanses, and long and almost deserted streets running at right angles and fringed by factories with lofty, interminable gray walls. During work-hours nobody passes along these streets, and on raising one's head one sees only lofty chimneys belching forth thick coal smoke above the roofs of big buildings with dusty window panes. And if any large cart entrance happens to be open one may espy deep yards crowded with drays and full of acrid vapor. The only sounds are the strident puffs of jets of steam, the dull rumbling of machinery, and the sudden rattle of ironwork lowered from the carts to the pavement. But on Sundays the factories do not work, and the district then falls into death-like silence. In summer time there is but bright sunshine heating the pavement, in winter some icy snow-laden wind rushing down the lonely streets. The population of Grenelle is said to be the worst of Paris, both the most vicious and the most wretched. The neighborhood of the Ecole Militaire attracts thither a swarm of worthless women, who bring in their train all the scum of the populace. In contrast to all this the gay bourgeois district of Passy rises up across the Seine; while the rich aristocratic quarters of the Invalides and the Faubourg St. Germain spread out close by. Thus the Beauchene works on the quay, as their owner laughingly said, turned their back upon misery and looked towards all the prosperity and gayety of this world.

Mathieu was very partial to the avenues, planted with fine trees, which radiate from the Champ de Mars and the Esplanade des Invalides, supplying great gaps for air and sunlight. But he was particularly fond of that long diversified Quai d'Orsay, which starts from the Rue du Bac in the very centre of the city, passes before the Palais Bourbon, crosses first the Esplanade des Invalides, and then the Champ de Mars, to end at the Boulevard de Grenelle, in the black factory region. How majestically it spread out, what fine old leafy trees there were round that bend of the Seine from the State Tobacco Works to the garden of the Eiffel Tower! The river winds along with sovereign gracefulness; the avenue stretches out under superb foliage. You can really saunter there amid delicious quietude, instinct as it were with all the charm and power of Paris.

It was thither that Mathieu wished to take his wife and the little ones that Sunday. But the distance was considerable, and some anxiety was felt respecting Rose's little legs. She was intrusted to Ambroise, who, although the youngest of the boys, was already energetic and determined. These two opened the march; then came Blaise and Denis, the twins, the parents bringing up the rear. Everything at first went remarkably well: they strolled on slowly in the gay sunshine. That beautiful winter afternoon was exquisitely pure and clear, and though it was very cold in the shade, all seemed golden and velvety in the stretches of bright light. There were a great many people out of doors— all the idle folks, clad in their Sunday best, whom the faintest sunshine draws in crowds to the promenades of Paris. Little Rose, feeling warm and gay, drew herself up as if to show the people that she was a big girl. She crossed the whole extent of the Champ de Mars without asking to be carried. And her three brothers strode along making the frozen pavement resound beneath their steps. Promenaders were ever turning round to watch them. In other cities of Europe the sight of a young married couple preceded by four children would have excited no comment, but here in Paris the spectacle was so unusual that remarks of astonishment, sarcasm, and even compassion were exchanged. Mathieu and Marianne divined, even if they did not actually hear, these comments, but they cared nothing for them. They bravely went their way, smiling at one another, and feeling convinced that the course they had taken in life was the right one, whatever other folks might think or say.

It was three o'clock when they turned their steps homeward; and Marianne, feeling rather tired, then took a little rest on a sofa in the drawing-room, where Zoe had previously lighted a good fire. The children, quieted by fatigue, were sitting round a little table, listening to a tale which Denis read from a story-book, when a visitor was announced. This proved to be Constance, who, after driving out with Maurice, had thought of calling to inquire after Marianne, whom she saw only once or twice a week, although the little pavilion was merely separated by a garden from the large house on the quay.

"Oh! are you poorly, my dear?" she inquired as she entered the room and perceived Marianne on the sofa.

"Oh! dear, no," replied the other, "but I have been out walking for the last two hours and am now taking some rest."

Mathieu had brought an armchair forward for his wife's rich, vain cousin, who, whatever her real feelings, certainly strove to appear amiable. She apologized for not being able to call more frequently, and

ÉMILE ZOLA

explained what a number of duties she had to discharge as mistress of her home. Meantime Maurice, clad in black velvet, hung round her petticoats, gazing from a distance at the other children, who one and all returned his scrutiny.

"Well, Maurice," exclaimed his mother, "don't you wish your little cousins good-day?"

He had to do as he was bidden and step towards them. But all five remained embarrassed. They seldom met, and had as yet had no opportunity to quarrel. The four little savages of Chantebled felt indeed almost out of their element in the presence of this young Parisian with bourgeois manners.

"And are all your little folks quite well?" resumed Constance, who, with her sharp eyes, was comparing her son with the other lads. "Ambroise has grown; his elder brothers also look very strong."

Her examination did not apparently result to Maurice's advantage. The latter was tall and looked sturdy, but he had quite a waxen complexion. Nevertheless, the glance that Constance gave the others was full of irony, disdain, and condemnation. When she had first heard that Marianne was likely to become a mother once more she had made no secret of her disapproval. She held to her old opinions more vigorously than ever.

Marianne, knowing full well that they would fall out if they discussed the subject of children, sought another topic of conversation. She inquired after Beauchene. "And Alexandre," said she, "why did you not bring him with you? I haven't seen him for a week!"

"Why," broke in Mathieu, "I told you he had gone shooting yesterday evening. He slept, no doubt, at Puymoreau, the other side of Chantebled, so as to be in the woods at daybreak this morning, and he probably won't be home till to-morrow."

"Ah! yes, I remember now. Well, it's nice weather to be in the woods."

This, however, was another perilous subject, and Marianne regretted having broached it, for, truth to tell, one never knew where Beauchene might really be when he claimed to have gone shooting. He availed himself so often of this pretext to absent himself from home that Constance was doubtless aware of the truth. But in the presence of that household, whose union was so perfect, she was determined to show a brave front.

"Well, you know," said she, "it is I who compel him to go about and take as much exercise as possible. He has a temperament that needs the open air. Shooting is very good for him."

At this same moment there came another ring at the door, announcing another visitor. And this time it was Madame Morange who entered the room, with her daughter Reine. She colored when she caught sight of Madame Beauchene, so keenly was she impressed by that perfect model of wealth and distinction, whom she ever strove to imitate. Constance, however, profited by the diversion of Valerie's arrival to declare that she unfortunately could not remain any longer, as a friend must now be waiting for her at home.

"Well, at all events, leave us Maurice," suggested Mathieu. "Here's Reine here now, and all six children can play a little while together. I will bring you the boy by and by, when he has had a little snack."

But Maurice had already once more sought refuge among his mother's skirts. And she refused the invitation. "Oh! no, no!" said she. "He has to keep to a certain diet, you know, and he must not eat anything away from home. Good-by; I must be off. I called only to inquire after you all in passing. Keep well; good-by."

Then she led her boy away, never speaking to Valerie, but simply shaking hands with her in a familiar, protecting fashion, which the other considered to be extremely distinguished. Reine, on her side, had smiled at Maurice, whom she already slightly knew. She looked delightful that day in her gown of thick blue cloth, her face smiling under her heavy black tresses, and showing such a likeness to her mother that she seemed to be the latter's younger sister.

Marianne, quite charmed, called the girl to her: "Come and kiss me, my dear! Oh! what a pretty young lady! Why, she is getting quite beautiful and tall. How old is she?"

"Nearly thirteen," Valerie replied.

She had seated herself in the armchair vacated by Constance, and Mathieu noticed what a keen expression of anxiety there was in her soft eyes. After mentioning that she also had called in passing to make inquiries, and declaring that both mother and children looked remarkably well, she relapsed into gloomy silence, scarcely listening to Marianne, who thanked her for having come. Thereupon it occurred to Mathieu to leave her with his wife. To him it seemed that she must have something on her mind, and perhaps she wished to make a confidante of Marianne.

"My dear Reine," said he, "come with these little ones into the dining-room. We will see what afternoon snack there is, and lay the cloth."

This proposal was greeted with shouts of delight, and all the children trooped into the dining-room with Mathieu. A quarter of an hour later, when everything was ready there, and Valerie came in, the latter's eyes looked very red, as if she had been weeping. And that evening, when Mathieu was alone with his wife, he learnt what the trouble was. Morange's scheme of leaving the Beauchene works and entering the service of the Credit National, where he would speedily rise to a high and lucrative position, his hope too of giving Reine a big dowry and marrying her off to advantage—all the ambitious dreams of rank and wealth in which his wife and he had indulged, now showed no likelihood of fulfilment, since it seemed probable that Valerie might again have a child. Both she and her husband were in despair over it, and though Marianne had done her utmost to pacify her friend and reconcile her to circumstances, there were reasons to fear that in her distracted condition she might do something desperate.

Four days later, when the Froments lunched with the Seguins du Hordel at the luxurious mansion in the Avenue d'Antin, they came upon similar trouble there. Seguin, who was positively enraged, did not scruple to accuse his wife of infidelity, and, on his side, he took to quite a bachelor life. He had been a gambler in his younger days, and had never fully cured himself of that passion, which now broke out afresh, like a fire which has only slumbered for a time. He spent night after night at his club, playing at baccarat, and could be met in the betting ring at every race meeting. Then, too, he glided into equivocal society and appeared at home only at intervals to vent his irritation and spite and jealousy upon his ailing wife.

She, poor woman, was absolutely guiltless of the charges preferred against her. But knowing her husband, and unwilling for her own part to give up her life of pleasure, she had practised concealment as long as possible. And now she was really very ill, haunted too by an unreasoning, irremovable fear that it would all end in her death. Mathieu, who had seen her but a few months previously looking so fair and fresh, was amazed to find her such a wreck. And on her side Valentine gazed, all astonishment, at Marianne, noticing with surprise how calm and strong the young woman seemed, and how limpid her clear and smiling eyes remained.

On the day of the Froments' visit Seguin had gone out early in the morning, and when they arrived he had not yet returned. Thus the lunch was for a short time kept waiting, and during the interval Celeste, the maid, entered the room where the visitors sat near her mistress, who was stretched upon a sofa, looking a perfect picture of distress. Valentine turned a questioning glance on the servant, who forthwith replied:

"No, madame, Monsieur has not come back yet. But that woman of my village is here. You know, madame, the woman I spoke to you about, Sophie Couteau, La Couteau as we call her at Rougemont, who brings nurses to Paris?"

"Well, what of it?" exclaimed Valentine, on the point of ordering Celeste to leave the room, for it seemed to her quite outrageous to be disturbed in this manner.

"Well, madame, she's here; and as I told you before, if you would intrust her with the matter now she would find a very good wet nurse for you in the country, and bring her here whenever she's wanted."

La Couteau had been standing behind the door, which had remained ajar, and scarcely had Celeste finished than, without waiting for an invitation, she boldly entered the room. She was a quick little wizened woman, with certain peasant ways, but considerably polished by her frequent journeys to Paris. So far as her small keen eyes and pointed nose went her long face was not unpleasant, but its expression of good nature was marred by her hard mouth, her thin lips, suggestive of artfulness and cupidity. Her gown of dark woollen stuff, her black cape, black mittens, and black cap with yellow ribbons, gave her the appearance of a respectable countrywoman going to mass in her Sunday best.

"Have you been a nurse?" Valentine inquired, as she scrutinized her.

"Yes, madame," replied La Couteau, "but that was ten years ago, when I was only twenty. It seemed to me that I wasn't likely to make much money by remaining a nurse, and so I preferred to set up as an agent to bring others to Paris."

As she spoke she smiled, like an intelligent woman who feels that those who give their services as wet nurses to bourgeois families are simply fools and dupes. However, she feared that she might have said too much on the point, and so she added: "But one does what one can, eh, madame? The doctor told me that I should never do for a nurse again, and so I thought that I might perhaps help the poor little dears in another manner."

"And you bring wet nurses to the Paris offices?"

"Yes, madame, twice a month. I supply several offices, but more particularly Madame Broquette's office in the Rue Roquepine. It's a very respectable place, where one runs no risk of being deceived—And so, if you like, madame, I will choose the very best I can find for you—the pick of the bunch, so to say. I know the business thoroughly, and you can rely on me."

As her mistress did not immediately reply, Celeste ventured to intervene, and began by explaining how it happened that La Couteau had called that day.

"When she goes back into the country, madame, she almost always takes a baby with her, sometimes a nurse's child, and sometimes the child of people who are not well enough off to keep a nurse in the house. And she takes these children to some of the rearers in the country. She just now came to see me before going round to my friend Madame Menoux, whose baby she is to take away with her."

Valentine became interested. This Madame Menoux was a haberdasher in the neighborhood and a great friend of Celeste's. She had married a former soldier, a tall handsome fellow, who now earned a hundred and fifty francs a month as an attendant at a museum. She was very fond of him, and had bravely set up a little shop, the profits from which doubled their income, in such wise that they lived very happily and almost at their ease. Celeste, who frequently absented herself from her duties to spend hours gossiping in Madame Menoux's little shop, was forever being scolded for this practice; but in the present instance Valentine, full of anxiety and curiosity, did not chide her. The maid was quite proud at being questioned, and informed her mistress that Madame Menoux's baby was a fine little boy, and that the mother had been attended by a certain Madame Rouche, who lived at the lower end of the Rue du Rocher.

"It was I who recommended her," continued the servant, "for a friend of mine whom she had attended had spoken to me very highly of her. No doubt she has not such a good position as Madame Bourdieu, who has so handsome a place in the Rue de Miromesnil, but she is less expensive, and so very kind and obliging."

Then Celeste suddenly ceased speaking, for she noticed that Mathieu's eyes were fixed upon her, and this, for reasons best known to herself, made her feel uncomfortable. He on his side certainly placed no confidence in this big dark girl with a head like that of a horse, who, it seemed to him, knew far too much.

Marianne joined in the conversation. "But why," asked she, "why does not this Madame Menoux, whom you speak about, keep her baby with her?"

Thereupon La Couteau turned a dark harsh glance upon this lady visitor, who, whatever course she might take herself, had certainly no right to prevent others from doing business.

"Oh! it's impossible," exclaimed Celeste, well pleased with the diversion. "Madame Menoux's shop is no bigger than my pocket-handkerchief, and at the back of it there is only one little room where she and her husband take their meals and sleep. And that room, too, overlooks a tiny courtyard where one can neither see nor breathe. The baby would not live a week in such a place. And, besides, Madame Menoux would not have time to attend to the child. She has never had a servant, and what with waiting on customers and having to cook meals in time for her husband's return from the museum, she never has a moment to spare. Oh! if she could, she would be very happy to keep the little fellow with her."

"It is true," said Marianne sadly; "there are some poor mothers whom I pity with all my heart. This person you speak of is not in poverty, and yet is reduced to this cruel separation. For my part, I should not be able to exist if a child of mine were taken away from me to some unknown spot and given to another woman."

La Couteau doubtless interpreted this as an attack upon herself. Assuming the kindly demeanor of one who dotes on children, the air which she always put on to prevail over hesitating mothers, she replied: "Oh, Rougemont is such a very pretty place. And then it's not far from Bayeux, so that folks are by no means savages there. The air is so pure, too, that people come there to recruit their health. And, besides, the little ones who are confided to us are well cared for, I assure you. One would have to be heartless to do otherwise than love such little angels."

However, like Celeste, she relapsed into silence on seeing how significantly Mathieu was looking at her. Perhaps, in spite of her rustic ways, she understood that there was a false ring in her voice. Besides, of what use was her usual patter about the salubrity of the region, since that lady, Madame Seguin, wished to have a nurse at her house? So she resumed: "Then it's understood, madame, I will bring you the best we have, a real treasure."

Valentine, now a little tranquillized as to her fears for herself, found strength to speak out. "No, no, I won't pledge myself in advance. I will send to see the nurses you bring to the office, and we shall see if there is one to suit me."

Then, without occupying herself further about the woman, she turned to Marianne, and asked: "Shall you nurse your baby yourself?"

ÉMILE ZOLA

"Certainly, as I did with the others. We have very decided opinions on that point, my husband and I."

"No doubt. I understand you: I should much like to do the same myself; but it is impossible."

La Couteau had remained there motionless, vexed at having come on a fruitless errand, and regretting the loss of the present which she would have earned by her obligingness in providing a nurse. She put all her spite into a glance which she shot at Marianne, who, thought she, was evidently some poor creature unable even to afford a nurse. However, at a sign which Celeste made her, she courtesied humbly and withdrew in the company of the maid.

A few minutes afterwards, Seguin arrived, and, repairing to the dining-room, they all sat down to lunch there. It was a very luxurious meal, comprising eggs, red mullet, game, and crawfish, with red and white Bordeaux wines and iced champagne. Such diet for Valentine and Marianne would never have met with Dr. Boutan's approval; but Seguin declared the doctor to be an unbearable individual whom nobody could ever please.

He, Seguin, while showing all politeness to his guests, seemed that day to be in an execrable temper. Again and again he levelled annoying and even galling remarks at his wife, carrying things to such a point at times that tears came to the unfortunate woman's eyes. Now that he scarcely set foot in the house he complained that everything was going wrong there. If he spent his time elsewhere it was, according to him, entirely his wife's fault. The place was becoming a perfect hell upon earth. And in everything, the slightest incident, the most common-place remark, he found an opportunity for jeers and gibes. These made Mathieu and Marianne extremely uncomfortable; but at last he let fall such a harsh expression that Valentine indignantly rebelled, and he had to apologize. At heart he feared her, especially when the blood of the Vaugelades arose within her, and she gave him to understand, in her haughty disdainful way, that she would some day revenge herself on him for his treatment.

However, seeking another outlet for his spite and rancor, he at last turned to Mathieu, and spoke of Chantebled, saying bitterly that the game in the covers there was fast becoming scarcer and scarcer, in such wise that he now had difficulty in selling his shooting shares, so that his income from the property was dwindling every year. He made no secret of the fact that he would much like to sell the estate, but where could he possibly find a purchaser for those unproductive woods, those sterile plains, those marshes and those tracts of gravel?

Mathieu listened to all this attentively, for during his long walks in the summer he had begun to take an interest in the estate. "Are you really of opinion that it cannot be cultivated?" he asked. "It's pitiful to see all that land lying waste and idle."

"Cultivate it!" cried Seguin. "Ah! I should like to see such a miracle! The only crops that one will ever raise on it are stones and frogs."

They had by this time eaten their dessert, and before rising from table Marianne was telling Valentine that she would much like to see and kiss her children, who had not been allowed to lunch with their elders on account of their supposed unruly ways, when a couple of visitors arrived in turn, and everything else was forgotten. One was Santerre the novelist, who of late had seldom called on the Seguins, and the other, much to Mathieu's dislike, proved to be Beauchene's sister, Seraphine, the Baroness de Lowicz. She looked at the young man in a bold, provoking, significant manner, and then, like Santerre, cast a sly glance of mocking contempt at Marianne and Valentine. She and the novelist between them soon turned the conversation on to subjects that appealed to their vicious tastes. And Santerre related that he had lately seen Doctor Gaude perform several operations at the Marbeuf Hospital. He had found there the usual set of society men who attend first performances at the theatres, and indeed there were also some women present.

And then he enlarged upon the subject, giving the crudest and most precise particulars, much to the delight of Seguin, who every now and again interpolated remarks of approval, while both Mathieu and Marianne grew more and more ill at ease. The young woman sat looking with amazement at Santerre as he calmly recapitulated horror after horror, to the evident enjoyment of the others. She remembered having read his last book, that love story which had seemed to her so supremely absurd, with its theories of the annihilation of the human species. And she at last glanced at Mathieu to tell him how weary she felt of all the semi-society and semi-medical chatter around her, and how much she would like to go off home, leaning on his arm, and walking slowly along the sunlit quays. He, for his part, felt a pang at seeing so much insanity rife amid those wealthy surroundings. He made his wife a sign that it was indeed time to take leave.

"What! are you going already!" Valentine then exclaimed. "Well, I dare not detain you if you feel tired." However, when Marianne begged her to kiss the children for her, she added: "Why, yes, it's true you have not seen them. Wait a moment, pray; I want you to kiss them yourself."

But when Celeste appeared in answer to the bell, she announced that Monsieur Gaston and Mademoiselle Lucie had gone out with their governess. And this made Seguin explode once more. All his rancor against his wife revived. The house was going to rack and ruin. She spent her days lying on a sofa. Since when had the governess taken leave to go out with the children without saying anything? One could not even see the children now in order to kiss them. It was a nice state of things. They were left to the servants; in fact, it was the servants now who controlled the house.

Thereupon Valentine began to cry.

"*Mon Dieu!*" said Marianne to her husband, when she found herself out of doors, able to breathe, and happy once more now that she was leaning on his arm; "why, they are quite mad, the people in that house."

"Yes," Mathieu responded, "they are mad, no doubt; but we must pity them, for they know not what happiness is."

VI

About nine o'clock one fine cold morning, a few days afterwards, as Mathieu, bound for his office, a little late through having lingered near his wife, was striding hastily across the garden which separated the pavilion from the factory yard, he met Constance and Maurice, who, clad in furs, were going out for a walk in the sharp air. Beauchene, who was accompanying them as far as the gate, bareheaded and ever sturdy and victorious, gayly exclaimed to his wife:

"Give the youngster a good spin on his legs! Let him take in all the fresh air he can. There's nothing like that and good food to make a man."

Mathieu, on hearing this, stopped short. "Has Maurice been poorly again?" he inquired.

"Oh, no!" hastily replied the boy's mother, with an appearance of great gayety, assumed perhaps from an unconscious desire to hide certain covert fears. "Only the doctor wants him to take exercise, and it is so fine this morning that we are going off on quite an expedition."

"Don't go along the quays," said Beauchene again. "Go up towards the Invalides. He'll have much stiffer marching to do when he's a soldier."

Then, the mother and the child having taken themselves off, he went back into the works with Mathieu, adding in his triumphant way: "That youngster, you know, is as strong as an oak. But women are always so nervous. For my part, I'm quite easy in mind about him, as you can see." And with a laugh he concluded: "When one has but one son, he keeps him."

That same day, about an hour later, a terrible dispute which broke out between old Moineaud's daughters, Norine and Euphrasie, threw the factory into a state of commotion. Norine's intrigue with Beauchene had ended in the usual way. He had soon tired of the girl and betaken himself to some other passing fancy, leaving her to her tears, her shame, and all the consequences of her fault; for although it had hitherto been possible for her to conceal her condition from her parents, she was unable to deceive her sister, who was her constant companion. The two girls were always bickering, and Norine had for some time lived in dread of scandal and exposure. And that day the trouble came to a climax, beginning with a trivial dispute about a bit of glass-paper in the workroom, then developing into a furious exchange of coarse, insulting language, and culminating in a frantic outburst from Euphrasie, who shrieked to the assembled work-girls all that she knew about her sister.

There was an outrageous scene: the sisters fought, clawing and scratching one another desperately, and could not be separated until Beauchene, Mathieu, and Morange, attracted by the extraordinary uproar, rushed into the workroom and restored a little order. Fortunately for Beauchene, Euphrasie did not know the whole truth, and Norine, after giving her employer a humble, supplicating glance, kept silence; but old Moineaud was present, and the public revelation of his daughter's shame sent him into a fury. He ordered Norine out of the works forthwith, and threatened to throw her out of window should he find her at home when he returned there in the evening. And Beauchene, both annoyed at the scandal and ashamed at being the primary cause of it, did not venture to interfere. It was only after the unhappy Norine had rushed off sobbing that he found strength of mind to attempt to pacify the father, and assert his authority in the workroom by threatening to dismiss one and all of the girls if the slightest scandal, the slightest noise, should ever occur there again.

Mathieu was deeply pained by the scene, but kept his own counsel. What most astonished him was the promptness with which Beauchene regained his self-possession as soon as Norine had fled, and the majesty with which he withdrew to his office after threatening the others and restoring order. Another whom the scene had painfully affected was Morange, whom Mathieu, to his surprise, found ghastly pale, with trembling hands, as if indeed he had had some share of responsibility in this unhappy business. But Morange, as he confided to Mathieu, was distressed for other reasons. The scene in the workroom, the revelation of Norine's condition, the fate awaiting the girl driven away into the bleak, icy streets, had revived all his own poignant worries with respect to Valerie. Mathieu had already heard of the latter's trouble from his wife, and he speedily grasped the accountant's meaning. It vaguely seemed to him also that Morange was yielding to the same unreasoning despair as Valerie, and was almost willing that she should take the desperate course which she had hinted to Marianne. But it was a very serious matter, and Mathieu did not wish to be in any way mixed up in it. Having tried his best to pacify the cashier, he sought forgetfulness of these painful incidents in his work.

That afternoon, however, a little girl, Cecile Moineaud, the old fitter's youngest daughter, slipped into his office, with a message from her mother, beseeching him to speak with her. He readily understood that the woman wished to see him respecting Norine, and in his usual compassionate way he consented to go. The interview took place in one of the adjacent streets, down which the cold winter wind was blowing. La Moineaude was there with Norine and another little girl of hers, Irma, a child eight years of age. Both Norine and her mother wept abundantly while begging Mathieu to help them. He alone knew the whole truth, and was in a position to approach Beauchene on the subject. La Moineaude was firmly determined to say nothing to her husband. She trembled for his future and that of her son Alfred, who was now employed at the works; for there was no telling what might happen if Beauchene's name should be mentioned. Life was indeed hard enough already, and what would become of them all should the family bread-winners be turned away from the factory? Norine certainly had no legal claim on Beauchene, the law being peremptory on that point; but, now that she had lost her employment, and was driven from home by her father, could he leave her to die of want in the streets? The girl tried to enforce her moral claim by asserting that she had always been virtuous before meeting Beauchene. In any case, her lot remained a very hard one. That Beauchene was the father of her child there could be no doubt; and at last Mathieu, without promising success, told the mother that he would do all he could in the matter.

He kept his word that same afternoon, and after a great deal of difficulty he succeeded. At first Beauchene fumed, stormed, denied, equivocated, almost blamed Mathieu for interfering, talked too of blackmail, and put on all sorts of high and mighty airs. But at heart the matter greatly worried him. What if Norine or her mother should go to his wife? Constance might close her eyes as long as she simply suspected things, but if complaints were formally, openly made to her, there would be a terrible scandal. On the other hand, however, should he do anything for the girl, it would become known, and everybody would regard him as responsible. And then there would be no end to what he called the blackmailing.

However, when Beauchene reached this stage Mathieu felt that the battle was gained. He smiled and answered: "Of course, one can never tell—the girl is certainly not malicious. But when women are driven beyond endurance, they become capable of the worst follies. I must say that she made no demands of me; she did not even explain what she wanted; she simply said that she could not remain in the streets in this bleak weather, since her father had turned her away from home. If you want my opinion, it is this: I think that one might at once put her to board at a proper place. Let us say that four or five months will elapse before she is able to work again; that would mean a round sum of five hundred francs in expenses. At that cost she might be properly looked after."

Beauchene walked nervously up and down, and then replied: "Well, I haven't a bad heart, as you know. Five hundred francs more or less will not inconvenience me. If I flew into a temper just now it was because the mere idea of being robbed and imposed upon puts me beside myself. But if it's a question of charity, why, then, do as you suggest. It must be understood, however, that I won't mix myself up in anything; I wish even to remain ignorant of what you do. Choose a nurse, place the girl where you please, and I will simply pay the bill. Neither more nor less."

Then he heaved a sigh of relief at the prospect of being extricated from this equivocal position, the worry of which he refused to acknowledge. And once more he put on the mien of a superior, victorious man, one who is certain that he will win all the battles of life. In fact, he even jested about the girl, and at last went off repeating his instructions: "See that my conditions are fully understood. I don't want to know anything about any child. Do whatever you please, but never let me hear another word of the matter."

That day was certainly one fertile in incidents, for in the evening there was quite an alarm at the Beauchenes. At the moment when they were about to sit down to dinner little Maurice fainted away and fell upon the floor. Nearly a quarter of an hour elapsed before the child could be revived, and meantime the distracted parents quarrelled and shouted, accusing one another of having compelled the lad to go out walking that morning in such cold, frosty weather. It was evidently that foolish outing which had chilled him. At least, this was what they said to one another by way of quieting their anxiety. Constance, while she held her boy in her arms, pictured him as dead. It occurred to her for the first time that she might possibly lose him. At this idea she experienced a terrible heart-pang, and a feeling of motherliness came upon her, so acute that it was like a revelation. The ambitious woman that was in her, she who dreamt of royalty for that only son, the future princely owner of the ever-growing family fortune, likewise suffered horribly. If she was to lose that son she would have no child left. Why had she none other? Was it not she who had willed it thus? At this thought a feeling of desperate regret shot through her like a red-hot blade, burning her cruelly to the very depths of her being. Maurice, however, at last recovered consciousness, and even sat down to the table and ate with a fair appetite. Then Beauchene immediately shrugged his shoulders, and began to jest about the unreasoning fears of women. And as time went by Constance herself ceased to think of the incident.

On the morrow, when Mathieu had to attend to the delicate mission which he had undertaken, he remembered the two women of whom Celeste, the maid, had spoken on the day of his visit to the Seguins. He at first dismissed all idea of that Madame Rouche, of whom the girl had spoken so strangely, but he thought of making some inquiries respecting Madame Bourdieu, who accommodated boarders at the little house where she resided in the Rue de Miromesnil. And he seemed to remember that this woman had attended Madame Morange at the time of Reine's birth, a circumstance which induced him to question the cashier.

At the very first words the latter seemed greatly disturbed. "Yes, a lady friend recommended Madame Bourdieu to my wife," said he; "but why do you ask me?"

And as he spoke he looked at Mathieu with an expression of anguish, as if that sudden mention of Madame Bourdieu's name signified that the young fellow had guessed his secret preoccupations. It was as though he had been abruptly surprised in wrong-doing. Perhaps, too, certain dim, haunting thoughts, which he had long been painfully revolving in his mind, without as yet being able to come to a decision, took shape at that moment. At all events, he turned pale and his lips trembled.

Then, as Mathieu gave him to understand that it was a question of placing Norine somewhere, he involuntarily let an avowal escape him.

"My wife was speaking to me of Madame Bourdieu only this morning," he began. "Oh! I don't know how it happened, but, as you are aware, Reine was born so many years ago that I can't give you any precise information. It seems that the woman has done well, and is now at the head of a first-class establishment. Inquire there yourself; I have no doubt you will find what you want there."

Mathieu followed this advice; but at the same time, as he had been warned that Madame Bourdieu's terms were rather high, he stifled his prejudices and began by repairing to the Rue du Rocher in order to reconnoitre Madame Rouche's establishment and make some inquiries of her. The mere aspect of the place chilled him. It was one of the black houses of old Paris, with a dark, evil-smelling passage, leading into a small yard which the nurse's few squalid rooms overlooked. Above the passage entrance was a yellow signboard which simply bore the name of Madame Rouche in big letters. She herself proved to be a person of five-or six-and-thirty, gowned in black and spare of figure, with a leaden complexion, scanty hair of no precise color, and a big nose of unusual prominence. With her low, drawling speech, her prudent, cat-like gestures, and her sour smile, he divined her to be a dangerous, unscrupulous woman. She told him that, as the accommodation at her disposal was so small, she only took boarders for a limited time, and this of course enabled him to curtail his inquiries. Glad to have done with her, he hurried off, oppressed by nausea and vaguely frightened by what he had seen of the place.

On the other hand, Madame Bourdieu's establishment, a little three-storied house in the Rue de Miromesnil, between the Rue La Boetie and the Rue de Penthievre, offered an engaging aspect, with its bright facade and muslin-curtained windows. And Madame Bourdieu, then two-and-thirty, rather short and stout, had a broad, pleasant white face, which had greatly helped her on the road to success. She expatiated to Mathieu on the preliminary training that was required by one of her profession, the cost of it, the efforts needed to make a position, the responsibilities, the inspections, the worries of all sorts that she had to face; and she plainly told the young man that her charge for a boarder would be two hundred francs a month. This was far more than he was empowered to give; however, after some further conversation, when Madame Bourdieu learnt that it was a question of four months' board, she became more accommodating, and agreed to accept a round sum of six hundred francs for the entire period, provided that the person for whom Mathieu was acting would consent to occupy a three-bedded room with two other boarders.

Altogether there were about a dozen boarders' rooms in the house, some of these having three, and even four, beds; while others, the terms for which were naturally higher, contained but one. Madame Bourdieu could accommodate as many as thirty boarders, and as a rule, she had some five-and-twenty staying on her premises. Provided they complied with the regulations, no questions were asked them. They were not required to say who they were or whence they came, and in most cases they were merely known by some Christian name which they chose to give.

Mathieu ended by agreeing to Madame Bourdieu's terms, and that same evening Norine was taken to her establishment. Some little trouble ensued with Beauchene, who protested when he learnt that five hundred francs would not suffice to defray the expenses. However, Mathieu managed affairs so diplomatically that at last the other not only became reconciled to the terms, but provided the money to purchase a little linen, and even agreed to supply pocket-money to the extent of ten francs a month. Thus, five days after Norine had entered Madame Bourdieu's establishment, Mathieu decided to return thither to hand the girl her first ten francs and tell her that he had settled everything.

He found her there in the boarders' refectory with some of her companions in the house—a tall, thin, severe-looking Englishwoman, with lifeless eyes and bloodless lips, who called herself Amy, and a pale red-haired girl with a tip-tilted nose and a big mouth, who was known as Victoire. Then, too, there was a young person of great beauty answering to the name of Rosine, a jeweller's daughter, so Norine told Mathieu, whose story was at once pathetic and horrible. The young man, while waiting to see Madame Bourdieu, who was engaged, sat for a time answering Norine's questions, and listening to the others, who conversed before him in a free and open way. His heart was wrung by much that he heard, and as soon as he could rid himself of Norine he returned to the waiting-room, eager to complete his business. There, however, two women who wished to consult Madame Bourdieu, and who sat chatting side by side on a sofa, told him that she was still engaged, so that he was compelled to tarry a little longer. He ensconced himself in a large armchair, and taking a newspaper from his pocket, began to read it. But he had not been thus occupied for many minutes before the door opened and a servant entered, ushering in a lady dressed in black and thickly veiled, whom she asked to be good enough to wait her turn. Mathieu was on the point of rising, for, though his back was turned to the door, he could see, in a looking-glass, that the new arrival was none other than Morange's wife, Valerie. After a moment's hesitation, however, the sight of her black gown and thick veil, which seemed to indicate that she desired to escape recognition, induced him to dive back into his armchair and feign extreme attention to his newspaper. She, on her side, had certainly not noticed him, but by glancing slantwise towards the looking-glass he could observe all her movements.

Meantime the conversation between the other women on the sofa continued, and to Mathieu's surprise it suddenly turned on Madame

Rouche, concerning whom one of them began telling the most horrible stories, which fully confirmed the young man's previous suspicions. These stories seemed to have a powerful fascination for Valerie, who sat in a corner, never stirring, but listening intently. She did not even turn her head towards the other women, but, beneath her veil, Mathieu could detect her big eyes glittering feverishly. She started but once. It was when one of the others inquired of her friend where that horrid creature La Rouche resided, and the other replied, "At the lower end of the Rue du Rocher."

Then their chatter abruptly ceased, for Madame Bourdieu made her appearance on the threshold of her private room. The gossips exchanged only a few words with her, and then, as Mathieu remained in his armchair, the high back of which concealed him from view, Valerie rose from her seat and followed Madame Bourdieu into the private room.

As soon as he was alone the young man let his newspaper fall upon his knees, and lapsed into a reverie, haunted by all the chatter he had heard, both there and in Norine's company, and shuddering at the thought of the dreadful secrets that had been revealed to him. How long an interval elapsed he could not tell, but at last he was suddenly roused by a sound of voices.

Madame Bourdieu was now escorting Valerie to the door. She had the same plump fresh face as usual, and even smiled in a motherly way; but the other was quivering, as with distress and grief. "You are not sensible, my dear child," said Madame Bourdieu to her. "It is simply foolish of you. Come, go home and be good."

Then, Valerie having withdrawn without uttering a word, Madame Bourdieu was greatly surprised to see Mathieu, who had risen from his chair. And she suddenly became serious, displeased with herself at having spoken in his presence. Fortunately, a diversion was created by the arrival of Norine, who came in from the refectory; and Mathieu then promptly settled his business and went off, after promising Norine that he would return some day to see her.

To make up for lost time he was walking hastily towards the Rue La Boetie, when, all at once, he came to a halt, for at the very corner of that street he again perceived Valerie, now talking to a man, none other than her husband. So Morange had come with her, and had waited for her in the street while she interviewed Madame Bourdieu. And now they both stood there consulting together, hesitating and evidently in distress. It was plain to Mathieu that a terrible combat was going on within them. They stamped about, moved hither and thither in a feverish way, then halted once more to resume their conversation in a whisper. At one moment the young man felt intensely relieved, for, turning into the Rue La Boetie, they walked on slowly, as if downcast and resigned, in the direction of Grenelle. But all at once they halted once more and exchanged a few words; and then Mathieu's heart contracted as he saw them retrace their steps along the Rue La Boetie and follow the Rue de la Pepiniere as far as the Rue du Rocher. He readily divined whither they were going, but some irresistible force impelled him to follow them; and before long, from an open doorway, in which he prudently concealed himself, he saw them look round to ascertain whether they were observed, and then slink, first the wife and afterwards the husband, into the dark passage of La Rouche's house. For a moment Mathieu lingered in his hiding-place, quivering, full of dread and horror; and when at last he turned his steps homeward it was with a heavy heart indeed.

The weeks went by, the winter ran its course, and March had come round, when the memory of all that the young fellow had heard and seen that day—things which he had vainly striven to forget—was revived in the most startling fashion. One morning at eight o'clock Morange abruptly called at the little pavilion in the Rue de la Federation, accompanied by his daughter Reine. The cashier was livid, haggard, distracted, and as soon as Reine had joined Mathieu's children, and could not hear what he said, he implored the young man to come with him. In a gasp he told the dreadful truth—Valerie was dying. Her daughter believed her to be in the country, but that was a mere fib devised to quiet the girl. Valerie was elsewhere, in Paris, and he, Morange, had a cab waiting below, but lacked the strength to go back to her alone, so poignant was his grief, so great his dread.

Mathieu was expecting a happy event that very day, and he at first told the cashier that he could not possibly go with him; but when he had informed Marianne that he believed that something dreadful had happened to the Moranges, she bravely bade him render all assistance. And then the two men drove, as Mathieu had anticipated, to the Rue du Rocher, and there found the hapless Valerie, not dying, but dead, and white, and icy cold. Ah! the desperate, tearless grief of the husband, who fell upon his knees at the bedside, benumbed, annihilated, as if he also felt death's heavy hand upon him.

For a moment, indeed, the young man anticipated exposure and scandal. But when he hinted this to La Rouche she faintly smiled. She had friends on many sides, it seemed. She had already reported Valerie's death at the municipal office, and the doctor, who would be sent to certify the demise, would simply ascribe it to natural causes. Such was the usual practice!

Then Mathieu bethought himself of leading Morange away; but the other, still plunged in painful stupor, did not heed him.

"No, no, my friend, I pray you, say nothing," he at last replied, in a very faint, distant voice, as though he feared to awaken the unfortunate woman who had fallen asleep forever. "I know what I have done; I shall never forgive myself. If she lies there, it is because I consented. Yet I adored her, and never wished her aught but happiness. I loved her too much, and I was weak. Still, I was the husband, and when her madness came upon her I ought to have acted sensibly, and have warned and dissuaded her. I can understand and excuse her, poor creature; but as for me, it is all over; I am a wretch; I feel horrified with myself."

All his mediocrity and tenderness of heart sobbed forth in this confession of his weakness. And his voice never gave sign of animation, never rose in a louder tone from the depths of his annihilated being, which would evermore be void. "She wished to be gay, and rich, and happy," he continued. "It was so legitimate a wish on her part, she was so intelligent and beautiful! There was only one delight for me, to content her tastes and satisfy her ambition. You know our new flat. We spent far too much money on it. Then came that story of the Credit National and the hope of speedily rising to fortune. And thus, when the trouble came, and I saw her distracted at the idea of having to renounce all her dreams, I became as mad as she was, and suffered her to do her will. We thought that our only means of escaping from everlasting penury and drudgery was to evade Nature, and now, alas! she lies there."

Morange's lugubrious voice, never broken by a sob, never rising to violence, but sounding like a distant, monotonous, mournful knell, rent Mathieu's heart. He sought words of consolation, and spoke of Reine.

"Ah, yes!" said the other, "I am very fond of Reine. She is so like her mother. You will keep her at your house till to-morrow, won't you? Tell her nothing; let her play; I will acquaint her with this dreadful misfortune. And don't worry me, I beg you, don't take me away. I promise you that I will keep very quiet: I will simply stay here, watching her. Nobody will even hear me; I shan't disturb any one."

Then his voice faltered and he stammered a few more incoherent phrases as he sank into a dream of his wrecked life.

Mathieu, seeing him so quiet, so overcome, at last decided to leave him there, and, entering the waiting cab, drove back to Grenelle. Ah! it was indeed relief for him to see the crowded, sunlit streets again, and to breathe the keen air which came in at both windows of the vehicle. Emerging from that horrid gloom, he breathed gladly beneath the vast sky, all radiant with healthy joy. And the image of Marianne arose before him like a consolatory promise of life's coming victory, an atonement for every shame and iniquity. His dear wife, whom everlasting hope kept full of health and courage, and through whom, even amid her pangs, love would triumph, while they both held themselves in readiness for to-morrow's allotted effort! The cab rolled on so slowly that Mathieu almost despaired, eager as he was to reach his bright little house, that he might once more take part in life's poem, that august festival instinct with so much suffering and so much joy, humanity's everlasting hymn, the coming of a new being into the world.

That very day, soon after his return, Denis and Blaise, Ambroise, Rose, and Reine were sent round to the Beauchenes', where they filled the house with their romping mirth. Maurice, however, was again ailing, and had to lie upon a sofa, disconsolate at being unable to take part in the play of the others. "He has pains in his legs," said his father to Mathieu, when he came round to inquire after Marianne; "he's growing so fast, and getting such a big fellow, you know."

Lightly as Beauchene spoke, his eyes even then wavered, and his face remained for a moment clouded. Perhaps, in his turn, he also had felt the passing of that icy breath from the unknown which one evening had made Constance shudder with dread whilst she clasped her swooning boy in her arms.

But at that moment Mathieu, who had left Marianne's room to answer Beauchene's inquiries, was summoned back again. And there he now found the sunlight streaming brilliantly, like a glorious greeting to new life. While he yet stood there, dazzled by the glow, the doctor said to him: "It is a boy."

Then Mathieu leant over his wife and kissed her lovingly. Her beautiful eyes were still moist with the tears of anguish, but she was already smiling with happiness.

"Dear, dear wife," said Mathieu, "how good and brave you are, and how I love you!"

"Yes, yes, I am very happy," she faltered, "and I must try to give you back all the love that you give me."

Ah! that room of battle and victory, it seemed radiant with triumphant glory. Elsewhere was death, darkness, shame, and crime, but here holy suffering had led to joy and pride, hope and trustfulness in the coming future. One single being born, a poor bare wee creature, raising the faint cry of a chilly fledgeling, and life's immense treasure was increased and eternity insured. Mathieu remembered one warm balmy spring night when, yonder at Chantebled, all the perfumes of fruitful nature had streamed into their room in the little hunting-box, and now around him amid equal rapture he beheld the ardent sunlight flaring, chanting the poem of eternal life that sprang from love the eternal.

VII

"I tell you that I don't need Zoe to give the child a bath," exclaimed Mathieu half in anger. "Stay in bed, and rest yourself!"

"But the servant must get the bath ready," replied Marianne, "and bring you some warm water."

She laughed as if amused by the dispute, and he ended by laughing also.

Two days previously they had re-installed themselves in the little pavilion on the verge of the woods near Janville which they rented from the Seguins. So impatient, indeed, were they to find themselves once more among the fields that in spite of the doctor's advice Marianne had made the journey but fifteen days after giving birth to her little boy. However, a precocious springtide brought with it that March such balmy warmth and sunshine that the only ill-effect she experienced was a little fatigue. And so, on the day after their arrival—Sunday—Mathieu, glad at being able to remain with her, insisted that she should rest in bed, and only rise about noon, in time for dejeuner.

"Why," he repeated, "I can very well attend to the child while you rest. You have him in your arms from morning till night. And, besides, if you only knew how pleased I am to be here again with you and the dear little fellow."

He approached her to kiss her gently, and with a fresh laugh she returned his kiss. It was quite true: they were both delighted to be back at Chantebled, which recalled to them such loving memories. That room, looking towards the far expanse of sky and all the countryside, renascent, quivering with sap, was gilded with gayety by the early springtide.

Marianne leant over the cradle which was near her, beside the bed. "The fact is," said she, "Master Gervais is sound asleep. Just look at him. You will never have the heart to wake him."

Then both father and mother remained for a moment gazing at their sleeping child. Marianne had passed her arm round her husband's neck and was clinging to him, as they laughed delightedly over the cradle in which the little one slumbered. He was a fine child, pink and white already; but only a father and mother could thus contemplate their offspring. As the baby opened his eyes, which were still full of all the mystery whence he had come, they raised exclamations full of emotion.

"You know, he saw me!"

"Certainly, and me too. He looked at me: he turned his head."

"Oh, the cherub!"

It was but an illusion, but that dear little face, still so soft and silent, told them so many things which none other would have heard! They found themselves repeated in the child, mingled as it were together; and detected extraordinary likenesses, which for hours and for days kept them discussing the question as to which of them he most resembled. Moreover, each proved very obstinate, declaring that he was the living portrait of the other.

As a matter of course, Master Gervais had no sooner opened his eyes than he began to shriek. But Marianne was pitiless: her rule was the bath first and milk afterwards. Zoe brought up a big jug of hot water, and then set out the little bath near the window in the sunlight. And Mathieu, all obstinacy, bathed the child, washing him with a soft sponge for some three minutes, while Marianne, from her bed, watched over the operation, jesting about the delicacy of touch that he displayed, as if the child were some fragile new-born divinity whom he feared to bruise with his big hands. At the same time they continued marvelling at the delightful scene. How pretty he looked in the water, his pink skin shining in the sunlight! And how well-behaved he was, for it was wonderful to see how quickly he ceased wailing and gave signs of satisfaction when he felt the all-enveloping caress of the warm water. Never had father and mother possessed such a little treasure.

"And now," said Mathieu, when Zoe had helped him to wipe the boy with a fine cloth, "and now we will weigh Master Gervais."

This was a complicated operation, which was rendered the more difficult by the extreme repugnance that the child displayed. He struggled and wriggled on the platform of the weighing scales to such a degree that it was impossible to arrive at his correct weight, in order to ascertain how much this had increased since the previous occasion. As a rule, the increase varied from six to seven ounces a week. The father generally lost patience over the operation, and the mother had to intervene.

"Here! put the scales on the table near my bed, and give me the little one in his napkin. We will see what the napkin weighs afterwards."

At this moment, however, the customary morning invasion took place. The other four children, who were beginning to know how to dress themselves, the elder ones helping the younger, and Zoe lending a hand at times, darted in at a gallop, like frolicsome escaped colts. Having thrown themselves on papa's neck and rushed upon mamma's bed to say good-morning, the boys stopped short, full of admiration and interest at the sight of Gervais in the scales. Rose, however, still rather uncertain on her legs, caught hold of the scales in her impatient efforts to climb upon the bed, and almost toppled everything over. "I want to see! I want to see!" she cried in her shrill voice.

At this the others likewise wished to meddle, and already stretched out their little hands, so that it became necessary to turn them out of doors.

"Now kindly oblige me by going to play outside," said Mathieu. "Take your hats and remain under the window, so that we may hear you."

Then, in spite of the complaints and leaps of Master Gervais, Marianne was at last able to obtain his correct weight. And what delight there was, for he had gained more than seven ounces during the week. After losing weight during the first three days, like all new-born children, he was now growing and filling out like a strong, healthy human plant. They could already picture him walking, sturdy and handsome. His mother, sitting up in bed, wrapped his swaddling clothes around him with her deft, nimble hands, jesting the while and answering each of his plaintive wails.

"Yes, yes, I know, we are very, very hungry. But it is all right; the soup is on the fire, and will be served to Monsieur smoking hot."

On awakening that morning she had made a real Sunday toilette: her superb hair was caught up in a huge chignon which disclosed the whiteness of her neck, and she wore a white flannel lace-trimmed dressing-jacket, which allowed but a little of her bare arms to be seen. Propped up by two pillows, she laughingly offered her breast to the child, who was already protruding his lips and groping with his hands. And when he found what he wanted he eagerly began to suck.

Mathieu, seeing that both mother and babe were steeped in sunshine, then went to draw one of the curtains, but Marianne exclaimed: "No, no, leave us the sun; it doesn't inconvenience us at all, it fills our veins with springtide."

He came back and lingered near the bed. The sun's rays poured over it, and life blazed there in a florescence of health and beauty. There is no more glorious blossoming, no more sacred symbol of living eternity than an infant at its mother's breast. It is like a prolongation of maternity's travail, when the mother continues giving herself to her babe, offering him the fountain of life that shall make him a man.

Scarce is he born to the world than she takes him back and clasps him to her bosom, that he may there again have warmth and nourishment. And nothing could be more simple or more necessary. Marianne, both for her own sake and that of her boy, in order that beauty and health might remain their portion, was naturally his nurse.

Little Gervais was still sucking when Zoe, after tidying the room, came up again with a big bunch of lilac, and announced that Monsieur and Madame Angelin had called, on their way back from an early walk, to inquire after Madame.

"Show them up," said Marianne gayly; "I can well receive them."

The Angelins were the young couple who, having installed themselves in a little house at Janville, ever roamed the lonely paths, absorbed in their mutual passion. She was delicious—dark, tall, admirably formed, always joyous and fond of pleasure. He, a handsome fellow, fair and square shouldered, had the gallant mien of a musketeer with his streaming moustache. In addition to their ten thousand francs a year, which enabled them to live as they liked, he earned a little money by painting pretty fans, flowery with roses and little women deftly postured. And so their life had hitherto been a game of love, an everlasting billing and cooing. Towards the close of the previous summer they had become quite intimate with the Froments, through meeting them well-nigh every day.

"Can we come in? Are we not intruding?" called Angelin, in his sonorous voice, from the landing.

Then Claire, his wife, as soon as she had kissed Marianne, apologized for having called so early.

"We only learnt last night, my dear," said she, "that you had arrived the day before. We didn't expect you for another eight or ten days. And so, as we passed the house just now, we couldn't resist calling. You will forgive us, won't you?" Then, never waiting for an answer, she added with the petulant vivacity of a tom-tit whom the open air had intoxicated: "Oh! so there is the new little gentleman—a boy, am I not right? And your health is good? But really I need not ask it. *Mon Dieu*, what a pretty little fellow he is! Look at him, Robert; how pretty he is! A real little doll! Isn't he funny now, isn't he funny! He is quite amusing."

Her husband, observing her gayety, drew near and began to admire the child by way of following her example. "Ah yes, he is really a pretty baby. But I have seen so many frightful ones—thin, puny, bluish little things, looking like little plucked chickens. When they are white and plump they are quite nice."

Mathieu began to laugh, and twitted the Angelins on having no child of their own. But on this point they held very decided opinions. They wished to enjoy life, unburdened by offspring, while they were young. As for what might happen in five or six years' time, that, of course, was another matter. Nevertheless, Madame Angelin could not help being struck by the delightful picture which Marianne, so fresh and gay, presented with her plump little babe at her breast in that white bed amid the bright sunshine.

At last she remarked: "There's one thing. I certainly could not feed a child. I should have to engage a nurse for any baby of mine."

"Of course!" her husband replied. "I would never allow you to feed it. It would be idiotic."

These words had scarcely passed his lips when he regretted them and apologized to Marianne, explaining that no mother possessed of means was nowadays willing to face the trouble and worry of nursing.

"Oh! for my part," Marianne responded, with her quiet smile, "if I had a hundred thousand francs a year I should nurse all my children, even were there a dozen of them. To begin with, it is so healthful, you know, both for mother and child: and if I didn't do my duty to the little one I should look on myself as a criminal, as a mother who grudged her offspring health and life."

Lowering her beautiful soft eyes towards her boy, she watched him with a look of infinite love, while he continued nursing gluttonously. And in a dreamy voice she continued: "To give a child of mine to another—oh no, never! I should feel too jealous. I want my children to be entirely my own. And it isn't merely a question of a child's physical health. I speak of his whole being, of the intelligence and heart that will come to him, and which he ought to derive from me alone. If I should find him foolish or malicious later on, I should think that his nurse had poisoned him. Dear little fellow! when he pulls like that it is as if he were drinking me up entirely."

Then Mathieu, deeply moved, turned towards the others, saying: "Ah! she is quite right. I only wish that every mother could hear her, and make it the fashion in France once more to suckle their infants. It would be sufficient if it became an ideal of beauty. And, indeed, is it not of the loftiest and brightest beauty?"

The Angelins complaisantly began to laugh, but they did not seem convinced. Just as they rose to take their leave an extraordinary uproar burst forth beneath the window, the piercing clamor of little wildings, freely romping in the fields. And it was all caused by Ambroise throwing a ball, which had lodged itself on a tree. Blaise and Denis were flinging stones at it to bring it down, and Rose called and jumped and stretched out her arms as if she hoped to be able to reach the ball. The Angelins stopped short, surprised and almost nervous.

"Good heavens!" murmured Claire, "what will it be when you have a dozen?"

"But the house would seem quite dead if they did not romp and shout," said Marianne, much amused. "Good-by, my dear. I will go to see you when I can get about."

The months of March and April proved superb, and all went well with Marianne. Thus the lonely little house, nestling amid foliage, was ever joyous. Each Sunday in particular proved a joy, for the father did not then have to go to his office. On the other days he started off early in the morning, and returned about seven o'clock, ever busily laden with work in the interval. And if his constant perambulations did not affect his good-humor, he was nevertheless often haunted by thoughts of the future. Formerly he had never been alarmed by the penury of his little home. Never had he indulged in any dream of ambition or wealth. Besides, he knew that his wife's only idea of happiness, like his own, was to live there in very simple fashion, leading a brave life of health, peacefulness, and love. But while he did not desire the power procured by a high position and the enjoyment offered by a large fortune, he could not help asking himself how he was to provide, were it ever so modestly, for his increasing family. What would he be able to do, should he have other children; how would he procure the necessaries of life each time that a fresh birth might impose fresh requirements upon him? One situated as he was must create resources, draw food from the earth step by step, each time a little mouth opened and cried its hunger aloud. Otherwise he would be guilty of criminal improvidence. And such reflections as these came upon him the more strongly as his penury had increased since the birth of Gervais—to such a point, indeed, that Marianne, despite prodigies of economy, no longer knew how to make her money last her till the end of the month. The slightest expenditure had to be debated; the very butter had to be spread thinly on the children's bread; and they had to continue wearing their blouses till they were well-nigh threadbare. To increase the embarrassment they grew every year, and cost more money. It had been necessary to send the three boys to a little school at Janville, which was as yet but a small expense. But would it not be necessary to send them the following year to a college, and where was the money for this to come from? A grave problem, a worry which grew from hour to hour, and which for Mathieu somewhat spoilt that charming spring whose advent was flowering the countryside.

The worst was that Mathieu deemed himself immured, as it were, in his position as designer at the Beauchene works. Even admitting that his salary should some day be doubled, it was not seven or eight thousand francs a year which would enable him to realize his dream of a numerous family freely and proudly growing and spreading like some happy forest, indebted solely for strength, health, and beauty to the good common mother of all, the earth, which gave to all its sap. And this was why, since his return to Janville, the earth, the soil had attracted him, detained him during his frequent walks, while he revolved vague but ever-expanding thoughts in his mind. He would pause for long minutes, now before a field of wheat, now on the verge of a leafy wood, now on the margin of a river whose waters glistened in the sunshine, and now amid the nettles of some stony moorland. All sorts of vague plans then rose within him, uncertain reveries of such vast scope, such singularity, that he had as yet spoken of them to nobody, not even his wife. Others would doubtless have mocked at him, for he had as yet but reached that dim, quivering hour when inventors feel the gust of their discovery sweep over them, before the idea that they are revolving presents itself with full precision to their minds. Yet why did he not address himself to the soil, man's everlasting provider and nurse? Why did he not clear and fertilize those far-spreading lands, those woods, those heaths, those stretches of stony ground which were left sterile around him? Since it was just that each man should bring his contribution to the common weal, create subsistence for himself and his offspring, why should not he, at the advent of each new child, supply a new field of fertile earth which would give that child food, without cost to the community? That was his sole idea; it took no more precise shape; at the thought of realizing it he was carried off into splendid dreams.

The Froments had been in the country fully a month when one evening Marianne, wheeling Gervais's little carriage in front of her, came as far as the bridge over the Yeuse to await Mathieu, who had promised to return early. Indeed, he got there before six o'clock. And

ÉMILE ZOLA

as the evening was fine, it occurred to Marianne to go as far as the Lepailleurs' mill down the river, and buy some new-laid eggs there.

"I'm willing," said Mathieu. "I'm very fond of their romantic old mill, you know; though if it were mine I should pull it down and build another one with proper appliances."

In the yard of the picturesque old building, half covered with ivy, with its mossy wheel slumbering amid water-lilies, they found the Lepailleurs, the man tall, dry, and carroty, the woman as carroty and as dry as himself, but both of them young and hardy. Their child Antonin was sitting on the ground, digging a hole with his little hands.

"Eggs?" La Lepailleur exclaimed; "yes, certainly, madame, there must be some."

She made no haste to fetch them, however, but stood looking at Gervais, who was asleep in his little vehicle.

"Ah! so that's your last. He's plump and pretty enough, I must say," she remarked.

But Lepailleur raised a derisive laugh, and with the familiarity which the peasant displays towards the bourgeois whom he knows to be hard up, he said: "And so that makes you five, monsieur. Ah, well! that would be a deal too many for poor folks like us."

"Why?" Mathieu quietly inquired. "Haven't you got this mill, and don't you own fields, to give labor to the arms that would come and whose labor would double and treble your produce?"

These simple words were like a whipstroke that made Lepailleur rear. And once again he poured forth all his spite. Ah! surely now, it wasn't his tumble-down old mill that would ever enrich him, since it had enriched neither his father nor his grandfather. And as for his fields, well, that was a pretty dowry that his wife had brought him, land in which nothing more would grow, and which, however much one might water it with one's sweat, did not even pay for manuring and sowing.

"But in the first place," resumed Mathieu, "your mill ought to be repaired and its old mechanism replaced, or, better still, you should buy a good steam-engine."

"Repair the mill! Buy an engine! Why, that's madness," the other replied. "What would be the use of it? As it is, people hereabouts have almost renounced growing corn, and I remain idle every other month."

"And then," continued Mathieu, "if your fields yield less, it is because you cultivate them badly, following the old routine, without proper care or appliances or artificial manure."

"Appliances! Artificial manure! All that humbug which has only sent poor folks to rack and ruin! Ah! I should just like to see you trying to cultivate the land better, and make it yield what it'll never yield any more."

Thereupon he quite lost his temper, became violent and brutal, launching against the ungrateful earth all the charges which his love of idleness and his obstinacy suggested. He had travelled, he had fought in Africa as a soldier, folks could not say that he had always lived in his hole like an ignorant beast. But, none the less, on leaving his regiment he had lost all taste for work and come to the conclusion that agriculture was doomed, and would never give him aught but dry bread to eat. The land would soon be bankrupt, and the peasantry no longer believed in it, so old and empty and worn out had it become. And even the sun got out of order nowadays; they had snow in July and thunderstorms in December, a perfect upsetting of seasons, which wrecked the crops almost before they were out of the ground.

"No, monsieur," said Lepailleur, "what you say is impossible; it's all past. The soil and work, there's nothing left of either. It's barefaced robbery, and though the peasant may kill himself with labor, he will soon be left without even water to drink. Children indeed! No, no! There's Antonin, of course, and for him we may just be able to provide. But I assure you that I won't even make Antonin a peasant against his will! If he takes to schooling and wishes to go to Paris, I shall tell him that he's quite right, for Paris is nowadays the only chance for sturdy chaps who want to make a fortune. So he will be at liberty to sell everything, if he chooses, and try his luck there. The only thing that I regret is that I didn't make the venture myself when there was still time."

Mathieu began to laugh. Was it not singular that he, a bourgeois with a bachelor's degree and scientific attainments, should dream of coming back to the soil, to the common mother of all labor and wealth, when this peasant, sprung from peasants, cursed and insulted the earth, and hoped that his son would altogether renounce it? Never had anything struck him as more significant. It symbolized that disastrous exodus from the rural districts towards the towns, an exodus which year by year increased, unhinging the nation and reducing it to anaemia.

"You are wrong," he said in a jovial way so as to drive all bitterness from the discussion. "Don't be unfaithful to the earth; she's an old mistress who would revenge herself. In your place I would lay myself out to obtain from her, by increase of care, all that I might want. As in the world's early days, she is still the great fruitful spouse, and she yields abundantly when she is loved in proper fashion."

But Lepailleur, raising his fists, retorted: "No, no; I've had enough of her!"

"And, by the way," continued Mathieu, "one thing which astonishes me is that no courageous, intelligent man has ever yet come forward to do something with all that vast abandoned estate yonder—that Chantebled—which old Seguin, formerly, dreamt of turning into a princely domain. There are great stretches of waste land, woods which one might partly fell, heaths and moorland which might easily be restored to cultivation. What a splendid task! What a work of creation for a bold man to undertake!"

This so amazed Lepailleur that he stood there openmouthed. Then his jeering spirit asserted itself: "But, my dear sir—excuse my saying it—you must be mad! Cultivate Chantebled, clear those stony tracts, wade about in those marshes! Why, one might bury millions there without reaping a single bushel of oats! It's a cursed spot, which my grandfather's father saw such as it is now, and which my grandson's son will see just the same. Ah! well, I'm not inquisitive, but it would really amuse me to meet the fool who might attempt such madness."

"*Mon Dieu*, who knows?" Mathieu quietly concluded. "When one only loves strongly one may work miracles."

La Lepailleur, after going to fetch a dozen eggs, now stood erect before her husband in admiration at hearing him talk so eloquently to a bourgeois. They agreed very well together in their avaricious rage at being unable to amass money by the handful without any great exertion, and in their ambition to make their son a gentleman, since only a gentleman could become wealthy. And thus, as Marianne was going off after placing the eggs under a cushion in Gervais' little carriage, the other complacently called her attention to Antonin, who, having made a hole in the ground, was now spitting into it.

"Oh! he's smart," said she; "he knows his alphabet already, and we are going to put him to school. If he takes after his father he will be no fool, I assure you."

It was on a Sunday, some ten days later, that the supreme revelation, the great flash of light which was to decide his life and that of those he loved, fell suddenly upon Mathieu during a walk he took with his wife and the children. They had gone out for the whole afternoon, taking a little snack with them in order that they might share it amid the long grass in the fields. And after scouring the paths, crossing the copses, rambling over the moorland, they came back to the verge of the woods and sat down under an oak. Thence the whole expanse spread out before them, from the little pavilion where they dwelt to the distant village of Janville. On their right was the great marshy plateau, from which broad, dry, sterile slopes descended; while lower ground stretched away on their left. Then, behind them, spread the woods with deep thickets parted by clearings, full of herbage which no scythe had ever touched. And not a soul was to be seen around them; there was naught save wild Nature, grandly quiescent under the bright sun of that splendid April day. The earth seemed to be dilating with all the sap amassed within it, and a flood of life could be felt rising and quivering in the vigorous trees, the spreading plants, and the impetuous growth of brambles and nettles which stretched invadingly over the soil. And on all sides a powerful, pungent odor was diffused.

"Don't go too far," Marianne called to the children; "we shall stay under this oak. We will have something to eat by and by."

Blaise and Denis were already bounding along, followed by Ambroise, to see who could run the fastest; but Rose pettishly called them back, for she preferred to play at gathering wild flowers. The open air fairly intoxicated the youngsters; the herbage rose, here and there, to their very shoulders. But they came back and gathered flowers; and after a time they set off at a wild run once more, one of the big brothers carrying the little sister on his back.

Mathieu, however, had remained absent-minded, with his eyes wandering hither and thither, throughout their walk. At times he did not hear Marianne when she spoke to him; he lapsed into reverie before some uncultivated tract, some copse overrun with brushwood, some spring which suddenly bubbled up and was then lost in mire. Nevertheless, she felt that there was no sadness nor feeling of indifference in his heart; for as soon as he returned to her he laughed once more with his soft, loving laugh. It was she who often sent him roaming about the country, even alone, for she felt that it would do him good; and although she had guessed that something very serious was passing through his mind, she retained full confidence, waiting till it should please him to speak to her.

Now, however, just as he had sunk once more into his reverie, his glance wandering afar, studying the great varied expanse of land, she raised a light cry: "Oh! look, look!"

Under the big oak tree she had placed Master Gervais in his little carriage, among wild weeds which hid its wheels. And while she handed a little silver mug, from which it was intended they should drink while taking their snack, she had noticed that the child raised his head and followed the movement of her hand, in which the silver sparkled beneath the sun-rays. Forthwith she repeated the experiment, and again the child's eyes followed the starry gleam.

"Ah! it can't be said that I'm mistaken, and am simply fancying it!" she exclaimed. "It is certain that he can see quite plainly now. My pretty pet, my little darling!"

She darted to the child to kiss him in celebration of that first clear glance. And then, too, came the delight of the first smile.

"Why, look!" in his turn said Mathieu, who was leaning over the child beside her, yielding to the same feeling of rapture, "there he is smiling at you now. But of course, as soon as these little fellows see clearly they begin to laugh."

She herself burst into a laugh. "You are right, he is laughing! Ah! how funny he looks, and how happy I am!"

Both father and mother laughed together with content at the sight of that infantile smile, vague and fleeting, like a faint ripple on the pure water of some spring.

Amid this joy Marianne called the four others, who were bounding under the young foliage around them: "Come, Rose! come, Ambroise! come, Blaise and Denis! It's time now; come at once to have something to eat."

They hastened up and the snack was set out on a patch of soft grass. Mathieu unhooked the basket which hung in front of the baby's little vehicle; and Marianne, having drawn some slices of bread-and-butter from it, proceeded to distribute them. Perfect silence ensued while all four children began biting with hearty appetite, which it was a pleasure to see. But all at once a scream arose. It came from Master Gervais, who was vexed at not having been served first.

"Ah! yes, it's true I was forgetting you," said Marianne gayly; "you shall have your share. There, open your mouth, you darling;" and, with an easy, simple gesture, she unfastened her dress-body; and then, under the sunlight which steeped her in golden radiance, in full view of the far-spreading countryside, where all likewise was bare—the soil, the trees, the plants, streaming with sap—having seated herself in the long grass, where she almost disappeared amid the swarming growth of

April's germs, the babe on her breast eagerly sucked in her warm milk, even as all the encompassing verdure was sucking life from the soil.

"How hungry you are!" she exclaimed. "Don't pinch me so hard, you little glutton!"

Meantime Mathieu had remained standing amid the enchantment of the child's first smile and the gayety born of the hearty hunger around him. Then his dream of creation came back to him, and he at last gave voice to those plans for the future which haunted him, and of which he had so far spoken to nobody: "Ah, well, it is high time that I should set to work and found a kingdom, if these children are to have enough soup to make them grow. Shall I tell you what I've thought—shall I tell you?"

Marianne raised her eyes, smiling and all attention. "Yes, tell me your secret if the time has come. Oh! I could guess that you had some great hope in you. But I did not ask you anything; I preferred to wait."

He did not give a direct reply, for at a sudden recollection his feelings rebelled. "That Lepailleur," said he, "is simply a lazy fellow and a fool in spite of all his cunning airs. Can there be any more sacrilegious folly than to imagine that the earth has lost her fruitfulness and is becoming bankrupt—she, the eternal mother, eternal life? She only shows herself a bad mother to her bad sons, the malicious, the obstinate, and the dull-witted, who do not know how to love and cultivate her. But if an intelligent son comes and devotes himself to her, and works her with the help of experience and all the new systems of science, you will soon see her quicken and yield tremendous harvests unceasingly. Ah! folks say in the district that this estate of Chantebled has never yielded and never will yield anything but nettles. Well, nevertheless, a man will come who will transform it and make it a new land of joy and abundance."

Then, suddenly turning round, with outstretched arm, and pointing to the spots to which he referred in turn, he went on: "Yonder in the rear there are nearly five hundred acres of little woods, stretching as far as the farms of Mareuil and Lillebonne. They are separated by clearings of excellent soil which broad gaps unite, and which could easily be turned into good pastures, for there are numerous springs. And, indeed, the springs become so abundant on the right, that they have changed that big plateau into a kind of marshland, dotted with ponds, and planted with reeds and rushes. But picture a man of bold mind, a clearer, a conqueror, who should drain those lands and rid them of superfluous water by means of a few canals which might easily be dug! Why, then a huge stretch of land would be reclaimed, handed

ÉMILE ZOLA

over to cultivation, and wheat would grow there with extraordinary vigor. But that is not all. There is the expanse before us, those gentle slopes from Janville to Vieux-Bourg, that is another five hundred acres, which are left almost uncultivated on account of their dryness, the stony poverty of their soil. So it is all very simple. One would merely have to take the sources up yonder, the waters, now stagnant, and carry them across those sterile slopes, which, when irrigated, would gradually develop extraordinary fertility. I have seen everything, I have studied everything. I feel that there are at least twelve hundred acres of land which a bold creator might turn into a most productive estate. Yonder lies a whole kingdom of corn, a whole new world to be created by labor, with the help of the beneficent waters and our father the sun, the source of eternal life."

Marianne gazed at him and admired him as he stood there quivering, pondering over all that he evoked from his dream. But she was frightened by the vastness of such hopes, and could not restrain a cry of disquietude and prudence.

"No, no, that is too much; you desire the impossible. How can you think that we shall ever possess so much—that our fortune will spread over the entire region? Think of the capital, the arms that would be needed for such a conquest!"

For a moment Mathieu remained silent on thus suddenly being brought back to reality. Then with his affectionate, sensible air, he began to laugh. "You are right; I have been dreaming and talking wildly," he replied. "I am not yet so ambitious as to wish to be King of Chantebled. But there is truth in what I have said to you; and, besides, what harm can there be in dreaming of great plans to give oneself faith and courage? Meantime I intend to try cultivating just a few acres, which Seguin will no doubt sell me cheaply enough, together with the little pavilion in which we live. I know that the unproductiveness of the estate weighs on him. And, later on, we shall see if the earth is disposed to love us and come to us as we go to her. Ah well, my dear, give that little glutton plenty of life, and you, my darlings, eat and drink and grow in strength, for the earth belongs to those who are healthy and numerous."

Blaise and Denis made answer by taking some fresh slices of bread-and-butter, while Rose drained the mug of wine and water which Ambroise handed her. And Marianne sat there like the symbol of blossoming Fruitfulness, the source of vigor and conquest, while Gervais heartily nursed on. He pulled so hard, indeed, that one could hear the sound of his lips. It was like the faint noise which attends the rise of a spring—a slender rill of milk that is to swell and become a river. Around her the mother heard that source springing up and spreading on all sides. She was not nourishing alone: the sap of April was dilating the land, sending a quiver through the woods, raising the long herbage which embowered her. And beneath her, from the bosom of the earth, which was ever in travail, she felt that flood of sap reaching and ever pervading her. And it was like a stream of milk flowing through the world, a stream of eternal life for humanity's eternal crop. And on that gay day of spring the dazzling, singing, fragrant countryside was steeped in it all, triumphal with that beauty of the mother, who, in the full light of the sun, in view of the vast horizon, sat there nursing her child.

VIII

On the morrow, after a morning's hard toil at his office at the works, Mathieu, having things well advanced, bethought himself of going to see Norine at Madame Bourdieu's. He knew that she had given birth to a child a fortnight previously, and he wished to ascertain the exact state of affairs, in order to carry to an end the mission with which Beauchene had intrusted him. As the other, however, had never again spoken to him on the subject, he simply told him that he was going out in the afternoon, without indicating the motive of his absence. At the same time he knew what secret relief Beauchene would experience when he at last learnt that the whole business was at an end—the child cast adrift and the mother following her own course.

On reaching the Rue de Miromesnil, Mathieu had to go up to Norine's room, for though she was to leave the house on the following Thursday, she still kept her bed. And at the foot of the bedstead, asleep in a cradle, he was surprised to see the infant, of which, he thought, she had already rid herself.

"Oh! is it you?" she joyously exclaimed. "I was about to write to you, for I wanted to see you before going away. My little sister here would have taken you the letter."

Cecile Moineaud was indeed there, together with the younger girl, Irma. The mother, unable to absent herself from her household duties, had sent them to make inquiries, and give Norine three big oranges, which glistened on the table beside the bed. The little girls had made the journey on foot, greatly interested by all the sights of the streets and the displays in the shop-windows. And now they were enraptured with the fine house in which they found their big sister sojourning, and full of curiosity with respect to the baby which slept under the cradle's muslin curtains.

Mathieu made the usual inquiries of Norine, who answered him gayly, but pouted somewhat at the prospect of having so soon to leave the house, where she had found herself so comfortable.

"We shan't easily find such soft mattresses and such good food, eh, Victoire?" she asked. Whereupon Mathieu perceived that another girl was present, a pale little creature with wavy red hair, tip-tilted nose, and long mouth, whom he had already seen there on the occasion of a previous visit. She slept in one of the two other beds which the room contained, and now sat beside it mending some linen. She was to leave the house on the morrow, having already sent her child to the Foundling Hospital; and in the meantime she was mending some things for Rosine, the well-to-do young person of great beauty whom Mathieu had previously espied, and whose story, according to Norine, was so sadly pathetic.

Victoire ceased sewing and raised her head. She was a servant girl by calling, one of those unlucky creatures who are overtaken by trouble when they have scarce arrived in the great city from their native village. "Well," said she, "it's quite certain that one won't be able to dawdle in bed, and that one won't have warm milk given one to drink before getting up. But, all the same, it isn't lively to see nothing but that big gray wall yonder from the window. And, besides, one can't go on forever doing nothing."

Norine laughed and jerked her head, as if she were not of this opinion. Then, as her little sisters embarrassed her, she wished to get rid of them.

"And so, my pussies," said she, "you say that papa's still angry with me, and that I'm not to go back home."

"Oh!" cried Cecile, "it's not so much that he's angry, but he says that all the neighbors would point their fingers at him if he let you come home. Besides, Euphrasie keeps his anger up, particularly since she's arranged to get married."

"What! Euphrasie going to be married? You didn't tell me that."

Norine looked very vexed, particularly when her sisters, speaking both together, told her that the future husband was Auguste Benard, a jovial young mason who lived on the floor above them. He had taken a fancy to Euphrasie, though she had no good looks, and was as thin, at eighteen, as a grasshopper. Doubtless, however, he considered her strong and hard-working.

"Much good may it do them!" said Norine spitefully. "Why, with her evil temper, she'll be beating him before six months are over. You can just tell mamma that I don't care a rap for any of you, and that I need nobody. I'll go and look for work, and I'll find somebody to help me. So, you hear, don't you come back here. I don't want to be bothered by you any more."

At this, Irma, but eight years old and tender-hearted, began to cry. "Why do you scold us? We didn't come to worry you. I wanted to ask you, too, if that baby's yours, and if we may kiss it before we go away."

Norine immediately regretted her spiteful outburst. She once more called the girls her "little pussies," kissed them tenderly, and told them that although they must run away now they might come back another day to see her if it amused them. "Thank mamma from me for her oranges. And as for the baby, well, you may look at it, but you mustn't touch it, for if it woke up we shouldn't be able to hear ourselves."

Then, as the two children leant inquisitively over the cradle, Mathieu also glanced at it, and saw a healthy, sturdy-looking child, with a square face and strong features. And it seemed to him that the infant was singularly like Beauchene.

At that moment, however, Madame Bourdieu came in, accompanied by a woman, whom he recognized as Sophie Couteau, "La Couteau," that nurse-agent whom he had seen at the Seguins' one day when she had gone thither to offer to procure them a nurse. She also certainly recognized this gentleman, whose wife, proud of being able to suckle her own children, had evinced such little inclination to help others to do business. She pretended, however, that she saw him for the first time; for she was discreet by profession and not even inquisitive, since so many matters were ever coming to her knowledge without the asking.

Little Cecile and little Irma went off at once; and then Madame Bourdieu, addressing Norine, inquired: "Well, my child, have you thought it over; have you quite made up your mind about that poor little darling, who is sleeping there so prettily? Here is the person I spoke to you about. She comes from Normandy every fortnight, bringing nurses to Paris; and each time she takes babies away with her to put them out to nurse in the country. Though you say you won't feed it, you surely need not cast off your child altogether; you might confide it to this person until you are in a position to take it back. Or else, if you have made up your mind to abandon it altogether, she will kindly take it to the Foundling Hospital at once."

Great perturbation had come over Norine, who let her head fall back on her pillow, over which streamed her thick fair hair, whilst her face darkened and she stammered: "*Mon Dieu, mon Dieu*! you are going to worry me again!"

Then she pressed her hands to her eyes as if anxious to see nothing more.

"This is what the regulations require of me, monsieur," said Madame Bourdieu to Mathieu in an undertone, while leaving the young mother for a moment to her reflections. "We are recommended to do all we can to persuade our boarders, especially when they are situated like this one, to nurse their infants. You are aware that this often saves not only the child, but the mother herself, from the sad future which threatens her. And so, however much she may wish to abandon the child, we leave it near her as long as possible, and feed it with the bottle, in the hope that the sight of the poor little creature may touch her heart and awaken feelings of motherliness in her. Nine times out of ten, as soon as she gives the child the breast, she is vanquished, and she keeps it. That is why you still see this baby here."

Mathieu, feeling greatly moved, drew near to Norine, who still lay back amid her streaming hair, with her hands pressed to her face. "Come," said he, "you are a goodhearted girl, there is no malice in you. Why not yourself keep that dear little fellow?"

Then she uncovered her burning, tearless face: "Did the father even come to see me?" she asked bitterly. "I can't love the child of a man who has behaved as he has! The mere thought that it's there, in that cradle, puts me in a rage."

"But that dear little innocent isn't guilty. It's he whom you condemn, yourself whom you punish, for now you will be quite alone, and he might prove a great consolation."

"No, I tell you no, I won't. I can't keep a child like that with nobody to help me. We all know what we can do, don't we? Well, it is of no use my questioning myself. I'm not brave enough, I'm not stupid enough to do such a thing. No, no, and no."

He said no more, for he realized that nothing would prevail over that thirst for liberty which she felt in the depths of her being. With a gesture he expressed his sadness, but he was neither indignant nor angry with her, for others had made her what she was.

"Well, it's understood, you won't be forced to feed it," resumed Madame Bourdieu, attempting a final effort. "But it isn't praiseworthy to abandon the child. Why not trust it to Madame here, who would put it out to nurse, so that you would be able to take it back some day, when you have found work? It wouldn't cost much, and no doubt the father would pay."

This time Norine flew into a passion. "He! pay? Ah! you don't know him. It's not that the money would inconvenience him, for he's a millionnaire. But all he wants is to see the little one disappear. If he had dared he would have told me to kill it! Just ask that gentleman if I speak the truth. You see that he keeps silent! And how am I to pay when I

ÉMILE ZOLA

haven't a copper, when to-morrow I shall be cast out-of-doors, perhaps, without work and without bread. No, no, a thousand times no, I can't!"

Then, overcome by an hysterical fit of despair, she burst into sobs. "I beg you, leave me in peace. For the last fortnight you have been torturing me with that child, by keeping him near me, with the idea that I should end by nursing him. You bring him to me, and set him on my knees, so that I may look at him and kiss him. You are always worrying me with him, and making him cry with the hope that I shall pity him and take him to my breast. But, *mon Dieu!* can't you understand that if I turn my head away, if I don't want to kiss him or even to see him, it is because I'm afraid of being caught and loving him like a big fool, which would be a great misfortune both for him and for me? He'll be far happier by himself! So, I beg you, let him be taken away at once, and don't torture me any more."

Sobbing violently, she again sank back in bed, and buried her dishevelled head in the pillows.

La Couteau had remained waiting, mute and motionless, at the foot of the bedstead. In her gown of dark woollen stuff and her black cap trimmed with yellow ribbons she retained the air of a peasant woman in her Sunday best. And she strove to impart an expression of compassionate good-nature to her long, avaricious, false face. Although it seemed to her unlikely that business would ensue, she risked a repetition of her customary speech.

"At Rougemont, you know, madame, your little one would be just the same as at home. There's no better air in the Department; people come there from Bayeux to recruit their health. And if you only knew how well the little ones are cared for! It's the only occupation of the district, to have little Parisians to coddle and love! And, besides, I wouldn't charge you dear. I've a friend of mine who already has three nurslings, and, as she naturally brings them up with the bottle, it wouldn't put her out to take a fourth for almost next to nothing. Come, doesn't that suit you—doesn't that tempt you?"

When, however, she saw that tears were Norine's only answer, she made an impatient gesture like an active woman who cannot afford to lose her time. At each of her fortnightly journeys, as soon as she had rid herself of her batch of nurses at the different offices, she hastened round the nurses' establishments to pick up infants, so as to take the train homewards the same evening together with two or three women who, as she put it, helped her "to cart the little ones about." On this occasion she was in a greater hurry, as Madame Bourdieu, who employed her in a variety of ways, had asked her to take Norine's child to the Foundling Hospital if she did not take it to Rougemont.

"And so," said La Couteau, turning to Madame Bourdieu, "I shall have only the other lady's child to take back with me. Well, I had better see her at once to make final arrangements. Then I'll take this one and carry it yonder as fast as possible, for my train starts at six o'clock."

When La Couteau and Madame Bourdieu had gone off to speak to Rosine, who was the "other lady" referred to, the room sank into silence save for the wailing and sobbing of Norine. Mathieu had seated himself near the cradle, gazing compassionately at the poor little babe, who was still peacefully sleeping. Soon, however, Victoire, the little servant girl, who had hitherto remained silent, as if absorbed in her sewing, broke the heavy silence and talked on slowly and interminably without raising her eyes from her needle.

"You were quite right in not trusting your child to that horrid woman!" she began. "Whatever may be done with him at the hospital, he will be better off there than in her hands. At least he will have a chance to live. And that's why I insisted, like you, on having mine taken there at once. You know I belong in that woman's region—yes, I come from Berville, which is barely four miles from Rougemont, and I can't help knowing La Couteau, for folks talk enough about her in our village. She's a nice creature and no mistake! And it's a fine trade that she plies, selling other people's milk. She was no better than she should be at one time, but at last she was lucky enough to marry a big, coarse, brutal fellow, whom at this time of day she leads by the nose. And he helps her. Yes, he also brings nurses to Paris and takes babies back with him, at busy times. But between them they have more murders on their consciences than all the assassins that have ever been guillotined. The mayor of Berville, a bourgeois who's retired from business and a worthy man, said that Rougemont was the curse of the Department. I know well enough that there's always been some rivalry between Rougemont and Berville; but, the folks of Rougemont ply a wicked trade with the babies they get from Paris. All the inhabitants have ended by taking to it, there's nothing else doing in the whole village, and you should just see how things are arranged so that there may be as many funerals as possible. Ah! yes, people don't keep their stock-in-trade on their hands. The more that die, the more they earn. And so one can understand that La Couteau always wants to take back as many babies as possible at each journey she makes."

Victoire recounted these dreadful things in her simple way, as one whom Paris has not yet turned into a liar, and who says all she knows, careless what it may be.

"And it seems things were far worse years ago," she continued. "I have heard my father say that, in his time, the agents would bring back four or five children at one journey—perfect parcels of babies, which they tied together and carried under their arms. They set them out in rows on the seats in the waiting-rooms at the station; and one day, indeed, a Rougemont agent forgot one child in a waiting-room, and there was quite a row about it, because when the child was found again it was dead. And then you should have seen in the trains what a heap of poor little things there was, all crying with hunger. It became pitiable in winter time, when there was snow and frost, for they were all shivering and blue with cold in their scanty, ragged swaddling-clothes. One or another often died on the way, and then it was removed at the next station and buried in the nearest cemetery. And you can picture what a state those who didn't die were in. At our place we care better for our pigs, for we certainly wouldn't send them travelling in that fashion. My father used to say that it was enough to make the very stones weep. Nowadays, however, there's more supervision; the regulations allow the agents to take only one nursling back at a time. But they know all sorts of tricks, and often take a couple. And then, too, they make arrangements; they have women who help them, and they avail themselves of those who may be going back into the country alone. Yes, La Couteau has all sorts of tricks to evade the law. And, besides, all the folks of Rougemont close their eyes—they are too much interested in keeping business brisk; and all they fear is that the police may poke their noses into their affairs. Ah! it is all very well for the Government to send inspectors every month, and insist on registers, and the Mayor's signature and the stamp of the Commune; why, it's just as if it did nothing. It doesn't prevent these women from quietly plying their trade and sending as many little ones as they can to kingdom-come. We've got a cousin at Rougemont who said to us one day: 'La Malivoire's precious lucky, she got rid of four more during last month.'"

Victoire paused for a moment to thread her needle. Norine was still weeping, while Mathieu listened, mute with horror, and with his eyes fixed upon the sleeping child.

"No doubt folks say less about Rougemont nowadays than they used to," the girl resumed; "but there's still enough to disgust one. We know three or four baby-farmers who are not worth their salt. The rule is to bring the little ones up with the bottle, you know; and you'd be horrified if you saw what bottles they are—never cleaned, always filthy, with the milk inside them icy cold in the winter and sour in the summer. La Vimeux, for her part, thinks that the bottle system costs too much, and so she feeds her children on soup. That clears them off all the quicker. At La Loiseau's you have to hold your nose when you go near the corner where the little ones sleep—their rags are so filthy. As for La Gavette, she's always working in the fields with her man, so that the three or four nurslings that she generally has are left in charge of the grandfather, an old cripple of seventy, who can't even prevent the fowls from coming to peck at the little ones.* And things are worse even at La Cauchois', for, as she has nobody at all to mind the children when she goes out working, she leaves them tied in their cradles, for fear lest they should tumble out and crack their skulls. You might visit all the houses in the village, and you would find the same thing everywhere. There isn't a house where the trade isn't carried on. Round our part there are places where folks make lace, or make cheese, or make cider; but at Rougemont they only make dead bodies."

All at once she ceased sewing, and looked at Mathieu with her timid, clear eyes.

"But the worst of all," she continued, "is La Couillard, an old thief who once did six months in prison, and who now lives a little way out of the village on the verge of the wood. No live child has ever left La Couillard's. That's her specialty. When you see an agent, like La Couteau, for instance, taking her a child, you know at once what's in the wind. La Couteau has simply bargained that the little one shall die. It's settled in a very easy fashion: the parents give a sum of three or four hundred francs on condition that the little one shall be kept till his first communion, and you may be quite certain that he dies within a week. It's only necessary to leave a window open near him, as a nurse used to do whom my father knew. At winter time, when she had half a dozen babies in her house, she would set the door wide open and then go out for a stroll. And, by the way, that little boy in the next room, whom La Couteau has just gone to see, she'll take him to La Couillard's, I'm sure;

---

* There is no exaggeration in what M. Zola writes on this subject. I have even read in French Government reports of instances in which nurslings have been devoured by pigs! And it is a well-known saying in France that certain Norman and Touraine villages are virtually "paved with little Parisians."—Trans.

ÉMILE ZOLA

for I heard the mother, Mademoiselle Rosine, agree with her the other day to give her a sum of four hundred francs down on the understanding that she should have nothing more to do in the matter."

At this point Victoire ceased speaking, for La Couteau came in to fetch Norine's child. Norine, who had emerged from her distress during the servant girl's stories, had ended by listening to them with great interest. But directly she perceived the agent she once more hid her face in her pillows, as though she feared to see what was about to happen. Mathieu, on his side, had risen from his chair and stood there quivering.

"So it's understood, I'm going to take the child," said La Couteau. "Madame Bourdieu has given me a slip of paper bearing the date of the birth and the address. Only I ought to have some Christian names. What do you wish the child to be called?"

Norine did not at first answer. Then, in a faint distressful voice, she said: "Alexandre."

"Alexandre, very well. But you would do better to give the boy a second Christian name, so as to identify him the more readily, if some day you take it into your head to run after him."

It was again necessary to tear a reply from Norine. "Honore," she said.

"Alexandre Honore—all right. That last name is yours, is it not?* And the first is the father's? That is settled; and now I've everything I need. Only it's four o'clock already, and I shall never get back in time for the six o'clock train if I don't take a cab. It's such a long way off—the other side of the Luxembourg. And a cab costs money. How shall we manage?"

While she continued whining, to see if she could not extract a few francs from the distressed girl, it suddenly occurred to Mathieu to carry out his mission to the very end by driving with her himself to the Foundling Hospital, so that he might be in a position to inform Beauchene that the child had really been deposited there, in his presence. So he told La Couteau that he would go down with her, take a cab, and bring her back.

"All right; that will suit me. Let us be off! It's a pity to wake the little one, since he's so sound asleep; but all the same, we must pack him off, since it's decided."

---

* Norine is, of course, a diminutive of Honorine, which is the feminine form of Honore.— Trans.

With her dry hands, which were used to handling goods of this description, she caught up the child, perhaps, however, a little roughly, forgetting her assumed wheedling good nature now that she was simply charged with conveying it to hospital. And the child awoke and began to scream loudly.

"Ah! dear me, it won't be amusing if he keeps up this music in the cab. Quick, let us be off."

But Mathieu stopped her. "Won't you kiss him, Norine?" he asked.

At the very first squeal that sorry mother had dipped yet lower under her sheets, carrying her hands to her ears, distracted as she was by the sound of those cries. "No, no," she gasped, "take him away; take him away at once. Don't begin torturing me again!"

Then she closed her eyes, and with one arm repulsed the child who seemed to be pursuing her. But when she felt that the agent was laying him on the bed, she suddenly shuddered, sat up, and gave a wild hasty kiss, which lighted on the little fellow's cap. She had scarcely opened her tear-dimmed eyes, and could have seen but a vague phantom of that poor feeble creature, wailing and struggling at the decisive moment when he was being cast into the unknown.

"You are killing me! Take him away; take him away!"

Once in the cab the child suddenly became silent. Either the jolting of the vehicle calmed him, or the creaking of the wheels filled him with emotion. La Couteau, who kept him on her knees, at first remained silent, as if interested in the people on the footwalks, where the bright sun was shining. Then, all of a sudden, she began to talk, venting her thoughts aloud.

"That little woman made a great mistake in not trusting the child to me. I should have put him out to nurse properly, and he would have grown up finely at Rougemont. But there! they all imagine that we simply worry them because we want to do business. But I just ask you, if she had given me five francs for myself and paid my return journey, would that have ruined her? A pretty girl like her oughtn't to be hard up for money. I know very well that in our calling there are some people who are hardly honest, who speculate and ask for commissions, and then put out nurslings at cheap rates and rob both the parents and the nurse. It's really not right to treat these dear little things as if they were goods—poultry or vegetables. When folks do that I can understand that their hearts get hardened, and that they pass the little ones on from hand to hand without any more care than if they were stock-in-trade. But then, monsieur, I'm an honest woman; I'm authorized by the mayor of our village; I hold a certificate of morality, which I can show to anybody. If ever you should come to Rougemont, just ask after Sophie Couteau there. Folks will tell you that I'm a hard-working woman, and don't owe a copper to a soul!"

Mathieu could not help looking at her to see how unblushingly she thus praised herself. And her speech struck him as if it were a premeditated reply to all that Victoire had related of her, for, with the keen scent of a shrewd peasant woman, she must have guessed that charges had been brought against her. When she felt that his piercing glance was diving to her very soul, she doubtless feared that she had not lied with sufficient assurance, and had somehow negligently betrayed herself; for she did not insist, but put on more gentleness of manner, and contented herself with praising Rougemont in a general way, saying what a perfect paradise it was, where the little ones were received, fed, cared for, and coddled as if they were all sons of princes. Then, seeing that the gentleman uttered never a word, she became silent once more. It was evidently useless to try to win him over. And meantime the cab rolled and rolled along; streets followed streets, ever noisy and crowded; and they crossed the Seine and at last drew near to the Luxembourg. It was only after passing the palace gardens that La Couteau again began:

"Well, it's that young person's own affair if she imagines that her child will be better off for passing through the Foundling. I don't attack the Administration, but you know, monsieur, there's a good deal to be said on the matter. At Rougemont we have a number of nurslings that it sends us, and they don't grow any better or die less frequently than the others. Well, well, people are free to act as they fancy; but all the same I should like you to know, as I do, all that goes on in there."

The cab had stopped at the top of the Rue Denfert-Rochereau, at a short distance from the former outer Boulevard. A big gray wall stretched out, the frigid facade of a State establishment, and it was through a quiet, simple, unobtrusive little doorway at the end of this wall that La Couteau went in with the child. Mathieu followed her, but he did not enter the office where a woman received the children. He felt too much emotion, and feared lest he should be questioned; it was, indeed, as if he considered himself an accomplice in a crime. Though La Couteau told him that the woman would ask him nothing, and the strictest secrecy was always observed, he preferred to wait in an anteroom, which led to several closed compartments, where the persons who came to deposit children were placed to wait their turn. And he watched the woman go off, carrying the little one, who still remained extremely well behaved, with a vacant stare in his big eyes.

Though the interval of waiting could not have lasted more than twenty minutes, it seemed terribly long to Mathieu. Lifeless quietude reigned in that stern, sad-looking anteroom, wainscoted with oak, and pervaded with the smell peculiar to hospitals. All he heard was the occasional faint wail of some infant, above which now and then rose a heavy, restrained sob, coming perhaps from some mother who was waiting in one of the adjoining compartments. And he recalled the "slide" of other days, the box which turned within the wall. The mother crept up, concealing herself much as possible from view, thrust her baby into the cavity as into an oven, gave a tug at the bell-chain, and then precipitately fled. Mathieu was too young to have seen the real thing; he had only seen it represented in a melodrama at the Port St. Martin Theatre.* But how many stories it recalled—hampers of poor little creatures brought up from the provinces and deposited at the hospital by carriers; the stolen babes of Duchesses, here cast into oblivion by suspicious-looking men; the hundreds of wretched work-girls too who had here rid themselves of their unfortunate children. Now, however, the children had to be deposited openly, and there was a staff which took down names and dates, while giving a pledge of inviolable secrecy. Mathieu was aware that some few people imputed to the suppression of the slide system the great increase in criminal offences. But each day public opinion condemns more and more the attitude of society in former times, and discards the idea that one must accept evil, dam it in, and hide it as if it were some necessary sewer; for the only course for a free community to pursue is to foresee evil and grapple with it, and destroy it in the bud. To diminish the number of cast-off children one must seek out the mothers, encourage them, succor them, and give them the means to be mothers in fact as well as in name. At that moment, however, Mathieu did not reason; it was his heart that was affected, filled with growing pity and anguish at the thought of all

---

* The "slide" system, which enabled a mother to deposit her child at the hospital without being seen by those within, ceased to be employed officially as far back as 1847; but the apparatus was long preserved intact, and I recollect seeing it in the latter years of the Second Empire, *cir.* 1867–70, when I was often at the artists' studios in the neighborhood. The aperture through which children were deposited in the sliding-box was close to the little door of which M. Zola speaks.—Trans.

the crime, all the shame, all the grief and distress that had passed through that anteroom in which he stood. What terrible confessions must have been heard, what a procession of suffering, ignominy, and wretchedness must have been witnessed by that woman who received the children in her mysterious little office! To her all the wreckage of the slums, all the woe lying beneath gilded life, all the abominations, all the tortures that remain unknown, were carried. There in her office was the port for the shipwrecked, there the black hole that swallowed up the offspring of frailty and shame. And while Mathieu's spell of waiting continued he saw three poor creatures arrive at the hospital. One was surely a work-girl, delicate and pretty though she looked, so thin, so pale too, and with so wild an air that he remembered a paragraph he had lately read in a newspaper, recounting how another such girl, after forsaking her child, had thrown herself into the river. The second seemed to him to be a married woman, some workman's wife, no doubt, overburdened with children and unable to provide food for another mouth; while the third was tall, strong, and insolent,—one of those who bring three or four children to the hospital one after the other. And all three women plunged in, and he heard them being penned in separate compartments by an attendant, while he, with stricken heart, realizing how heavily fate fell on some, still stood there waiting.

When La Couteau at last reappeared with empty arms she said never a word, and Mathieu put no question to her. Still in silence, they took their seats in the cab; and only some ten minutes afterwards, when the vehicle was already rolling through bustling, populous streets, did the woman begin to laugh. Then, as her companion, still silent and distant, did not condescend to ask her the cause of her sudden gayety, she ended by saying aloud:

"Do you know why I am laughing? If I kept you waiting a bit longer, it was because I met a friend of mine, an attendant in the house, just as I left the office. She's one of those who put the babies out to nurse in the provinces.* Well, my friend told me that she was going to Rougemont to-morrow with two other attendants, and that among others they would certainly have with them the little fellow I had just left at the hospital."

---

* There are only about 600 beds at the Hopital des Enfants Assistes, and the majority of the children deposited there are perforce placed out to purse in the country.—Trans.

Again did she give vent to a dry laugh which distorted her wheedling face. And she continued: "How comical, eh? The mother wouldn't let me take the child to Rougemont, and now it's going there just the same. Ah! some things are bound to happen in spite of everything."

Mathieu did not answer, but an icy chill had sped through his heart. It was true, fate pitilessly took its own course. What would become of that poor little fellow? To what early death, what life of suffering or wretchedness, or even crime, had he been thus brutally cast?

But the cab continued rolling on, and for a long while neither Mathieu nor La Couteau spoke again. It was only when the latter alighted in the Rue de Miromesnil that she began to lament, on seeing that it was already half-past five o'clock, for she felt certain that she would miss her train, particularly as she still had some accounts to settle and that other child upstairs to fetch. Mathieu, who had intended to keep the cab and drive to the Northern terminus, then experienced a feeling of curiosity, and thought of witnessing the departure of the nurse-agents. So he calmed La Couteau by telling her that if she would make haste he would wait for her. And as she asked for a quarter of an hour, it occurred to him to speak to Norine again, and so he also went upstairs.

When he entered Norine's room he found her sitting up in bed, eating one of the oranges which her little sisters had brought her. She had all the greedy instincts of a plump, pretty girl; she carefully detached each section of the orange, and, her eyes half closed the while, her flesh quivering under her streaming outspread hair, she sucked one after another with her fresh red lips, like a pet cat lapping a cup of milk. Mathieu's sudden entry made her start, however, and when she recognized him she smiled faintly in an embarrassed way.

"It's done," he simply said.

She did not immediately reply, but wiped her fingers on her handkerchief. However, it was necessary that she should say something, and so she began: "You did not tell me you would come back—I was not expecting you. Well, it's done, and it's all for the best. I assure you there was no means of doing otherwise."

Then she spoke of her departure, asked the young man if he thought she might regain admittance to the works, and declared that in any case she should go there to see if the master would have the audacity to turn her away. Thus she continued while the minutes went slowly by. The conversation had dropped, Mathieu scarcely replying to her, when

La Couteau, carrying the other child in her arms, at last darted in like a gust of wind. "Let's make haste, let's make haste!" she cried. "They never end with their figures; they try all they can to leave me without a copper for myself!"

But Norine detained her, asking: "Oh! is that Rosine's baby? Pray do show it me." Then she uncovered the infant's face, and exclaimed: "Oh! how plump and pretty he is!" And she began another sentence: "What a pity! Can one have the heart—" But then she remembered, paused, and changed her words: "Yes, how heartrending it is when one has to forsake such little angels."

"Good-by! Take care of yourself!" cried La Couteau; "you will make me miss my train. And I've got the return tickets, too; the five others are waiting for me at the station! Ah! what a fuss they would make if I got there too late!"

Then, followed by Mathieu, she hurried away, bounding down the stairs, where she almost fell with her little burden. But soon she threw herself back in the cab, which rolled off.

"Ah! that's a good job! And what do you say of that young person, monsieur? She wouldn't lay out fifteen francs a month on her own account, and yet she reproaches that good Mademoiselle Rosine, who has just given me four hundred francs to have her little one taken care of till his first communion. Just look at him—a superb child, isn't he? What a pity it is that the finest are often those who die the first."

Mathieu looked at the infant on the woman's knees. His garments were very white, of fine texture, trimmed with lace, as if he were some little condemned prince being taken in all luxury to execution. And the young man remembered that Norine had told him that the child was the offspring of crime. Born amid secrecy, he was now, for a fixed sum, to be handed over to a woman who would quietly suppress him by simply leaving some door or window wide open. Young though the boy was, he already had a finely-formed face, that suggested the beauty of a cherub. And he was very well behaved; he did not raise the faintest wail. But a shudder swept through Mathieu. How abominable!

La Couteau quickly sprang from the cab as soon as they reached the courtyard of the St. Lazare Station. "Thank you, monsieur, you have been very kind," said she. "And if you will kindly recommend me to any ladies you may know, I shall quite at their disposal."

Then Mathieu, having alighted on the pavement in his turn, saw a scene which detained him there a few moments longer. Amid all the scramble of passengers and luggage, five women of peasant aspect, each carrying an infant, were darting in a scared, uneasy way hither and thither, like crows in trouble, with big yellow beaks quivering and black wings flapping with anxiety. Then, on perceiving La Couteau, there was one general caw, and all five swooped down upon her with angry, voracious mien. And, after a furious exchange of cries and explanations, the six banded themselves together, and, with cap-strings waving and skirts flying, rushed towards the train, carrying the little ones, like birds of prey who feared delay in returning to the charnel-house.

And Mathieu remained alone in the great crowd. Thus every year did these crows of ill omen carry off from Paris no fewer than 20,000 children, who were never, never seen again! Ah! that great question of the depopulation of France! Not merely were there those who were resolved to have no children, not only were infanticide and crime of other kinds rife upon all sides, but one-half of the babes saved from those dangers were killed. Thieves and murderesses, eager for lucre, flocked to the great city from the four points of the compass, and bore away all the budding Life that their arms could carry in order that they might turn it to Death! They beat down the game, they watched in the doorways, they sniffed from afar the innocent flesh on which they preyed. And the babes were carted to the railway stations; the cradles, the wards of hospitals and refuges, the wretched garrets of poor mothers, without fires and without bread—all, all were emptied! And the packages were heaped up, moved carelessly hither and thither, sent off, distributed to be murdered either by foul deed or by neglect. The raids swept on like tempest blasts; Death's scythe never knew dead season, at every hour it mowed down budding life. Children who might well have lived were taken from their mothers, the only nurses whose milk would have nourished them, to be carted away and to die for lack of proper nutriment.

A rush of blood warmed Mathieu's heart when, all at once, he thought of Marianne, so strong and healthy, who would be waiting for him on the bridge over the Yeuse, in the open country, with their little Gervais at her breast. Figures that he had seen in print came back to his mind. In certain regions which devoted themselves to baby-farming the mortality among the nurslings was fifty per cent; in the best of them it was forty, and seventy in the worst. It was calculated that in one century seventeen millions of nurslings had died. Over a long period the mortality had remained at from one hundred to one

ÉMILE ZOLA

hundred and twenty thousand per annum. The most deadly reigns, the greatest butcheries of the most terrible conquerors, had never resulted in such massacre. It was a giant battle that France lost every year, the abyss into which her whole strength sank, the charnel-place into which every hope was cast. At the end of it is the imbecile death of the nation. And Mathieu, seized with terror at the thought, rushed away, eager to seek consolation by the side of Marianne, amid the peacefulness, the wisdom, and the health which were their happy lot.

IX

One Thursday morning Mathieu went to lunch with Dr. Boutan in the rooms where the latter had resided for more than ten years, in the Rue de l'Universite, behind the Palais-Bourbon. By a contradiction, at which he himself often laughed, this impassioned apostle of fruitfulness had remained a bachelor. His extensive practice kept him in a perpetual hurry, and he had little time free beyond his dejeuner hour. Accordingly, whenever a friend wished to have any serious conversation with him, he preferred to invite him to his modest table, to partake more or less hastily of an egg, a cutlet, and a cup of coffee.

Mathieu wished to ask the doctor's advice on a grave subject. After a couple of weeks' reflection, his idea of experimenting in agriculture, of extricating that unappreciated estate of Chantebled from chaos, preoccupied him to such a degree that he positively suffered at not daring to come to a decision. The imperious desire to create, to produce life, health, strength, and wealth grew within him day by day. Yet what fine courage and what a fund of hope he needed to venture upon an enterprise which outwardly seemed so wild and rash, and the wisdom of which was apparent to himself alone. With whom could he discuss such a matter, to whom could he confide his doubts and hesitation? When the idea of consulting Boutan occurred to him, he at once asked the doctor for an appointment. Here was such a confidant as he desired, a man of broad, brave mind, one who worshipped life, who was endowed with far-seeing intelligence, and who would therefore at once look beyond the first difficulties of execution.

As soon as they were face to face on either side of the table, Mathieu began to pour forth his confession, recounting his dream—his poem, as he called it. And the doctor listened without interrupting, evidently won over by the young man's growing, creative emotion. When at last Boutan had to express an opinion he replied: "*Mon Dieu*, my friend, I can tell you nothing from a practical point of view, for I have never even planted a lettuce. I will even add that your project seems to me so hazardous that any one versed in these matters whom you might consult would assuredly bring forward substantial and convincing arguments to dissuade you. But you speak of this affair with such superb confidence and ardor and affection, that I feel convinced you would succeed. Moreover, you flatter my own views, for I have long endeavored to show that, if numerous families are ever to flourish again in France, people must again love and worship the soil, and desert the towns, and lead a fruitful fortifying country life. So how can I disapprove your plans? Moreover, I suspect that, like all people who ask advice, you simply came here in the hope that you would find in me a brother ready, in principle at all events, to wage the same battle."

At this they both laughed heartily. Then, on Boutan inquiring with what capital he would start operations, Mathieu quietly explained that he did not mean to borrow money and thus run into debt; he would begin, if necessary, with very few acres indeed, convinced as he was of the conquering power of labor. His would be the head, and he would assuredly find the necessary arms. His only worry was whether he would be able to induce Seguin to sell him the old hunting-box and the few acres round it on a system of yearly payments, without preliminary disbursement. When he spoke to the doctor on this subject, the other replied:

"Oh! I think he is very favorably disposed. I know that he would be delighted to sell that huge, unprofitable estate, for with his increasing pecuniary wants he is very much embarrassed by it. You are aware, no doubt, that things are going from bad to worse in his household."

Then the doctor broke off to inquire: "And our friend Beauchene, have you warned him of your intention to leave the works?"

"Why, no, not yet," said Mathieu; "and I would ask you to keep the matter private, for I wish to have everything settled before informing him."

Lunching quickly, they had now got to their coffee, and the doctor offered to drive Mathieu back to the works, as he was going there himself, for Madame Beauchene had requested him to call once a week, in order that he might keep an eye on Maurice's health. Not only did the lad still suffer from his legs, but he had so weak and delicate a stomach that he had to be dieted severely.

"It's the kind of stomach one finds among children who have not been brought up by their own mothers," continued Boutan. "Your plucky wife doesn't know that trouble; she can let her children eat whatever they fancy. But with that poor little Maurice, the merest trifle, such as four cherries instead of three, provokes indigestion. Well, so it is settled, I will drive you back to the works. Only I must first make a call in the Rue Roquepine to choose a nurse. It won't take me long, I hope. Quick! let us be off."

When they were together in the brougham, Boutan told Mathieu that it was precisely for the Seguins that he was going to the nurse-agency. There was a terrible time at the house in the Avenue d'Antin. A few months previously Valentine had given birth to a daughter, and her husband had obstinately resolved to select a fit nurse for the child himself, pretending that he knew all about such matters. And he had chosen a big, sturdy young woman of monumental appearance. Nevertheless, for two months past Andree, the baby, had been pining away, and the doctor had discovered, by analyzing the nurse's milk, that it was deficient in nutriment. Thus the child was simply perishing of starvation. To change a nurse is a terrible thing, and the Seguins' house was in a tempestuous state. The husband rushed hither and thither, banging the doors and declaring that he would never more occupy himself about anything.

"And so," added Boutan, "I have now been instructed to choose a fresh nurse. And it is a pressing matter, for I am really feeling anxious about that poor little Andree."

"But why did not the mother nurse her child?" asked Mathieu.

The doctor made a gesture of despair. "Ah! my dear fellow, you ask me too much. But how would you have a Parisienne of the wealthy bourgeoisie undertake the duty, the long brave task of nursing a child, when she leads the life she does, what with receptions and dinners and soirees, and absences and social obligations of all sorts? That little Madame Seguin is simply trifling when she puts on an air of deep distress and says that she would so much have liked to nurse her infant, but that it was impossible since she had no milk. She never even tried! When her first child was born she could doubtless have nursed it. But to-day, with the imbecile, spoilt life she leads, it is quite certain that she is incapable of making such an effort. The worst is, my dear fellow, as any doctor will tell you, that after three or four generations of mothers who do not feed their children there comes a generation that cannot do so. And so, my friend, we are fast coming, not only in France, but in other countries where the odious wet-nurse system is in vogue, to a race of wretched, degenerate women, who will be absolutely powerless to nourish their offspring."

Mathieu then remembered what he had witnessed at Madame Bourdieu's and the Foundling Hospital. And he imparted his impressions to Boutan, who again made a despairing gesture. There was a great work of social salvation to be accomplished, said he. No doubt a number of philanthropists were trying their best to improve things, but private effort could not cope with such widespread need. There must be general measures; laws must be passed to save the nation. The mother must be protected and helped, even in secrecy, if she asked for it; she must be cared for, succored, from the earliest period, and right through all the long months during which she fed her babe. All sorts of establishments would have to be founded—refuges, convalescent homes, and so forth; and there must be protective enactments, and large sums of money voted to enable help to be extended to all mothers, whatever they might be. It was only by such preventive steps that one could put a stop to the frightful hecatomb of newly-born infants, that incessant loss of life which exhausted the nation and brought it nearer and nearer to death every day.

"And," continued the doctor, "it may all be summed up in this verity: 'It is a mother's duty to nurse her child.' And, besides, a mother, is she not the symbol of all grandeur, all strength, all beauty? She represents the eternity of life. She deserves a social culture, she should be religiously venerated. When we know how to worship motherhood, our country will be saved. And this is why, my friend, I should like a mother feeding her babe to be adopted as the highest expression of human beauty. Ah! how can one persuade our Parisiennes, all our French women, indeed, that woman's beauty lies in being a mother with an infant on her knees? Whenever that fashion prevails, we shall be the sovereign nation, the masters of the world!"

He ended by laughing in a distressed way, in his despair at being unable to change manners and customs, aware as he was that the nation could be revolutionized only by a change in its ideal of true beauty.

"To sum up, then, I believe in a child being nursed only by its own mother. Every mother who neglects that duty when she can perform it is a criminal. Of course, there are instances when she is physically incapable of accomplishing her duty, and in that case there is the feeding-bottle, which, if employed with care and extreme cleanliness, only sterilized milk being used, will yield a sufficiently good result. But to send a child away to be nursed means almost certain death; and as for the nurse in the house, that is a shameful transaction, a source of incalculable evil, for both the employer's child and the nurse's child frequently die from it."

Just then the doctor's brougham drew up outside the nurse-agency in the Rue Roquepine.

"I dare say you have never been in such a place, although you are the father of five children," said Boutan to Mathieu, gaily.

"No, I haven't."

"Well, then, come with me. One ought to know everything."

The office in the Rue Roquepine was the most important and the one with the best reputation in the district. It was kept by Madame Broquette, a woman of forty, with a dignified if somewhat blotched face, who was always very tightly laced in a faded silk gown of dead-leaf hue. But if she represented the dignity and fair fame of the establishment in its intercourse with clients, the soul of the place, the ever-busy manipulator, was her husband, Monsieur Broquette, a little man with a pointed nose, quick eyes, and the agility of a ferret. Charged with the police duties of the office, the supervision and training of the nurses, he received them, made them clean themselves, taught them to smile and put on pleasant ways, besides penning them in their various rooms and preventing them from eating too much. From morn till night he was ever prowling about, scolding and terrorizing those dirty, ill-behaved, and often lying and thieving women. The building, a dilapidated private house, with a damp ground floor, to which alone clients were admitted, had two upper stories, each comprising six rooms arranged as dormitories, in which the nurses and their infants slept. There was no end to the arrivals and departures there: the peasant women were ever galloping through the place, dragging trunks about, carrying babes in swaddling clothes, and filling the rooms and the passages with wild cries and vile odors. And amid all this the house had another inmate, Mademoiselle Broquette, Herminie as she was called, a long, pale, bloodless girl of fifteen, who mooned about languidly among that swarm of sturdy young women.

Boutan, who knew the house well, went in, followed by Mathieu. The central passage, which was fairly broad, ended in a glass door, which admitted one to a kind of courtyard, where a sickly conifer stood on a round patch of grass, which the dampness rotted. On the right of the passage was the office, whither Madame Broquette, at the request of her customers, summoned the nurses, who waited in a neighboring room, which was simply furnished with a greasy deal table in the centre. The furniture of the office was some old Empire stuff, upholstered in red velvet. There was a little mahogany centre table, and a gilt clock. Then, on the left of the passage, near the kitchen, was the general refectory, with two long tables, covered with oilcloth, and surrounded by straggling chairs, whose straw seats were badly damaged. Just a make-believe sweep with a broom was given there every day: one could divine long-amassed, tenacious dirt in every dim corner; and the place reeked with an odor of bad cookery mingled with that of sour milk.

When Boutan thrust open the office door he saw that Madame Broquette was busy with an old gentleman, who sat there inspecting a party of nurses. She recognized the doctor, and made a gesture of regret. "No matter, no matter," he exclaimed; "I am not in a hurry: I will wait."

Through the open door Mathieu had caught sight of Mademoiselle Herminie, the daughter of the house, ensconced in one of the red velvet armchairs near the window, and dreamily perusing a novel there, while her mother, standing up, extolled her goods in her most dignified way to the old gentleman, who gravely contemplated the procession of nurses and seemed unable to make up his mind.

"Let us have a look at the garden," said the doctor, with a laugh.

One of the boasts of the establishment, indeed, as set forth in its prospectus, was a garden and a tree in it, as if there were plenty of good air there, as in the country. They opened the glass door, and on a bench near the tree they saw a plump girl, who doubtless had just arrived, pretending to clean a squealing infant. She herself looked sordid, and had evidently not washed since her journey. In one corner there was an overflow of kitchen utensils, a pile of cracked pots and greasy and rusty saucepans. Then, at the other end, a French window gave access to the nurses' waiting-room, and here again there was a nauseous spectacle of dirt and untidiness.

All at once Monsieur Broquette darted forward, though whence he had come it was hard to say. At all events, he had seen Boutan, who was a client that needed attention. "Is my wife busy, then?" said he. "I cannot allow you to remain waiting here, doctor. Come, come, I pray you."

With his little ferreting eyes he had caught sight of the dirty girl cleaning the child, and he was anxious that his visitors should see nothing further of a character to give them a bad impression of the establishment. "Pray, doctor, follow me," he repeated, and understanding that an example was necessary, he turned to the girl, exclaiming, "What business have you to be here? Why haven't you gone upstairs to wash and dress? I shall fling a pailful of water in your face if you don't hurry off and tidy yourself."

Then he forced her to rise and drove her off, all scared and terrified, in front of him. When she had gone upstairs he led the two gentlemen to the office entrance and began to complain: "Ah! doctor, if you only knew what trouble I have even to get those girls to wash their hands! We who are so clean! who put all our pride in keeping the house clean. If ever a speck of dust is seen anywhere it is certainly not my fault."

Since the girl had gone upstairs a fearful tumult had arisen on the upper floors, whence also a vile smell descended. Some dispute, some battle, seemed to be in progress. There were shouts and howls, followed by a furious exchange of vituperation.

"Pray excuse me," at last exclaimed Monsieur Broquette; "my wife will receive you in a minute."

Thereupon he slipped off and flew up the stairs with noiseless agility. And directly afterwards there was an explosion. Then the house suddenly sank into death-like silence. All that could be heard was the voice of Madame in the office, as, in a very dignified manner, she kept on praising her goods.

"Well, my friend," said Boutan to Mathieu, while they walked up and down the passage, "all this, the material side of things, is nothing. What you should see and know is what goes on in the minds of all these people. And note that this is a fair average place. There are others which are real dens, and which the police sometimes have to close. No doubt there is a certain amount of supervision, and there are severe regulations which compel the nurses to bring certificates of morality, books setting forth their names, ages, parentage, the situations they have held, and so on, with other documents on which they have immediately to secure a signature from the Prefecture, where the final authorization is granted them. But these precautions don't prevent fraud and deceit of various kinds. The women assert that they have only recently begun nursing, when they have been doing it for months; they show you superb children which they have borrowed and which they assert to be their own. And there are many other tricks to which they resort in their eagerness to make money."

As the doctor and Mathieu chatted on, they paused for a moment near the door of the refectory, which chanced to be open, and there, among other young peasant women, they espied La Couteau hastily partaking of cold meat. Doubtless she had just arrived from Rougemont, and, after disposing of the batch of nurses she had brought with her, was seeking sustenance for the various visits which she would have to make before returning home. The refectory, with its wine-stained tables and greasy walls, cast a smell like that of a badly-kept sink.

"Ah! so you know La Couteau!" exclaimed Boutan, when Mathieu had told him of his meetings with the woman. "Then you know the depths of crime. La Couteau is an ogress! And yet, think of it, with our fine social organization, she is more or less useful, and perhaps I myself shall be happy to choose one of the nurses that she has brought with her."

At this moment Madame Broquette very amiably asked the visitors into her office. After long reflection, the old gentleman had gone off without selecting any nurse, but saying that he would return some other time.

"There are folks who don't know their own minds," said Madame Broquette sententiously. "It isn't my fault, and I sincerely beg you to excuse me, doctor. If you want a good nurse you will be satisfied, for I have just received some excellent ones from the provinces. I will show you."

Herminie, meanwhile, had not condescended to raise her nose from her novel. She remained ensconced in her armchair, still reading, with a weary, bored expression on her anaemic countenance. Mathieu, after sitting down a little on one side, contented himself with looking on, while Boutan stood erect, attentive to every detail, like a commander reviewing his troops. And the procession began.

Having opened a door which communicated with the common room, Madame Broquette, assuming the most noble airs, leisurely introduced the pick of her nurses, in groups of three, each with her infant in her arms. About a dozen were thus inspected: short ones with big heavy limbs, tall ones suggesting maypoles, dark ones with coarse stiff hair, fair ones with the whitest of skins, quick ones and slow ones, ugly ones and others who were pleasant-looking. All, however, wore the same nervous, silly smile, all swayed themselves with embarrassed timidity, the anxious mien of the bondswoman at the slave market, who fears that she may not find a purchaser. They clumsily tried to put on graceful ways, radiant with internal joy directly a customer seemed to nibble, but clouding over and casting black glances at their companions when the latter seemed to have the better chance. Out of the dozen the doctor began by setting three aside, and finally he detained but one, in order that he might study her more fully.

"One can see that Monsieur le Docteur knows his business," Madame Broquette allowed herself to say, with a flattering smile. "I don't often have such pearls. But she has only just arrived, otherwise she would probably have been engaged already. I can answer for her as I could for myself, for I have put her out before."

The nurse was a dark woman of about twenty-six, of average height, built strongly enough, but having a heavy, common face with a hard-looking jaw. Having already been in service, however, she held herself fairly well.

"So that child is not your first one?" asked the doctor.

"No, monsieur, he's my third."

Then Boutan inquired into her circumstances, studied her papers, took her into Madame Broquette's private room for examination, and on his return make a minute inspection of her child, a strong plump boy, some three months old, who in the interval had remained very quiet on an armchair. The doctor seemed satisfied, but he suddenly raised his head to ask, "And that child is really your own?"

"Oh! monsieur, where could I have got him otherwise?"

"Oh! my girl, children are borrowed, you know."

Then he paused for a moment, still hesitating and looking at the young woman, embarrassed by some feeling of doubt, although she seemed to embody all requirements. "And are you all quite well in your family?" he asked; "have none of your relatives ever died of chest complaints?"

"Never, monsieur."

"Well, of course you would not tell me if they had. Your books ought to contain a page for information of that kind. And you, are you of sober habits? You don't drink?"

"Oh! monsieur."

This time the young woman bristled up, and Boutan had to calm her. Then her face brightened with pleasure as soon as the doctor—with the gesture of a man who is taking his chance, for however careful one may be there is always an element of chance in such matters—said to her: "Well, it is understood, I engage you. If you can send your child away at once, you can go this evening to the address I will give you. Let me see, what is your name?"

"Marie Lebleu."

Madame Broquette, who, without presuming to interfere with a doctor, had retained her majestic air which so fully proclaimed the high respectability of her establishment, now turned towards her daughter: "Herminie, go to see if Madame Couteau is still there."

Then, as the girl slowly raised her pale dreamy eyes without stirring from her chair, her mother came to the conclusion that she had better execute the commission herself. A moment later she came back with La Couteau.

The doctor was now settling money matters. Eighty francs a month for the nurse; and forty-five francs for her board and lodging at the agency and Madame Broquette's charges. Then there was the question of her child's return to the country, which meant another thirty francs, without counting a gratuity to La Couteau.

"I'm going back this evening," said the latter; "I'm quite willing to take the little one with me. In the Avenue d'Antin, did you say? Oh! I know, there's a lady's maid from my district in that house. Marie can go there at once. When I've settled my business, in a couple of hours, I will go and rid her of her baby."

On entering the office, La Couteau had glanced askance at Mathieu, without, however, appearing to recognize him. He had remained on his chair silently watching the scene—first an inspection as of cattle at a market, and then a bargaining, the sale of a mother's milk. And by degrees pity and revolt had filled his heart. But a shudder passed through him when La Couteau turned towards the quiet, fine-looking child, of which she promised to rid the nurse. And once more he pictured her with her five companions at the St.-Lazare railway station, each, like some voracious crow, with a new-born babe in her clutches. It was the pillaging beginning afresh; life and hope were again being stolen from Paris. And this time, as the doctor said, a double murder was threatened; for, however careful one may be, the employer's child often dies from another's milk, and the nurse's child, carried back into the country like a parcel, is killed with neglect and indigestible pap.

But everything was now settled, and so the doctor and his companion drove away to Grenelle. And there, at the very entrance of the Beauchene works, came a meeting which again filled Mathieu with emotion. Morange, the accountant, was returning to his work after dejeuner, accompanied by his daughter Reine, both of them dressed in deep mourning. On the morrow of Valerie's funeral, Morange had returned to his work in a state of prostration which almost resembled forgetfulness. It was clear that he had abandoned all ambitious plans of quitting the works to seek a big fortune elsewhere. Still he could not make up his mind to leave his flat, though it was now too large for him, besides being too expensive. But then his wife had lived in those rooms, and he wished to remain in them. And, moreover, he desired to provide his daughter with all comfort. All the affection of his weak heart was now given to that child, whose resemblance to her mother distracted him. He would gaze at her for hours with tears in his eyes. A great passion was springing up within him; his one dream now was to dower her richly and seek happiness through her, if indeed he could ever be happy again. Thus feelings of avarice had come to him; he economized with respect to everything that was not connected with her, and secretly sought supplementary work in order that he might give her more luxury and increase her dower. Without her he would have died of weariness and self-abandonment. She was indeed fast becoming his very life.

"Why, yes," said she with a pretty smile, in answer to a question which Boutan put to her, "it is I who have brought poor papa back. I wanted to be sure that he would take a stroll before setting to work again. Other wise he shuts himself up in his room and doesn't stir."

Morange made a vague apologetic gesture. At home, indeed, overcome as he was by grief and remorse, he lived in his bedroom in the company of a collection of his wife's portraits, some fifteen photographs, showing her at all ages, which he had hung on the walls.

"It is very fine to-day, Monsieur Morange," said Boutan, "you do right in taking a stroll."

The unhappy man raised his eyes in astonishment, and glanced at the sun as if he had not previously noticed it. "That is true, it is fine weather—and besides it is very good for Reine to go out a little."

Then he tenderly gazed at her, so charming, so pink and white in her black mourning gown. He was always fearing that she must feel bored during the long hours when he left her at home, alone with the servant. To him solitude was so distressful, so full of the wife whom he mourned, and whom he accused himself of having killed.

"Papa won't believe that one never feels *ennui* at my age," said the girl gayly. "Since my poor mamma is no longer there, I must needs be a little woman. And, besides, the Baroness sometimes calls to take me out."

Then she gave a shrill cry on seeing a brougham draw up close to the curb. A woman was leaning out of the window, and she recognized her.

"Why, papa, there is the Baroness! She must have gone to our house, and Clara must have told her that I had accompanied you here."

This, indeed, was what had happened. Morange hastily led Reine to the carriage, from which Seraphine did not alight. And when his daughter had sprung in joyously, he remained there another moment, effusively thanking the Baroness, and delighted to think that his dear child was going to amuse herself. Then, after watching the brougham till it disappeared, he entered the factory, looking suddenly aged and shrunken, as if his grief had fallen on his shoulders once more, so

ÉMILE ZOLA

overwhelming him that he quite forgot the others, and did not even take leave of them.

"Poor fellow!" muttered Mathieu, who had turned icy cold on seeing Seraphine's bright mocking face and red hair at the carriage window.

Then he was going to his office when Beauchene beckoned to him from one of the windows of the house to come in with the doctor. The pair of them found Constance and Maurice in the little drawing-room, whither the father had repaired to finish his coffee and smoke a cigar. Boutan immediately attended to the child, who was much better with respect to his legs, but who still suffered from stomachic disturbance, the slightest departure from the prescribed diet leading to troublesome complications.

Constance, though she did not confess it, had become really anxious about the boy, and questioned the doctor, and listened to him with all eagerness. While she was thus engaged Beauchene drew Mathieu on one side.

"I say," he began, laughing, "why did you not tell me that everything was finished over yonder? I met the pretty blonde in the street yesterday."

Mathieu quietly replied that he had waited to be questioned in order to render an account of his mission, for he had not cared to be the first to raise such a painful subject. The money handed to him for expenses had proved sufficient, and whenever the other desired it, he could produce receipts for his various disbursements. He was already entering into particulars when Beauchene jovially interrupted him.

"You know what happened here? She had the audacity to come and ask for work, not of me of course, but of the foreman of the women's work-room. Fortunately I had foreseen this and had given strict orders; so the foreman told her that considerations of order and discipline prevented him from taking her back. Her sister Euphrasie, who is to be married next week, is still working here. Just fancy them having another set-to! Besides, her place is not here."

Then he went to take a little glass of cognac which stood on the mantelpiece.

Mathieu had learnt only the day before that Norine, on leaving Madame Bourdieu's, had sought a temporary refuge with a female friend, not caring to resume a life of quarrelling at her parents' home. Besides her attempt to regain admittance at Beauchene's, she had applied at two other establishments; but, as a matter of fact, she did not evince any particular ardor in seeking to obtain work. Four months' idleness and coddling had altogether disgusted her with a factory hand's life, and the inevitable was bound to happen. Indeed Beauchene, as he came back sipping his cognac, resumed: "Yes, I met her in the street. She was quite smartly dressed, and leaning on the arm of a big, bearded young fellow, who did nothing but make eyes at her. It was certain to come to that, you know. I always thought so."

Then he was stepping towards his wife and the doctor, when he remembered something else, came back, and asked Mathieu in a yet lower tone, "What was it you were telling me about the child?" And as soon as Mathieu had related that he had taken the infant to the Foundling Hospital so as to be certain that it was deposited there, he warmly pressed his hand. "That's perfect. Thank you, my dear fellow; I shall be at peace now."

He felt, indeed, intensely relieved, hummed a lively air, and then took his stand before Constance, who was still consulting the doctor. She was holding little Maurice against her knees, and gazing at him with the jealous love of a good bourgeoise, who carefully watched over the health of her only son, that son whom she wished to make a prince of industry and wealth. All at once, however, in reply to a remark from Boutan, she exclaimed: "Why then, doctor, you think me culpable? You really say that a child, nursed by his mother, always has a stronger constitution than others, and can the better resist the ailments of childhood?"

"Oh! there is no doubt of it, madame."

Beauchene, ceasing to chew his cigar, shrugged his shoulders, and burst into a sonorous laugh: "Oh! don't you worry, that youngster will live to be a hundred! Why, the Burgundian who nursed him was as strong as a rock! But, I say, doctor, you intend then to make the Chambers pass a law for obligatory nursing by mothers?"

At this sally Boutan also began to laugh. "Well, why not?" said he.

This at once supplied Beauchene with material for innumerable jests. Why, such a law would completely upset manners and customs, social life would be suspended, and drawing-rooms would become deserted! Posters would be placarded everywhere bearing the inscription: "Closed on account of nursing."

"Briefly," said Beauchene, in conclusion, "you want to have a revolution."

"A revolution, yes," the doctor gently replied, "and we will effect it."

X

Mathieu finished studying his great scheme, the clearing and cultivation of Chantebled, and at last, contrary to all prudence but with all the audacity of fervent faith and hope, it was resolved upon. He warned Beauchene one morning that he should leave the works at the end of the month, for on the previous day he had spoken to Seguin, and had found him quite willing to sell the little pavilion and some fifty acres around it on very easy terms. As Mathieu had imagined, Seguin's affairs were in a very muddled state, for he had lost large sums at the gaming table and spent money recklessly on women, leading indeed a most disastrous life since trouble had arisen in his home. And so he welcomed the transaction which Mathieu proposed to him, in the hope that the young man would end by ridding him of the whole of that unprofitable estate should his first experiment prove successful. Then came other interviews between them, and Seguin finally consented to sell on a system of annual payments, spread over a term of years, the first to be made in two years' time from that date. As things stood, the property seemed likely to remain unremunerative forever, and so there was nothing risked in allowing the purchaser a couple of years' credit. However, they agreed to meet once more and settle the final details before a formal deed of sale was drawn up. And one Monday morning, therefore, about ten o'clock, Mathieu set out for the house in the Avenue d'Antin in order to complete the business.

That morning, as it happened, Celeste the maid received in the linen room, where she usually remained, a visit from her friend Madame Menoux, the little haberdasher of the neighborhood, in whose tiny shop she was so fond of gossiping. They had become more intimate than ever since La Couteau, at Celeste's instigation, had taken Madame Menoux's child, Pierre, to Rougemont, to be put out to nurse there in the best possible way for the sum of thirty francs a month. La Couteau had also very complaisantly promised to call each month at one or another of her journeys in order to receive the thirty francs, thereby saving the mother the trouble of sending the money by post, and also enabling her to obtain fresh news of her child. Thus, each time a payment became due, if La Couteau's journey happened to be delayed a single day, Madame Menoux grew terribly frightened, and hastened off to Celeste to make inquiries of her. And, moreover, she was glad to have an opportunity of conversing with this girl, who came from the very part where her little Pierre was being reared.

"You will excuse, me, won't you, mademoiselle, for calling so early," said she, "but you told me that your lady never required you before nine o'clock. And I've come, you know, because I've had no news from over yonder, and it occurred to me that you perhaps might have received a letter."

Blonde, short and thin, Madame Menoux, who was the daughter of a poor clerk, had a slender pale face, and a pleasant, but somewhat sad, expression. From her own slightness of build probably sprang her passionate admiration for her big, handsome husband, who could have crushed her between his fingers. If she was slight, however, she was endowed with unconquerable tenacity and courage, and she would have killed herself with hard work to provide him with the coffee and cognac which he liked to sip after each repast.

"Ah! it's hard," she continued, "to have had to send our Pierre so far away. As it is, I don't see my husband all day, and now I've a child whom I never see at all. But the misfortune is that one has to live, and how could I have kept the little fellow in that tiny shop of mine, where from morning till night I never have a moment to spare! Yet, I can't help crying at the thought that I wasn't able to keep and nurse him. When my husband comes home from the museum every evening, we do nothing but talk about him, like a pair of fools. And so, according to you, mademoiselle, that place Rougemont is very healthy, and there are never any nasty illnesses about there?"

But at this moment she was interrupted by the arrival of another early visitor, whose advent she hailed with a cry of delight.

"Oh! how happy I am to see you, Madame Couteau! What a good idea it was of mine to call here!"

Amid exclamations of joyous surprise, the nurse-agent explained that she had arrived by the night train with a batch of nurses, and had started on her round of visits as soon as she had deposited them in the Rue Roquepine.

"After bidding Celeste good-day in passing," said she, "I intended to call on you, my dear lady. But since you are here, we can settle our accounts here, if you are agreeable."

Madame Menoux, however, was looking at her very anxiously. "And how is my little Pierre?" she asked.

"Why, not so bad, not so bad. He is not, you know, one of the strongest; one can't say that he's a big child. Only he's so pretty and nice-looking with his rather pale face. And it's quite certain that if there are bigger babies than he is, there are smaller ones too."

She spoke more slowly as she proceeded, and carefully sought words which might render the mother anxious, without driving her to despair. These were her usual tactics in order to disturb her customers' hearts, and then extract as much money from them as possible. On this occasion she must have guessed that she might carry things so far as to ascribe a slight illness to the child.

"However, I must really tell you, because I don't know how to lie; and besides, after all, it's my duty—Well, the poor little darling has been ill, and he's not quite well again yet."

Madame Menoux turned very pale and clasped her puny little hands: "*Mon Dieu*! he will die of it."

"No, no, since I tell you that he's already a little better. And certainly he doesn't lack good care. You should just see how La Loiseau coddles him! When children are well behaved they soon get themselves loved. And the whole house is at his service, and no expense is spared The doctor came twice, and there was even some medicine. And that costs money."

The last words fell from La Couteau's lips with the weight of a club. Then, without leaving the scared, trembling mother time to recover, the nurse-agent continued: "Shall we go into our accounts, my dear lady?"

Madame Menoux, who had intended to make a payment before returning to her shop, was delighted to have some money with her. They looked for a slip of paper on which to set down the figures; first the month's nursing, thirty francs; then the doctor, six francs; and indeed, with the medicine, that would make ten francs.

"Ah! and besides, I meant to tell you," added La Couteau, "that so much linen was dirtied during his illness that you really ought to add three francs for the soap. That would only be just; and besides, there were other little expenses, sugar, and eggs, so that in your place, to act like a good mother, I should put down five francs. Forty-five francs altogether, will that suit you?"

In spite of her emotion Madame Menoux felt that she was being robbed, that the other was speculating on her distress. She made a gesture of surprise and revolt at the idea of having to give so much money—that money which she found so hard to earn. No end of cotton and needles had to be sold to get such a sum together! And her distress, between the necessity of economy on the one hand and her maternal anxiety on the other, would have touched the hardest heart.

"But that will make another half-month's money," said she.

At this La Couteau put on her most frigid air: "Well, what would you have? It isn't my fault. One can't let your child die, so one must incur the necessary expenses. And then, if you haven't confidence in me, say so; send the money and settle things direct. Indeed, that will greatly relieve me, for in all this I lose my time and trouble; but then, I'm always stupid enough to be too obliging."

When Madame Menoux, again quivering and anxious, had given way, another difficulty arose. She had only some gold with her, two twenty-franc pieces and one ten-franc piece. The three coins lay glittering on the table. La Couteau looked at them with her yellow fixed eyes.

"Well, I can't give you your five francs change," she said, "I haven't any change with me. And you, Celeste, have you any change for this lady?"

She risked asking this question, but put it in such a tone and with such a glance that the other immediately understood her. "I have not a copper in my pocket," she replied.

Deep silence fell. Then, with bleeding heart and a gesture of cruel resignation, Madame Menoux did what was expected of her.

"Keep those five francs for yourself, Madame Couteau, since you have to take so much trouble. And, *mon Dieu*! may all this money bring me good luck, and at least enable my poor little fellow to grow up a fine handsome man like his father."

"Oh! as for that I'll warrant it," cried the other, with enthusiasm. "Those little ailments don't mean anything—on the contrary. I see plenty of little folks, I do; and so just remember what I tell you, yours will become an extraordinarily fine child. There won't be better."

When Madame Menoux went off, La Couteau had lavished such flattery and such promises upon her that she felt quite light and gay; no longer regretting her money, but dreaming of the day when little Pierre would come back to her with plump cheeks and all the vigor of a young oak.

As soon as the door had closed behind the haberdasher, Celeste began to laugh in her impudent way: "What a lot of fibs you told her! I don't believe that her child so much as caught a cold," she exclaimed.

La Couteau began by assuming a dignified air: "Say that I'm a liar at once. The child isn't well, I assure you."

ÉMILE ZOLA

The maid's gayety only increased at this. "Well now, you are really comical, putting on such airs with me. I know you, remember, and I know what is meant when the tip of your nose begins to wriggle."

"The child is quite puny," repeated her friend, more gently.

"Oh! I can believe that. All the same I should like to see the doctor's prescriptions, and the soap and the sugar. But, you know, I don't care a button about the matter. As for that little Madame Menoux, it's here to-day and gone to-morrow. She has her business, and I have mine. And you, too, have yours, and so much the better if you get as much out of it as you can."

But La Couteau changed the conversation by asking the maid if she could not give her a drop of something to drink, for night travelling did upset her stomach so. Thereupon Celeste, with a laugh, took a bottle half-full of malaga and a box of biscuits from the bottom of a cupboard. This was her little secret store, stolen from the still-room. Then, as the other expressed a fear that her mistress might surprise them, she made a gesture of insolent contempt. Her mistress! Why, she had her nose in her basins and perfumery pots, and wasn't at all likely to call till she had fixed herself up so as to look pretty.

"There are only the children to fear," added Celeste; "that Gaston and that Lucie, a couple of brats who are always after one because their parents never trouble about them, but let them come and play here or in the kitchen from morning till night. And I don't dare lock this door, for fear they should come rapping and kicking at it."

When, by way of precaution, she had glanced down the passage and they had both seated themselves at table, they warmed and spoke out their minds, soon reaching a stage of easy impudence and saying everything as if quite unconscious how abominable it was. While sipping her wine Celeste asked for news of the village, and La Couteau spoke the brutal truth, between two biscuits. It was at the Vimeux' house that the servant's last child, born in La Rouche's den, had died a fortnight after arriving at Rougemont, and the Vimeux, who were more or less her cousins, had sent her their friendly remembrances and the news that they were about to marry off their daughter. Then, at La Gavette's, the old grandfather, who looked after the nurslings while the family was at work in the fields, had fallen into the fire with a baby in his arms. Fortunately they had been pulled out of it, and only the little one had been roasted. La Cauchois, though at heart she wasn't downcast, now had some fears that she might be worried, because four little ones had gone off from her house all in a body, a window being forgetfully left open at night-time. They were all four little Parisians, it seemed—two foundlings and two that had come from Madame Bourdieu's. Since the beginning of the year as many had died at Rougemont as had arrived there, and the mayor had declared that far too many were dying, and that the village would end by getting a bad reputation. One thing was certain, La Couillard would be the very first to receive a visit from the gendarmes if she didn't so arrange matters as to keep at least one nursling alive every now and then.

"Ah? that Couillard!" added the nurse-agent. "Just fancy, my dear, I took her a child, a perfect little angel—the boy of a very pretty young person who was stopping at Madame Bourdieu's. She paid four hundred francs to have him brought up until his first communion, and he lived just five days! Really now, that wasn't long enough! La Couillard need not have been so hasty. It put me in such a temper! I asked her if she wanted to dishonor me. What will ruin me is my good heart. I don't know how to refuse when folks ask me to do them a service. And God in Heaven knows how fond I am of children! I've always lived among them, and in future, if anybody who's a friend of mine gives me a child to put out to nurse, I shall say: 'We won't take the little one to La Couillard, for it would be tempting Providence. But after all, I'm an honest woman, and I wash my hands of it, for if I do take the cherubs over yonder I don't nurse them. And when one's conscience is at ease one can sleep quietly.'"

"Of course," chimed in Celeste, with an air of conviction.

While they thus waxed maudlin over their malaga, there arose a horrible red vision—a vision of that terrible Rougemont, paved with little Parisians, the filthy, bloody village, the charnel-place of cowardly murder, whose steeple pointed so peacefully to the skies in the midst of the far-spreading plain.

But all at once a rush was heard in the passage, and the servant hastened to the door to rid herself of Gaston and Lucie, who were approaching. "Be off! I don't want you here. Your mamma has told you that you mustn't come here."

Then she came back into the room quite furious. "That's true!" said she; "I can do nothing but they must come to bother me. Why don't they stay a little with the nurse?"

"Oh! by the way," interrupted La Couteau, "did you hear that Marie Lebleu's little one is dead? She must have had a letter about it.

Such a fine child it was! But what can one expect? it's a nasty wind passing. And then you know the saying, 'A nurse's child is the child of sacrifice!'"

"Yes, she told me she had heard of it," replied Celeste, "but she begged me not to mention it to madame, as such things always have a bad effect. The worst is that if her child's dead madame's little one isn't much better off."

At this La Couteau pricked up her ears. "Ah! so things are not satisfactory?"

"No, indeed. It isn't on account of her milk; that's good enough, and she has plenty of it. Only you never saw such a creature—such a temper! always brutal and insolent, banging the doors and talking of smashing everything at the slightest word. And besides, she drinks like a pig—as no woman ought to drink."

La Couteau's pale eyes sparkled with gayety, and she briskly nodded her head as if to say that she knew all this and had been expecting it. In that part of Normandy, in and around Rougemont, all the women drank more or less, and the girls even carried little bottles of brandy to school with them in their baskets. Marie Lebleu, however, was a woman of the kind that one picks up under the table, and, indeed, it might be said that since the birth of her last child she had never been quite sober.

"I know her, my dear," exclaimed La Couteau; "she is impossible. But then, that doctor who chose her didn't ask my opinion. And, besides, it isn't a matter that concerns me. I simply bring her to Paris and take her child back to the country. I know nothing about anything else. Let the gentlefolks get out of their trouble by themselves."

This sentiment tickled Celeste, who burst out laughing. "You haven't an idea," said she, "of the infernal life that Marie leads here! She fights people, she threw a water-bottle at the coachman, she broke a big vase in madame's apartments, she makes them all tremble with constant dread that something awful may happen. And, then, if you knew what tricks she plays to get something to drink! For it was found out that she drank, and all the liqueurs were put under lock and key. So you don't know what she devised? Well, last week she drained a whole bottle of Eau de Melisse, and was ill, quite ill, from it. Another time she was caught sipping some Eau de Cologne from one of the bottles in madame's dressing-room. I now really believe that she treats herself to some of the spirits of wine that are given her for the warmer!—it's enough to make one die of laughing. I'm always splitting my sides over it, in my little corner."

Then she laughed till the tears came into her eyes; and La Couteau, on her side highly amused, began to wriggle with a savage delight. All at once, however, she calmed down and exclaimed, "But, I say, they will turn her out of doors?"

"Oh! that won't be long. They would have done so already if they had dared."

But at this moment the ringing of a bell was heard, and an oath escaped Celeste. "Good! there's madame ringing for me now! One can never be at peace for a moment."

La Couteau, however, was already standing up, quite serious, intent on business and ready to depart.

"Come, little one, don't be foolish, you must do your work. For my part I have an idea. I'll run to fetch one of the nurses whom I brought this morning, a girl I can answer for as for myself. In an hour's time I'll be back here with her, and there will be a little present for you if you help me to get her the situation."

She disappeared while the maid, before answering a second ring, leisurely replaced the malaga and the biscuits at the bottom of the cupboard.

At ten o'clock that day Seguin was to take his wife and their friend Santerre to Mantes, to lunch there, by way of trying an electric motor-car, which he had just had built at considerable expense. He had become fond of this new "sport," less from personal taste, however, than from his desire to be one of the foremost in taking up a new fashion. And a quarter of an hour before the time fixed for starting he was already in his spacious "cabinet," arrayed in what he deemed an appropriate costume: a jacket and breeches of greenish ribbed velvet, yellow shoes, and a little leather hat. And he poked fun at Santerre when the latter presented himself in town attire, a light gray suit of delicate effect.

Soon after Valentine had given birth to her daughter Andree, the novelist had again become a constant frequenter of the house in the Avenue d'Antin. He was intent on resuming the little intrigue that he had begun there and felt confident of victory. Valentine, on her side, after a period of terror followed by great relief, had set about making up for lost time, throwing herself more wildly than ever into the vortex of fashionable life. She had recovered her good looks and youthfulness, and had never before experienced such a desire to divert herself, leaving her children more and more to the care of servants, and going about, hither and thither, as her fancy listed, particularly since her husband did the same in his sudden fits of jealousy and brutality, which broke out every now and again in the most imbecile fashion without the slightest cause. It was the collapse of all family life, with the threat of a great disaster in the future; and Santerre lived there in the midst of it, helping on the work of destruction.

He gave a cry of rapture when Valentine at last made her appearance gowned in a delicious travelling dress, with a cavalier toque on her head. But she was not quite ready, for she darted off again, saying that she would be at their service as soon as she had seen her little Andree, and given her last orders to the nurse.

"Well, make haste," cried her husband. "You are quite unbearable, you are never ready."

It was at this moment that Mathieu called, and Seguin received him in order to express his regret that he could not that day go into business matters with him. Nevertheless, before fixing another appointment, he was willing to take note of certain conditions which the other wished to stipulate for the purpose of reserving to himself the exclusive right of purchasing the remainder of the Chantebled estate in portions and at fixed dates. Seguin was promising that he would carefully study this proposal when he was cut short by a sudden tumult—distant shouts, wild hurrying to and fro, and a violent banging of doors.

"Why! what is it? what is it?" he muttered, turning towards the shaking walls.

The door suddenly opened and Valentine reappeared, distracted, red with fear and anger, and carrying her little Andree, who wailed and struggled in her arms.

"There, there, my pet," gasped the mother, "don't cry, she shan't hurt you any more. There, it's nothing, darling; be quiet, do."

Then she deposited the little girl in a large armchair, where she at once became quiet again. She was a very pretty child, but still so puny, although nearly four months old, that there seemed to be nothing but her beautiful big eyes in her pale little face.

"Well, what is the matter?" asked Seguin, in astonishment.

"The matter, is, my friend, that I have just found Marie lying across the cradle as drunk as a market porter, and half stifling the child. If I had been a few moments later it would have been all over. Drunk at ten o'clock in the morning! Can one understand such a thing? I had noticed that she drank, and so I hid the liqueurs, for I hoped to be able to keep her, since her milk is so good. But do you know what she had drunk? Why, the methylated spirits for the warmer! The empty bottle had remained beside her."

"But what did she say to you?"

"She simply wanted to beat me. When I shook her, she flew at me in a drunken fury, shouting abominable words. And I had time only to escape with the little one, while she began barricading herself in the room, where she is now smashing the furniture! There! just listen!"

Indeed, a distant uproar of destruction reached them. They looked one at the other, and deep silence fell, full of embarrassment and alarm.

"And then?" Seguin ended by asking in his curt dry voice.

"Well, what can I say? That woman is a brute beast, and I can't leave Andree in her charge to be killed by her. I have brought the child here, and I certainly shall not take her back. I will even own that I won't run the risk of going back to the room. You will have to turn the girl out of doors, after paying her wages."

"I! I!" cried Seguin. Then, walking up and down as if spurring on the anger which was rising within him, he burst forth: "I've had enough, you know, of all these idiotic stories! This house has become a perfect hell upon earth all through that child! There will soon be nothing but fighting here from morning till night. First of all it was pretended that the nurse whom I took the trouble to choose wasn't healthy. Well, then a second nurse is engaged, and she gets drunk and stifles the child. And now, I suppose, we are to have a third, some other vile creature who will prey on us and drive us mad. No, no, it's too exasperating, I won't have it."

Valentine, her fears now calmed, became aggressive. "What won't you have? There is no sense in what you say. As we have a child we must have a nurse. If I had spoken of nursing the little one myself you would have told me I was a fool. You would have found the house more uninhabitable than ever, if you had seen me with the child always in my arms. But I won't nurse—I can't. As you say, we will take a third nurse; it's simple enough, and we'll do so at once and risk it."

Seguin had abruptly halted in front of Andree, who, alarmed by the sight of his stern dark figure began to cry. Blinded as he was by anger, he perhaps failed to see her, even as he failed to see Gaston and Lucie, who had hastened in at the noise of the dispute and stood near the door, full of curiosity and fear. As nobody thought of sending them away they remained there, and saw and heard everything.

"The carriage is waiting," resumed Seguin, in a voice which he strove to render calm. "Let us make haste, let us go."

Valentine looked at him in stupefaction. "Come, be reasonable," said she. "How can I leave this child when I have nobody to whom I can trust her?"

"The carriage is waiting for us," he repeated, quivering; "let us go at once."

And as his wife this time contented herself with shrugging her shoulders, he was seized with one of those sudden fits of madness which impelled him to the greatest violence, even when people were present, and made him openly display his rankling poisonous sore, that absurd jealousy which had upset his life. As for that poor little puny, wailing child, he would have crushed her, for he held her to be guilty of everything, and indeed it was she who was now the obstacle to that excursion he had planned, that pleasure trip which he had promised himself, and which now seemed to him of such supreme importance. And 'twas so much the better if friends were there to hear him. So in the vilest language he began to upbraid his wife, not only reproaching her for the birth of that child, but even denying that the child was his. "You will only be content when you have driven me from the house!" he finished in a fury. "You won't come? Well then, I'll go by myself!"

And thereupon he rushed off like a whirlwind, without a word to Santerre, who had remained silent, and without even remembering that Mathieu still stood there awaiting an answer. The latter, in consternation at hearing all these things, had not dared to withdraw lest by doing so he should seem to be passing judgment on the scene. Standing there motionless, he turned his head aside, looked at little Andree who was still crying, and at Gaston and Lucie, who, silent with fright, pressed one against the other behind the armchair in which their sister was wailing.

Valentine had sunk upon a chair, stifling with sobs, her limbs trembling. "The wretch! Ah, how he treats me! To accuse me thus, when he knows how false it is! Ah! never more; no, never more! I would rather kill myself; yes, kill myself!"

Then Santerre, who had hitherto stood on one side, gently drew near to her and ventured to take her hand with a gesture of affectionate compassion, while saying in an undertone: "Come, calm yourself. You know very well that you are not alone, that you are not forsaken. There are some things which cannot touch you. Calm yourself, cease weeping, I beg you. You distress me dreadfully."

He made himself the more gentle since the husband had been the more brutal; and he leant over her yet the more closely, and again lowered his voice till it became but a murmur. Only a few words could be heard: "It is wrong of you to worry yourself like this. Forget all that folly. I told you before that he doesn't know how to behave towards a woman."

Twice was that last remark repeated with a sort of mocking pity; and she smiled vaguely amid her drying tears, in her turn murmuring: "You are kind, you are. Thank you. And you are quite right. . . Ah! if I could only be a little happy!"

Then Mathieu distinctly saw her press Santerre's hand as if in acceptance of his consolation. It was the logical, fatal outcome of the situation—given a wife whom her husband had perverted, a mother who refused to nurse her babe. And yet a cry from Andree suddenly set Valentine erect, awaking to the reality of her position. If that poor creature were so puny, dying for lack of her mother's milk, the mother also was in danger from her refusal to nurse her and clasp her to her breast like a buckler of invincible defence. Life and salvation one through the other, or disaster for both, such was the law. And doubtless Valentine became clearly conscious of her peril, for she hastened to take up the child and cover her with caresses, as if to make of her a protecting rampart against the supreme madness to which she had felt prompted. And great was the distress that came over her. Her other children were there, looking and listening, and Mathieu also was still waiting. When she perceived him her tears gushed forth again, and she strove to explain things, and even attempted to defend her husband.

"Excuse him, there are moments when he quite loses his head. *Mon Dieu!* What will become of me with this child? Yet I can't nurse her now, it is too late. It is frightful to be in such a position without knowing what to do. Ah! what will become of me, good Lord?"

Santerre again attempted to console her, but she no longer listened to him, and he was about to defer all further efforts till another time when unexpected intervention helped on his designs.

Celeste, who had entered noiselessly, stood there waiting for her mistress to allow her to speak. "It is my friend who has come to see me, madame," said she; "you know, the person from my village, Sophie Couteau, and as she happens to have a nurse with her—"

"There is a nurse here?"

"Oh! yes, madame, a very fine one, an excellent one."

Then, on perceiving her mistress's radiant surprise, her joy at this relief, she showed herself zealous: "Madame must not tire herself by holding the little one. Madame hasn't the habit. If madame will allow me, I will bring the nurse to her."

Heaving a sigh of happy deliverance, Valentine had allowed the servant to take the child from her. So Heaven had not abandoned her! However, she began to discuss the matter, and was not inclined to have the nurse brought there. She somehow feared that if the other one, who was drunk in her room, should come out and meet the new arrival, she would set about beating them all and breaking everything. At last she insisted on taking Santerre and Mathieu into the linen-room, saying that the latter must certainly have some knowledge of these matters, although he declared the contrary. Only Gaston and Lucie were formally forbidden to follow.

"You are not wanted," said their mother, "so stay here and play. But we others will all go, and as softly as possible, please, so that that drunken creature may not suspect anything."

Once in the linen-room, Valentine ordered all the doors to be carefully secured. La Couteau was standing there with a sturdy young person of five-and-twenty, who carried a superb-looking infant in her arms. She had dark hair, a low forehead, and a broad face, and was very respectably dressed. And she made a little courtesy like a well-trained nurse, who has already served with gentlefolks and knows how to behave. But Valentine's embarrassment remained extreme; she looked at the nurse and at the babe like an ignorant woman who, though her elder children had been brought up in a room adjoining her own, had never troubled or concerned herself about anything. In her despair, seeing that Santerre kept to himself, she again appealed to Mathieu, who once more excused himself. And it was only then that La Couteau, after glancing askance at the gentleman who, somehow or other, always turned up whenever she had business to transact, ventured to intervene:

"Will madame rely on me? If madame will kindly remember, I once before ventured to offer her my services, and if she had accepted them she would have saved herself no end of worry. That Marie Lebleu is impossible, and I certainly could have warned madame of it at the time when I came to fetch Marie's child. But since madame's doctor had chosen her, it was not for me to speak. Oh! she has good milk, that's quite sure; only she also has a good tongue, which is always dry. So if madame will now place confidence in me—"

Then she rattled on interminably, expatiating on the respectability of her calling, and praising the value of the goods she offered.

"Well, madame, I tell you that you can take La Catiche with your eyes shut. She's exactly what you want, there's no better in Paris. Just look how she's built, how sturdy and how healthy she is! And her child, just look at it! She's married, she even has a little girl of four at the village with her husband. She's a respectable woman, which is more than can be said for a good many nurses. In a word, madame, I know her and can answer for her. If you are not pleased with her I myself will give you your money back."

In her haste to get it all over Valentine made a great gesture of surrender. She even consented to pay one hundred francs a month, since La Catiche was a married woman. Moreover, La Couteau explained that she would not have to pay the office charges, which would mean a saving of forty-five francs, though, perhaps, madame would not forget all the trouble which she, La Couteau, had taken. On the other hand, there would, of course, be the expense of taking La Catiche's child back to the village, a matter of thirty francs. Valentine liberally promised to double that sum; and all seemed to be settled, and she felt delivered, when she suddenly bethought herself of the other nurse, who had barricaded herself in her room. How could they get her out in order to install La Catiche in her place?

"What!" exclaimed La Couteau, "does Marie Lebleu frighten you? She had better not give me any of her nonsense if she wants me ever to find her another situation. I'll speak to her, never fear."

Celeste thereupon placed Andree on a blanket, which was lying there, side by side with the infant of which the new nurse had rid herself a moment previously, and undertook to conduct La Couteau to Marie Lebleu's room. Deathlike silence now reigned there, but the nurse-agent only had to give her name to secure admittance. She went in, and for a few moments one only heard her dry curt voice. Then, on coming out, she tranquillized Valentine, who had gone to listen, trembling.

"I've sobered her, I can tell you," said she. "Pay her her month's wages. She's packing her box and going off."

Then, as they went back into the linen-room, Valentine settled pecuniary matters and added five francs for this new service. But a final difficulty arose. La Couteau could not come back to fetch La Catiche's child in the evening, and what was she to do with it during the rest of the day? "Well, no matter," she said at last, "I'll take it; I'll deposit it at the office, before I go my round. They'll give it a bottle there, and it'll have to grow accustomed to the bottle now, won't it?"

"Of course," the mother quietly replied.

Then, as La Couteau, on the point of leaving, after all sorts of bows and thanks, turned round to take the little one, she made a gesture of hesitation on seeing the two children lying side by side on the blanket.

"The devil!" she murmured; "I mustn't make a mistake."

This seemed amusing, and enlivened the others. Celeste fairly exploded, and even La Catiche grinned broadly; while La Couteau caught up the child with her long claw-like hands and carried it away. Yet another gone, to be carted away yonder in one of those ever-recurring *razzias* which consigned the little babes to massacre!

Mathieu alone had not laughed. He had suddenly recalled his conversation with Boutan respecting the demoralizing effects of that nurse trade, the shameful bargaining, the common crime of two mothers, who each risked the death of her child—the idle mother who bought another's services, the venal mother who sold her milk. He felt cold at heart as he saw one child carried off still full of life, and the other remain there already so puny. And what would be fate's course? Would not one or the other, perhaps both of them be sacrificed?

Valentine, however, was already leading both him and Santerre to the spacious salon again; and she was so delighted, so fully relieved, that she had recovered all her cavalier carelessness, her passion for noise and pleasure. And as Mathieu was about to take his leave, he heard the triumphant Santerre saying to her, while for a moment he retained her hand in his clasp: "Till to-morrow, then." And she, who had cast her buckler of defence aside, made answer: "Yes—yes, to-morrow."

A week later La Catiche was the acknowledged queen of the house. Andree had recovered a little color, and was increasing in weight daily. And in presence of this result the others bowed low indeed. There was every disposition to overlook all possible faults on the nurse's part. She was the third, and a fourth would mean the child's death; so that she was an indispensable, a providential helper, one whose services must be retained at all costs. Moreover, she seemed to have no defects, for she was a calm, cunning, peasant woman, one who knew how to rule her employers and extract from them all that was to be extracted. Her conquest of the Seguins was effected with extraordinary skill. At first some unpleasantness seemed likely, because Celeste was, on her own side, pursuing a similar course; but they were both too intelligent to do otherwise than come to an understanding. As their departments were distinct, they agreed that they could prosecute parallel invasions. And from that moment they even helped one another, divided the empire, and preyed upon the house in company.

La Catiche sat upon a throne, served by the other domestics, with her employers at her feet. The finest dishes were for her; she had her special wine, her special bread, she had everything most delicate and most nourishing that could be found. Gluttonous, slothful, and proud, she strutted about, bending one and all to her fancies. The others gave way to her in everything to avoid sending her into a temper which might have spoilt her milk. At her slightest indisposition everybody was distracted. One night she had an attack of indigestion, and all the doctors in the neighborhood were rung up to attend on her. Her only real defect, perhaps, was a slight inclination for pilfering; she appropriated some linen that was lying about, but madame would not hear of the matter being mentioned.

There was also the chapter of the presents which were heaped on her in order to keep her in good temper. Apart from the regulation present when the child cut its first tooth, advantage was taken of various other occasions, and a ring, a brooch, and a pair of earrings were given her. Naturally she was the most adorned nurse in the Champs-Elysees, with superb cloaks and the richest of caps, trimmed with long ribbons which flared in the sunlight. Never did lady lead a life of more sumptuous idleness. There were also the presents which she extracted for her husband and her little girl at the village. Parcels were sent them by express train every week. And on the morning when news came that her own baby, carried back by La Couteau, had died from the effects of a bad cold, she was presented with fifty francs as if in payment for the loss of her child. Little Andree, meanwhile, grew ever stronger, and thus La Catiche rose higher and higher, with the whole house bending low beneath her tyrannical sway.

On the day when Mathieu called to sign the deed which was to insure him the possession of the little pavilion of Chantebled with some fifty acres around it, and the privilege of acquiring other parts of the estate on certain conditions, he found Seguin on the point of starting for Le Havre, where a friend, a wealthy Englishman, was waiting for him with his yacht, in order that they might have a month's trip round the coast of Spain.

"Yes," said Seguin feverishly, alluding to some recent heavy losses at the gaming table, "I'm leaving Paris for a time—I have no luck here just now. But I wish you plenty of courage and all success, my dear sir. You know how much I am interested in the attempt you are about to make."

A little later that same day Mathieu was crossing the Champs-Elysees, eager to join Marianne at Chantebled, moved as he was by the decisive step he had taken, yet quivering also with faith and hope, when in a deserted avenue he espied a cab waiting, and recognized Santerre inside it. Then, as a veiled lady furtively sprang into the vehicle, he turned round wondering: Was that not Valentine? And as the cab drove off he felt convinced it was.

There came other meetings when he reached the main avenue; first Gaston and Lucie, already tired of play, and dragging about their puny limbs under the careless supervision of Celeste, who was busy laughing with a grocer's man; while farther off La Catiche, superb and royal, decked out like the idol of venal motherhood, was giving little Andree an outing, with her long purple ribbons streaming victoriously in the sunshine.

XI

O n the day when the first blow with the pick was dealt, Marianne, with Gervais in her arms, came and sat down close by, full of happy emotion at this work of faith and hope which Mathieu was so boldly undertaking. It was a clear, warm day in the middle of June, with a pure, broad sky that encouraged confidence. And as the children had been given a holiday, they played about in the surrounding grass, and one could hear the shrill cries of little Rose while she amused herself with running after the three boys.

"Will you deal the first blow?" Mathieu gayly asked his wife.

But she pointed to her baby. "No, no, I have my work. Deal it yourself, you are the father."

He stood there with two men under his orders, but ready himself to undertake part of the hard manual toil in order to help on the realization of his long thought of, ripening scheme. With great prudence and wisdom he had assured himself a modest livelihood for a year of effort, by an intelligent scheme of association and advances repayable out of profits, which would enable him to wait for his first harvest. And it was his life that he risked on that future crop, should the earth refuse his worship and his labor. But he was a faithful believer, one who felt certain of conquering, since love and determination were his.

"Well then, here goes!" he gallantly cried. "May the earth prove a good mother to us!"

Then he dealt the first blow with his pick.

The work was begun to the left of the old pavilion, in a corner of that extensive marshy tableland, where little streams coursed on all sides through the reeds which sprang up everywhere. It was at first simply a question of draining a few acres by capturing these streams and turning them into canals, in order to direct them afterwards over the dry sandy slopes which descended towards the railway line. After an attentive examination Mathieu had discovered that the work might easily be executed, and that water-furrows would suffice, such was the disposition and nature of the ground. This, indeed, was his real discovery, not to mention the layer of humus which he felt certain would be found amassed on the plateau, and the wondrous fertility which it would display as soon as a ploughshare had passed through it. And so with his pick he now began to open the trench which was to drain the damp soil above, and fertilize the dry, sterile, thirsty ground below.

The open air, however, had doubtless given Gervais an appetite, for he began to cry. He was now a strong little fellow, three months and a half old, and never neglected mealtime. He was growing like one of the young trees in the neighboring wood, with hands which did not easily release what they grasped, with eyes too full of light, now all laughter and now all tears, and with the ever open beak of a greedy bird, that raised a tempest whenever his mother kept him waiting.

"Yes, yes, I know you are there," said she; "come, don't deafen us any longer."

Then she gave him the breast and he became quiet, simply purring like a happy little kitten. The beneficent source had begun to flow once more, as if it were inexhaustible. The trickling milk murmured unceasingly. One might have said that it could be heard descending and spreading, while Mathieu on his side continued opening his trench, assisted by the two men whose apprenticeship was long since past.

He rose up at last, wiped his brow, and with his air of quiet certainty exclaimed: "It's only a trade to learn. In a few months' time I shall be nothing but a peasant. Look at that stagnant pond there, green with water-plants. The spring which feeds it is yonder in that big tuft of herbage. And when this trench has been opened to the edge of the slope, you will see the pond dry up, and the spring gush forth and take its course, carrying the beneficent water away."

"Ah!" said Marianne, "may it fertilize all that stony expanse, for nothing can be sadder than dead land. How happy it will be to quench its thirst and live again!"

Then she broke off to scold Gervais: "Come, young gentleman, don't pull so hard," said she. "Wait till it comes; you know very well that it's all for you."

Meantime the blows of the pickaxes rang out, the trench rapidly made its way through the fat, moist soil, and soon the water would flow into the parched veins of the neighboring sandy tracts to endow them with fruitfulness. And the light trickling of the mother's milk also continued with the faint murmur of an inexhaustible source, flowing from her breast into the mouth of her babe, like a fountain of eternal life. It ever and ever flowed, it created flesh, intelligence, and labor, and strength. And soon its whispering would mingle with the babble of the delivered spring as it descended along the trenches to the dry hot lands. And at last there would be but one and the same stream, one and the same river, gradually overflowing and carrying life to all the earth, a mighty river of nourishing milk flowing through the world's veins, creating without a pause, and producing yet more youth and more health at each return of springtide.

Four months later, when Mathieu and his men had finished the autumn ploughing, there came the sowing on the same spot. Marianne was there again, and it was such a very mild gray day that she was still able to sit down, and once more gayly give the breast to little Gervais. He was already eight months old and had become quite a personage. He grew a little more every day, always in his mother's arms, on that warm breast whence he sucked life. He was like the seed which clings to the seed-pod so long as it is not ripe. And at that first quiver of November, that approach of winter through which the germs would slumber in the furrows, he pressed his chilly little face close to his mother's warm bosom, and nursed on in silence as if the river of life were lost, buried deep beneath the soil.

"Ah!" said Marianne, laughing, "you are not warm, young gentleman, are you? It is time for you to take up your winter quarters."

Just then Mathieu, with his sower's bag at his waist, was returning towards them, scattering the seed with broad rhythmical gestures. He had heard his wife, and he paused to say to her: "Let him nurse and sleep till the sun comes back. He will be a man by harvest time." And, pointing to the great field which he was sowing with his assistants, he added: "All this will grow and ripen when our Gervais has begun to walk and talk—just look, see our conquest!"

He was proud of it. From ten to fifteen acres of the plateau were now rid of the stagnant pools, cleared and levelled; and they spread out in a brown expanse, rich with humus, while the water-furrows which intersected them carried the streams to the neighboring slopes. Before cultivating those dry lands one must yet wait until the moisture should have penetrated and fertilized them. That would be the work of the future, and thus, by degrees, life would be diffused through the whole estate.

"Evening is coming on," resumed Mathieu, "I must make haste."

Then he set off again, throwing the seed with his broad rhythmical gesture. And while Marianne, gravely smiling, watched him go, it occurred to little Rose to follow in his track, and take up handfuls of earth, which she scattered to the wind. The three boys perceived her, and Blaise and Denis then hastened up, followed by Ambroise, all gleefully imitating their father's gesture, and darting hither and thither around him. And for a moment it was almost as if Mathieu with the sweep of his arm not only cast the seed of expected corn into the furrows, but also sowed those dear children, casting them here and there without cessation, so that a whole nation of little sowers should spring up and finish populating the world.

Two months more went by, and January had arrived with a hard frost, when one day the Froments unexpectedly received a visit from Seguin and Beauchene, who had come to try their luck at wild-duck shooting, among such of the ponds on the plateau as had not yet been drained. It was a Sunday, and the whole family was gathered in the roomy kitchen, cheered by a big fire. Through the clear windows one could see the far-spreading countryside, white with rime, and stiffly slumbering under that crystal casing, like some venerated saint awaiting April's resurrection. And, that day, when the visitors presented themselves, Gervais also was slumbering in his white cradle, rendered somnolent by the season, but plump even as larks are in the cold weather, and waiting, he also, simply for life's revival, in order to reappear in all the triumph of his acquired strength.

The family had gayly partaken of dejeuner, and now, before nightfall, the four children had gathered round a table by the window, absorbed in a playful occupation which delighted them. Helped by Ambroise, the twins, Blaise and Denis, were building a whole village out of pieces of cardboard, fixed together with paste. There were houses, a town hall, a church, a school. And Rose, who had been forbidden to touch the scissors, presided over the paste, with which she smeared herself even to her hair. In the deep quietude, through which their laughter rang at intervals, their father and mother had remained seated side by side in front of the blazing fire, enjoying that delightful Sunday peace after the week's hard work.

They lived there very simply, like genuine peasants, without any luxury, any amusement, save that of being together. Their gay, bright kitchen was redolent of that easy primitive life, lived so near the earth, which frees one from fictitious wants, ambition, and the longing for pleasure. And no fortune, no power could have brought such quiet delight as that afternoon of happy intimacy, while the last-born slept so soundly and quietly that one could not even hear him breathe.

Beauchene and Seguin broke in upon the quiet like unlucky sportsmen, with their limbs weary and their faces and hands icy cold.

Amid the exclamations of surprise which greeted them, they complained of the folly that had possessed them to venture out of Paris in such bleak weather.

"Just fancy, my dear fellow," said Beauchene, "we haven't seen a single duck! It's no doubt too cold. And you can't imagine what a bitter wind blows on the plateau, amid those ponds and bushes bristling with icicles. So we gave up the idea of any shooting. You must give us each a glass of hot wine, and then we'll get back to Paris."

Seguin, who was in even a worse humor, stood before the fire trying to thaw himself; and while Marianne made haste to warm some wine, he began to speak of the cleared fields which he had skirted. Under the icy covering, however, beneath which they stiffly slumbered, hiding the seed within them, he had guessed nothing of the truth, and already felt anxious about this business of Mathieu's, which looked anything but encouraging. Indeed, he already feared that he would not be paid his purchase money, and so made bold to speak ironically.

"I say, my dear fellow, I am afraid you have lost your time," he began; "I noticed it all as I went by, and it did not seem promising. But how can you hope to reap anything from rotten soil in which only reeds have been growing for centuries?"

"One must wait," Mathieu quietly answered. "You must come back and see it all next June."

But Beauchene interrupted them. "There is a train at four o'clock, I think," said he; "let us make haste, for it would annoy us tremendously to miss it, would it not, Seguin?"

So saying, he gave him a gay, meaning glance. They had doubtless planned some little spree together, like husbands bent on availing themselves to the utmost of the convenient pretext of a day's shooting. Then, having drunk some wine and feeling warmed and livelier, they began to express astonishment at their surroundings.

"It stupefies me, my dear fellow," declared Beauchene, "that you can live in this awful solitude in the depth of winter. It is enough to kill anybody. I am all in favor of work, you know; but, dash it! one must have some amusement too."

"But we do amuse ourselves," said Mathieu, waving his hand round that rustic kitchen in which centred all their pleasant family life.

The two visitors followed his gesture, and gazed in amazement at the walls covered with utensils, at the rough furniture, and at the table on which the children were still building their village after offering their cheeks to be kissed. No doubt they were unable to understand what pleasure there could possibly be there, for, suppressing a jeering laugh, they shook their heads. To them it was really an extraordinary life, a life of most singular taste.

"Come and see my little Gervais," said Marianne softly. "He is asleep; mind, you must not wake him."

For politeness' sake they both bent over the cradle, and expressed surprise at finding a child but ten months old so big. He was very good, too. Only, as soon as he should wake, he would no doubt deafen everybody. And then, too, if a fine child like that sufficed to make life happy, how many people must be guilty of spoiling their lives! The visitors came back to the fireside, anxious only to be gone now that they felt enlivened.

"So it's understood," said Mathieu, "you won't stay to dinner with us?"

"Oh, no, indeed!" they exclaimed in one breath.

Then, to attenuate the discourtesy of such a cry, Beauchene began to jest, and accepted the invitation for a later date when the warm weather should have arrived.

"On my word of honor, we have business in Paris," he declared. "But I promise you that when it's fine we will all come and spend a day here—yes, with our wives and children. And you will then show us your work, and we shall see if you have succeeded. So good-by! All my good wishes, my dear fellow! Au revoir, cousin! Au revoir, children; be good!"

Then came more kisses and hand-shakes, and the two men disappeared. And when the gentle silence had fallen once more Mathieu and Marianne again found themselves in front of the bright fire, while the children completed the building of their village with a great consumption of paste, and Gervais continued sleeping soundly. Had they been dreaming? Mathieu wondered. What sudden blast from all the shame and suffering of Paris had blown into their far-away quiet? Outside, the country retained its icy rigidity. The fire alone sang the song of hope in life's future revival. And, all at once, after a few minutes' reverie the young man began to speak aloud, as if he had at last just found the answer to all sorts of grave questions which he had long since put to himself.

"But those folks don't love; they are incapable of loving! Money, power, ambition, pleasure—yes, all those things may be theirs, but not love! Even the husbands who deceive their wives do not really love their mistresses. They have never glowed with the supreme desire, the divine desire which is the world's very soul, the brazier of eternal life. And that explains everything. Without desire there is no love, no courage, and no hope. By love alone can one create. And if love be restricted in its mission there is but failure. Yes, they lie and deceive, because they do not love. Then they suffer and lapse into moral and physical degradation. And at the end lies the collapse of our rotten society, which breaks up more and more each day before our eyes. That, then, is the truth I was seeking. It is desire and love that save. Whoever loves and creates is the revolutionary saviour, the maker of men for the new world which will shortly dawn."

Never before had Mathieu so plainly understood that he and his wife were different from others. This now struck him with extraordinary force. Comparisons ensued, and he realized that their simple life, free from the lust of wealth, their contempt for luxury and worldly vanities, all their common participation in toil which made them accept and glorify life and its duties, all that mode of existence of theirs which was at once their joy and their strength, sprang solely from the source of eternal energy: the love with which they glowed. If, later on, victory should remain with them, if they should some day leave behind them work of value and health and happiness, it would be solely because they had possessed the power of love and the courage to love freely, harvesting, in an ever-increasing family, both the means of support and the means of conquest. And this sudden conviction filled Mathieu with such a glow that he leant towards his wife, who sat there deeply moved by what he said, and kissed her ardently upon the lips. It was divine love passing like a flaming blast. But she, though her own eyes were sparkling, laughingly scolded him, saying: "Hush, hush, you will wake Gervais."

Then they remained there hand in hand, pressing each other's fingers amid the silence. Evening was coming on, and at last the children, their village finished, raised cries of rapture at seeing it standing there among bits of wood, which figured trees. And then the softened glances of the parents strayed now through the window towards the crops sleeping beneath the crystalline rime, and now towards their last-born's cradle, where hope was likewise slumbering.

Again did two long months go by. Gervais had just completed his first year, and fine weather, setting in early, was hastening the awaking of the earth. One morning, when Marianne and the children went to join Mathieu on the plateau, they raised shouts of wonder, so completely had the sun transformed the expanse in a single week. It was now all green velvet, a thick endless carpet of sprouting corn, of tender, delicate emerald hue. Never had such a marvellous crop been seen. And thus, as the family walked on through the mild, radiant April morning, amid the country now roused from winter's sleep, and quivering with fresh youth, they all waxed merry at the sight of that healthfulness, that progressing fruitfulness, which promised the fulfilment of all their hopes. And their rapture yet increased when, all at once, they noticed that little Gervais also was awaking to life, acquiring decisive strength. As he struggled in his little carriage and his mother removed him from it, behold! he took his flight, and, staggering, made four steps; then hung to his father's legs with his little fists. A cry of extraordinary delight burst forth.

"Why! he walks, he walks!"

Ah! those first lispings of life, those successive flights of the dear little ones; the first glance, the first smile, the first step—what joy do they not bring to parents' hearts! They are the rapturous *etapes* of infancy, for which father and mother watch, which they await impatiently, which they hail with exclamations of victory, as if each were a conquest, a fresh triumphal entry into life. The child grows, the child becomes a man. And there is yet the first tooth, forcing its way like a needle-point through rosy gums; and there is also the first stammered word, the "pa-pa," the "mam-ma," which one is quite ready to detect amid the vaguest babble, though it be but the purring of a kitten, the chirping of a bird. Life does its work, and the father and the mother are ever wonderstruck with admiration and emotion at the sight of that efflorescence alike of their flesh and their souls.

"Wait a moment," said Marianne, "he will come back to me. Gervais! Gervais!"

And after a little hesitation, a false start, the child did indeed return, taking the four steps afresh, with arms extended and beating the air as if they were balancing-poles.

"Gervais! Gervais!" called Mathieu in his turn. And the child went back to him; and again and again did they want him to repeat the journey, amid their mirthful cries, so pretty and so funny did they find him.

Then, seeing that the four other children began playing rather roughly with him in their enthusiasm, Marianne carried him away. And once more, on the same spot, on the young grass, did she give him the breast. And again did the stream of milk trickle forth.

Close by that spot, skirting the new field, there passed a crossroad, in rather bad condition, leading to a neighboring village. And on this road a cart suddenly came into sight, jolting amid the ruts, and driven by a peasant—who was so absorbed in his contemplation of the land which Mathieu had cleared, that he would have let his horse climb upon a heap of stones had not a woman who accompanied him abruptly pulled the reins. The horse then stopped, and the man in a jeering voice called out: "So this, then, is your work, Monsieur Froment?"

Mathieu and Marianne thereupon recognized the Lepailleurs, the people of the mill. They were well aware that folks laughed at Janville over the folly of their attempt—that mad idea of growing wheat among the marshes of the plateau. Lepailleur, in particular, distinguished himself by the violent raillery he levelled at this Parisian, a gentleman born, with a good berth, who was so stupid as to make himself a peasant, and fling what money he had to that rascally earth, which would assuredly swallow him and his children and his money all together, without yielding even enough wheat to keep them in bread. And thus the sight of the field had stupefied him. It was a long while since he had passed that way, and he had never thought that the seed would sprout so thickly, for he had repeated a hundred times that nothing would germinate, so rotten was all the land. Although he almost choked with covert anger at seeing his predictions thus falsified, he was unwilling to admit his error, and put on an air of ironical doubt.

"So you think it will grow, eh? Well, one can't say that it hasn't come up. Only one must see if it can stand and ripen." And as Mathieu quietly smiled with hope and confidence, he added, striving to poison his joy: "Ah! when you know the earth you'll find what a hussy she is. I've seen plenty of crops coming on magnificently, and then a storm, a gust of wind, a mere trifle, has reduced them to nothing! But you are young at the trade as yet; you'll get your experience in misfortune."

His wife, who nodded approval on hearing him talk so finely, then addressed herself to Marianne: "Oh! my man doesn't say that to discourage you, madame. But the land you know, is just like children. There are some who live and some who die; some who give one pleasure, and others who kill one with grief. But, all considered, one always bestows more on them than one gets back, and in the end one finds oneself duped. You'll see, you'll see."

Without replying, Marianne, moved by these malicious predictions, gently raised her trustful eyes to Mathieu. And he, though for a moment irritated by all the ignorance, envy, and imbecile ambition which he felt were before him, contented himself with jesting. "That's it, we'll see. When your son Antoine becomes a prefect, and I have twelve peasant daughters ready, I'll invite you to their weddings, for it's your mill that ought to be rebuilt, you know, and provided with a fine engine, so as to grind all the corn of my property yonder, left and right, everywhere!"

The sweep of his arm embraced such a far expanse of ground that the miller, who did not like to be derided, almost lost his temper. He lashed his horse with his whip, and the cart jolted on again through the ruts.

"Wheat in the ear is not wheat in the mill," said he. "Au revoir, and good luck to you, all the same."

"Thanks, au revoir."

Then, while the children still ran about, seeking early primroses among the mosses, Mathieu came and sat down beside Marianne, who, he saw, was quivering. He said nothing to her, for he knew that she possessed sufficient strength and confidence to surmount, unaided, such fears for the future as threats might kindle in her womanly heart. But he simply set himself there, so near her that he touched her, looking and smiling at her the while. And she immediately became calm again and likewise smiled, while little Gervais, whom the words of the malicious could not as yet disturb, nursed more eagerly than ever, with a purr of rapturous satisfaction. The milk was ever trickling, bringing flesh to little limbs which grew stronger day by day, spreading through the earth, filling the whole world, nourishing the life which increased hour by hour. And was not this the answer which faith and hope returned to all threats of death?—the certainty of life's victory, with fine children ever growing in the sunlight, and fine crops ever rising from the soil at each returning spring! To-morrow, yet once again, on the glorious day of harvest, the corn will have ripened, the children will be men!

And it was thus, indeed, three months later, when the Beauchenes and the Seguins, keeping their promise, came—husbands, wives, and children—to spend a Sunday afternoon at Chantebled. The Froments had even prevailed on Morange to be of the party with Reine, in their desire to draw him for a day, at any rate, from the dolorous prostration in which he lived. As soon as all these fine folks had alighted from the train it was decided to go up to the plateau to see the famous fields, for everybody was curious about them, so extravagant and inexplicable did the idea of Mathieu's return to the soil, and transformation into a peasant, seem to them. He laughed gayly, and at least he succeeded in surprising them when he waved his hand towards the great expanse under the broad blue sky, that sea of tall green stalks whose ears were already heavy and undulated at the faintest breeze. That warm splendid afternoon, the far-spreading fields looked like the very triumph of fruitfulness, a growth of germs which the humus amassed through centuries had nourished with prodigious sap, thus producing this first formidable crop, as if to glorify the eternal source of life which sleeps in the earth's flanks. The milk had streamed, and the corn now grew on all sides with overflowing energy, creating health and strength, bespeaking man's labor and the kindliness, the solidarity of the world. It was like a beneficent, nourishing ocean, in which all hunger would be appeased, and in which to-morrow might arise, amid that tide of wheat whose waves were ever carrying good news to the horizon.

True, neither Constance nor Valentine was greatly touched by the sight of the waving wheat, for other ambitions filled their minds: and Morange, though he stared with his vague dim eyes, did not even seem to see it. But Beauchene and Seguin marvelled, for they remembered their visit in the month of January, when the frozen ground had been wrapt in sleep and mystery. They had then guessed nothing, and now they were amazed at this miraculous awakening, this conquering fertility, which had changed a part of the marshy tableland into a field of living wealth. And Seguin, in particular, did not cease praising and admiring, certain as he now felt that he would be paid, and already hoping that Mathieu would soon take a further portion of the estate off his hands.

Then, as soon as they had walked to the old pavilion, now transformed into a little farm, and had seated themselves in the garden, pending dinner-time, the conversation fell upon children. Marianne, as it happened, had weaned Gervais the day before, and he was there among the ladies, still somewhat unsteady on his legs, and yet boldly going from one to the other, careless of his frequent falls on his back or his nose. He was a gay-spirited child who seldom lost his temper, doubtless because his health was so good. His big clear eyes were ever laughing; he offered his little hands in a friendly way, and was very white, very pink, and very sturdy—quite a little man indeed, though but fifteen and a half months old. Constance and Valentine admired him, while Marianne jested and turned him away each time that he greedily put out his little hands towards her.

"No, no, monsieur, it's over now. You will have nothing but soup in future."

"Weaning is such a terrible business," then remarked Constance. "Did he let you sleep last night?"

"Oh! yes, he had good habits, you know; he never troubled me at night. But this morning he was stupefied and began to cry. Still, you see, he is fairly well behaved already. Besides, I never had more trouble than this with the other ones."

Beauchene was standing there, listening, and, as usual, smoking a cigar. Constance appealed to him:

"You are lucky. But you, dear, remember—don't you?—what a life Maurice led us when his nurse went away. For three whole nights we were unable to sleep."

"But just look how your Maurice is playing!" exclaimed Beauchene. "Yet you'll be telling me again that he is ill."

"Oh! I no longer say that, my friend; he is quite well now. Besides, I was never anxious; I know that he is very strong."

A great game of hide-and-seek was going on in the garden, along the paths and even over the flower-beds, among the eight children who were assembled there. Besides the four of the house—Blaise, Denis, Ambroise, and Rose—there were Gaston and Lucie, the two elder children of the Seguins, who had abstained, however, from bringing their other daughter—little Andree. Then, too, both Reine and Maurice were present. And the latter now, indeed, seemed to be all right upon his legs, though his square face with its heavy jaw still remained somewhat pale. His mother watched him running about, and felt so happy and so vain at the realization of her dream that she became quite amiable even towards these poor relatives the Froments, whose retirement into the country seemed to her like an incomprehensible downfall, which forever thrust them out of her social sphere.

"Ah! well," resumed Beauchene, "I've only one boy, but he's a sturdy fellow, I warrant it; isn't he, Mathieu?"

These words had scarcely passed his lips when he must have regretted them. His eyelids quivered and a little chill came over him as his glance met that of his former designer. For in the latter's clear eyes he beheld, as it were, a vision of that other son, Norine's ill-fated child, who had been cast into the unknown. Then there came a pause, and amid the shrill cries of the boys and girls playing at hide-and-seek a number of little shadows flitted through the sunlight: they were the shadows of the poor doomed babes who scarce saw the light before they were carried off from homes and hospitals to be abandoned in corners, and die of cold, and perhaps even of starvation!

Mathieu had been unable to answer a word. And his emotion increased when he noticed Morange huddled up on a chair, and gazing with blurred, tearful eyes at little Gervais, who was laughingly toddling hither and thither. Had a vision come to him also? Had the phantom of his dead wife, shrinking from the duties of motherhood and murdered in a hateful den, risen before him in that sunlit garden, amid all the turbulent mirth of happy, playful children?

"What a pretty girl your daughter Reine is!" said Mathieu, in the hope of drawing the accountant from his haunting remorse. "Just look at her running about!—so girlish still, as if she were not almost old enough to be married."

Morange slowly raised his head and looked at his daughter. And a smile returned to his eyes, still moist with tears. Day by day his adoration increased. As Reine grew up he found her more and more like her mother, and all his thoughts became centred in her. His one yearning was that she might be very beautiful, very happy, very rich. That would be a sign that he was forgiven—that would be the only joy for which he could yet hope. And amid it all there was a vague feeling of jealousy at the thought that a husband would some day take her from him, and that he would remain alone in utter solitude, alone with the phantom of his dead wife.

"Married?" he murmured; "oh! not yet. She is only fourteen."

At this the others expressed surprise: they would have taken her to be quite eighteen, so womanly was her precocious beauty already.

"As a matter of fact," resumed her father, feeling flattered, "she has already been asked in marriage. You know that the Baroness de Lowicz is kind enough to take her out now and then. Well, she told me that an arch-millionnaire had fallen in love with Reine—but he'll have to wait! I shall still be able to keep her to myself for another five or six years at least!"

He no longer wept, but gave a little laugh of egotistical satisfaction, without noticing the chill occasioned by the mention of Seraphine's name; for even Beauchene felt that his sister was hardly a fit companion for a young girl.

Then Marianne, anxious at seeing the conversation drop, began, questioning Valentine, while Gervais at last slyly crept to her knees.

"Why did you not bring your little Andree?" she inquired. "I should have been so pleased to kiss her. And she would have been able to play with this little gentleman, who, you see, does not leave me a moment's peace."

But Seguin did not give his wife time to reply. "Ah! no, indeed!" he exclaimed; "in that case I should not have come. It is quite enough to have to drag the two others about. That fearful child has not ceased deafening us ever since her nurse went away."

Valentine then explained that Andree was not really well behaved. She had been weaned at the beginning of the previous week, and La Catiche, after terrorizing the household for more than a year, had plunged it by her departure into anarchy. Ah! that Catiche, she might compliment herself on all the money she had cost! Sent away almost by force, like a queen who is bound to abdicate at last, she had been loaded with presents for herself and her husband, and her little girl at the village! And now it had been of little use to take a dry-nurse in her place, for Andree did not cease shrieking from morning till night. They had discovered, too, that La Catiche had not only carried off with her a large quantity of linen, but had left the other servants quite spoilt, disorganized, so that a general clearance seemed necessary.

"Oh!" resumed Marianne, as if to smooth things, "when the children are well one can overlook other worries."

"Why, do you imagine that Andree is well?" cried Seguin, giving way to one of his brutal fits. "That Catiche certainly set her right at first, but I don't know what happened afterwards, for now she is simply skin and bones." Then, as his wife wished to protest, he lost his temper. "Do you mean to say that I don't speak the truth? Why, look at our two others yonder: they have papier-mache faces, too! It is evident that you don't look after them enough. You know what a poor opinion Santerre has of them!"

For him Santerre's opinion remained authoritative. However, Valentine contented herself with shrugging her shoulders; while the others, feeling slightly embarrassed, looked at Gaston and Lucie, who amid the romping of their companions, soon lost breath and lagged behind, sulky and distrustful.

"But, my dear friend," said Constance to Valentine, "didn't our good Doctor Boutan tell you that all the trouble came from your not nursing your children yourself? At all events, that was the compliment that he paid me."

At the mention of Boutan a friendly shout arose. Oh! Boutan, Boutan! he was like all other specialists. Seguin sneered; Beauchene jested about the legislature decreeing compulsory nursing by mothers; and only Mathieu and Marianne remained silent.

"Of course, my dear friend, we are not jesting about you," said Constance, turning towards the latter. "Your children are superb, and nobody says the contrary."

Marianne gayly waved her hand, as if to reply that they were free to make fun of her if they pleased. But at this moment she perceived that Gervais, profiting by her inattention, was busy seeking his "paradise lost." And thereupon she set him on the ground: "Ah, no, no, monsieur!" she exclaimed. "I have told you that it is all over. Can't you see that people would laugh at us?"

Then for her and her husband came a delightful moment. He was looking at her with deep emotion. Her duty accomplished, she was now returning to him, for she was spouse as well as mother. Never had he thought her so beautiful, possessed of so strong and so calm a beauty, radiant with the triumph of happy motherhood, as though indeed a spark of something divine had been imparted to her by that river of milk that had streamed from her bosom. A song of glory seemed to sound, glory to the source of life, glory to the true mother, to the one who nourishes, her travail o'er. For there is none other; the rest are imperfect and cowardly, responsible for incalculable disasters. And on seeing her thus, in that glory, amid her vigorous children, like the good goddess of Fruitfulness, Mathieu felt that he adored her. Divine passion swept by—the glow which makes the fields palpitate, which rolls on through the waters, and floats in the wind, begetting millions and millions of existences. And 'twas delightful the ecstasy into which they both sank, forgetfulness of all else, of all those others who were there. They saw them no longer; they felt but one desire, to say that they loved each other, and that the season had come when love blossoms afresh. His lips protruded, she offered hers, and then they kissed.

"Oh! don't disturb yourselves!" cried Beauchene merrily. "Why, what is the matter with you?"

"Would you like us to move away?" added Seguin.

But while Valentine laughed wildly, and Constance put on a prudish air, Morange, in whose voice tears were again rising, spoke these words, fraught with supreme regret: "Ah! you are right!"

Astonished at what they had done, without intention of doing it, Mathieu and Marianne remained for a moment speechless, looking at one another in consternation. And then they burst into a hearty laugh, gayly excusing themselves. To love! to love! to be able to love! Therein lies all health, all will, and all power.

XII

Four years went by. And during those four years Mathieu and Marianne had two more children, a daughter at the end of the first year and a son at the expiration of the third. And each time that the family thus increased, the estate at Chantebled was increased also—on the first occasion by fifty more acres of rich soil reclaimed among the marshes of the plateau, and the second time by an extensive expanse of wood and moorland which the springs were beginning to fertilize. It was the resistless conquest of life, it was fruitfulness spreading in the sunlight, it was labor ever incessantly pursuing its work of creation amid obstacles and suffering, making good all losses, and at each succeeding hour setting more energy, more health, and more joy in the veins of the world.

On the day when Mathieu called on Seguin to purchase the wood and moorland, he lunched with Dr. Boutan, whom he found in an execrable humor. The doctor had just heard that three of his former patients had lately passed through the hands of his colleague Gaude, the notorious surgeon to whose clinic at the Marbeuf Hospital society Paris flocked as to a theatre. One of these patients was none other than Euphrasie, old Moineaud's eldest daughter, now married to Auguste Benard, a mason, and already the mother of three children. She had doubtless resumed her usual avocations too soon after the birth of her last child, as often happens in working-class families where the mother is unable to remain idle. At all events, she had for some time been ailing, and had finally been removed to the hospital. Mathieu had for a while employed her young sister Cecile, now seventeen, as a servant in the house at Chantebled, but she was of poor health and had returned to Paris, where, curiously enough, she also entered Doctor Gaude's clinic. And Boutan waxed indignant at the methods which Gaude employed. The two sisters, the married woman and the girl, had been discharged as cured, and so far, this might seem to be the case; but time, in Boutan's opinion, would bring round some terrible revenges.

One curious point of the affair was that Beauchene's dissolute sister, Seraphine, having heard of these so-called cures, which the newspapers had widely extolled, had actually sought out the Benards and the Moineauds to interview Euphrasie and Cecile on the subject. And in the result she likewise had placed herself in Gaude's hands. She certainly was of little account, and, whatever might become of her, the world would be none the poorer by her death. But Boutan pointed out that during the fifteen years that Gaude's theories and practices had prevailed in France, no fewer than half a million women had been treated accordingly, and, in the vast majority of cases, without any such treatment being really necessary. Moreover, Boutan spoke feelingly of the after results of such treatment—comparative health for a few brief years, followed in some cases by a total loss of muscular energy, and in others by insanity of a most violent form; so that the padded cells of the madhouses were filling year by year with the unhappy women who had passed through the hands of Gaude and his colleagues. From a social point of view also the effects were disastrous. They ran counter to all Boutan's own theories, and blasted all his hopes of living to see France again holding a foremost place among the nations of the earth.

"Ah!" said he to Mathieu, "if people were only like you and your good wife!"

During those four years at Chantebled the Froments had been ever founding, creating, increasing, and multiplying, again and again proving victorious in the eternal battle which life wages against death, thanks to that continual increase both of offspring and of fertile land which was like their very existence, their joy and their strength. Desire passed like a gust of flame—desire divine and fruitful, since they possessed the power of love, kindliness, and health. And their energy did the rest—that will of action, that quiet bravery in the presence of the labor that is necessary, the labor that has made and that regulates the earth. But during the first two years they had to struggle incessantly. There were two disastrous winters with snow and ice, and March brought hail-storms and hurricanes which left the crops lying low. Even as Lepailleur had threateningly predicted with a laugh of impotent envy, it seemed as if the earth meant to prove a bad mother, ungrateful to them for their toil, indifferent to their losses. During those two years they only extricated themselves from trouble thanks to the second fifty acres that they purchased from Seguin, to the west of the plateau, a fresh expanse of rich soil which they reclaimed amid the marshes, and which, in spite of frost and hail, yielded a prodigious first harvest. As the estate gradually expanded, it also grew stronger, better able to bear ill-luck.

But Mathieu and Marianne also had great family worries. Their five elder children gave them much anxiety, much fatigue. As with the soil, here again there was a daily battle, endless cares and endless fears. Little

Gervais was stricken with fever and narrowly escaped death. Rose, too, one day filled them with the direst alarm, for she fell from a tree in their presence, but fortunately with no worse injury than a sprain. And, on the other hand, they were happy in the three others, Blaise, Denis, and Ambroise, who proved as healthy as young oak-trees. And when Marianne gave birth to her sixth child, on whom they bestowed the gay name of Claire, Mathieu celebrated the new pledge of their affection by further acquisitions.

Then, during the two ensuing years, their battles and sadness and joy all resulted in victory once more. Marianne gave birth, and Mathieu conquered new lands. There was ever much labor, much life expended, and much life realized and harvested. This time it was a question of enlarging the estate on the side of the moorlands, the sandy, gravelly slopes where nothing had grown for centuries. The captured sources of the tableland, directed towards those uncultivated tracts, gradually fertilized them, covered them with increasing vegetation. There were partial failures at first, and defeat even seemed possible, so great was the patient determination which the creative effort demanded. But here, too, the crops at last overflowed, while the intelligent felling of a part of the purchased woods resulted in a large profit, and gave Mathieu an idea of cultivating some of the spacious clearings hitherto overgrown with brambles.

And while the estate spread the children grew. It had been necessary to send the three elder ones—Blaise, Denis, and Ambroise—to a school in Paris, whither they gallantly repaired each day by the first train, returning only in the evening. But the three others, little Gervais and the girls Rose and Claire, were still allowed all freedom in the midst of Nature. Marianne, however, gave birth to a seventh child, amid circumstances which caused Mathieu keen anxiety. For a moment, indeed, he feared that he might lose her. But her healthful temperament triumphed over all, and the child—a boy, named Gregoire—soon drank life and strength from her breast, as from the very source of existence. When Mathieu saw his wife smiling again with that dear little one in her arms, he embraced her passionately, and triumphed once again over every sorrow and every pang. Yet another child, yet more wealth and power, yet an additional force born into the world, another field ready for to-morrow's harvest.

And 'twas ever the great work, the good work, the work of fruitfulness spreading, thanks to the earth and to woman, both victorious over destruction, offering fresh means of subsistence each time a fresh child was born, and loving, willing, battling, toiling even amid suffering, and ever tending to increase of life and increase of hope.

THEN TWO MORE YEARS ROLLED on. And during those two years Mathieu and Marianne had yet another child, a girl. And again, at the same time as the family increased, the estate of Chantebled was increased also—on one side by five-and-seventy acres of woodland stretching over the plateau as far as the fields of Mareuil, and on the other by five-and-seventy acres of sloping moorland, extending to the village of Monval, alongside the railway line. But the principal change was that, as the old hunting-box, the little dilapidated pavilion, no longer offered sufficient accommodation, a whole farmstead had to be erected—stone buildings, and barns, and sheds, and stables, and cowhouses—for farm hands and crops and animals, whose number increased at each enlargement of the estate.

It was the resistless conquest of life; it was fruitfulness spreading in the sunlight; it was labor ever incessantly pursuing its work of creation amid obstacles and suffering, ever making good all losses, and at each succeeding hour setting more energy, more health, and more joy in the veins of the world.

But during those two years, while Chantebled grew, while labor and worry and victory alternated, Mathieu suddenly found himself mixed up in a terribly tragedy. He was obliged to come to Paris at times—more often indeed than he cared—now through his business relations with Seguin, now to sell, now to buy, now to order one thing or another. He often purchased implements and appliances at the Beauchene works, and had thus kept up intercourse with Morange, who once more seemed a changed man. Time had largely healed the wound left by his wife's death, particularly as she seemed to live again in Reine, to whom he was more attached than ever. Reine was no longer a child; she had become a woman. Still her father hoped to keep her with him some years yet, while working with all diligence, saving and saving every penny that he could spare, in order to increase her dowry.

But the inevitable was on the march, for the girl had become the constant companion of Seraphine. The latter, however depraved she might be, had certainly in the first instance entertained no idea of corrupting the child whom she patronized. She had at first taken her solely to such places of amusement as were fit for her years and understanding. But little by little the descent had come. Reine, too, as she grew into a woman, amid the hours of idleness when she was left alone by her father—who, perforce, had to spend his days at the Beauchene works—developed an ardent temperament and a thirst for every frivolous pleasure. And by degrees the once simply petted child became a participator in Seraphine's own reckless and dissolute life.

When the end came, and Reine found herself in dire trouble because of a high State functionary, a married man, a friend of Seraphine's—both women quite lost their heads. Such a blow might kill Morange. Everything must be hidden from him; but how? Thereupon Seraphine devised a plan. She obtained permission for Reine to accompany her on a visit into the country; but while the fond father imagined that his daughter was enjoying herself among society folk at a chateau in the Loiret, she was really hiding in Paris. It was indeed a repetition of her mother's tragic story, with this difference—that Seraphine addressed herself to no vulgar Madame Rouche, but to an assistant of her own surgeon, Gaude, a certain Sarraille, who had a dingy den of a clinic in the Passage Tivoli.

It was a bright day in August, and Mathieu, who had come to Paris to make some purchases at the Beauchene works, was lunching alone with Morange at the latter's flat, when Seraphine arrived there breathless and in consternation. Reine, she said, had been taken ill in the country, and she had brought her back to Paris to her own flat. But it was not thither; it was to Sarraille's den that she drove Morange and Mathieu. And there the frightful scene which had been enacted at La Rouche's at the time of Valerie's death was repeated. Reine, too, was dead—dead like her mother! And Morange, in a first outburst of fury threatened both Seraphine and Sarraille with the scaffold. For half an hour there was no mastering him, but all at once he broke down. To lose his daughter as he had lost his wife, it was too appalling; the blow was too great; he had strength left only to weep. Sarraille, moreover, defended himself; he swore that he had known nothing of the truth, that the deceased had simply come to him for legitimate treatment, and that both she and the Baroness had deceived him. Then Seraphine on her side took hold of Morange's hands, protesting her devotion, her frightful grief, her fear, too, lest the reputation of the poor dear girl should be dragged through the mire, if he (the father) did not keep the terrible secret. She accepted her share of responsibility and blame, admitted that she had been very culpable, and spoke of eternal remorse. But might the terrible truth be buried in the dead girl's grave, might there be none but pure flowers strewn upon that grave, might she who lay therein be regretted by all who had known her, as one snatched away in all innocence of youth and beauty!

And Morange yielded to his weakness of heart, stifling the while with sobs, and scarce repeating that word "Murderers!" which had sprung from his lips so impulsively a little while before. He thought, too, of the scandal, an autopsy, a court of law, the newspapers recounting the crime, his daughter's memory covered with mire, and—No! no! he could have none of that. Whatever Seraphine might be, she had spoken rightly.

Then his powerlessness to avenge his daughter completed his prostration. It was as if he had been beaten almost to the point of death; every one of his limbs was bruised, his head seemed empty, his heart cold and scarce able to beat. And he sank into a sort of second childhood, clasping his hands and stammering plaintively, terrified, and beseeching compassion, like one whose sufferings are too hard to bear.

And when Mathieu sought to console him he muttered: "Oh, it is all over. They have both gone, one after the other, and I alone am guilty. The first time it was I who lied to Reine, telling her that her mother was travelling; and then she in her turn lied to me the other day with that story an invitation to a chateau in the country. Ah! if eight years ago I had only opposed my poor Valerie's madness, my poor Reine would still be alive to-day. . . Yes, it is all my fault; I alone killed them by my weakness. I am their murderer."

Shivering, deathly cold, he went on amid his sobs: "And, wretched fool that I have been, I have killed them through loving them too much. They were so beautiful, and it was so excusable for them to be rich and gay and happy. One after the other they took my heart from me, and I lived only in them and by them and for them. When one had left me, the other became my all in all, and for her, my daughter, I again indulged in the dream of ambition which had originated with her mother. And yet I killed them both, and my mad desire to rise and conquer fortune led me to that twofold crime. Ah! when I think that even this morning I still dared to esteem myself happy at having but that one child, that daughter to cherish! What foolish blasphemy against love and life! She is dead now, dead like her mother, and I am alone, with nobody to love and nobody to love me—neither wife nor daughter, neither desire nor will, but alone—ah! all alone, forever!"

It was the cry of supreme abandonment that he raised, while sinking to the floor strengthless, with a great void within him; and all he could do was to press Mathieu's hands and stammer: "Leave me—tell me nothing. You alone were right. I refused the offers of life, and life has now taken everything from me."

Mathieu, in tears himself, kissed him and lingered yet a few moments longer in that tragic den, feeling more moved than he had ever felt before. And when he went off he left the unhappy Morange in the charge of Seraphine, who now treated him like a little ailing child whose will-power was entirely gone.

And at Chantebled, as time went on, Mathieu and Marianne founded, created, increased, and multiplied. During the two years which elapsed, they again proved victorious in the eternal battle which life wages against death, thanks to that continual increase both of offspring and of fertile land which was like their very existence, their joy, and their strength. Desire passed like a gust of flame—desire divine and fruitful, since they possessed the power of love, kindliness, and health. And their energy did the rest—that will of action, that quiet bravery in the presence of the labor that is necessary, the labor that has made and that regulates the world. They were, however, still in the hard, trying, earlier stage of their work of conquest, and they often wept with grief and anxiety. Many were their cares, too, in transforming the old pavilion into a farm. The outlay was considerable, and at times it seemed as if the crops would never pay the building accounts. Moreover, as the enterprise grew in magnitude, and there came more and more cattle, more and more horses, a larger staff of both men and girls became necessary, to say nothing of additional implements and appliances, and the increase of supervision which left the Froments little rest. Mathieu controlled the agricultural part of the enterprise, ever seeking improved methods for drawing from the earth all the life that slumbered within it. And Marianne watched over the farmyard, the dairy, the poultry, and showed herself a first-class accountant, keeping the books, and receiving and paying money. And thus, in spite of recurring worries, strokes of bad luck and inevitable mistakes, fortune smiled on them athwart all worries and losses, so brave and sensible did they prove in their incessant daily struggle.

Apart, too, from the new buildings, the estate was increased by five-and-seventy acres of woodland, and five-and-seventy acres of sandy sloping soil. Mathieu's battle with those sandy slopes became yet keener, more and more heroic as his field of action expanded; but he ended by conquering, by fertilizing them yet more each season, thanks to the fructifying springs which he directed through them upon every side. And in the same way he cut broad roads through the new woods which he purchased on the plateau, in order to increase the means of communication and carry into effect his idea of using the clearings as pasture for his cattle, pending the time when he might largely devote himself to stock-raising. In this wise, then, the battle went on, and spread incessantly in all directions; and the chances of decisive victory likewise increased, compensation for possible loss on one side being found on another where the harvest proved prodigious.

And, like the estate, the children also grew. Blaise and Denis, the twins, now already fourteen years of age, reaped prize after prize at school, putting their younger brother, Ambroise, slightly to shame, for his quick and ingenious mind was often busy with other matters than his lessons. Gervais, the girls Rose and Claire, as well as the last-born boy, little Gregoire, were yet too young to be trusted alone in Paris, and so they continued growing in the open air of the country, without any great mishap befalling them. And at the end of those two years Marianne gave birth to her eighth child, this time a girl, named Louise; and when Mathieu saw her smiling with the dear little babe in her arms, he embraced her passionately, and triumphed once again over every sorrow and every pang. Yet another child, yet more wealth and power, yet an additional force born into the world, another field ready for to-morrow's harvest.

And 'twas ever the great work, the good work, the work of fruitfulness spreading, thanks to the earth and thanks to woman, both victorious over destruction, offering fresh means of subsistence each time a fresh child was born, and loving, willing, battling, toiling, even amid suffering, and ever tending to increase of life and increase of hope.

THEN TWO MORE YEARS ROLLED on, and during those two years Mathieu and Marianne had yet another child, another daughter, whom they called Madeleine. And once again the estate of Chantebled was increased; this time by all the marshland whose ponds and whose springs remained to be drained and captured on the west of the plateau. The whole of this part of the property was now acquired by the Froments— two hundred acres of land where, hitherto, only water plants had grown, but which now was given over to cultivation, and yielded abundant crops. And the new springs, turned into canals on every side, again carried beneficent life to the sandy slopes, and fertilized them. It was life's resistless conquest; it was fruitfulness spreading in the sunlight; it was labor ever incessantly pursuing its work of creation amid obstacles and suffering, making good all losses, and at each succeeding hour setting more energy, more health, and more joy in the veins of the world.

This time it was Seguin himself who asked Mathieu to purchase a fresh part of the estate, pressing him even to take all that was left of it, woods and moorland—extending over some five hundred acres. Nowadays Seguin was often in need of money, and in order to do business he offered Mathieu lower terms and all sorts of advantages; but the other prudently declined the proposals, keeping steadfastly to his original intentions, which were that he would proceed with his work of creation step by step, in accordance with his exact means and requirements. Moreover, a certain difficulty arose with regard to the purchase of the remaining moors, for enclosed by this land, eastward, near the railway line, were a few acres belonging to Lepailleur, the miller, who had never done anything with them. And so Mathieu preferred to select what remained of the marshy plateau, adding, however, that he would enter into negotiations respecting the moorland later on, when the miller should have consented to sell his enclosure. He knew that, ever since his property had been increasing, Lepailleur had regarded him with the greatest jealousy and hatred, and he did not think it advisable to apply to him personally, certain as he felt that he would fail in his endeavor. Seguin, however, pretended that if he took up the matter he would know how to bring the miller to reason, and even secure the enclosure for next to nothing. And indeed, thinking that he might yet induce Mathieu to purchase all the remaining property, he determined to see Lepailleur and negotiate with him before even signing the deed which was to convey to Mathieu the selected marshland on the plateau.

But the outcome proved as Mathieu had foreseen. Lepailleur asked such a monstrous price for his few acres enclosed within the estate that nothing could be done. When he was approached on the subject by Seguin, he made little secret of the rage he felt at Mathieu's triumph. He had told the young man that he would never succeed in reaping an ear of wheat from that uncultivated expanse, given over to brambles for centuries past; and yet now it was covered with abundant crops! And this had increased the miller's rancor against the soil; he hated it yet more than ever for its harshness to him, a peasant's son, and its kindliness towards that bourgeois, who seemed to have fallen from heaven expressly to revolutionize the region. Thus, in answer to Seguin, he declared with a sneer that since sorcerers had sprung up who were able to make wheat sprout from stones, his patch of ground was now worth its weight in gold. Several years previously, no doubt, he had offered Seguin the enclosure for a trifle; but times had changed, and he now crowed loudly over the other's folly in not entertaining his previous offer.

On the other hand, there seemed little likelihood of his turning the enclosure to account himself, for he was more disgusted than ever with the tilling of the soil. His disposition had been further embittered by the birth of a daughter, whom he would willingly have dispensed with, anxious as he was with respect to his son Antonin, now a lad of twelve, who proved so sharp and quick at school that he was regarded by the folks of Janville as a little prodigy. Mathieu had mortally offended the father and mother by suggesting that Antonin should be sent to an agricultural college—a very sensible suggestion, but one which exasperated them, determined as they were to make him a gentleman.

As Lepailleur would not part with his enclosure on any reasonable terms, Seguin had to content himself for the time with selling Mathieu the selected marshland on the plateau. A deed of conveyance having been prepared, they exchanged signatures. And then, on Seguin's hands, there still remained nearly two hundred and fifty acres of woods in the direction of Lillebonne, together with the moorlands stretching to Vieux-Bourg, in which Lepailleur's few acres were enclosed.

It was on the occasion of the visits which he paid Seguin in reference to these matters that Mathieu became acquainted with the terrible break-up of the other's home. The very rooms of the house in the Avenue d'Antin, particularly the once sumptuous "cabinet," spoke of neglect and abandonment. The desire to cut a figure in society, and to carry the "fad" of the moment to extremes, ever possessed Seguin; and thus he had for a while renounced his pretended artistic tastes for certain new forms of sport—the motor-car craze, and so forth. But his only real passion was horseflesh, and to this he at last returned. A racing stable which he set up quickly helped on his ruin. Women and gaming had been responsible for the loss of part of his large fortune, and now horses were devouring the remainder. It was said, too, that he gambled at the bourse, in the hope of recouping himself for his losses on the turf, and by way, too, of affecting an air of power and influence, for he allowed it to be supposed that he obtained information direct from members of the Government. And as his losses increased and downfall threatened him, all that remained of the *bel esprit* and moralist, once so prone to discuss literature and social philosophy with Santerre, was an embittered, impotent individual—one who had proclaimed himself a pessimist for fashion's sake, and was now caught in his own trap; having so spoilt his existence that he was now but an artisan of corruption and death.

All was disaster in his home. Celeste the maid had long since been dismissed, and the children were now in the charge of a certain German governess called Nora, who virtually ruled the house. Her position with respect to Seguin was evident to one and all; but then, what of Seguin's wife and Santerre? The worst was, that this horrible life, which seemed to be accepted on either side, was known to the children, or, at all events, to the elder daughter Lucie, yet scarcely in her teens. There had been terrible scenes with this child, who evinced a mystical disposition, and was ever talking of becoming a nun when she grew up. Gaston, her brother, resembled his father; he was brutal in his ways, narrow-minded, supremely egotistical. Very different was the little girl Andree, whom La Catiche had suckled. She had become a pretty child—so affectionate, docile, and gay, that she scarcely complained even of her brother's teasing, almost bullying ways. "What a pity," thought Mathieu, "that so lovable a child should have to grow up amid such surroundings!"

And then his thoughts turned to his own home—to Chantebled. The debts contracted at the outset of his enterprise had at last been paid, and he alone was now the master there, resolved to have no other partners than his wife and children. It was for each of his children that he conquered a fresh expanse of land. That estate would remain their home, their source of nourishment, the tie linking them together, even if they became dispersed through the world in a variety of social positions. And thus how decisive was that growth of the property, the acquisition of that last lot of marshland which allowed the whole plateau to be cultivated! There might now come yet another child, for there would be food for him; wheat would grow to provide him with daily bread. And when the work was finished, when the last springs were captured, and the land had been drained and cleared, how prodigious was the scene at springtide!—with the whole expanse, as far as eye could see, one mass of greenery, full of the promise of harvest. Therein was compensation for every tear, every worry and anxiety of the earlier days of labor.

Meantime Mathieu, amid his creative work, received Marianne's gay and courageous assistance. And she was not merely a skilful helpmate, taking a share in the general management, keeping the accounts, and watching over the home. She remained both a loving and well-loved spouse, and a mother who nursed, reared, and educated her little ones in order to give them some of her own sense and heart. As Boutan remarked, it is not enough for a woman to have a child; she should also possess healthy moral gifts in order that she may bring it up in creditable fashion. Marianne, for her part, made it her pride to obtain everything from her children by dint of gentleness and grace. She was listened to, obeyed, and worshipped by them, because she was so beautiful, so kind, and so greatly beloved. Her task was scarcely easy, since she had eight children already; but in all things she proceeded in a very orderly fashion, utilizing the elder to watch over the younger ones, giving each a little share of loving authority, and extricating herself from every embarrassment by setting truth and justice above one and all. Blaise and Denis, the twins, who were now sixteen, and Ambroise, who was nearly fourteen, did in a measure escape her authority, being largely in their father's hands. But around her she had the five others—from Rose, who was eleven, to Louise, who was two years old; between them, at intervals of a couple of years, coming Gervais, Claire, and Gregoire. And each time that one flew away, as it were, feeling his wings strong enough for flight, there appeared another to nestle beside her. And it was again a daughter, Madeleine, who came at the expiration of those two years. And when Mathieu saw his wife erect and smiling again, with the dear little girl at her breast, he embraced her passionately and triumphed once again over every sorrow and every pang. Yet another child, yet more wealth and power, yet an additional force born into the world, another field ready for to-morrow's harvest.

And 'twas ever the great work, the good work, the work of fruitfulness spreading, thanks to the earth and thanks to woman, both victorious over destruction, offering fresh means of subsistence each time a fresh child was born, and loving, willing, battling, toiling even amid suffering, and ever tending to increase of life and increase of hope.

XIII

Two more years went by, and during those two years Mathieu and Marianne had yet another daughter; and this time, as the family increased, Chantebled also was increased by all the woodland extending eastward of the plateau to the distant farms of Mareuil and Lillebonne. All the northern part of the property was thus acquired: more than five hundred acres of woods, intersected by clearings which roads soon connected together. And those clearings, transformed into pasture-land, watered by the neighboring springs, enabled Mathieu to treble his live-stock and attempt cattle-raising on a large scale. It was the resistless conquest of life, it was fruitfulness spreading in the sunlight, it was labor ever incessantly pursuing its work of creation amid obstacles and suffering, making good all losses, and at each succeeding hour setting more energy, more health, and more joy in the veins of the world.

Since the Froments had become conquerors, busily founding a little kingdom and building up a substantial fortune in land, the Beauchenes no longer derided them respecting what they had once deemed their extravagant idea in establishing themselves in the country. Astonished and anticipating now the fullest success, they treated them as well-to-do relatives, and occasionally visited them, delighted with the aspect of that big, bustling farm, so full of life and prosperity. It was in the course of these visits that Constance renewed her intercourse with her former schoolfellow, Madame Angelin, the Froments' neighbor. A great change had come over the Angelins; they had ended by purchasing a little house at the end of the village, where they invariably spent the summer, but their buoyant happiness seemed to have departed. They had long desired to remain unburdened by children, and now they eagerly longed to have a child, and none came, though Claire, the wife, was as yet but six-and-thirty. Her husband, the once gay, handsome musketeer, was already turning gray and losing his eyesight—to such a degree, indeed, that he could scarcely see well enough to continue his profession as a fan-painter.

When Madame Angelin went to Paris she often called on Constance, to whom, before long, she confided all her worries. She had been in a doctor's hands for three years, but all to no avail, and now during the last six months she had been consulting a person in the Rue de Miromesnil, a certain Madame Bourdieu, said she.

Constance at first made light of her friend's statements, and in part declined to believe her. But when she found herself alone she felt disquieted by what she had heard. Perhaps she would have treated the matter as mere idle tittle-tattle, if she had not already regretted that she herself had no second child. On the day when the unhappy Morange had lost his only daughter, and had remained stricken down, utterly alone in life, she had experienced a vague feeling of anguish. Since that supreme loss the wretched accountant had been living on in a state of imbecile stupefaction, simply discharging his duties in a mechanical sort of way from force of habit. Scarcely speaking, but showing great gentleness of manner, he lived as one who was stranded, fated to remain forever at Beauchene's works, where his salary had now risen to eight thousand francs a year. It was not known what he did with this amount, which was considerable for a man who led such a narrow regular life, free from expenses and fancies outside his home—that flat which was much too big for him, but which he had, nevertheless, obstinately retained, shutting himself up therein, and leading a most misanthropic life in fierce solitude.

It was his grievous prostration which had at one moment quite upset and affected Constance, so that she had even sobbed with the desolate man—she whose tears flowed so seldom! No doubt a thought that she might have had other children than Maurice came back to her in certain bitter hours of unconscious self-examination, when from the depths of her being, in which feelings of motherliness awakened, there rose vague fear, sudden dread, such as she had never known before.

Yet Maurice, her son, after a delicate youth which had necessitated great care, was now a handsome fellow of nineteen, still somewhat pale, but vigorous in appearance. He had completed his studies in a fairly satisfactory manner, and was already helping his father in the management of the works. And his adoring mother had never set higher hopes upon his head. She already pictured him as the master of that great establishment, whose prosperity he would yet increase, thereby rising to royal wealth and power.

Constance's worship for that only son, to-morrow's hero; increased the more since his father day by day declined in her estimation, till she regarded him in fact with naught but contempt and disgust. It was a logical downfall, which she could not stop, and the successive phases of which she herself fatally precipitated. At the outset she had overlooked his infidelity; then from a spirit of duty and to save him from irreparable folly she had sought to retain him near her; and finally, failing in her endeavor, she had begun to feel loathing and disgust. He was now two-and-forty, he drank too much, he ate too much, he smoked too much. He was growing corpulent and scant of breath, with hanging lips and heavy eyelids; he no longer took care of his person as formerly, but went about slipshod, and indulged in the coarsest pleasantries. But it was more particularly away from his home that he sank into degradation, indulging in the low debauchery which had ever attracted him. Every now and again he disappeared from the house and slept elsewhere; then he concocted such ridiculous falsehoods that he could not be believed, or else did not take the trouble to lie at all. Constance, who felt powerless to influence him, ended by allowing him complete freedom.

The worst was, that the dissolute life he led grievously affected the business. He who had been such a great and energetic worker had lost both mental and bodily vigor; he could no longer plan remunerative strokes of business; he no longer had the strength to undertake important contracts. He lingered in bed in the morning, and remained for three or four days without once going round the works, letting disorder and waste accumulate there, so that his once triumphal stock-takings now year by year showed a falling-off. And what an end it was for that egotist, that enjoyer, so gayly and noisily active, who had always professed that money—capital increased tenfold by the labor of others—was the only desirable source of power, and whom excess of money and excess of enjoyment now cast with appropriate irony to slow ruin, the final paralysis of the impotent.

But a supreme blow was to fall on Constance and fill her with horror of her husband. Some anonymous letters, the low, treacherous revenge of a dismissed servant, apprised her of Beauchene's former intrigue with Norine, that work-girl who had given birth to a boy, spirited away none knew whither. Though ten years had elapsed since that occurrence, Constance could not think of it without a feeling of revolt. Whither had that child been sent? Was he still alive? What ignominious existence was he leading? She was vaguely jealous of the boy. The thought that her husband had two sons and she but one was painful to her, now that all her motherly nature was aroused. But she devoted herself yet more ardently to her fondly loved Maurice; she made a demi-god of him, and for his sake even sacrificed her just rancor. She indeed came to the conclusion that he must not suffer from his father's indignity, and so it was for him that, with extraordinary strength of will, she ever preserved a proud demeanor, feigning that she was ignorant of everything, never addressing a reproach to her husband, but remaining, in the presence of others, the same respectful wife as formerly. And even when they were alone together she kept silence and avoided explanations and quarrels. Never even thinking of the possibility of revenge, she seemed, in the presence of her husband's profligacy, to attach herself more firmly to her home, clinging to her son, and protected by him from thought of evil as much as by her own sternness of heart and principles. And thus sorely wounded, full of repugnance but hiding her contempt, she awaited the triumph of that son who would purify and save the house, feeling the greatest faith in his strength, and quite surprised and anxious whenever, all at once, without reasonable cause, a little quiver from the unknown brought her a chill, affecting her heart as with remorse for some long-past fault which she no longer remembered.

That little quiver came back while she listened to all that Madame Angelin confided to her. And at last she became quite interested in her friend's case, and offered to accompany her some day when she might be calling on Madame Bourdieu. In the end they arranged to meet one Thursday afternoon for the purpose of going together to the Rue de Miromesnil.

As it happened, that same Thursday, about two o'clock, Mathieu, who had come to Paris to see about a threshing-machine at Beauchene's works, was quietly walking along the Rue La Boetie when he met Cecile Moineaud, who was carrying a little parcel carefully tied round with string. She was now nearly twenty-one, but had remained slim, pale, and weak, since passing through the hands of Dr. Gaude. Mathieu had taken a great liking to her during the few months she had spent as a servant at Chantebled; and later, knowing what had befallen her at the hospital, he had regarded her with deep compassion. He had busied himself to find her easy work, and a friend of his had given her some cardboard boxes to paste together, the only employment that did not tire her thin weak hands. So childish had she remained that one would have taken her for a young girl suddenly arrested in her growth. Yet her slender fingers were skilful, and she contrived to earn some two francs a day in making the little boxes. And as she suffered greatly at her parents' home, tortured by her brutal surroundings there, and robbed of her earnings week by week, her dream was to secure a home of her own, to find a little money that would enable her to install herself in a room where she might live in peace and quietness. It had occurred to Mathieu to give her a pleasant surprise some day by supplying her with the small sum she needed.

"Where are you running so fast?" he gayly asked her.

The meeting seemed to take her aback, and she answered in an evasive, embarrassed way: "I am going to the Rue de Miromesnil for a call I have to make."

Noticing his kindly air, however, she soon told him the truth. Her sister, that poor creature Norine, had just given birth to another child, her third, at Madame Bourdieu's establishment. A gentleman who had been protecting her had cast her adrift, and she had been obliged to sell her few sticks of furniture in order to get together a couple of hundred francs, and thus secure admittance to Madame Bourdieu's house, for the mere idea of having to go to a hospital terrified her. Whenever she might be able to get about again, however, she would find herself in the streets, with the task of beginning life anew at one-and-thirty years of age.

"She never behaved unkindly to me," resumed Cecile. "I pity her with all my heart, and I have been to see her. I am taking her a little chocolate now. Ah! if you only saw her little boy! he is a perfect love!"

The poor girl's eyes shone, and her thin, pale face became radiant with a smile. The instinct of maternity remained keen within her, though she could never be a mother.

"What a pity it is," she continued, "that Norine is so obstinately determined on getting rid of the baby, just as she got rid of the others. This little fellow, it's true, cries so much that she has had to give him the breast. But it's only for the time being; she says that she can't see him starve while he remains near her. But it quite upsets me to think that one can get rid of one's children; I had an idea of arranging things very differently. You know that I want to leave my parents, don't you? Well, I thought of renting a room and of taking my sister and her little boy with me. I would show Norine how to cut out and paste up those little boxes, and we might live, all three, happily together."

"And won't she consent?" asked Mathieu.

"Oh! she told me that I was mad; and there's some truth in that, for I have no money even to rent a room. Ah! if you only knew how it distresses me."

Mathieu concealed his emotion, and resumed in his quiet way: "Well, there are rooms to be rented. And you would find a friend to help you. Only I am much afraid that you will never persuade your sister to keep her child, for I fancy that I know her ideas on that subject. A miracle would be needed to change them."

Quick-witted as she was, Cecile darted a glance at him. The friend he spoke of was himself. Good heavens would her dream come true? She ended by bravely saying: "Listen, monsieur; you are so kind that you really ought to do me a last favor. It would be to come with me and see Norine at once. You alone can talk to her and prevail on her perhaps. But let us walk slowly, for I am stifling, I feel so happy."

Mathieu, deeply touched, walked on beside her. They turned the corner of the Rue de Miromesnil, and his own heart began to beat as they climbed the stairs of Madame Bourdieu's establishment. Ten years ago! Was it possible? He recalled everything that he had seen and heard in that house. And it all seemed to date from yesterday, for the building had not changed; indeed, he fancied that he could recognize the very grease-spots on the doors on the various landings.

Following Cecile to Norine's room, he found Norine up and dressed, but seated at the side of her bed and nursing her babe.

"What! is it you, monsieur?" she exclaimed, as soon as she recognized her visitor. "It is very kind of Cecile to have brought you. Ah! *mon Dieu* what a lot of things have happened since I last saw you! We are none of us any the younger."

He scrutinized her, and she did indeed seem to him much aged. She was one of those blondes who fade rapidly after their thirtieth year. Still, if her face had become pasty and wore a weary expression, she remained pleasant-looking, and seemed as heedless, as careless as ever.

Cecile wished to bring matters to the point at once. "Here is your chocolate," she began. "I met Monsieur Froment in the street, and he is so kind and takes so much interest in me that he is willing to help me in carrying out my idea of renting a room where you might live and work with me. So I begged him to come up here and talk with you, and prevail on you to keep that poor little fellow of yours. You see, I don't want to take you unawares; I warn you in advance."

Norine started with emotion, and began to protest. "What is all this again?" said she. "No, no, I don't want to be worried. I'm too unhappy as it is."

But Mathieu immediately intervened, and made her understand that if she reverted to the life she had been leading she would simply sink lower and lower. She herself had no illusions on that point; she spoke bitterly enough of her experiences. Her youth had flown, her good-looks were departing, and the prospect seemed hopeless enough. But then what could she do? When one had fallen into the mire one had to stay there.

"Ah! yes, ah! yes," said she; "I've had enough of that infernal life which some folks think so amusing. But it's like a stone round my neck; I can't get rid of it. I shall have to keep to it till I'm picked up in some corner and carried off to die at a hospital."

She spoke these words with the fierce energy of one who all at once clearly perceives the fate which she cannot escape. Then she glanced at her infant, who was still nursing. "He had better go his way and I'll go mine," she added. "Then we shan't inconvenience one another."

This time her voice softened, and an expression of infinite tenderness passed over her desolate face. And Mathieu, in astonishment, divining the new emotion that possessed her, though she did not express it, made haste to rejoin: "To let him go his way would be the shortest way to kill him, now that you have begun to give him the breast."

"Is it my fault?" she angrily exclaimed. "I didn't want to give it to him; you know what my ideas were. And I flew into a passion and almost fought Madame Bourdieu when she put him in my arms. But then how could I hold out? He cried so dreadfully with hunger, poor little mite, and seemed to suffer so much, that I was weak enough to let him nurse just a little. I didn't intend to repeat it, but the next day he cried again, and so I had to continue, worse luck for me! There was no pity shown me; I've been made a hundred times more unhappy than I should have been, for, of course, I shall soon have to get rid of him as I got rid of the others."

Tears appeared in her eyes. It was the oft-recurring story of the girl-mother who is prevailed upon to nurse her child for a few days, in the hope that she will grow attached to the babe and be unable to part from it. The chief object in view is to save the child, because its best nurse is its natural nurse, the mother. And Norine, instinctively divining the trap set for her, had struggled to escape it, and repeated, sensibly enough, that one ought not to begin such a task when one meant to throw it up in a few days' time. As soon as she yielded she was certain to be caught; her egotism was bound to be vanquished by the wave of pity, love, and hope that would sweep through her heart. The poor, pale, puny infant had weighed but little the first time he took the breast. But every morning afterwards he had been weighed afresh, and on the wall at the foot of the bed had been hung the diagram indicating the daily difference of weight. At first Norine had taken little interest in the matter, but as the line gradually ascended, plainly indicating how much the child was profiting, she gave it more and more attention. All at once, as the result of an indisposition, the line had dipped down; and since then she had always feverishly awaited the weighing, eager to see if the line would once more ascend. Then, a continuous rise having set in, she laughed with delight. That little line, which ever ascended, told her that her child was saved, and that all the weight and strength he acquired was derived from her—from her milk, her blood, her flesh. She was completing the appointed work; and motherliness, at last awakened within her, was blossoming in a florescence of love.

"If you want to kill him," continued Mathieu, "you need only take him from your breast. See how eagerly the poor little fellow is nursing!"

This was indeed true. And Norine burst into big sobs: "*Mon Dieu!* you are beginning to torture me again. Do you think that I shall take any pleasure in getting rid of him now? You force me to say things which make me weep at night when I think of them. I shall feel as if my very vitals were being torn out when this child is taken from me! There, are you both pleased that you have made me say it? But what good does it do to put me in such a state, since nobody can remedy things, and he must needs go to the foundlings, while I return to the gutter, to wait for the broom that's to sweep me away?"

But Cecile, who likewise was weeping, kissed and kissed the child, and again reverted to her dream, explaining how happy they would be, all three of them, in a nice room, which she pictured full of endless joys, like some Paradise. It was by no means difficult to cut out and paste up the little boxes. As soon as Norine should know the work, she, who was strong, might perhaps earn three francs a day at it. And five francs a day between them, would not that mean fortune, the rearing of the child, and all evil things forgotten, at an end? Norine, more weary than ever, gave way at last, and ceased refusing.

"You daze me," she said. "I don't know. Do as you like—but certainly it will be great happiness to keep this dear little fellow with me."

Cecile, enraptured, clapped her hands; while Mathieu, who was greatly moved, gave utterance to these deeply significant words: "You have saved him, and now he saves you."

Then Norine at last smiled. She felt happy now; a great weight had been lifted from her heart. And carrying her child in her arms she insisted on accompanying her sister and their friend to the first floor.

During the last half-hour Constance and Madame Angelin had been deep in consultation with Madame Bourdieu. The former had not given her name, but had simply played the part of an obliging friend accompanying another on an occasion of some delicacy. Madame Bourdieu, with the keen scent characteristic of her profession, divined a possible customer in that inquisitive lady who put such strange questions to her. However, a rather painful scene took place, for realizing that she could not forever deceive Madame Angelin with false hopes, Madame Bourdieu decided to tell the truth—her case was hopeless. Constance, however, at last made a sign to entreat her to continue deceiving her friend, if only for charity's sake. The other, therefore, while conducting her visitors to the landing, spoke a few hopeful words to Madame Angelin: "After all, dear madame," said she, "one must never despair. I did wrong to speak as I did just now. I may yet be mistaken. Come back to see me again."

At this moment Mathieu and Cecile were still on the landing in conversation with Norine, whose infant had fallen asleep in her arms. Constance and Madame Angelin were so surprised at finding the farmer of Chantebled in the company of the two young women that they pretended they did not see him. All at once, however, Constance, with the help of memory, recognized Norine, the more readily perhaps as she was now aware that Mathieu had, ten years previously, acted as her husband's intermediary. And a feeling of revolt and the wildest fancies instantly arose within her. What was Mathieu doing in that house? whose child was it that the young woman carried in her arms? At that moment the other child seemed to peer forth from the past; she saw it in swaddling clothes, like the infant there; indeed, she almost confounded one with the other, and imagined that it was indeed her husband's illegitimate son that was sleeping in his mother's arms before her. Then all the satisfaction she had derived from what she had heard Madame Bourdieu say departed, and she went off furious and ashamed, as if soiled and threatened by all the vague abominations which she had for some time felt around her, without knowing, however, whence came the little chill which made her shudder as with dread.

As for Mathieu, he saw that neither Norine nor Cecile had recognized Madame Beauchene under her veil, and so he quietly continued explaining to the former that he would take steps to secure for her from the Assistance Publique—the official organization for the relief of the poor—a cradle and a supply of baby linen, as well as immediate pecuniary succor, since she undertook to keep and nurse her child. Afterwards he would obtain for her an allowance of thirty francs a month for at least one year. This would greatly help the sisters, particularly in the earlier stages of their life together in the room which they had settled to rent. When Mathieu added that he would take upon himself the preliminary outlay of a little furniture and so forth, Norine insisted upon kissing him.

"Oh! it is with a good heart," said she. "It does one good to meet a man like you. And come, kiss my poor little fellow, too; it will bring him good luck."

On reaching the Rue La Boetie it occurred to Mathieu, who was bound for the Beauchene works, to take a cab and let Cecile alight near her parents' home, since it was in the neighborhood of the factory. But she explained to him that she wished, first of all, to call upon her sister Euphrasie in the Rue Caroline. This street was in the same direction, and so Mathieu made her get into the cab, telling her that he would set her down at her sister's door.

She was so amazed, so happy at seeing her dream at last on the point of realization, that as she sat in the cab by the side of Mathieu she did not know how to thank him. Her eyes were quite moist, all smiles and tears.

"You must not think me a bad daughter, monsieur," said she, "because I'm so pleased to leave home. Papa still works as much as he is able, though he does not get much reward for it at the factory. And mamma does all she can at home, though she hasn't much strength left her nowadays. Since Victor came back from the army, he has married and has children of his own, and I'm even afraid that he'll have more than he can provide for, as, while he was in the army, he seems to have lost all taste for work. But the sharpest of the family is that lazybones Irma, my younger sister, who's so pretty and so delicate-looking, perhaps because she's always ill. As you may remember, mamma used to fear that Irma might turn out badly like Norine. Well, not at all! Indeed, she's the only one of us who is likely to do well, for she's going to marry a clerk in the post-office. And so the only ones left at home are myself and Alfred. Oh! he is a perfect bandit! That is the plain truth. He committed a theft the other day, and one had no end of trouble to get him out of the hands of the police commissary. But all the same, mamma has a weakness for him, and lets him take all my earnings. Yes, indeed, I've had quite enough of him, especially as he is always terrifying me out of my wits, threatening to beat and even kill me, though he well knows that ever since my illness the slightest noise throws me into a faint. And as, all considered, neither papa nor mamma needs me, it's quite excusable, isn't it, that I should prefer living quietly alone. It is my right, is it not, monsieur?"

She went on to speak of her sister Euphrasie, who had fallen into a most wretched condition, said she, ever since passing through Dr. Gaude's hands. Her home had virtually been broken up, she had become decrepit, a mere bundle of rags, unable even to handle a broom. It made one tremble to see her. Then, after a pause, just as the cab was reaching the Rue Caroline, the girl continued: "Will you come up to see her? You might say a few kind words to her. It would please me, for I'm going on a rather unpleasant errand. I thought that she would have strength enough to make some little boxes like me, and thus earn a few pence for herself; but she has kept the work I gave her more than a month now, and if she really cannot do it I must take it back."

Mathieu consented, and in the room upstairs he beheld one of the most frightful, poignant spectacles that he had ever witnessed. In the centre of that one room where the family slept and ate, Euphrasie sat on a straw-bottomed chair; and although she was barely thirty years of age, one might have taken her for a little old woman of fifty; so thin and so withered did she look that she resembled one of those fruits, suddenly deprived of sap, that dry up on the tree. Her teeth had fallen, and of her hair she only retained a few white locks. But the more characteristic mark of this mature senility was a wonderful loss of muscular strength, an almost complete disappearance of will, energy, and power of action, so that she now spent whole days, idle, stupefied, without courage even to raise a finger.

When Cecile told her that her visitor was M. Froment, the former chief designer at the Beauchene works, she did not even seem to recognize him; she no longer took interest in anything. And when her sister spoke of the object of her visit, asking for the work with which she had entrusted her, she answered with a gesture of utter weariness: "Oh! what can you expect! It takes me too long to stick all those little bits of cardboard together. I can't do it; it throws me into a perspiration."

Then a stout woman, who was cutting some bread and butter for the three children, intervened with an air of quiet authority: "You ought to take those materials away, Mademoiselle Cecile. She's incapable of doing anything with them. They will end by getting dirty, and then your people won't take them back."

This stout woman was a certain Madame Joseph, a widow of forty and a charwoman by calling, whom Benard, the husband, had at first engaged to come two hours every morning to attend to the housework, his wife not having strength enough to put on a child's shoes or to set a pot on the fire. At first Euphrasie had offered furious resistance to this intrusion of a stranger, but, her physical decline progressing, she had been obliged to yield. And then things had gone from bad to worse, till Madame Joseph became supreme in the household. Between times there had been terrible scenes over it all; but the wretched Euphrasie, stammering and shivering, had at last resigned herself to the position, like some little old woman sunk into second childhood and already cut off from the world. That Benard and Madame Joseph were not bad-hearted in reality was shown by the fact that although Euphrasie was now but an useless encumbrance, they kept her with them, instead of flinging her into the streets as others would have done.

"Why, there you are again in the middle of the room!" suddenly exclaimed the fat woman, who each time that she went hither and thither found it necessary to avoid the other's chair. "How funny it is that you can never put yourself in a corner! Auguste will be coming in for his four o'clock snack in a moment, and he won't be at all pleased if he doesn't find his cheese and his glass of wine on the table."

Without replying, Euphrasie nervously staggered to her feet, and with the greatest trouble dragged her chair towards the table. Then she sat down again limp and very weary.

Just as Madame Joseph was bringing the cheese, Benard, whose workshop was near by, made his appearance. He was still a full-bodied, jovial fellow, and began to jest with his sister-in-law while showing great politeness towards Mathieu, whom he thanked for taking interest in his unhappy wife's condition. "*Mon Dieu*, monsieur," said he, "it isn't her fault; it is all due to those rascally doctors at the hospital. For a year or so one might have thought her cured, but you see what has now become of her. Ah! it ought not to be allowed! You are no doubt aware that they treated Cecile just the same. And there was another, too, a baroness, whom you must know. She called here the other day to see Euphrasie, and, upon my word, I didn't recognize her. She used to be such a fine woman, and now she looks a hundred years old. Yes, yes, I say that the doctors ought to be sent to prison."

He was about to sit down to table when he stumbled against Euphrasie's chair. She sat watching him with an anxious, semi-stupefied expression. "There you are, in my way as usual!" said he; "one is always tumbling up against you. Come, make a little room, do."

He did not seem to be a very terrible customer, but at the sound of his voice she began to tremble, full of childish fear, as if she were threatened with a thrashing. And this time she found strength enough to drag her chair as far as a dark closet, the door of which was open. She there sought refuge, ensconcing herself in the gloom, amid which one could vaguely espy her shrunken, wrinkled face, which suggested that of some very old great-grandmother, who was taking years and years to die.

Mathieu's heart contracted as he observed that senile terror, that shivering obedience on the part of a woman whose harsh, dry, aggressively quarrelsome disposition he so well remembered. Industrious, self-willed, full of life as she had once been, she was now but a limp human rag. And yet her case was recorded in medical annals as one of the renowned Gaude's great miracles of cure. Ah! how truly had Boutan spoken in saying that people ought to wait to see the real results of those victorious operations which were sapping the vitality of France.

Cecile, however, with eager affection, kissed the three children, who somehow continued to grow up in that wrecked household. Tears came to her eyes, and directly Madame Joseph had given her back the work-materials entrusted to Euphrasie she hurried Mathieu away. And, as they reached the street, she said: "Thank you, Monsieur Froment; I can go home on foot now—. How frightful, eh? Ah! as I told you, we shall be in Paradise, Norine and I, in the quiet room which you have so kindly promised to rent for us."

On reaching Beauchene's establishment Mathieu immediately repaired to the workshops, but he could obtain no precise information respecting his threshing-machine, though he had ordered it several months previously. He was told that the master's son, Monsieur Maurice, had gone out on business, and that nobody could give him an answer, particularly as the master himself had not put in an appearance at the works that week. He learnt, however, that Beauchene had returned from a journey that very day, and must be indoors with his wife. Accordingly, he resolved to call at the house, less on account of the threshing-machine than to decide a matter of great interest to him, that of the entry of one of his twin sons, Blaise, into the establishment.

This big fellow had lately left college, and although he had only completed his nineteenth year, he was on the point of marrying a portionless young girl, Charlotte Desvignes, for whom he had conceived a romantic attachment ever since childhood. His parents, seeing in this match a renewal of their own former loving improvidence, had felt moved, and unwilling to drive the lad to despair. But, if he was to marry, some employment must first be found for him. Fortunately this could be managed. While Denis, the other of the twins, entered a technical school, Beauchene, by way of showing his esteem for the increasing fortune of his good cousins, as he now called the Froments, cordially offered to give Blaise a situation at his establishment.

On being ushered into Constance's little yellow salon, Mathieu found her taking a cup of tea with Madame Angelin, who had come back with her from the Rue de Miromesnil. Beauchene's unexpected arrival on the scene had disagreeably interrupted their private converse. He had returned from one of the debauches in which he so frequently indulged under the pretext of making a short business journey, and, still slightly intoxicated, with feverish, sunken eyes and clammy tongue, he was wearying the two women with his impudent, noisy falsehoods.

"Ah! my dear fellow!" he exclaimed on seeing Mathieu, "I was just telling the ladies of my return from Amiens—. What wonderful duck pates they have there!"

Then, on Mathieu speaking to him of Blaise, he launched out into protestations of friendship. It was understood, the young fellow need only present himself at the works, and in the first instance he should be put with Morange, in order that he might learn something of the business mechanism of the establishment. Thus talking, Beauchene puffed and coughed and spat, exhaling meantime the odor of tobacco, alcohol, and musk, which he always brought back from his "sprees," while his wife smiled affectionately before the others as was her wont, but directed at him glances full of despair and disgust whenever Madame Angelin turned her head.

As Beauchene continued talking too much, owning for instance that he did not know how far the thresher might be from completion, Mathieu noticed Constance listening anxiously. The idea of Blaise entering the establishment had already rendered her grave, and now her husband's apparent ignorance of important business matters distressed her. Besides, the thought of Norine was reviving in her mind; she remembered the girl's child, and almost feared some fresh understanding between Beauchene and Mathieu. All at once, however, she gave a cry of great relief: "Ah! here is Maurice."

Her son was entering the room—her son, the one and only god on whom she now set her affection and pride, the crown-prince who to-morrow would become king, who would save the kingdom from perdition, and who would exalt her on his right hand in a blaze of glory. She deemed him handsome, tall, strong, and as invincible in his nineteenth year as all the knights of the old legends. When he explained that he had just profitably compromised a worrying transaction in which his father had rashly embarked, she pictured him repairing disasters and achieving victories. And she triumphed more than ever on hearing him promise that the threshing-machine should be ready before the end of that same week.

"You must take a cup of tea, my dear," she exclaimed. "It would do you good; you worry your mind too much."

Maurice accepted the offer, and gayly replied: "Oh! do you know, an omnibus almost crushed me just now in the Rue de Rivoli!"

At this his mother turned livid, and the cup which she held escaped from her hand. Ah! God, was her happiness at the mercy of an accident? Then once again the fearful threat sped by, that icy gust which came she knew not whence, but which ever chilled her to her bones.

"Why, you stupid," said Beauchene, laughing, "it was he who crushed the omnibus, since here he is, telling you the tale. Ah! my poor Maurice, your mother is really ridiculous. I know how strong you are, and I'm quite at ease about you."

That day Madame Angelin returned to Janville with Mathieu. They found themselves alone in the railway carriage, and all at once, without any apparent cause, tears started from the young woman's eyes. At this she apologized, and murmured as if in a dream: "To have a child, to rear him, and then lose him—ah! certainly one's grief must then be poignant. Yet one has had him with one; he has grown up, and one has known for years all the joy of having him at one's side. But when one never has a child—never, never—ah! come rather suffering and mourning than such a void as that!"

And meantime, at Chantebled, Mathieu and Marianne founded, created, increased, and multiplied, again proving victorious in the eternal battle which life wages against death, thanks to that continual increase both of offspring and of fertile land, which was like their very existence, their joy and their strength. Desire passed like a gust of flame, desire divine and fruitful, since they possessed the power of love, of kindliness, and health. And their energy did the rest—that will of action, that quiet bravery in the presence of the labor that is necessary, the labor that has made and that regulates the world. Yet even during those two years it was not without constant struggling that they achieved victory. True, victory was becoming more and more certain as the estate expanded. The petty worries of earlier days had disappeared, and the chief question was now one of ruling sensibly and equitably. All the land had been purchased northward on the plateau, from the farm of Mareuil to the farm of Lillebonne; there was not a copse that did not belong to the Froments, and thus beside the surging sea of corn there rose a royal park of centenarian trees. Apart from the question of felling portions of the wood for timber, Mathieu was not disposed to retain the remainder for mere beauty's sake; and accordingly avenues were devised connecting the broad clearings, and cattle were then turned into this part of the property. The ark of life, increased by hundreds of animals, expanded, burst through the great trees. There was a fresh growth of fruitfulness: more and more cattle-sheds had to be built, sheepcotes had to be created, and manure came in loads and loads to endow the land with wondrous fertility. And now yet other children might come, for floods of milk poured forth, and there were herds and flocks to clothe and nourish them. Beside the ripening crops the woods waved their greenery, quivering with the eternal seeds that germinated in their shade, under the dazzling sun. And only one more stretch of land, the sandy slopes on the east, remained to be conquered in order that the kingdom might be complete. Assuredly this compensated one for all former tears, for all the bitter anxiety of the first years of toil.

Then, while Mathieu completed his conquest, there came to Marianne during those two years the joy of marrying one of her children even while she was again *enceinte*, for, like our good mother the earth, she also remained fruitful. 'Twas a delightful fete, full of infinite hope, that wedding of Blaise and Charlotte; he a strong young fellow of nineteen, she an adorable girl of eighteen summers, each loving the other with a love of nosegay freshness that had budded, even in childhood's hour, along the flowery paths of Chantebled. The eight other children were all there: first the big brothers, Denis, Ambroise, and Gervais, who were now finishing their studies; next Rose, the eldest girl, now fourteen, who promised to become a woman of healthy beauty and happy gayety of disposition; then Claire, who was still a child, and

Gregoire, who was only just going to college; without counting the very little ones, Louise and Madeleine.

Folks came out of curiosity from the surrounding villages to see the gay troop conduct their big brother to the municipal offices. It was a marvellous cortege, flowery like springtide, full of felicity, which moved every heart. Often, moreover, on ordinary holidays, when for the sake of an outing the family repaired in a band to some village market, there was such a gallop in traps, on horseback, and on bicycles, while the girls' hair streamed in the wind and loud laughter rang out from one and all, that people would stop to watch the charming cavalcade. "Here are the troops passing!" folks would jestingly exclaim, implying that nothing could resist those Froments, that the whole countryside was theirs by right of conquest, since every two years their number increased. And this time, at the expiration of those last two years it was again to a daughter, Marguerite, that Marianne gave birth. For a while she remained in a feverish condition, and there were fears, too, that she might be unable to nurse her infant as she had done all the others. Thus, when Mathieu saw her erect once more and smiling, with her dear little Marguerite at her breast, he embraced her passionately, and triumphed once again over every sorrow and every pang. Yet another child, yet more wealth and power, yet an additional force born into the world, another field ready for to-morrow's harvest!

And 'twas ever the great work, the good work, the work of fruitfulness spreading, thanks to the earth and thanks to woman, both victorious over destruction, offering fresh means of subsistence each time a fresh child was born, and loving, willing, battling, toiling, even amid suffering, and ever tending to increase of life and increase of hope.

ÉMILE ZOLA

XIV

Two more years went by, and during those two years yet another child, this time a boy, was born to Mathieu and Marianne. And on this occasion, at the same time as the family increased, the estate of Chantebled was increased also by all the heatherland extending to the east as far as the village of Vieux-Bourg. And this time the last lot was purchased, the conquest of the estate was complete. The 1250 acres of uncultivated soil which Seguin's father, the old army contractor, had formerly purchased in view of erecting a palatial residence there were now, thanks to unremitting effort, becoming fruitful from end to end. The enclosure belonging to the Lepailleurs, who stubbornly refused to sell it, alone set a strip of dry, stony, desolate land amid the broad green plain. And it was all life's resistless conquest; it was fruitfulness spreading in the sunlight; it was labor ever incessantly pursuing its work of creation amid obstacles and suffering, making good all losses, and at each succeeding hour setting more energy, more health, and more joy in the veins of the world.

Blaise, now the father of a little girl some ten months old, had been residing at the Beauchene works since the previous winter. He occupied the little pavilion where his mother had long previously given birth to his brother Gervais. His wife Charlotte had conquered the Beauchenes by her fair grace, her charming, bouquet-like freshness, to such a point, indeed, that even Constance had desired to have her near her. The truth was that Madame Desvignes had made adorable creatures of her two daughters, Charlotte and Marthe. At the death of her husband, a stockbroker's confidential clerk, who had died, leaving her at thirty years of age in very indifferent circumstances, she had gathered her scanty means together and withdrawn to Janville, her native place, where she had entirely devoted herself to her daughters' education. Knowing that they would be almost portionless, she had brought them up extremely well, in the hope that this might help to find them husbands, and it so chanced that she proved successful.

Affectionate intercourse sprang up between her and the Froments; the children played together; and it was, indeed, from those first games that came the love-romance which was to end in the marriage of Blaise and Charlotte. By the time the latter reached her eighteenth birthday and married, Marthe her sister, then fourteen years old, had become the inseparable companion of Rose Froment, who was of the same age and as pretty as herself, though dark instead of fair. Charlotte, who had a more delicate, and perhaps a weaker, nature than her gay, sensible sister, had become passionately fond of drawing and painting, which she had learnt at first simply by way of accomplishment. She had ended, however, by painting miniatures very prettily, and, as her mother remarked, her proficiency might prove a resource to her in the event of misfortune. Certainly there was some of the bourgeois respect and esteem for a good education in the fairly cordial greeting which Constance extended to Charlotte, who had painted a miniature portrait of her, a good though a flattering likeness.

On the other hand, Blaise, who was endowed with the creative fire of the Froments, ever striving, ever hard at work, became a valuable assistant to Maurice as soon as a brief stay in Morange's office had made him familiar with the business of the firm. Indeed it was Maurice who, finding that his father seconded him less and less, had insisted on Blaise and Charlotte installing themselves in the little pavilion, in order that the former's services might at all times be available. And Constance, ever on her knees before her son, could in this matter only obey respectfully. She evinced boundless faith in the vastness of Maurice's intellect. His studies had proved fairly satisfactory; if he was somewhat slow and heavy, and had frequently been delayed by youthful illnesses, he had, nevertheless, diligently plodded on. As he was far from talkative, his mother gave out that he was a reflective, concentrated genius, who would astonish the world by actions, not by speech. Before he was even fifteen she said of him, in her adoring way: "Oh! he has a great mind." And, naturally enough, she only acknowledged Blaise to be a necessary lieutenant, a humble assistant, one whose hand would execute the sapient young master's orders. The latter, to her thinking, was now so strong and so handsome, and he was so quickly reviving the business compromised by the father's slow collapse, that surely he must be on the high-road to prodigious wealth, to that final great triumph, indeed, of which she had been dreaming so proudly, so egotistically, for so many years.

But all at once the thunderbolt fell. It was not without some hesitation that Blaise had agreed to make the little pavilion his home, for he knew that there was an idea of reducing him to the status of a mere piece of machinery. But at the birth of his little girl he bravely decided to accept the proposal, and to engage in the battle of life even as his father had engaged in it, mindful of the fact that he also might in time have a large family. But it so happened that one morning, when he went up to the house to ask Maurice for some instructions, he heard from Constance herself that the young man had spent a very bad night, and that she had therefore prevailed on him to remain in bed. She did not evince any great anxiety on the subject; the indisposition could only be due to a little fatigue. Indeed, for a week past the two cousins had been tiring themselves out over the delivery of a very important order, which had set the entire works in motion. Besides, on the previous day Maurice, bareheaded and in perspiration, had imprudently lingered in a draught in one of the sheds while a machine was being tested.

That evening he was seized with intense fever, and Boutan was hastily summoned. On the morrow, alarmed, though he scarcely dared to say it, by the lightning-like progress of the illness, the doctor insisted on a consultation, and two of his colleagues being summoned, they soon agreed together. The malady was an extremely infectious form of galloping consumption, the more violent since it had found in the patient a field where there was little to resist its onslaught. Beauchene was away from home, travelling as usual. Constance, for her part, in spite of the grave mien of the doctors, who could not bring themselves to tell her the brutal truth, remained, in spite of growing anxiety, full of a stubborn hope that her son, the hero, the demi-god necessary for her own life, could not be seriously ill and likely to die. But only three days elapsed, and during the very night that Beauchene returned home, summoned by a telegram, the young fellow expired in her arms.

In reality his death was simply the final decomposition of impoverished, tainted, bourgeois blood, the sudden disappearance of a poor, mediocre being who, despite a facade of seeming health, had been ailing since childhood. But what an overwhelming blow it was both for the mother and for the father, all whose dreams and calculations it swept away! The only son, the one and only heir, the prince of industry, whom they had desired with such obstinate, scheming egotism, had passed away like a shadow; their arms clasped but a void, and the frightful reality arose before them; a moment had sufficed, and they were childless.

Blaise was with the parents at the bedside at the moment when Maurice expired. It was then about two in the morning, and as soon as possible he telegraphed the news of the death to Chantebled. Nine o'clock was striking when Marianne, very pale, quite upset, came into the yard to call Mathieu.

"Maurice is dead! . . . *Mon Dieu*! an only son; poor people!"

They stood there thunderstruck, chilled and trembling. They had simply heard that the young man was poorly; they had not imagined him to be seriously ill.

"Let me go to dress," said Mathieu; "I shall take the quarter-past ten o'clock train. I must go to kiss them."

Although Marianne was expecting her eleventh child before long, she decided to accompany her husband. It would have pained her to be unable to give this proof of affection to her cousins, who, all things considered, had treated Blaise and his young wife very kindly. Moreover, she was really grieved by the terrible catastrophe. So she and her husband, after distributing the day's work among the servants, set out for Janville station, which they reached just in time to catch the quarter-past ten o'clock train. It was already rolling on again when they recognized the Lepailleurs and their son Antonin in the very compartment where they were seated.

Seeing the Froments thus together in full dress, the miller imagined that they were going to a wedding, and when he learnt that they had a visit of condolence to make, he exclaimed: "Oh! so it's just the contrary. But no matter, it's an outing, a little diversion nevertheless."

Since Mathieu's victory, since the whole of the estate of Chantebled had been conquered and fertilized, Lepailleur had shown some respect for his bourgeois rival. Nevertheless, although he could not deny the results hitherto obtained, he did not altogether surrender, but continued sneering, as if he expected that some rending of heaven or earth would take place to prove him in the right. He would not confess that he had made a mistake; he repeated that he knew the truth, and that folks would some day see plainly enough that a peasant's calling was the very worst calling there could be, since the dirty land had gone bankrupt and would yield nothing more. Besides, he held his revenge—that enclosure which he left barren, uncultivated, by way of protest against the adjoining estate which it intersected. The thought of this made him ironical.

"Well," he resumed in his ridiculously vain, scoffing way, "we are going to Paris too. Yes, we are going to install this young gentleman there."

He pointed as he spoke to his son Antonin, now a tall, carroty fellow of eighteen, with an elongated head. A few light-colored bristles were already sprouting on his chin and cheeks, and he wore town attire, with a silk hat and gloves, and a bright blue necktie. After astonishing Janville by his success at school, he had displayed so much repugnance to manual work that his father had decided to make "a Parisian" of him.

"So it is decided; you have quite made up your mind?" asked Mathieu in a friendly way.

"Why, yes; why should I force him to toil and moil without the least hope of ever enriching himself? Neither my father nor I ever managed to put a copper by with that wretched old mill of ours. Why, the mill-stones wear away with rot more than with grinding corn. And the wretched fields, too, yield far more pebbles than crowns. And so, as he's now a scholar, he may as well try his fortune in Paris. There's nothing like city life to sharpen a man's wits."

Madame Lepailleur, who never took her eyes from her son, but remained in admiration before him as formerly before her husband, now exclaimed with an air of rapture: "Yes, yes, he has a place as a clerk with Maitre Rousselet, the attorney. We have rented a little room for him; I have seen about the furniture and the linen, and to-day's the great day; he will sleep there to-night, after we have dined, all three, at a good restaurant. Ah! yes, I'm very pleased; he's making a start now."

"And he will perhaps end by being a minister of state," said Mathieu, with a smile; "who knows? Everything is possible nowadays."

It all typified the exodus from the country districts towards the towns, the feverish impatience to make a fortune, which was becoming general. Even the parents nowadays celebrated their child's departure, and accompanied the adventurer on his way, anxious and proud to climb the social ladder with him. And that which brought a smile to the lips of the farmer of Chantebled, the bourgeois who had become a peasant, was the thought of the double change: the miller's son going to Paris, whereas he had gone to the earth, the mother of all strength and regeneration.

Antonin, however, had also begun to laugh with the air of an artful idler who was more particularly attracted by the free dissipation of Paris life. "Oh! minister?" said he, "I haven't much taste for that. I would much sooner win a million at once so as to rest afterwards."

Delighted with this display of wit, the Lepailleurs burst into noisy merriment. Oh! their boy would do great things, that was quite certain!

Marianne, her heart oppressed by thought of the mourning which awaited her, had hitherto kept silent. She now asked, however, why little

Therese did not form one of the party. Lepailleur dryly replied that he did not choose to embarrass himself with a child but six years old, who did not know how to behave. Her arrival had upset everything in the house; things would have been much better if she had never been born. Then, as Marianne began to protest, saying that she had seldom seen a more intelligent and prettier little girl, Madame Lepailleur answered more gently: "Oh! she's sharp; that's true enough; but one can't send girls to Paris. She'll have to be put somewhere, and it will mean a lot of trouble, a lot of money. However, we mustn't talk about all that this morning, since we want to enjoy ourselves."

At last the train reached Paris, and the Lepailleurs, leaving the Northern terminus, were caught and carried off by the impetuously streaming crowd.

When Mathieu and Marianne alighted from their cab on the Quai d'Orsay, in front of the Beauchenes' residence, they recognized the Seguins' brougham drawn up beside the foot pavement. And within it they perceived the two girls, Lucie and Andree, waiting mute and motionless in their light-colored dresses. Then, as they approached the door, they saw Valentine come out, in a very great hurry as usual. On recognizing them, however, she assumed an expression of deep pity, and spoke the words required by the situation:

"What a frightful misfortune, is it not? an only son!"

Then she burst out into a flood of words: "You have hastened here, I see, as I did; it is only natural. I heard of the catastrophe only by chance less than an hour ago. And you see my luck! My daughters were dressed, and I myself was dressing to take them to a wedding—a cousin of our friend Santerre is marrying a diplomatist. And, in addition, I am engaged for the whole afternoon. Well, although the wedding is fixed for a quarter-past eleven, I did not hesitate, but drove here before going to the church. And naturally I went upstairs alone. My daughters have been waiting in the carriage. We shall no doubt be a little late for the wedding. But no matter! You will see the poor parents in their empty house, near the body, which, I must say, they have laid out very nicely on the bed. Oh! it is heartrending."

Mathieu was looking at her, surprised to see that she did not age. The fiery flame of her wild life seemed to scorch and preserve her. He knew that her home was now completely wrecked. Seguin openly lived with Nora, the governess, for whom he had furnished a little house. It was there even that he had given Mathieu an appointment to sign the final transfer of the Chantebled property. And since Gaston had entered the military college of St. Cyr, Valentine had only her two daughters with her in the spacious, luxurious mansion of the Avenue d'Antin, which ruin was slowly destroying.

"I think," resumed Madame Seguin, "that I shall tell Gaston to obtain permission to attend the funeral. For I am not sure whether his father is in Paris. It's just the same with our friend Santerre; he's starting on a tour to-morrow. Ah! not only do the dead leave us, but it is astonishing what a number of the living go off and disappear! Life is very sad, is it not, dear madame?"

As she spoke a little quiver passed over her face; the dread of the coming rupture, which she had felt approaching for several months past, amid all the skilful preparations of Santerre, who had been long maturing some secret plan, which she did not as yet divine. However, she made a devout ecstatic gesture, and added: "Well, we are in the hands of God."

Marianne, who was still smiling at the ever-motionless girls in the closed brougham, changed the subject. "How tall they have grown, how pretty they have become! Your Andree looks adorable. How old is your Lucie now? She will soon be of an age to marry."

"Oh! don't let her hear you," retorted Valentine; "you would make her burst into tears! She is seventeen, but for sense she isn't twelve. Would you believe it, she began sobbing this morning and refusing to go to the wedding, under the pretence that it would make her ill? She is always talking of convents; we shall have to come to a decision about her. Andree, though she is only thirteen, is already much more womanly. But she is a little stupid, just like a sheep. Her gentleness quite upsets me at times; it jars on my nerves."

Then Valentine, on the point of getting into her carriage, turned to shake hands with Marianne, and thought of inquiring after her health. "Really," said she, "I lose my head at times. I was quite forgetting. And the baby you're expecting will be your eleventh child, will it now? How terrible! Still it succeeds with you. And, ah! those poor people whom you are going to see, their house will be quite empty now."

When the brougham had rolled away it occurred to Mathieu and Marianne that before seeing the Beauchenes it might be advisable for them to call at the little pavilion, where their son or their daughter-in-law might be able to give them some useful information. But neither Blaise nor Charlotte was there. They found only a servant who was watching over the little girl, Berthe. This servant declared that she had not seen Monsieur Blaise since the previous day, for he had remained at the Beauchenes' near the body. And as for Madame, she also had gone there early that morning, and had left instructions that Berthe was to be brought to her at noon, in order that she might not have to come back to give her the breast. Then, as Marianne in surprise began to put some questions, the girl explained matters: "Madame took a box of drawing materials with her. I fancy that she is painting a portrait of the poor young man who is dead."

As Mathieu and Marianne crossed the courtyard of the works, they felt oppressed by the grave-like silence which reigned in that great city of labor, usually so full of noise and bustle. Death had suddenly passed by, and all the ardent life had at once ceased, the machinery had become cold and mute, the workshops silent and deserted. There was not a sound, not a soul, not a puff of that vapor which was like the very breath of the place. Its master dead, it had died also. And the distress of the Froments increased when they passed from the works into the house, amid absolute solitude; the connecting gallery was wrapt in slumber, the staircase quivered amid the heavy silence, all the doors were open, as in some uninhabited house, long since deserted. They found no servant in the antechamber, and even the dim drawing-room, where the blinds of embroidered muslin were lowered, while the armchairs were arranged in a circle, as on reception days, when numerous visitors were expected, at first seemed to them to be empty. But at last they detected a shadowy form moving slowly to and fro in the middle of the room. It was Morange, bareheaded and frock-coated; he had hastened thither at the first news with the same air as if he had been repairing to his office. He seemed to be at home; it was he who received the visitors in a scared way, overcome as he was by this sudden demise, which recalled to him his daughter's abominable death. His heart-wound had reopened; he was livid, all in disorder, with his long gray beard streaming down, while he stepped hither and thither without a pause, making all the surrounding grief his own.

As soon as he recognized the Froments he also spoke the words which came from every tongue: "What a frightful misfortune, an only son!"

Then he pressed their hands, and whispered and explained that Madame Beauchene, feeling quite exhausted, had withdrawn for a few moments, and that Beauchene and Blaise were making necessary arrangements downstairs. And then, resuming his maniacal

weary and limp, his strength undermined by his dissolute life, the slow disorganization of his faculties. He had sobbed like a child before his dead son, all his vanity crushed, all his calculations destroyed. The thunderbolt had sped by, and nothing remained. In a minute his life had been swept away; the world was now all black and void. And he remained livid, in consternation at it all, his bloated face swollen with grief, his heavy eyelids red with tears.

When he perceived the Froments, weakness again came upon him, and he staggered towards them with open arms, once more stifling with sobs.

"Ah! my dear friends, what a terrible blow! And I wasn't here! When I got here he had lost consciousness; he did not recognize me—. Is it possible? A lad who was in such good health! I cannot believe it. It seems to me that I must be dreaming, and that he will get up presently and come down with me into the workshops!"

They kissed him, they pitied him, struck down like this upon his return from some carouse or other, still intoxicated, perhaps, and tumbling into the midst of such an awful disaster, his prostration increased by the stupor following upon debauchery. His beard, moist with his tears, still stank of tobacco and musk.

Although he scarcely knew the Angelins, he pressed them also in his arms. "Ah! my poor friends, what a terrible blow! What a terrible blow!"

Then Blaise in his turn came to kiss his parents. In spite of his grief, and the horrible night he had spent, his face retained its youthful freshness. Yet tears coursed down his cheeks, for, working with Maurice day by day, he had conceived real friendship for him.

The silence fell again. Morange, as if unconscious of what went on around him, as if he were quite alone there, continued walking softly hither and thither like a somnambulist. Beauchene, with haggard mien, went off, and then came back carrying some little address-books. He turned about for another moment, and finally sat down at a writing-table which had been brought out of Maurice's room. Little accustomed as he was to grief, he instinctively sought to divert his mind, and began searching in the little address-books for the purpose of drawing up a list of the persons who must be invited to the funeral. But his eyes became blurred, and with a gesture he summoned Blaise, who, after going into the bedchamber to glance at his wife's sketch, was now returning to the drawing-room. Thereupon the young man, standing erect beside the writing-table, began to dictate the names in a low voice; and then, amid the deep silence sounded a low and monotonous murmur.

The minutes slowly went by. The visitors were still waiting for Constance. At last a little door of the death-chamber slowly opened, and she entered that chamber noiselessly, without anybody knowing that she was there. She looked like a spectre emerging out of the darkness into the pale light of the tapers. She had not yet wept; her face was livid, contracted, hardened by cold rage. Her little figure, instead of bending, seemed to have grown taller beneath the injustice of destiny, as if borne up by furious rebellion. Yet her loss did not surprise her. She had immediately felt that she had expected it, although but a minute before the death she had stubbornly refused to believe it possible. But the thought of it had remained latent within her for long months, and frightful evidence thereof now burst forth. She suddenly heard the whispers of the unknown once more, and understood them; she knew the meaning of those shivers which had chilled her, those vague, terror-fraught regrets at having no other child! And that which had been threatening her had come; irreparable destiny had willed it that her only son, the salvation of the imperilled home, the prince of to-morrow, who was to share his empire with her, should be swept away like a withered leaf. It was utter downfall; she sank into an abyss. And she remained tearless; fury dried her tears within her. Yet, good mother that she had always been, she suffered all the torment of motherliness exasperated, poisoned by the loss of her child.

She drew near to Charlotte and paused behind her, looking at the profile of her dead son resting among the flowers. And still she did not weep. She slowly gazed over the bed, filled her eyes with the dolorous scene, then carried them again to the paper, as if to see what would be left her of that adored son—those few pencil strokes—when the earth should have taken him forever. Charlotte, divining that somebody was behind her, started and raised her head. She did not speak; she had felt frightened. But both women exchanged a glance. And what a heart pang came to Constance, amid that display of death, in the presence of the void, the nothingness that was hers, as she gazed on the other's face, all love and health and beauty, suggesting some youthful star, whence promise of the future radiated through the fine gold of wavy hair.

But yet another pang came to Constance at that moment: words which were being whispered in the drawing-room, near the door of the bedchamber, reached her distinctly. She did not move, but remained erect behind Charlotte, who had resumed her work. And eagerly lending ear, she listened, not showing herself as yet, although she had already seen Marianne and Madame Angelin seated near the doorway, almost among the folds of the hangings.

"Ah!" Madame Angelin was saying, "the poor mother had a presentiment of it, as it were. I saw that she felt very anxious when I told her my own sad story. There is no hope for me; and now death has passed by, and no hope remains for her."

Silence ensued once more; then, prompted by some connecting train of thought, she went on: "And your next child will be your eleventh, will it not? Eleven is not a number; you will surely end by having twelve!"

As Constance heard those words she shuddered in another fit of that fury which dried up her tears. By glancing sideways she could see that mother of ten children, who was now expecting yet an eleventh child. She found her still young, still fresh, overflowing with joy and health and hope. And she was there, like the goddess of fruitfulness, nigh to the funeral bier at that hour of the supreme rending, when she, Constance, was bowed down by the irretrievable loss of her only child.

But Marianne was answering Madame Angelin: "Oh I don't think that at all likely. Why, I'm becoming an old woman. You forget that I am already a grandmother. Here, look at that!"

So saying, she waved her hand towards the servant of her daughter-in-law, Charlotte, who, in accordance with the instructions she had received, was now bringing the little Berthe in order that her mother might give her the breast. The servant had remained at the drawing-room door, hesitating, disliking to intrude on all that mourning; but the child good-humoredly waved her fat little fists, and laughed lightly. And Charlotte, hearing her, immediately rose and tripped across the salon to take the little one into a neighboring room.

"What a pretty child!" murmured Madame Angelin. "Those little ones are like nosegays; they bring brightness and freshness wherever they come."

Constance for her part had been dazzled. All at once, amid the semi-obscurity, starred by the flames of the tapers, amid the deathly atmosphere, which the odor of the roses rendered the more oppressive, that laughing child had set a semblance of budding springtime, the fresh, bright atmosphere of a long promise of life. And it typified the victory of fruitfulness; it was the child's child, it was Marianne reviving in her son's daughter. A grandmother already, and she was only forty-one years old! Marianne had smiled at that thought. But the hatchet-stroke rang out yet more frightfully in Constance's heart. In her case the tree was cut down to its very root, the sole scion had been lopped off, and none would ever sprout again.

For yet another moment she remained alone amid that nothingness, in that room where lay her son's remains. Then she made up her mind and passed into the drawing-room, with the air of a frozen spectre. They all rose, kissed her, and shivered as their lips touched her cold cheeks, which her blood was unable to warm. Profound compassion wrung them, so frightful was her calmness. And they sought kind words to say to her, but she curtly stopped them.

"It is all over," said she; "there is nothing to be said. Everything is ended, quite ended."

Madame Angelin sobbed, Angelin himself wiped his poor fixed, blurred eyes. Marianne and Mathieu shed tears while retaining Constance's hands in theirs. And she, rigid and still unable to weep, refused consolation, repeating in monotonous accents: "It is finished; nothing can give him back to me. Is it not so? And thus there remains nothing; all is ended, quite ended."

She needed to be brave, for visitors would soon be arriving in a stream. But a last stab in the heart was reserved for her. Beauchene, who since her arrival had begun to cry again, could no longer see to write. Moreover, his hand trembled, and he had to leave the writing-table and fling himself into an armchair, saying to Blaise: "There sit down there, and continue to write for me."

Then Constance saw Blaise seat himself at her son's writing-table, in his place, dip his pen in the inkstand and begin to write with the very same gesture that she had so often seen Maurice make. That Blaise, that son of the Froments! What! her dear boy was not yet buried, and a Froment already replaced him, even as vivacious, fast-growing plants overrun neighboring barren fields. That stream of life flowing around her, intent on universal conquest, seemed yet more threatening; grandmothers still bore children, daughters suckled already, sons laid hands upon vacant kingdoms. And she remained alone; she had but her unworthy, broken-down, worn-out husband beside her; while Morange, the maniac, incessantly walking to and fro, was like the symbolical spectre of human distress, one whose heart and strength and reason had been carried away in the frightful death of his only daughter. And not a sound came from the cold and empty works; the works themselves were dead.

The funeral ceremony two days later was an imposing one. The five hundred workmen of the establishment followed the hearse, notabilities of all sorts made up an immense cortege. It was much noticed that an old workman, father Moineaud, the oldest hand of the works, was one of the pall-bearers. Indeed, people thought it touching, although the worthy old man dragged his legs somewhat, and looked quite out of his element in a frock coat, stiffened as he was by thirty years' hard toil. In the cemetery, near the grave, Mathieu felt surprised on being approached by an old lady who alighted from one of the mourning-coaches.

"I see, my friend," said she, "that you do not recognize me."

He made a gesture of apology. It was Seraphine, still tall and slim, but so fleshless, so withered that one might have thought she was a hundred years old. Cecile had warned Mathieu of it, yet if he had not seen her himself he would never have believed that her proud insolent beauty, which had seemed to defy time and excesses, could have faded so swiftly. What frightful, withering blast could have swept over her?

"Ah! my friend," she continued, "I am more dead than the poor fellow whom they are about to lower into that grave. Come and have a chat with me some day. You are the only person to whom I can tell everything."

The coffin was lowered, the ropes gave out a creaking sound, and there came a little thud—the last. Beauchene, supported by a relative, looked on with dim, vacant eyes. Constance, who had had the bitter courage to come, and had now wept all the tears in her body, almost fainted. She was carried away, driven back to her home, which would now forever be empty, like one of those stricken fields that remain barren, fated to perpetual sterility. Mother earth had taken back her all.

And at Chantebled Mathieu and Marianne founded, created, increased, and multiplied, again proving victorious in the eternal battle which life wages against death, thanks to that continual increase, both of offspring and of fertile land, which was like their very existence, their joy and their strength. Desire passed like a gust of flame, desire divine and fruitful, since they possessed the power of love, kindliness, and health. And their energy did the rest—that will of action, that quiet bravery in the presence of the labor that is requisite, the labor that has made and that regulates the world.

Still, during those two years it was not without constant battling that victory remained to them. At last it was complete. Piece by piece

Seguin had sold the entire estate, of which Mathieu was now king, thanks to his prudent system of conquest, that of increasing his empire by degrees as he gradually felt himself stronger. The fortune which the idler had disdained and dissipated had passed into the hands of the toiler, the creator. There were 1250 acres, spreading from horizon to horizon; there were woods intersected by broad meadows, where flocks and herds pastured; there was fat land overflowing with harvests, in the place of marshes that had been drained; there was other land, each year of increasing fertility, in the place of the moors which the captured springs now irrigated. The Lepailleurs' uncultivated enclosure alone remained, as if to bear witness to the prodigy, the great human effort which had quickened that desert of sand and mud, whose crops would henceforth nourish so many happy people. Mathieu devoured no other man's share; he had brought his share into being, increasing the common wealth, subjugating yet another small portion of this vast world, which is still so scantily peopled and so badly utilized for human happiness. The farm, the homestead, had sprung up and grown in the centre of the estate like a prosperous township, with inhabitants, servants, and live stock, a perfect focus of ardent triumphal life. And what sovereign power was that of the happy fruitfulness which had never wearied of creating, which had yielded all these beings and things that had been increasing and multiplying for twelve years past, that invading town which was but a family's expansion, those trees, those plants, those grain crops, those fruits whose nourishing stream ever rose under the dazzling sun! All pain and all tears were forgotten in that joy of creation, the accomplishment of due labor, the conquest of the future conducting to the infinite of Action.

Then, while Mathieu completed his work of conquest, Marianne during those two years had the happiness of seeing a daughter born to her son Blaise, even while she herself was expecting another child. The branches of the huge tree had begun to fork, pending the time when they would ramify endlessly, like the branches of some great royal oak spreading afar over the soil. There would be her children's children, her grandchildren's children, the whole posterity increasing from generation to generation. And yet how carefully and lovingly she still assembled around her her own first brood, from Blaise and Denis the twins, now one-and-twenty, to the last born, the wee creature who sucked in life from her bosom with greedy lips. There were some of all ages in the brood—a big fellow, who was already a father; others who went to school; others who still had to be dressed in the morning; there were boys, Ambroise, Gervais, Gregoire, and another; there were girls, Rose, nearly old enough to marry; Claire, Louise, Madeleine, and Marguerite, the last of whom could scarcely toddle. And it was a sight to see them roam over the estate like a troop of colts, following one another at varied pace, according to their growth. She knew that she could not keep them all tied to her apron-strings; it would be sufficient happiness if the farm kept two or three beside her; she resigned herself to seeing the younger ones go off some day to conquer other lands. Such was the law of expansion; the earth was the heritage of the most numerous race. Since they had number on their side, they would have strength also; the world would belong to them. The parents themselves had felt stronger, more united at the advent of each fresh child. If in spite of terrible cares they had always conquered, it was because their love, their toil, the ceaseless travail of their heart and will, gave them the victory. Fruitfulness is the great conqueress; from her come the pacific heroes who subjugate the world by peopling it. And this time especially, when at the lapse of those two years Marianne gave birth to a boy, Nicolas, her eleventh child, Mathieu embraced her passionately, triumphing over every sorrow and every pang. Yet another child; yet more wealth and power; yet an additional force born into the world; another field ready for to-morrow's harvest.

And 'twas ever the great work, the good work, the work of fruitfulness spreading, thanks to the earth and thanks to woman, both victorious over destruction, offering fresh means of subsistence each time a fresh child was born, and loving, willing, battling, toiling even amid suffering, and ever tending to increase of life and increase of hope.

XV

A mid the deep mourning life slowly resumed its course at the Beauchene works. One effect of the terrible blow which had fallen on Beauchene was that for some weeks he remained quietly at home. Indeed, he seemed to have profited by the terrible lesson, for he no longer coined lies, no longer invented pressing business journeys as a pretext for dissipation. He even set to work once more, and busied himself about the factory, coming down every morning as in his younger days. And in Blaise he found an active and devoted lieutenant, on whom he each day cast more and more of the heavier work. Intimates were most struck, however, by the manner in which Beauchene and his wife drew together again. Constance was most attentive to her husband; Beauchene no longer left her, and they seemed to agree well together, leading a very retired life in their quiet house, where only relatives were now received.

Constance, on the morrow of Maurice's sudden death, was like one who has just lost a limb. It seemed to her that she was no longer whole; she felt ashamed of being, as it were, disfigured. Mingled, too, with her loving sorrow for Maurice there was humiliation at the thought that she was no longer a mother, that she no longer had any heir-apparent to her kingdom beside her. To think that she had been so stubbornly determined to have but one son, one child, in order that he might become the sole master of the family fortune, the all-powerful monarch of the future. Death had stolen him from her, and the establishment now seemed to be less her own, particularly since that fellow Blaise and his wife and his child, representing those fruitful and all-invading Froments, were installed there. She could no longer console herself for having welcomed and lodged them, and her one passionate, all-absorbing desire was to have another son, and thereby reconquer her empire.

This it was which led to her reconciliation with her husband, and for six months they lived together on the best of terms. Then, however, came another six months, and it was evident that they no longer agreed so well together, for Beauchene took himself off at times under the pretext of seeking fresh air, and Constance remained at home, feverish, her eyes red with weeping.

One day Mathieu, who had come to Grenelle to see his daughter-in-law, Charlotte, was lingering in the garden playing with little Berthe, who had climbed upon his knees, when he was surprised by the sudden approach of Constance, who must have seen him from her windows. She invented a pretext to draw him into the house, and kept him there nearly a quarter of an hour before she could make up her mind to speak her thoughts. Then, all at once, she began: "My dear Mathieu, you must forgive me for mentioning a painful matter, but there are reasons why I should do so. Nearly fifteen years ago, I know it for a fact, my husband had a child by a girl who was employed at the works. And I also know that you acted as his intermediary on that occasion, and made certain arrangements with respect to that girl and her child—a boy, was it not?"

She paused for a reply. But Mathieu, stupefied at finding her so well informed, and at a loss to understand why she spoke to him of that sorry affair after the lapse of so many years, could only make a gesture by which he betrayed both his surprise and his anxiety.

"Oh!" said she, "I do not address any reproach to you; I am convinced that your motives were quite friendly, even affectionate, and that you wished to hush up a scandal which might have been very unpleasant for me. Moreover, I do not desire to indulge in recriminations after so long a time. My desire is simply for information. For a long time I did not care to investigate the statements whereby I was informed of the affair. But the recollection of it comes back to me and haunts me persistently, and it is natural that I should apply to you. I have never spoken a word on the subject to my husband, and indeed it is best for our tranquillity that I should not attempt to extort a detailed confession from him. One circumstance which has induced me to speak to you is that on an occasion when I accompanied Madame Angelin to a house in the Rue de Miromesnil, I perceived you there with that girl, who had another child in her arms. So you have not lost sight of her, and you must know what she is doing, and whether her first child is alive, and in that case where he is, and how he is situated."

Mathieu still refrained from replying, for Constance's increasing feverishness put him on his guard, and impelled him to seek the motive of such a strange application on the part of one who was as a rule so proud and so discreet. What could be happening? Why did she strive to provoke confidential revelations which might have far-reaching effects? Then, as she closely scanned him with her keen eyes, he sought to answer her with kind, evasive words.

"You greatly embarrass me. And, besides, I know nothing likely to interest you. What good would it do yourself or your husband to stir up all the dead past? Take my advice, forget what people may have told you—you are so sensible and prudent—"

But she interrupted him, caught hold of his hands, and held them in her warm, quivering grasp. Never before had she so behaved, forgetting and surrendering herself so passionately. "I repeat," said she, "that nobody has anything to fear from me—neither my husband, nor that girl, nor the child. Cannot you understand me? I am simply tormented; I suffer at knowing nothing. Yes, it seems to me that I shall feel more at ease when I know the truth. It is for myself that I question you, for my own peace of mind. . . Ah! if I could only tell you, if I could tell you!"

He began to divine many things; it was unnecessary for her to be more explicit. He knew that during the past year she and her husband had been hoping for the advent of a second child, and that none had come. As a woman, Constance felt no jealousy of Norine, but as a mother she was jealous of her son. She could not drive the thought of that child from her mind; it ever and ever returned thither like a mocking insult now that her hopes of replacing Maurice were fading fast. Day by day did she dream more and more passionately of the other woman's son, wondering where he was, what had become of him, whether he were healthy, and whether he resembled his father.

"I assure you, my dear Mathieu," she resumed, "that you will really bring me relief by answering me. Is he alive? Tell me simply whether he is alive. But do not tell me a lie. If he is dead I think that I shall feel calmer. And yet, good heavens! I certainly wish him no evil."

Then Mathieu, who felt deeply touched, told her the simple truth.

"Since you insist on it, for the benefit of your peace of mind, and since it is to remain entirely between us and to have no effect on your home, I see no reason why I should not confide to you what I know. But that is very little. The child was left at the Foundling Hospital in my presence. Since then the mother, having never asked for news, has received none. I need not add that your husband is equally ignorant, for he always refused to have anything to do with the child. Is the lad still alive? Where is he? Those are things which I cannot tell you. A long inquiry would be necessary. If, however, you wish for my opinion, I think it probable that he is dead, for the mortality among these poor cast-off children is very great."

Constance looked at him fixedly. "You are telling me the real truth? You are hiding nothing?" she asked. And as he began to protest, she went on: "Yes, yes, I have confidence in you. And so you believe that he is dead! Ah! to think of all those children who die, when so many women would be happy to save one, to have one for themselves. Well, if you haven't been able to tell me anything positive, you have at least done your best. Thank you."

During the ensuing months Mathieu often found himself alone with Constance, but she never reverted to the subject. She seemed to set her energy on forgetting all about it, though he divined that it still haunted her. Meantime things went from bad to worse in the Beauchene household. The husband gradually went back to his former life of debauchery, in spite of all the efforts of Constance to keep him near her. She, for her part, clung to her fixed idea, and before long she consulted Boutan. There was a terrible scene that day between husband and wife in the doctor's presence. Constance raked up the story of Norine and cast it in Beauchene's teeth, while he upbraided her in a variety of ways. However, Boutan's advice, though followed for a time, proved unavailing, and she at last lost confidence in him. Then she spent months and months in consulting one and another. She placed herself in the hands of Madame Bourdieu, she even went to see La Rouche, she applied to all sorts of charlatans, exasperated to fury at finding that there was no real succor for her. She might long ago have had a family had she so chosen. But she had elected otherwise, setting all her egotism and pride on that only son whom death had snatched away; and now the motherhood she longed for was denied her.

For nearly two years did Constance battle, and at last in despair she was seized with the idea of consulting Dr. Gaude. He told her the brutal truth; it was useless for her to address herself to charlatans; she would simply be robbed by them; there was absolutely no hope for her. And Gaude uttered those decisive words in a light, jesting way, as though surprised and amused by her profound grief. She almost fainted on the stairs as she left his flat, and for a moment indeed death seemed welcome. But by a great effort of will she recovered self-possession, the courage to face the life of loneliness that now lay before her. Moreover, another idea vaguely dawned upon her, and the first time she found herself alone with Mathieu she again spoke to him of Norine's boy.

"Forgive me," said she, "for reverting to a painful subject, but I am suffering too much now that I know there is no hope for me. I am haunted by the thought of that illegitimate child of my husband's. Will you do me a great service? Make the inquiry you once spoke to me about, try to find out if he is alive or dead. I feel that when I know the facts peace may perhaps return to me."

Mathieu was almost on the point of answering her that, even if this child were found again, it could hardly cure her of her grief at having no child of her own. He had divined her agony at seeing Blaise take Maurice's place at the works now that Beauchene had resumed his dissolute life, and daily intrusted the young man with more and more authority. Blaise's home was prospering too; Charlotte had now given birth to a second child, a boy, and thus fruitfulness was invading the place and usurpation becoming more and more likely, since Constance could never more have an heir to bar the road of conquest. Without penetrating her singular feelings, Mathieu fancied that she perhaps wished to sound him to ascertain if he were not behind Blaise, urging on the work of spoliation. She possibly imagined that her request would make him anxious, and that he would refuse to make the necessary researches. At this idea he decided to do as she desired, if only to show her that he was above all the base calculations of ambition.

"I am at your disposal, cousin," said he. "It is enough for me that this inquiry may give you a little relief. But if the lad is alive, am I to bring him to you?"

"Oh! no, no, I do not ask that!" And then, gesticulating almost wildly, she stammered: "I don't know what I want, but I suffer so dreadfully that I am scarce able to live!"

In point of fact a tempest raged within her, but she really had no settled plan. One could hardly say that she really thought of that boy as a possible heir. In spite of her hatred of all conquerors from without, was it likely that she would accept him as a conqueror, in the face of her outraged womanly feelings and her bourgeois horror of illegitimacy? And yet if he were not her son, he was at least her husband's. And perhaps an idea of saving her empire by placing the works in the hands of that heir was dimly rising within her, above all her prejudices and her rancor. But however that might be, her feelings for the time remained confused, and the only clear thing was her desperate torment at being now and forever childless, a torment which goaded her on to seek another's child with the wild idea of making that child in some slight degree her own.

Mathieu, however, asked her, "Am I to inform Beauchene of the steps I take?"

"Do you as you please," she answered. "Still, that would be the best."

That same evening there came a complete rupture between herself and her husband. She threw in Beauchene's face all the contempt and loathing that she had felt for him for years. Hopeless as she was, she revenged herself by telling him everything that she had on her heart and mind. And her slim dark figure, upborne by bitter rage, assumed such redoubtable proportions in his eyes that he felt frightened by her and fled. Henceforth they were husband and wife in name only. It was logic on the march, it was the inevitable disorganization of a household reaching its climax, it was rebellion against nature's law and indulgence in vice leading to the gradual decline of a man of intelligence, it was a hard worker sinking into the sloth of so-called pleasure; and then, death having snatched away the only son, the home broke to pieces— the wife—fated to childlessness, and the husband driven away by her, rolling through debauchery towards final ruin.

But Mathieu, keeping his promise to Constance, discreetly began his researches. And before he even consulted Beauchene it occurred to him to apply at the Foundling Hospital. If, as he anticipated, the child were dead, the affair would go no further. Fortunately enough he remembered all the particulars: the two names, Alexandre-Honore, given to the child, the exact date of the deposit at the hospital, indeed all the little incidents of the day when he had driven thither with La Couteau. And when he was received by the director of the establishment, and had explained to him the real motives of his inquiries, at the same time giving his name, he was surprised by the promptness and precision of the answer: Alexandre-Honore, put out to nurse with the woman Loiseau at Rougemont, had first kept cows, and had then tried the calling of a locksmith; but for three months past he had been in apprenticeship with a wheelwright, a certain Montoir, residing at Saint-Pierre, a hamlet in the vicinity of Rougemont. Thus the lad lived; he was fifteen years old, and that was all. Mathieu could obtain no further information respecting either his physical health or his morality.

When Mathieu found himself in the street again, slightly dazed, he remembered that La Couteau had told him that the child would be sent to Rougemont. He had always pictured it dying there, carried off by the hurricane which killed so many babes, and lying in the silent village cemetery paved with little Parisians. To find the boy alive, saved from the massacre, came like a surprise of destiny, and brought vague anguish, a fear of some terrible catastrophe to Mathieu's heart. At the same time, since the boy was living, and he now knew where to seek him, he felt that he must warn Beauchene. The matter was becoming serious, and it seemed to him that he ought not to carry the inquiry any further without the father's authorization.

That same day, then, before returning to Chantebled, he repaired to the factory, where he was lucky enough to find Beauchene, whom Blaise's absence on business had detained there by force. Thus he was in a very bad humor, puffing and yawning and half asleep. It was nearly three o'clock, and he declared that he could never digest his lunch properly unless he went out afterwards. The truth was that since his rupture with his wife he had been devoting his afternoons to paying attentions to a girl serving at a beer-house.

"Ah! my good fellow," he muttered as he stretched himself. "My blood is evidently thickening. I must bestir myself, or else I shall be in a bad way."

However, he woke up when Mathieu had explained the motive of his visit. At first he could scarcely understand it, for the affair seemed to him so extraordinary, so idiotic.

"Eh? What do you say? It was my wife who spoke to you about that child? It is she who has taken it into her head to collect information and start a search?"

His fat apoplectical face became distorted, his anger was so violent that he could scarcely stutter. When he heard, however, of the mission with which his wife had intrusted Mathieu, he at last exploded: "She is mad! I tell you that she is raving mad! Were such fancies ever seen? Every morning she invents something fresh to distract me!"

Without heeding this interruption, Mathieu quietly finished his narrative: "And so I have just come back from the Foundling Hospital, where I learnt that the boy is alive. I have his address—and now what am I to do?"

This was the final blow. Beauchene clenched his fists and raised his arms in exasperation. "Ah! well, here's a nice state of things! But why on earth does she want to trouble me about that boy? He isn't hers! Why can't she leave us alone, the boy and me? It's my affair. And I ask you if it is at all proper for my wife to send you running about after him? Besides, I hope that you are not going to bring him to her. What on earth could we do with that little peasant, who may have every vice? Just picture him coming between us. I tell you that she is mad, mad, mad!"

He had begun to walk angrily to and fro. All at once he stopped: "My dear fellow, you will just oblige me by telling her that he is dead."

But he turned pale and recoiled. Constance stood on the threshold and had heard him. For some time past she had been in the habit of stealthily prowling around the offices, like one on the watch for something. For a moment, at the sight of the embarrassment which both men displayed, she remained silent. Then, without even addressing her husband, she asked: "He is alive, is he not?"

Mathieu could but tell her the truth. He answered with a nod. Then Beauchene, in despair, made a final effort: "Come, be reasonable, my dear. As I was saying only just now, we don't even know what this youngster's character is. You surely don't want to upset our life for the mere pleasure of doing so?"

Standing there, lean and frigid, she gave him a harsh glance; then, turning her back on him, she demanded the child's name, and the names of the wheelwright and the locality. "Good, you say Alexandre-Honore, with Montoir the wheelwright, at Saint-Pierre, near Rougemont, in Calvados. Well, my friend, oblige me by continuing your researches; endeavor to procure me some precise information about this boy's habits and disposition. Be prudent, too; don't give anybody's name. And thanks for what you have done already; thanks for all you are doing for me."

Thereupon she took herself off without giving any further explanation, without even telling her husband of the vague plans she was forming. Beneath her crushing contempt he had grown calm again. Why should he spoil his life of egotistical pleasure by resisting that mad creature? All that he need do was to put on his hat and betake himself to his usual diversions. And so he ended by shrugging his shoulders.

"After all, let her pick him up if she chooses, it won't be my doing. Act as she asks you, my dear fellow; continue your researches and try to content her. Perhaps she will then leave me in peace. But I've had quite enough of it for to-day; good-by, I'm going out."

With the view of obtaining some information of Rougemont, Mathieu at first thought of applying to La Couteau, if he could find her again; for which purpose it occurred to him that he might call on Madame Bourdieu in the Rue de Miromesnil. But another and more certain means suggested itself. He had been led to renew his intercourse with the Seguins, of whom he had for a time lost sight; and, much to his surprise, he had found Valentine's former maid, Celeste, in the Avenue d'Antin once more. Through this woman, he thought, he might reach La Couteau direct.

The renewal of the intercourse between the Froments and the Seguins was due to a very happy chance. Mathieu's son Ambroise, on leaving college, had entered the employment of an uncle of Seguin's, Thomas du Hordel, one of the wealthiest commission merchants in Paris; and this old man, who, despite his years, remained very sturdy, and still directed his business with all the fire of youth, had conceived a growing fondness for Ambroise, who had great mental endowments and a real genius for commerce. Du Hordel's own children had consisted of two daughters, one of whom had died young, while the other had married a madman, who had lodged a bullet in his head and had left her childless and crazy like himself. This partially explained the deep grandfatherly interest which Du Hordel took in young Ambroise, who was the handsomest of all the Froments, with a clear complexion, large black eyes, brown hair that curled naturally, and manners of much refinement and elegance. But the old man was further captivated by the young fellow's spirit of enterprise, the four modern languages which he spoke so readily, and the evident mastery which he would some day show in the management of a business which extended over the five parts of the world. In his childhood, among his brothers and sisters, Ambroise had always been the boldest, most captivating and self-assertive. The others might be better than he, but he reigned over them like a handsome, ambitious, greedy boy, a future man of gayety and conquest. And this indeed he proved to be; by the charm of his victorious intellect he conquered old Du Hordel in a few months, even as later on he was destined to vanquish everybody and everything much as he pleased. His strength lay in his power of pleasing and his power of action, a blending of grace with the most assiduous industry.

About this time Seguin and his uncle, who had never set foot in the house of the Avenue d'Antin since insanity had reigned there, drew together again. Their apparent reconciliation was the outcome of a drama shrouded in secrecy. Seguin, hard up and in debt, cast off by Nora, who divined his approaching ruin, and preyed upon by other voracious creatures, had ended by committing, on the turf, one of those indelicate actions which honest people call thefts. Du Hordel, on being apprised of the matter, had hastened forward and had paid what was due in order to avoid a frightful scandal. And he was so upset by the extraordinary muddle in which he found his nephew's home, once all prosperity, that remorse came upon him as if he were in some degree responsible for what had happened, since he had egotistically kept away from his relatives for his own peace's sake. But he was more particularly won over by his grandniece Andree, now a delicious young girl well-nigh eighteen years of age, and therefore marriageable. She alone sufficed to attract him to the house, and he was greatly distressed by the dangerous state of abandonment in which he found her.

Her father continued dragging out his worthless life away from home. Her mother, Valentine, had just emerged from a frightful crisis, her final rupture with Santerre, who had made up his mind to marry a very wealthy old lady, which, after all, was the logical destiny of such a crafty exploiter of women, one who behind his affectation of cultured pessimism had the vilest and greediest of natures. Valentine, distracted by this rupture, had now thrown herself into religion, and, like her husband, disappeared from the house for whole days. She was said to be an active helpmate of old Count de Navarede, the president of a society of Catholic propaganda. Gaston, her son, having left Saint-Cyr three months previously, was now at the Cavalry School of Saumur, so fired with passion for a military career that he already spoke of remaining a bachelor, since a soldier's sword should be his only love, his only spouse. Then Lucie, now nineteen years old, and full of mystical exaltation, had already entered an Ursuline convent for her novitiate. And in the big empty home, whence father, mother, brother and sister fled, there remained but the gentle and adorable Andree, exposed to all the blasts of insanity which even now swept through the household, and so distressed by loneliness, that her uncle, Du Hordel, full of compassionate affection, conceived the idea of giving her a husband in the person of young Ambroise, the future conqueror.

This plan was helped on by the renewed presence of Celeste the maid. Eight years had elapsed since Valentine had been obliged to dismiss this woman for immorality; and during those eight years Celeste, weary of service, had tried a number of equivocal callings of which she did not speak. She had ended by turning up at Rougemont, her native place, in bad health and such a state of wretchedness, that for the sake of a living she went out as a charwoman there. Then she gradually recovered her health, and accumulated a little stock of clothes, thanks to the protection of the village priest, whom she won over by an affectation of extreme piety. It was at Rougemont, no doubt, that she planned her return to the Seguins, of whose vicissitudes she was informed by La Couteau, the latter having kept up her intercourse with Madame Menoux, the little haberdasher of the neighborhood.

Valentine, shortly after her rupture with Santerre, one day of furious despair, when she had again dismissed all her servants, was surprised by the arrival of Celeste, who showed herself so repentant, so devoted, and so serious-minded, that her former mistress felt touched. She made her weep on reminding her of her faults, and asking her to swear before God that she would never repeat them; for Celeste now went to confession and partook of the holy communion, and carried with her a certificate from the Cure of Rougemont vouching for her deep piety and high morality. This certificate acted decisively on Valentine, who, unwilling to remain at home, and weary of the troubles of housekeeping, understood what precious help she might derive from this woman. On her side Celeste certainly relied upon power being surrendered to her. Two months later, by favoring Lucie's excessive partiality to religious practices, she had helped her into a convent. Gaston showed himself only when he secured a few days' leave. And so Andree alone remained at home, impeding by her presence the great general pillage that Celeste dreamt of. The maid therefore became a most active worker on behalf of her young mistress's marriage.

Andree, it should be said, was comprised in Ambroise's universal conquest. She had met him at her uncle Du Hordel's house for a year before it occurred to the latter to marry them. She was a very gentle girl, a little golden-haired sheep, as her mother sometimes said. And that handsome, smiling young man, who evinced so much kindness towards her, became the subject of her thoughts and hopes whenever she suffered from loneliness and abandonment. Thus, when her uncle prudently questioned her, she flung herself into his arms, weeping big tears of gratitude and confession. Valentine, on being approached, at first manifested some surprise. What, a son of the Froments! Those Froments had already taken Chantebled from them, and did they now want to take one of their daughters? Then, amid the collapse of fortune and household, she could find no reasonable objection to urge. She had never been attached to Andree. She accused La Catiche, the nurse, of having made the child her own. That gentle, docile, emotional little sheep was not a Seguin, she often remarked. Then, while feigning to defend the girl, Celeste embittered her mother against her, and inspired her with a desire to see the marriage promptly concluded, in order that she might free herself from her last cares and live as she wished. Thus, after a long chat with Mathieu, who promised his consent, it remained only for Du Hordel to assure himself of Seguin's approval before an application in due form was made. It was difficult, however, to find Seguin in a suitable frame of mind. So weeks were lost, and it became necessary to pacify Ambroise, who was very much in love, and was doubtless warned by his all-invading genius that this loving and simple girl would bring him a kingdom in her apron.

One day when Mathieu was passing along the Avenue d'Antin, it occurred to him to call at the house to ascertain if Seguin had re-appeared there, for he had suddenly taken himself off without warning, and had gone, so it was believed, to Italy. Then, as Mathieu found himself alone with Celeste, the opportunity seemed to him an excellent one to discover La Couteau's whereabouts. He asked for news of her, saying that a friend of his was in need of a good nurse.

"Well, monsieur, you are in luck's way," the maid replied; "La Couteau is to bring a child home to our neighbor, Madame Menoux, this very day. It is nearly four o'clock now, and that is the time when she promised to come. You know Madame Menoux's place, do you not? It is the third shop in the first street on the left." Then she apologized for being unable to conduct him thither: "I am alone," she said; "we still have no news of the master. On Wednesdays Madame presides at the meeting of her society, and Mademoiselle Andree has just gone out walking with her uncle."

Mathieu hastily repaired to Madame Menoux's shop. From a distance he saw her standing on the threshold; age had made her thinner than ever; at forty she was as slim as a young girl, with a long and pointed face. Silent labor consumed her; for twenty years she had been desperately selling bits of cotton and packages of needles without ever making a fortune, but pleased, nevertheless, at being able to add her modest gains to her husband's monthly salary in order to provide him with sundry little comforts. His rheumatism would no doubt soon compel him to relinquish his post as a museum attendant, and how would they be able to manage with his pension of a few hundred francs per annum if she did not keep up her business? Moreover, they had met with no luck. Their first child had died, and some years had elapsed before the birth of a second boy, whom they had greeted with delight, no doubt, though he would prove a heavy burden to them, especially as they had now decided to take him back from the country. Thus Mathieu found the worthy woman in a state of great emotion, waiting for the child on the threshold of her shop, and watching the corner of the avenue.

"Oh! it was Celeste who sent you, monsieur! No, La Couteau hasn't come yet. I'm quite astonished at it; I expect her every moment. Will you kindly step inside, monsieur, and sit down?"

He refused the only chair which blocked up the narrow passage where scarcely three customers could have stood in a row. Behind a glass partition one perceived the dim back shop, which served as kitchen and dining-room and bedchamber, and which received only a little air from a damp inner yard which suggested a sewer shaft.

"As you see, monsieur, we have scarcely any room," continued Madame Menoux; "but then we pay only eight hundred francs rent, and where else could we find a shop at that price? And besides, I have been here for nearly twenty years, and have worked up a little regular custom in the neighborhood. Oh! I don't complain of the place myself, I'm not big, there is always sufficient room for me. And as my husband comes home only in the evening, and then sits down in his armchair to smoke his pipe, he isn't so much inconvenienced. I do all I can for him, and he is reasonable enough not to ask me to do more. But with a child I fear that it will be impossible to get on here."

The recollection of her first boy, her little Pierre, returned to her, and her eyes filled with tears. "Ah! monsieur, that was ten years ago, and I can still see La Couteau bringing him back to me, just as she'll be bringing the other by and by. I was told so many tales; there was such good air at Rougemont, and the children led such healthy lives, and my boy had such rosy cheeks, that I ended by leaving him there till he was five years old, regretting that I had no room for him here. And no, you can't have an idea of all the presents that the nurse wheedled out of me, of all the money that I paid! It was ruination! And then, all at once, I had just time to send for the boy, and he was brought back to me as thin and pale and weak, as if he had never tasted good bread in his life. Two months later he died in my arms. His father fell ill over it, and if we hadn't been attached to one another, I think we should both have gone and drowned ourselves."

Scarce wiping her eyes she feverishly returned to the threshold, and again cast a passionate expectant glance towards the avenue. And when she came back, having seen nothing, she resumed: "So you will understand our emotion when, two years ago, though I was thirty-seven, I again had a little boy. We were wild with delight, like a young married couple. But what a lot of trouble and worry! We had to put the little fellow out to nurse as we let the other one, since we could not possibly keep him here. And even after swearing that he should not go to Rougemont we ended by saying that we at least knew the place, and that he would not be worse off there than elsewhere. Only we sent him to La Vimeux, for we wouldn't hear any more of La Loiseau since she sent Pierre back in such a fearful state. And this time, as the little fellow is now two years old, I was determined to have him home again, though I don't even know where I shall put him. I've been waiting for an hour now, and I can't help trembling, for I always fear some catastrophe."

She could not remain in the shop, but remained standing by the doorway, with her neck outstretched and her eyes fixed on the street corner. All at once a deep cry came from her: "Ah! here they are!"

Leisurely, and with a sour, harassed air, La Couteau came in and placed the sleeping child in Madame Menoux's arms, saying as she did so: "Well, your George is a tidy weight, I can tell you. You won't say that I've brought you this one back like a skeleton."

Quivering, her legs sinking beneath her for very joy, the mother had been obliged to sit down, keeping her child on her knees, kissing him, examining him, all haste to see if he were in good health and likely to live. He had a fat and rather pale face, and seemed big, though puffy. When she had unfastened his wraps, her hands trembling the while with nervousness, she found that he was pot-bellied, with small legs and arms.

"He is very big about the body," she murmured, ceasing to smile, and turning gloomy with renewed fears.

"Ah, yes! complain away!" said La Couteau. "The other was too thin; this one will be too fat. Mothers are never satisfied!"

At the first glance Mathieu had detected that the child was one of those who are fed on pap, stuffed for economy's sake with bread and water, and fated to all the stomachic complaints of early childhood. And at the sight of the poor little fellow, Rougemont, the frightful slaughter-place, with its daily massacre of the innocents, arose in his memory, such as it had been described to him in years long past. There was La Loiseau, whose habits were so abominably filthy that her nurslings rotted as on a manure heap; there was La Vimeux, who never purchased a drop of milk, but picked up all the village crusts and made bran porridge for her charges as if they had been pigs; there was La Gavette too, who, being always in the fields, left her nurslings in the charge of a paralytic old man, who sometimes let them fall into the fire; and there was La Cauchois, who, having nobody to watch the babes, contented herself with tying them in their cradles, leaving them in the company of fowls which came in bands to peck at their eyes. And the scythe of death swept by; there was wholesale assassination; doors were left wide open before rows of cradles, in order to make room for fresh bundles despatched from Paris. Yet all did not die; here, for instance, was one brought home again. But even when they came back alive they carried with them the germs of death, and another hecatomb ensued, another sacrifice to the monstrous god of social egotism.

"I'm tired out; I must sit down," resumed La Couteau, seating herself on the narrow bench behind the counter. "Ah! what a trade! And to think that we are always received as if we were heartless criminals and thieves!"

She also had become withered, her sunburnt, tanned face suggesting more than ever the beak of a bird of prey. But her eyes remained very keen, sharpened as it were by ferocity. She no doubt failed to get rich fast enough, for she continued wailing, complaining of her calling, of the increasing avarice of parents, of the demands of the authorities, of the warfare which was being declared against nurse-agents on all sides. Yes, it was a lost calling, said she, and really God must have abandoned her that she should still be compelled to carry it on at forty-five years of age. "It will end by killing me," she added; "I shall always get more kicks than money at it. How unjust it is! Here have I brought you back a superb child, and yet you look anything but pleased—it's enough to disgust one of doing one's best!"

In thus complaining her object perhaps was to extract from the haberdasher as large a present as possible. Madame Menoux was certainly disturbed by it all. Her boy woke up and began to wail loudly, and it became necessary to give him a little lukewarm milk. At last, when the accounts were settled, the nurse-agent, seeing that she would have ten francs for herself, grew calmer. She was about to take her leave when Madame Menoux, pointing to Mathieu, exclaimed: "This gentleman wished to speak to you on business."

Although La Couteau had not seen the gentleman for several years past, she had recognized him perfectly well. Still she had not even turned towards him, for she knew him to be mixed up in so many matters that his discretion was a certainty. And so she contented herself with saying: "If monsieur will kindly explain to me what it is I shall be quite at his service."

"I will accompany you," replied Mathieu; "we can speak together as we walk along."

"Very good, that will suit me well, for I am rather in a hurry."

Once outside, Mathieu resolved that he would try no ruses with her. The best course was to tell her plainly what he wanted, and then to buy her silence. At the first words he spoke she understood him. She well remembered Norine's child, although in her time she had carried dozens of children to the Foundling Hospital. The particular circumstances of that case, however, the conversation which had taken place, her drive with Mathieu in a cab, had all remained engraved on her memory. Moreover, she had found that child again, at Rougemont, five days later; and she even remembered that her friend the hospital-attendant had left it with La Loiseau. But she had occupied herself no more about it afterwards; and she believed that it was now dead, like so many others. When she heard Mathieu speak of the hamlet of Saint-Pierre, of Montoir the wheelwright, and of Alexandre-Honore, now fifteen, who must be in apprenticeship there, she evinced great surprise.

"Oh, you must be mistaken, monsieur," she said; "I know Montoir at Saint-Pierre very well. And he certainly has a lad from the Foundling, of the age you mention, at his place. But that lad came from La Cauchois; he is a big carroty fellow named Richard, who arrived at our village some days before the other. I know who his mother was; she was an English woman called Amy, who stopped more than once at Madame Bourdieu's. That ginger-haired lad is certainly not your Norine's boy. Alexandre-Honore was dark."

"Well, then," replied Mathieu, "there must be another apprentice at the wheelwright's. My information is precise, it was given me officially."

After a moment's perplexity La Couteau made a gesture of ignorance, and admitted that Mathieu might be right. "It's possible," said she; "perhaps Montoir has two apprentices. He does a good business, and as I haven't been to Saint-Pierre for some months now I can say nothing certain. Well, and what do you desire of me, monsieur?"

He then gave her very clear instructions. She was to obtain the most precise information possible about the lad's health, disposition, and conduct, whether the schoolmaster had always been pleased with him, whether his employer was equally satisfied, and so forth. Briefly, the inquiry was to be complete. But, above all things, she was to carry it on in such a way that nobody should suspect anything, neither the boy himself nor the folks of the district. There must be absolute secrecy.

"All that is easy," replied La Couteau, "I understand perfectly, and you can rely on me. I shall need a little time, however, and the best plan will be for me to tell you of the result of my researches when I next come to Paris. And if it suits you you will find me to-day fortnight, at two o'clock, at Broquette's office in the Rue Roquepine. I am quite at home there, and the place is like a tomb."

Some days later, as Mathieu was again at the Beauchene works with his son Blaise, he was observed by Constance, who called him to her and questioned him in such direct fashion that he had to tell her what steps he had taken. When she heard of his appointment with La Couteau for the Wednesday of the ensuing week, she said to him in her resolute way: "Come and fetch me. I wish to question that woman myself. I want to be quite certain on the matter."

In spite of the lapse of fifteen years Broquette's nurse-office in the Rue Roquepine had remained the same as formerly, except that Madame Broquette was dead and had been succeeded by her daughter Herminie. The sudden loss of that fair, dignified lady, who had possessed such a decorative presence and so ably represented the high morality and respectability of the establishment, had at first seemed a severe one. But it so happened that Herminie, a tall, slim, languid creature that she was, gorged with novel-reading, also proved in her way a distinguished figurehead for the office. She was already thirty and was still unmarried, feeling indeed nothing but loathing for all the mothers laden with whining children by whom she was surrounded. Moreover, M. Broquette, her father, though now more than five-and-seventy, secretly remained the all-powerful, energetic director of the place, discharging all needful police duties, drilling new nurses like recruits, remaining ever on the watch and incessantly perambulating the three floors of his suspicious, dingy lodging-house.

La Couteau was waiting for Mathieu in the doorway. On perceiving Constance, whom she did not know, for she had never previously met her, she seemed surprised. Who could that lady be? what had she to do with the affair? However, she promptly extinguished the bright gleam of curiosity which for a moment lighted up her eyes; and as Herminie, with distinguished nonchalance, was at that moment exhibiting a party of nurses to two gentlemen in the office, she took her visitors into the empty refectory, where the atmosphere was as usual tainted by a horrible stench of cookery.

"You must excuse me, monsieur and madame," she exclaimed, "but there is no other room free just now. The place is full."

Then she carried her keen glances from Mathieu to Constance, preferring to wait until she was questioned, since another person was now in the secret.

"You can speak out," said Mathieu. "Did you make the inquiries I spoke to you about?"

"Certainly, monsieur. They were made, and properly made, I think."

"Then tell us the result: I repeat that you can speak freely before this lady."

"Oh! monsieur, it won't take me long. You were quite right: there were two apprentices at the wheelwright's at Saint-Pierre, and one of them was Alexandre-Honore, the pretty blonde's child, the same that we took together over yonder. He had been there, I found, barely two months, after trying three or four other callings, and that explains my ignorance of the circumstance. Only he's a lad who can stay nowhere, and so three weeks ago he took himself off."

Constance could not restrain an exclamation of anxiety: "What! took himself off?"

"Yes, madame, I mean that he ran away, and this time it is quite certain that he has left the district, for he disappeared with three hundred francs belonging to Montoir, his master."

La Couteau's dry voice rang as if it were an axe dealing a deadly blow. Although she could not understand the lady's sudden pallor and despairing emotion, she certainly seemed to derive cruel enjoyment from it.

"Are you quite sure of your information?" resumed Constance, struggling against the facts. "That is perhaps mere village tittle-tattle."

"Tittle-tattle, madame? Oh! when I undertake to do anything I do it properly. I spoke to the gendarmes. They have scoured the whole district, and it is certain that Alexandre-Honore left no address behind him when he went off with those three hundred francs. He is still on the run. As for that I'll stake my name on it."

This was indeed a hard blow for Constance. That lad, whom she fancied she had found again, of whom she dreamt incessantly, and on whom she had based so many unacknowledgable plans of vengeance, escaped her, vanished once more into the unknown! She was distracted by it as by some pitiless stroke of fate, some fresh and irreparable defeat. However, she continued the interrogatory.

"Surely you did not merely see the gendarmes? you were instructed to question everybody."

"That is precisely what I did, madame. I saw the schoolmaster, and I spoke to the other persons who had employed the lad. They all told me that he was a good-for-nothing. The schoolmaster remembered that he had been a liar and a bully. Now he's a thief; that makes him perfect. I can't say otherwise than I have said, since you wanted to know the plain truth."

La Couteau thus emphasized her statements on seeing that the lady's suffering increased. And what strange suffering it was; a heart-pang at each fresh accusation, as if her husband's illegitimate child had become in some degree her own! She ended indeed by silencing the nurse-agent.

"Thank you. The boy is no longer at Rougemont, that is all we wished to know."

La Couteau thereupon turned to Mathieu, continuing her narrative, in order to give him his money's worth.

"I also made the other apprentice talk a bit," said she; "you know, that big carroty fellow, Richard, whom I spoke to you about. He's another whom I wouldn't willingly trust. But it's certain that he doesn't know where his companion has gone. The gendarmes think that Alexandre is in Paris."

Thereupon Mathieu in his turn thanked the woman, and handed her a bank-note for fifty francs—a gift which brought a smile to her face and rendered her obsequious, and, as she herself put it, "as discreetly silent as the grave." Then, as three nurses came into the refectory, and Monsieur Broquette could be heard scrubbing another's hands in the kitchen, by way of teaching her how to cleanse herself of her native dirt, Constance felt nausea arise within her, and made haste to follow her companion away. Once in the street, instead of entering the cab which was waiting, she paused pensively, haunted by La Couteau's final words.

"Did you hear?" she exclaimed. "That wretched lad may be in Paris."

"That is probable enough; they all end by stranding here."

Constance again hesitated, reflected, and finally made up her mind to say in a somewhat tremulous voice: "And the mother, my friend; you know where she lives, don't you? Did you not tell me that you had concerned yourself about her?"

"Yes, I did."

"Then listen—and above all, don't be astonished; pity me, for I am really suffering. An idea has just taken possession of me; it seems to me that if the boy is in Paris, he may have found his mother. Perhaps he is with her, or she may at least know where he lodges. Oh! don't tell me that it is impossible. On the contrary, everything is possible."

Surprised and moved at seeing one who usually evinced so much calmness now giving way to such fancies as these, Mathieu promised that he would make inquiries. Nevertheless, Constance did not get into the cab, but continued gazing at the pavement. And when she once more raised her eyes, she spoke to him entreatingly, in an embarrassed, humble manner: "Do you know what we ought to do? Excuse me, but it is a service I shall never forget. If I could only know the truth at once it might calm me a little. Well, let us drive to that woman's now. Oh! I won't go up; you can go alone, while I wait in the cab at the street corner. And perhaps you will obtain some news."

It was an insane idea, and he was at first minded to prove this to her. Then, on looking at her, she seemed to him so wretched, so painfully tortured, that without a word, making indeed but a kindly gesture of compassion, he consented. And the cab carried them away.

The large room in which Norine and Cecile lived together was at Grenelle, near the Champ de Mars, in a street at the end of the Rue de la Federation. They had been there for nearly six years now, and in the earlier days had experienced much worry and wretchedness. But the child whom they had to feed and save had on his side saved them also. The motherly feelings slumbering in Norine's heart had awakened with passionate intensity for that poor little one as soon as she had given him the breast and learnt to watch over him and kiss him. And it was also wondrous to see how that unfortunate creature Cecile regarded the child as in some degree her own. He had indeed two mothers, whose thoughts were for him alone. If Norine, during the first few months, had often wearied of spending her days in pasting little boxes together, if even thoughts of flight had at times come to her, she had always been restrained by the puny arms that were clasped around her neck. And now she had grown calm, sensible, diligent, and very expert at the light work which Cecile had taught her. It was a sight to see them both, gay and closely united in their little home, which was like a convent cell, spending their days at their little table; while between them was their child, their one source of life, of hard-working courage and happiness.

Since they had been living thus they had made but one good friend, and this was Madame Angelin. As a delegate of the Poor Relief Service, intrusted with one of the Grenelle districts, Madame Angelin had found Norine among the pensioners over whom she was appointed to watch. A feeling of affection for the two mothers, as she called the sisters, had sprung up within her, and she had succeeded in inducing the authorities to prolong the child's allowance of thirty francs a month for a period of three years. Then she had obtained scholastic assistance for him, not to mention frequent presents which she brought—clothes, linen, and even money—for apart from official matters, charitable people often intrusted her with fairly large sums, which she distributed among the most meritorious of the poor mothers whom she visited. And even nowadays she occasionally called on the sisters, well pleased to spend an hour in that nook of quiet toil, which the laughter and the play of the child enlivened. She there felt herself to be far away from the world, and suffered less from her own misfortunes. And Norine kissed her hands, declaring that without her the little household of the two mothers would never have managed to exist.

When Mathieu appeared there, cries of delight arose. He also was a friend, a saviour—the one who, by first taking and furnishing the large room, had founded the household. It was a very clean room, almost coquettish with its white curtains, and rendered very cheerful by its two large windows, which admitted the golden radiance of the afternoon sun. Norine and Cecile were working at the table, cutting out cardboard and pasting it together, while the little one, who had come home from school, sat between them on a high chair, gravely handling a pair of scissors and fully persuaded that he was helping them.

"Oh! is it you? How kind of you to come to see us! Nobody has called for five days past. Oh! we don't complain of it. We are so happy alone together! Since Irma married a clerk she has treated us with disdain. Euphrasie can no longer come down her stairs. Victor and his wife live so far away. And as for that rascal Alfred, he only comes up here to see if he can find something to steal. Mamma called five days ago to tell us that papa had narrowly escaped being killed at the works on the previous day. Poor mamma! she is so worn out that before long she won't be able to take a step."

While the sisters thus rattled on both together, one beginning a sentence and the other finishing it, Mathieu looked at Norine, who, thanks to that peaceful and regular life, had regained in her thirty-sixth year a freshness of complexion that suggested a superb, mature fruit gilded by the sun. And even the slender Cecile had acquired strength, the strength which love's energy can impart even to a childish form.

All at once, however, she raised a loud exclamation of horror: "Oh! he has hurt himself, the poor little fellow." And at once she snatched the scissors from the child, who sat there laughing with a drop of blood at the tip of one of his fingers.

"Oh! good Heavens," murmured Norine, who had turned quite pale, "I feared that he had slit his hand."

For a moment Mathieu wondered if he would serve any useful purpose by fulfilling the strange mission he had undertaken. Then it seemed to him that it might be as well to say at least a word of warning to the young woman who had grown so calm and quiet, thanks to the life of work which she had at last embraced. And he proceeded very prudently, only revealing the truth by slow degrees. Nevertheless, there came a moment when, after reminding Norine of the birth of Alexandre-Honore, it became necessary for him to add that the boy was living.

The mother looked at Mathieu in evident consternation. "He is living, living! Why do you tell me that? I was so pleased at knowing nothing."

"No doubt; but it is best that you should know. I have even been assured that he must now be in Paris, and I wondered whether he might have found you, and have come to see you."

At this she lost all self-possession. "What! Have come to see me! Nobody has been to see me. Do you think, then, that he might come? But I don't want him to do so! I should go mad! A big fellow of fifteen falling on me like that—a lad I don't know and don't care for! Oh! no, no; prevent it, I beg of you; I couldn't—I couldn't bear it!"

With a gesture of utter distraction she had burst into tears, and had caught hold of the little one near her, pressing him to her breast as if to shield him from the other, the unknown son, the stranger, who by his resurrection threatened to thrust himself in some degree in the younger lad's place.

"No, no!" she cried. "I have but one child; there is only one I love; I don't want any other."

Cecile had risen, greatly moved, and desirous of bringing her sister to reason. Supposing that the other son should come, how could she turn him out of doors? At the same time, though her pity was aroused for the abandoned one, she also began to bewail the loss of their happiness. It became necessary for Mathieu to reassure them both by saying that he regarded such a visit as most improbable. Without telling them the exact truth, he spoke of the elder lad's disappearance, adding, however, that he must be ignorant even of his mother's name. Thus, when he left the sisters, they already felt relieved and had again turned to their little boxes while smiling at their son, to whom they had once more intrusted the scissors in order that he might cut out some paper men.

Down below, at the street corner, Constance, in great impatience, was looking out of the cab window, watching the house-door.

"Well?" she asked, quivering, as soon as Mathieu was near her.

"Well, the mother knows nothing and has seen nobody. It was a foregone conclusion."

She sank down as if from some supreme collapse, and her ashen face became quite distorted. "You are right, it was certain," said she; "still one always hopes." And with a gesture of despair she added: "It is all ended now. Everything fails me, my last dream is dead."

Mathieu pressed her hand and remained waiting for her to give an address in order that he might transmit it to the driver. But she seemed to have lost her head and to have forgotten where she wished to go. Then, as she asked him if he would like her to set him down anywhere, he replied that he wished to call on the Seguins. The fear of finding herself alone again so soon after the blow which had fallen on her thereupon gave her the idea of paying a visit to Valentine, whom she had not seen for some time past.

"Get in," she said to Mathieu; "we will go to the Avenue d'Antin together."

The vehicle rolled off and heavy silence fell between them; they had not a word to say to one another. However, as they were reaching their destination, Constance exclaimed in a bitter voice: "You must give my husband the good news, and tell him that the boy has disappeared. Ah! what a relief for him!"

Mathieu, on calling in the Avenue d'Antin, had hoped to find the Seguins assembled there. Seguin himself had returned to Paris, nobody knew whence, a week previously, when Andree's hand had been formally asked of him; and after an interview with his uncle Du Hordel he had evinced great willingness and cordiality. Indeed, the wedding had immediately been fixed for the month of May, when the Froments also hoped to marry off their daughter Rose. The two weddings, it was thought, might take place at Chantebled on the same day, which would be delightful. This being arranged, Ambroise was accepted as fiance, and to his great delight was able to call at the Seguins' every day, about five o'clock, to pay his court according to established usage. It was on account of this that Mathieu fully expected to find the whole family at home.

When Constance asked for Valentine, however, a footman informed her that Madame had gone out. And when Mathieu in his turn asked for Seguin, the man replied that Monsieur was also absent. Only Mademoiselle was at home with her betrothed. On learning this the visitors went upstairs.

"What! are you left all alone?" exclaimed Mathieu on perceiving the young couple seated side by side on a little couch in the big room on the first floor, which Seguin had once called his "cabinet."

"Why, yes, we are alone in the house," Andree answered with a charming laugh. "We are very pleased at it."

They looked adorable, thus seated side by side—she so gentle, of such tender beauty—he with all the fascinating charm that was blended with his strength.

"Isn't Celeste there at any rate?" again inquired Mathieu.

"No, she has disappeared we don't know where." And again they laughed like free frolicsome birds ensconced in the depths of some lonely forest.

"Well, you cannot be very lively all alone like this."

"Oh! we don't feel at all bored, we have so many things to talk about. And then we look at one another. And there is never an end to it all."

Though her heart bled, Constance could not help admiring them. Ah, to think of it! Such grace, such health, such hope! While in her home all was blighted, withered, destroyed, that race of Froments seemed destined to increase forever! For this again was a conquest—those two children left free to love one another, henceforth alone in that sumptuous mansion which to-morrow would belong to them. Then, at another thought, Constance turned towards Mathieu: "Are you not also marrying your eldest daughter?" she asked.

"Yes, Rose," Mathieu gayly responded. "We shall have a grand fete at Chantebled next May! You must all of you come there."

'Twas indeed as she had thought: numbers prevailed, life proved victorious. Chantebled had been conquered from the Seguins, and now their very house would soon be invaded by Ambroise, while the Beauchene works themselves had already half fallen into the hands of Blaise.

"We will go," she answered, quivering. "And may your good luck continue—that is what I wish you."

XVI

Amid the general delight attending the double wedding which was to prove, so to say, a supreme celebration of the glory of Chantebled, it had occurred to Mathieu's daughter Rose to gather the whole family together one Sunday, ten days before the date appointed for the ceremony. She and her betrothed, followed by the whole family, were to repair to Janville station in the morning to meet the other affianced pair, Ambroise and Andree, who were to be conducted in triumph to the farm where they would all lunch together. It would be a kind of wedding rehearsal, she exclaimed with her hearty laugh; they would be able to arrange the programme for the great day. And her idea enraptured her to such a point, she seemed to anticipate so much delight from this preliminary festival, that Mathieu and Marianne consented to it.

Rose's marriage was like the supreme blossoming of years of prosperity, and brought a finishing touch to the happiness of the home. She was the prettiest of Mathieu's daughters, with dark brown hair, round gilded cheeks, merry eyes, and charming mouth. And she had the most equable of dispositions, her laughter ever rang out so heartily! She seemed indeed to be the very soul, the good fairy, of that farm teeming with busy life. But beneath the invariable good humor which kept her singing from morning till night there was much common sense and energy of affection, as her choice of a husband showed. Eight years previously Mathieu had engaged the services of one Frederic Berthaud, the son of a petty farmer of the neighborhood. This sturdy young fellow had taken a passionate interest in the creative work of Chantebled, learning and working there with rare activity and intelligence. He had no means of his own at all. Rose, who had grown up near him, knew however that he was her father's preferred assistant, and when he returned to the farm at the expiration of his military service she, divining that he loved her, forced him to acknowledge it. Thus she settled her own future life; she wished to remain near her parents, on that farm which had hitherto held all her happiness. Neither Mathieu nor Marianne was surprised at this. Deeply touched, they signified their approval of a choice in which affection for themselves had so large a part. The family ties seemed to be drawn yet closer, and increase of joy came to the home.

So everything was settled, and it was agreed that on the appointed Sunday Ambroise should bring his betrothed Andree and her mother, Madame Seguin, to Janville by the ten o'clock train. A couple of hours previously Rose had already begun a battle with the object of prevailing upon the whole family to repair to the railway station to meet the affianced pair.

"But come, my children, it is unreasonable," Marianne gently exclaimed. "It is necessary that somebody should stay at home. I shall keep Nicolas here, for there is no need to send children of five years old scouring the roads. I shall also keep Gervais and Claire. But you may take all the others if you like, and your father shall lead the way."

Rose, however, still merrily laughing, clung to her plan. "No, no, mamma, you must come as well; everybody must come; it was promised. Ambroise and Andree, you see, are like a royal couple from a neighboring kingdom. My brother Ambroise, having won the hand of a foreign princess, is going to present her to us. And so, to do them the honors of our own empire, we, Frederic and I, must go to meet them, attended by the whole Court. You form the Court and you cannot do otherwise than come. Ah what a fine sight it will be when we spread out through the country on our way home again!"

Marianne, amused by her daughter's overflowing gayety, ended by laughing and giving way.

"This will be the order of the march," resumed Rose. "Oh! I've planned everything, as you will see! As for Frederic and myself, we shall go on our bicycles—that is the most modern style. We will also take my maids of honor, my little sisters Louise, Madeleine, and Marguerite, eleven, nine, and seven years old, on their bicycles. They will look very well behind me. Then Gregoire can follow on his wheel; he is thirteen, and will do as a page, bringing up the rear of my personal escort. All the rest of the Court will have to pack itself into the chariot—I mean the big family wagon, in which there is room for eight. You, as Queen Mother, may keep your last little prince, Nicolas, on your knees. Papa will only have to carry himself proudly, as befits the head of a dynasty. And my brother Gervais, that young Hercules of seventeen, shall drive, with Claire, who at fifteen is so remarkable for common sense, beside him on the box-seat. As for the illustrious twins, those high and mighty lords, Denis and Blaise, we will call for them at Janville, since they are waiting for us there, at Madame Desvignes'."

Thus did Rose rattle on, exulting over the scheme she had devised. She danced, sang, clapped her hands, and finally exclaimed: "Ah! for a pretty cortege this will be fine indeed."

She was animated by such joyous haste that she made the party start much sooner than was necessary, and they reached Janville at half-past nine. It was true, however, that they had to call for the others there. The house in which Madame Desvignes had taken refuge after her husband's death, and which she had now occupied for some twelve years, living there in a very quiet retired way on the scanty income she had managed to save, was the first in the village, on the high road. For a week past her elder daughter Charlotte, Blaise's wife, had come to stay there with her children, Berthe and Christophe, who needed change of air; and on the previous evening they had been joined by Blaise, who was well pleased to spend Sunday with them.

Madame Desvignes' younger daughter, Marthe, was delighted whenever her sister thus came to spend a few weeks in the old home, bringing her little ones with her, and once more occupying the room which had belonged to her in her girlish days. All the laughter and playfulness of the past came back again, and the one dream of worthy Madame Desvignes, amid her pride at being a grandmamma, was of completing her life-work, hitherto so prudently carried on, by marrying off Marthe in her turn. As a matter of fact it had seemed likely that there might be three instead of two weddings at Chantebled that spring. Denis, who, since leaving a scientific school had embarked in fresh technical studies, often slept at the farm and nearly every Sunday he saw Marthe, who was of the same age as Rose and her constant companion. The young girl, a pretty blonde like her sister Charlotte, but of a less impulsive and more practical nature, had indeed attracted Denis, and, dowerless though she was, he had made up his mind to marry her, since he had discovered that she possessed the sterling qualities that help one on to fortune. But in their chats together both evinced good sense and serene confidence, without sign of undue haste. Particularly was this the case with Denis, who was very methodical in his ways and unwilling to place a woman's happiness in question until he could offer her an assured position. Thus, of their own accord, they had postponed their marriage, quietly and smilingly resisting the passionate assaults of Rose, whom the idea of three weddings on the same day had greatly excited. At the same time, Denis continued visiting Madame Desvignes, who, on her side, equally prudent and confident, received him much as if he were her son. That morning he had even quitted the farm at seven o'clock, saying that he meant to surprise Blaise in bed; and thus he also was to be met at Janville.

As it happened, the fete of Janville fell on Sunday, the second in May. Encompassing the square in front of the railway station were roundabouts, booths, shooting galleries, and refreshment stalls. Stormy showers during the night had cleansed the sky, which was of a pure blue, with a flaming sun, whose heat in fact was excessive for the season. A good many people were already assembled on the square—all the idlers of the district, bands of children, and peasants of the surrounding country, eager to see the sights; and into the midst of this crowd fell the Froments—first the bicyclists, next the wagon, and then the others who had been met at the entry of the village.

"We are producing our little effect!" exclaimed Rose as she sprang from her wheel.

This was incontestable. During the earlier years the whole of Janville had looked harshly on those Froments, those bourgeois who had come nobody knew whence, and who, with overweening conceit, had talked of making corn grow in land where there had been nothing but crops of stones for centuries past. Then the miracle, Mathieu's extraordinary victory, had long hurt people's vanity and thereby increased their anger. But everything passes away; one cannot regard success with rancor, and folks who grow rich always end by being in the right. Thus, nowadays, Janville smiled complacently on that swarming family which had grown up beside it, forgetting that in former times each fresh birth at Chantebled had been regarded as quite scandalous by the gossips. Besides, how could one resist such a happy display of strength and power, such a merry invasion, when, as on that festive Sunday, the whole family came up at a gallop, conquering the roads, the streets, and the squares? What with the father and mother, the eleven children—six boys and five girls—and two grandchildren already, there were fifteen of them. The eldest boys, the twins, were now four-and-twenty, and still so much alike that people occasionally mistook one for the other as in their cradle days, when Marianne had been obliged to open their eyes to identify them, those of Blaise being gray, and those of Denis black. Nicolas, the youngest boy, at the other end of the family scale, was as yet but five years old; a delightful little urchin was he, a precocious little man whose energy and courage were quite amusing. And between the twins and that youngster came the eight other children: Ambroise, the future husband, who was already on the road to every conquest; Rose, so brimful of life; who likewise was on the eve of marrying; Gervais, with his square brow and wrestler's limbs, who would soon be fighting the good fight of agriculture; Claire, who was silent and hardworking, and lacked beauty, but possessed a strong heart and a housewife's sensible head. Next Gregoire, the undisciplined, self-willed schoolboy, who was ever beating the hedges in search of adventures; and then the three last girls: Louise, plump and good natured; Madeleine, delicate and of dreamy mind; Marguerite, the least pretty but the most loving of the trio. And when, behind their father and their mother, the eleven came along one after the other, followed too by Berthe and Christophe, representing yet another generation, it was a real procession that one saw, as, for instance, on that fine Sunday on the Grand Place of Janville, already crowded with holiday-making folks. And the effect was irresistible; even those who were scarcely pleased with the prodigious success of Chantebled felt enlivened and amused at seeing the Froments galloping about and invading the place. So much health and mirth and strength accompanied them, as if earth with her overflowing gifts of life had thus profusely created them for to-morrow's everlasting hopes.

"Let those who think themselves more numerous come forward!" Rose resumed gayly. "And then we will count one another."

"Come, be quiet!" said her mother, who, after alighting from the wagon, had set Nicolas on the ground. "You will end by making people hoot us."

"Hoot us! Why, they admire us: just look at them! How funny it is, mamma, that you are not prouder of yourself and of us!"

"Why, I am so very proud that I fear to humiliate others."

They all began to laugh. And Mathieu, standing near Marianne, likewise felt proud at finding himself, as he put it, among "the sacred battalion" of his sons and daughters. To that battalion worthy Madame Desvignes herself belonged, since her daughter Charlotte was adding soldiers to it and helping it to become an army. Such as it was indeed, this was only the beginning; later on the battalion would be seen ever increasing and multiplying, becoming a swarming victorious race, great-grandchildren following grandchildren, till there were fifty of them, and a hundred, and two hundred, all tending to increase the happiness and beauty of the world. And in the mingled amazement and amusement of Janville gathered around that fruitful family there was certainly some of the instinctive admiration which is felt for the strength and the healthfulness which create great nations.

"Besides, we have only friends now," remarked Mathieu. "Everybody is cordial with us!"

"Oh, everybody!" muttered Rose. "Just look at the Lepailleurs yonder, in front of that booth."

The Lepailleurs were indeed there—the father, the mother, Antonin, and Therese. In order to avoid the Froments they were pretending to take great interest in a booth, where a number of crudely-colored china ornaments were displayed as prizes for the winners at a "lucky-wheel." They no longer even exchanged courtesies with the Chantebled folks; for in their impotent rage at such ceaseless prosperity they had availed themselves of a petty business dispute to break off all relations. Lepailleur regarded the creation of Chantebled as a personal insult, for he had not forgotten his jeers and challenges with respect to those moorlands, from which, in his opinion, one would never reap anything but stones. And thus, when he had well examined the china ornaments, it occurred to him to be insolent, with which object he turned round and stared at the Froments, who, as the train they were expecting would not arrive for another quarter of an hour, were gayly promenading through the fair.

The miller's bad temper had for the last two months been increased by the return of his son Antonin to Janville under very deplorable circumstances. This young fellow, who had set off one morning to conquer Paris, sent there by his parents, who had a blind confidence in his fine handwriting, had remained with Maitre Rousselet the attorney for four years as a petty clerk, dull-witted and extremely idle. He had not made the slightest progress in his profession, but had gradually sunk into debauchery, cafe-life, drunkenness, gambling, and facile amours. To him the conquest of Paris meant greedy indulgence in the coarsest pleasures such as he had dreamt of in his village. It consumed all his money, all the supplies which he extracted from his mother by continual promises of victory, in which she implicitly believed, so great was her faith in him. But he ended by grievously suffering in health, turned thin and yellow, and actually began to lose his hair at three-and-twenty, so that his mother, full of alarm, brought him home one day, declaring that he worked too hard, and that she would not allow him to kill himself in that fashion. It leaked out, however, later on, that Maitre Rousselet had summarily dismissed him. Even before this was known his return home did not fail to make his father growl. The miller partially guessed the truth, and if he did not openly vent his anger, it was solely from pride, in order that he might not have to confess his mistake with respect to the brilliant career which he had predicted for Antonin. At home, when the doors were closed, Lepailleur revenged himself on his wife, picking the most frightful quarrels with her since he had discovered her frequent remittances of money to their son. But she held her own against him, for even as she had formerly admired him, so at present she admired her boy. She sacrificed, as it were, the father to the son, now that the latter's greater learning brought her increased surprise. And so the household was all disagreement as a result of that foolish attempt, born of vanity, to make their heir a Monsieur, a Parisian. Antonin for his part sneered and shrugged his shoulders at it all, idling away his time pending the day when he might be able to resume a life of profligacy.

When the Froments passed by, it was a fine sight to see the Lepailleurs standing there stiffly and devouring them with their eyes. The father puckered his lips in an attempt to sneer, and the mother jerked her head with an air of bravado. The son, standing there with his hands in his pockets, presented a sorry sight with his bent back, his bald head, and pale face. All three were seeking to devise something disagreeable when an opportunity presented itself.

"Why, where is Therese?" exclaimed La Lepailleur. "She was here just now: what has become of her? I won't have her leave me when there are all these people about!"

It was quite true, for the last moment Therese had disappeared. She was now ten years old and very pretty, quite a plump little blonde, with wild hair and black eyes which shone brightly. But she had a terribly impulsive and wilful nature, and would run off and disappear for hours at a time, beating the hedges and scouring the countryside in search of birds'-nests and flowers and wild fruit. If her mother, however, made such a display of alarm, darting hither and thither to find her, just as the Froments passed by, it was because she had become aware of some scandalous proceedings during the previous week. Therese's ardent dream was to possess a bicycle, and she desired one the more since her parents stubbornly refused to content her, declaring in fact that those machines might do for bourgeois but were certainly not fit for well-behaved girls. Well, one afternoon, when she had gone as usual into the fields, her mother, returning from market, had perceived her on a deserted strip of road, in company with little Gregoire Froment, another young wanderer whom she often met in this wise, in spots known only to themselves. The two made a very suitable pair, and were ever larking and rambling along the paths, under the leaves, beside the ditches. But the abominable thing was that, on this occasion, Gregoire, having seated Therese on his own bicycle, was supporting her at the waist and running alongside, helping her to direct the machine. Briefly it was a real bicycle lesson which the little rascal was giving, and which the little hussy took with all the pleasure in the world. When Therese returned home that evening she had her ears soundly boxed for her pains.

"Where can that little gadabout have got to?" La Lepailleur continued shouting. "One can no sooner take one's eyes off her than she runs away."

Antonin, however, having peeped behind the booth containing the china ornaments, lurched back again, still with his hands in his pockets, and said with his vicious sneer: "Just look there, you'll see something."

And indeed, behind the booth, his mother again found Therese and Gregoire together. The lad was holding his bicycle with one hand and explaining some of the mechanism of it, while the girl, full of admiration and covetousness, looked on with glowing eyes. Indeed she could not resist her inclination, but laughingly let Gregoire raise her in order to seat her for a moment on the saddle, when all at once her mother's terrible voice burst forth: "You wicked hussy! what are you up to there again? Just come back at once, or I'll settle your business for you."

Then Mathieu also, catching sight of the scene, sternly summoned Gregoire: "Please to place your wheel with the others. You know what I have already said to you, so don't begin again."

It was war. Lepailleur impudently growled ignoble threats, which fortunately were lost amid the strains of a barrel organ. And the two families separated, going off in different directions through the growing holiday-making crowd.

"Won't that train ever come, then?" resumed Rose, who with joyous impatience was at every moment turning to glance at the clock of the little railway station on the other side of the square. "We have still ten minutes to wait: whatever shall we do?"

As it happened she had stopped in front of a hawker who stood on the footway with a basketful of crawfish, crawling, pell-mell, at his feet. They had certainly come from the sources of the Yeuse, three leagues away. They were not large, but they were very tasty, for Rose herself had occasionally caught some in the stream. And thus a greedy but also playful fancy came to her.

"Oh, mamma!" she cried, "let us buy the whole basketful. It will be for the feast of welcome, you see; it will be our present to the royal couple we are awaiting. People won't say that Our Majesties neglect to do things properly when they are expecting other Majesties. And I will cook them when we get back, and you'll see how well I shall succeed."

At this the others began to poke fun at her, but her parents ended by doing as she asked, big child as she was, who in the fulness of her happiness hardly knew what amusement to seek. However, as by way of pastime she obstinately sought to count the crawfish, quite an affair ensued: some of them pinched her, and she dropped them with a little shriek; and, amid it all, the basket fell over and then the crawfish hurriedly crawled away. The boys and girls darted in pursuit of them, there was quite a hunt, in which even the serious members of the family at last took part. And what with the laughter and eagerness of one and all, the big as well as the little, the whole happy brood, the sight was so droll and gay that the folks of Janville again drew near and good-naturedly took their share of the amusement.

All at once, however, arose a distant rumble of wheels and an engine whistled.

"Ah, good Heavens! here they are!" cried Rose, quite scared; "quick, quick, or the reception will be missed."

A scramble ensued, the owner of the crawfish was paid, and there was just time to shut the basket and carry it to the wagon. The whole family was already running off, invading the little station, and ranging itself in good order along the arrival platform.

"No, no, not like that," Rose repeated. "You don't observe the right order of precedence. The queen mother must be with the king her husband, and then the princes according to their height. Frederic must place himself on my right. And it's for me, you know, to make the speech of welcome."

The train stopped. When Ambroise and Andree alighted they were at first much surprised to find that everybody had come to meet them, drawn up in a row with solemn mien. When Rose, however began to deliver a pompous little speech, treating her brother's betrothed like some foreign princess, whom she had orders to welcome in the name of the king, her father, the young couple began to laugh, and even prolonged the joke by responding in the same style. The railway men looked on and listened, gaping. It was a fine farce, and the Froments were delighted at showing themselves so playful on that warm May morning.

But Marianne suddenly raised an exclamation of surprise: "What! has not Madame Seguin come with you? She gave me so many promises that she would."

In the rear of Ambroise and Andree Celeste the maid had alone alighted from the train. And she undertook to explain things: "Madame charged me," said she, "to say that she was really most grieved. Yesterday she still hoped that she would be able to keep her promise. Only in the evening she received a visit from Monsieur de Navarede, who is presiding to-day, Sunday, at a meeting of his Society, and of course Madame could not do otherwise than attend it. So she requested me to accompany the young people, and everything is satisfactory, for here they are, you see."

As a matter of fact nobody regretted the absence of Valentine, who always moped when she came into the country. And Mathieu expressed the general opinion in a few words of polite regret: "Well, you must tell her how much we shall miss her. And now let us be off."

Celeste, however, intervened once more. "Excuse me, monsieur, but I cannot remain with you. No. Madame particularly told me to go back to her at once, as she will need me to dress her. And, besides, she is always bored when she is alone. There is a train for Paris at a quarter past ten, is there not? I will go back by it. Then I will be here at eight o'clock this evening to take Mademoiselle home. We settled all that in looking through a time-table. Till this evening, monsieur."

"Till this evening, then, it's understood."

Thereupon, leaving the maid in the deserted little station, all the others returned to the village square, where the wagon and the bicycles were waiting.

"Now we are all assembled," exclaimed Rose, "and the real fete is about to begin. Let me organize the procession for our triumphal return to the castle of our ancestors."

"I am very much afraid that your procession will be soaked," said Marianne. "Just look at the rain approaching!"

During the last few moments there had appeared in the hitherto spotless sky a huge, livid cloud, rising from the west and urged along by a sudden squall. It presaged a return of the violent stormy showers of the previous night.

"Rain! Oh, we don't care about that," the girl responded with an air of superb defiance. "It will never dare to come down before we get home."

Then, with a comical semblance of authority, she disposed her people in the order which she had planned in her mind a week previously. And the procession set off through the admiring village, amid the smiles of all the good women hastening to their doorsteps, and then spread out along the white road between the fertile fields, where bands of startled larks took wing, carrying their clear song to the heavens. It was really magnificent.

At the head of the party were Rose and Frederic, side by side on their bicycles, opening the nuptial march with majestic amplitude. Behind them followed the three maids of honor, the younger sisters, Louise, Madeleine, and Marguerite, the tallest first, the shortest last, and each on a wheel proportioned to her growth. And with berets* on their heads, and their hair down their backs, waving in the breeze, they looked adorable, suggesting a flight of messenger swallows skimming over the ground and bearing good tidings onward. As for Gregoire the page, restive and always ready to bolt, he did not behave very well; for he actually tried to pass the royal couple at the head of the procession, a proceeding which brought him various severe admonitions until he fell back, as duty demanded, to his deferential and modest post. On the other hand, as the three maids of honor began to sing the ballad of Cinderella on her way to the palace of Prince Charming, the royal couple condescendingly declared that the song was appropriate and of pleasing effect, whatever might be the requirements of etiquette. Indeed, Rose, Frederic, and Gregoire also ended by singing the ballad, which rang out amid the serene, far-spreading countryside like the finest music in the world.

Then, at a short distance in the rear, came the chariot, the good old family wagon, which was now crowded. According to the prearranged programme it was Gervais who held the ribbons, with Claire beside him. The two strong horses trotted on in their usual leisurely fashion, in spite of all the gay whip-cracking of their driver, who also wished to contribute to the music. Inside there were now seven people for six places, for if the three children were small, they were at the same time so restless that they fully took up their share of room. First, face to face, there were Ambroise and Andree, the betrothed couple who

* The beret is the Pyreneean tam-o'-shanter.

ÉMILE ZOLA

were being honored by this glorious welcome. Then, also face to face, there were the high and mighty rulers of the region, Mathieu and Marianne, the latter of whom kept little Nicolas, the last prince of the line, on her knees, he braying the while like a little donkey, because he felt so pleased. Then the last places were occupied by the rulers' granddaughter and grandson, Mademoiselle Berthe and Monsieur Christophe, who were as yet unable to walk long distances. And the chariot rolled on with much majesty, albeit that for fear of the rain the curtains of stout white linen had already been half-drawn, thus giving the vehicle, at a distance, somewhat of the aspect of a miller's van.

Further back yet, as a sort of rear-guard, was a group on foot, composed of Blaise, Denis, Madame Desvignes, and her daughters Charlotte and Marthe. They had absolutely refused to take a fly, finding it more pleasant to walk the mile and a half which separated Chantebled from Janville. If the rain should fall, they would manage to find shelter somewhere. Besides, Rose had declared that a suite on foot was absolutely necessary to give the procession its full significance. Those five last comers would represent the multitude, the great concourse of people which follows sovereigns and acclaims them. Or else they might be the necessary guard, the men-at-arms, who watched for the purpose of foiling a possible attack from some felon neighbor. At the same time it unfortunately happened that worthy Madame Desvignes could not walk very fast, so that the rear-guard was soon distanced, to such a degree indeed that it became merely a little lost group, far away.

Still this did not disconcert Rose, but rather made her laugh the more. At the first bend of the road she turned her head, and when she saw her rear-guard more than three hundred yards away she raised cries of admiration. "Oh! just look, Frederic! What an interminable procession! What a deal of room we take up! The cortege is becoming longer and longer, and the road won't be long enough for it very soon."

Then, as the three maids of honor and the page began to jeer impertinently, "just try to be respectful," she said. "Count a little. There are six of us forming the vanguard. In the chariot there are nine, and six and nine make fifteen. Add to them the five of the rear-guard, and we have twenty. Wherever else is such a family seen? Why, the rabbits who watch us pass are mute with stupor and humiliation."

Then came another laugh, and once more they all took up the song of Cinderella on her way to the palace of Prince Charming.

It was at the bridge over the Yeuse that the first drops of rain, big drops they were, began to fall. The big livid cloud, urged on by a terrible wind, was galloping across the sky, filling it with the clamor of a tempest. And almost immediately afterwards the rain-drops increased in volume and in number, lashed by so violent a squall that the water poured down as if by the bucketful, or as if some huge sluice-gate had suddenly burst asunder overhead. One could no longer see twenty yards before one. In two minutes the road was running with water like the bed of a torrent.

Then there was a *sauve-qui-peut* among the procession. It was learnt later on that the people of the rear-guard had luckily been surprised near a peasant's cottage, in which they had quietly sought refuge. Then the folks in the wagon simply drew their curtains, and halted beneath the shelter of a wayside tree for fear lest the horses should take fright under such a downpour. They called to the bicyclists ahead of them to stop also, instead of obstinately remaining in such a deluge. But their words were lost amid the rush of water. However, the little girls and the page took a proper course in crouching beside a thick hedge, though the betrothed couple wildly continued on their way.

Frederic, the more reasonable of the two, certainly had sense enough to say: "This isn't prudent on our part. Let us stop like the others, I beg you."

But from Rose, all excitement, transported by her blissful fever, and insensible, so it seemed, to the pelting of the rain, he only drew this answer: "Pooh! what does it matter, now that we are soaking? It is by stopping we might do ourselves harm. Let us make haste, all haste. In three minutes we shall be at home and able to make fine sport of those laggards when they arrive in another quarter of an hour."

They had just crossed the Yeuse bridge, and they swept on side by side, although the road was far from easy, being a continual ascent for a thousand yards or so between rows of lofty poplars.

"I assure you that we are doing wrong," the young man repeated. "They will blame me, and they will be right."

"Oh! well," cried she, "I'm amusing myself. This bicycle bath is quite funny. Leave me, then, if you don't love me enough to follow me."

He followed her, however, pressed close beside her, and sought to shelter her a little from the slanting rain. And it was a wild, mad race on the part of that young couple, almost linked together, their elbows touching as they sped on and on, as if lifted from the ground, carried off by all that rushing, howling water which poured down so ragefully. It was as though a thunder-blast bore them along. But at the very moment when they sprang from their bicycles in the yard of the farm the rain ceased, and the sky became blue once more.

Rose was laughing like a lunatic, and looked very flushed, but she was soaked to such a point that water streamed from her clothes, her hair, her hands. You might have taken her for some fairy of the springs who had overturned her urn on herself.

"Well, the fete is complete," she exclaimed breathlessly. "All the same, we are the first home."

She then darted upstairs to comb her hair and change her gown. But to gain just a few minutes, eager as she was to cook the crawfish, she did not take the trouble to put on dry linen. She wished the pot to be on the fire with the water, the white wine, the carrots and spices, before the family arrived. And she came and went, attending to the fire and filling the whole kitchen with her gay activity, like a good housewife who was glad to display her accomplishments, while her betrothed, who had also come downstairs again after changing his clothes, watched her with a kind of religious admiration.

At last, when the whole family had arrived, the folks of the brake and the pedestrians also, there came a rather sharp explanation. Mathieu and Marianne were angry, so greatly had they been alarmed by that rush through the storm.

"There was no sense in it, my girl," Marianne repeated. "Did you at least change your linen?"

"Why yes, why yes!" replied Rose. "Where are the crawfish?"

Mathieu meantime was lecturing Frederic. "You might have broken your necks," said he; "and, besides, it is by no means good to get soaked with cold water when one is hot. You ought to have stopped her."

"Well, she insisted on going on, and whenever she insists on anything, you know, I haven't the strength to prevent her."

At last Rose, in her pretty way, put an end to the reproaches. "Come, that's enough scolding; I did wrong, no doubt. But won't anybody compliment me on my *court-bouillon*? Have you ever known crawfish to smell as nice as that?"

The lunch was wonderfully gay. As they were twenty, and wished to have a real rehearsal of the wedding feast, the table had been set in a large gallery adjoining the ordinary dining-room. This gallery was still bare, but throughout the meal they talked incessantly of how they would embellish it with shrubs, garlands of foliage, and clumps of flowers. During the dessert they even sent for a ladder with the view of indicating on the walls the main lines of the decorations.

For a moment or so Rose, previously so talkative, had lapsed into silence. She had eaten heartily, but all the color had left her face, which had assumed a waxy pallor under her heavy hair, which was still damp. And when she wished to ascend the ladder herself to indicate how some ornament should be placed, her legs suddenly failed her, she staggered, and then fainted away.

Everybody was in consternation, but she was promptly placed in a chair, where for a few minutes longer she remained unconscious. Then, on coming to her senses, she remained for a moment silent, oppressed as by a feeling of pain, and apparently failing to understand what had taken place. Mathieu and Marianne, terribly upset, pressed her with questions, anxious as they were to know if she felt better. She had evidently caught cold, and this was the fine result of her foolish ride.

By degrees the girl recovered her composure, and again smiled. She then explained that she now felt no pain, but that it had suddenly seemed to her as if a heavy paving-stone were lying on her chest; then this weight had melted away, leaving her better able to breathe. And, indeed, she was soon on feet once more, and finished giving her views respecting the decoration of the gallery, in such wise that the others ended by feeling reassured, and the afternoon passed away joyously in the making of all sorts of splendid plans. Little was eaten at dinner, for they had done too much honor to the crawfish at noon. And at nine o'clock, as soon as Celeste arrived for Andree, the gathering broke up. Ambroise was returning to Paris that same evening. Blaise and Denis were to take the seven o'clock train the following morning. And Rose, after accompanying Madame Desvignes and her daughters to the road, called to them through the darkness: "Au revoir, come back soon." She was again full of gayety at the thought of the general rendezvous which the family had arranged for the approaching weddings.

Neither Mathieu nor Marianne went to bed at once, however. Though they did not even speak of it together, they thought that Rose looked very strange, as if, indeed, she were intoxicated. She had again staggered on returning to the house, and though she only complained of some slight oppression, they prevailed on her to go to bed. After she had retired to her room, which adjoined their own, Marianne went several times to see if she were well wrapped up and were sleeping peacefully, while Mathieu remained anxiously thoughtful beside the lamp. At last the girl fell asleep, and the parents, leaving the door of communication open, then exchanged a few words in an undertone, in their desire to tranquillize each other. It would surely be nothing; a good night's rest would suffice to restore Rose to her wonted health. Then in their turn they went to bed, the whole farm lapsed into silence, surrendering itself to slumber until the first cockcrow. But all at once, about four o'clock, shortly before daybreak, a stifled call, "Mamma! mamma!" awoke both Mathieu and Marianne, and they sprang out of bed, barefooted, shivering, and groping for the candle. Rose was again stifling, struggling against another attack of extreme violence. For the second time, however, she soon regained consciousness and appeared relieved, and thus the parents, great as was their distress, preferred to summon nobody but to wait till daylight. Their alarm was caused particularly by the great change they noticed in their daughter's appearance; her face was swollen and distorted, as if some evil power had transformed her in the night. But she fell asleep again, in a state of great prostration; and they no longer stirred for fear of disturbing her slumber. They remained there watching and waiting, listening to the revival of life in the farm around them as the daylight gradually increased. Time went by; five and then six o'clock struck. And at about twenty minutes to seven Mathieu, on looking into the yard, and there catching sight of Denis, who was to return to Paris by the seven o'clock train, hastened down to tell him to call upon Boutan and beg the doctor to come at once. Then, as soon as his son had started, he rejoined Marianne upstairs, still unwilling to call or warn anybody. But a third attack followed, and this time it was the thunderbolt.

Rose had half risen in bed, her arms thrown out, her mouth distended as she gasped "Mamma! mamma!"

Then in a sudden fit of revolt, a last flash of life, she sprang from her bed and stepped towards the window, whose panes were all aglow with the rising sun. And for a moment she leant there, her legs bare, her shoulders bare, and her heavy hair falling over her like a royal mantle. Never had she looked more beautiful, more dazzling, full of strength and love.

But she murmured: "Oh! how I suffer! It is all over, I am going to die."

Her father darted towards her; her mother sustained her, throwing her arms around her like invincible armor which would shield her from all harm.

"Don't talk like that, you unhappy girl! It is nothing; it is only another attack which will pass away. Get into bed again, for mercy's sake. Your old friend Boutan is on his way here. You will be up and well again to-morrow."

"No, no, I am going to die; it is all over."

She fell back in their arms; they only had time to lay her on her bed. And the thunderbolt fell: without a word, without a glance, in a few minutes she died of congestion of the lungs.

Ah! the imbecile thunderbolt! Ah! the scythe, which with a single stroke blindly cuts down a whole springtide! It was all so brutally sudden, so utterly unexpected, that at first the stupefaction of Marianne and Mathieu was greater than their despair. In response to their cries the whole farm hastened up, the fearful news filled the place, and then all sank into the deep silence of death—all work, all life ceasing. And the other children were there, scared and overcome: little Nicolas, who did not yet understand things; Gregoire, the page of the previous day; Louise, Madeleine, and Marguerite, the three maids of honor, and their elders, Claire and Gervais, who felt the blow more deeply. And there were yet the others journeying away, Blaise, Denis, and Ambroise, travelling to Paris at that very moment, in ignorance of the unforeseen, frightful hatchet-stroke which had fallen on the family. Where would the terrible tidings reach them? In what cruel distress would they return! And the doctor who would soon arrive too! But all at once, amid the terror and confusion, there rang out the cries of Frederic, the poor dead girl's affianced lover. He shrieked his despair aloud, he was half mad, he wished to kill himself, saying that he was the murderer and that he ought to have prevented Rose from so rashly riding home through the storm! He had to be led away and watched for fear of some fresh misfortune. His sudden frenzy had gone to every heart; sobs burst forth and lamentations arose from the woful parents, from the brothers, the sisters, from the whole of stricken Chantebled, which death thus visited for the first time.

Ah, God! Rose on that bed of mourning, white, cold, and dead! She, the fairest, the gayest, the most loved! She, before whom all the others were ever in admiration—she of whom they were so proud, so fond! And to think that this blow should fall in the midst of hope, bright hope in long life and sterling happiness, but ten days before her wedding, and on the morrow of that day of wild gayety, all jests and laughter! They could again see her, full of life and so adorable with her happy youthful fancies—that princely reception and that royal procession. It had seemed as if those two coming weddings, celebrated the same day, would be like the supreme florescence of the family's long happiness and prosperity. Doubtless they had often experienced trouble and had even wept at times, but they had drawn closer together and consoled one another on such occasions; none had ever been cut off from the good-night embraces which healed every sore. And now the best was gone, death had come to say that absolute joy existed for none, that the most valiant, the happiest; never reaped the fulness of their hopes. There was no life without death. And they paid their share of the debt of human wretchedness, paid it the more dearly since they had made for themselves a larger sum of life. When everything germinates and grows around one, when one has determined on unreserved fruitfulness; on continuous creation and increase, how awful is the recall to the ever-present dim abyss in which the world is fashioned, on the day when misfortune falls, digs its first pit, and carries off a loved one! It is like a sudden snapping, a rending of the hopes which seemed to be endless, and a feeling of stupefaction comes at the discovery that one cannot live and love forever!

Ah! how terrible were the two days that followed: the farm itself lifeless, without sound save that of the breathing of the cattle, the whole family gathered together, overcome by the cruel spell of waiting, ever in tears while the poor corpse remained there under a harvest of flowers. And there was this cruel aggravation, that on the eve of the funeral, when the body had been laid in the coffin, it was brought down into that gallery where they had lunched so merrily while discussing how magnificently they might decorate it for the two weddings. It was there that the last funeral watch, the last wake, took place, and there were no evergreen shrubs, no garlands of foliage, merely four tapers which burnt there amid a wealth of white roses gathered in the morning, but already fading. Neither the mother nor the father was willing to go to bed that night. They remained, side by side, near the child whom mother-earth was taking back from them. They could see her quite little again, but sixteen months old, at the time of their first sojourn at Chantebled in the old tumbledown shooting-box, when she had just been weaned and they were wont to go and cover her up at nighttime. They saw her also, later on, in Paris, hastening to them in the morning, climbing up and pulling their bed to pieces with triumphant laughter. And they saw her yet more clearly, growing and becoming more beautiful even as Chantebled did, as if, indeed, she herself bloomed with all the health and beauty of that now fruitful land. Yet she was no more, and whenever the thought returned to them that they would never see her again, their hands sought one another, met in a woful clasp, while from their crushed and mingling hearts it seemed as if all life, all future, were flowing away to nihility. Now that a breach had been made, would not every other happiness be carried off in turn? And though the ten other children were there, from the little one five years old to the twins who were four-and-twenty, all clad in black, all gathered in tears around their sleeping sister, like a sorrow-stricken battalion rendering funeral honors, neither the father nor the mother saw or counted them: their hearts were rent by the loss of the daughter who had departed, carrying away with her some of their own flesh. And in that long bare gallery which the four candles scarcely lighted, the dawn at last arose upon that death watch, that last leave-taking.

Then grief again came with the funeral procession, which spread out along the white road between the lofty poplars and the green corn, that road over which Rose had galloped so madly through the storm. All the relations of the Froments, all their friends, all the district, had come to pay a tribute of emotion at so sudden and swift a death. Thus, this time, the cortege did stretch far away behind the hearse, draped with white and blooming with white roses in the bright sunshine. The whole family was present; the mother and the sisters had declared that they would only quit their loved one when she had been lowered into her last resting-place. And after the family came the friends, the Beauchenes, the Seguins, and others. But Mathieu and Marianne, worn out, overcome by suffering, no longer recognized people amid their tears. They only remembered on the morrow that they must have seen Morange, if indeed it were really Morange—that silent, unobtrusive, almost shadowy gentleman, who had wept while pressing their hands. And in like fashion Mathieu fancied that, in some horrible dream, he had seen Constance's spare figure and bony profile drawing near to him in the cemetery after the coffin had been lowered into the grave, and addressing vague words of consolation to him, though he fancied that her eyes flashed the while as if with abominable exultation.

What was it that she had said? He no longer knew. Of course her words must have been appropriate, even as her demeanor was that of a mourning relative. But a memory returned to him, that of other words which she had spoken when promising to attend the two weddings.

She had then in bitter fashion expressed a wish that the good fortune of Chantebled might continue. But they, the Froments, so fruitful and so prosperous, were now stricken in their turn, and their good fortune had perhaps departed forever! Mathieu shuddered; his faith in the future was shaken; he was haunted by a fear of seeing prosperity and fruitfulness vanish, now that there was that open breach.

XVII

A year later the first child born to Ambroise and Andree, a boy, little Leonce, was christened. The young people had been married very quietly six weeks after the death of Rose. And that christening was to be the first outing for Mathieu and Marianne, who had not yet fully recovered from the terrible shock of their eldest daughter's death. Moreover, it was arranged that after the ceremony there should simply be a lunch at the parents' home, and that one and all should afterwards be free to return to his or her avocations. It was impossible for the whole family to come, and, indeed, apart from the grandfather and grandmother, only the twins, Denis and Blaise, and the latter's wife Charlotte, were expected, together with the godparents. Beauchene, the godfather, had selected Madame Seguin as his *commere*, for, since the death of Maurice, Constance shuddered at the bare thought of touching a child. At the same time she had promised to be present at the lunch, and thus there would be ten of them, sufficient to fill the little dining-room of the modest flat in the Rue de La Boetie, where the young couple resided pending fortune's arrival.

It was a very pleasant morning. Although Mathieu and Marianne had been unwilling to set aside their black garments even for this rejoicing, they ended by evincing some gentle gayety before the cradle of that little grandson, whose advent brought them a renewal of hope. Early in the winter a fresh bereavement had fallen on the family; Blaise had lost his little Christophe, then two and a half years old, through an attack of croup. Charlotte, however, was already at that time again *enceinte*, and thus the grief of the first days had turned to expectancy fraught with emotion.

The little flat in the Rue de La Boetie seemed very bright and fragrant; it was perfumed by the fair grace of Andree and illumined by the victorious charm of Ambroise, that handsome loving couple who, arm in arm, had set out so bravely to conquer the world. During the lunch, too, there was the formidable appetite and jovial laughter of Beauchene, who gave the greatest attention to his *commere* Valentine, jesting and paying her the most extravagant court, which afforded her much amusement, prone as she still was to play a girlish part, though she was already forty-five and a grandmother like Marianne. Constance alone remained grave, scarce condescending to bend her thin lips into a faint smile, while a shadow of deep pain passed over her withered face every time that she glanced round that gay table, whence new strength, based on the invincible future, arose in spite of all the recent mourning.

At about three o'clock Blaise rose from the table, refusing to allow Beauchene to take any more Chartreuse.

"It's true, he is right, my children," Beauchene ended by exclaiming in a docile way. "We are very comfortable here, but it is absolutely necessary that we should return to the works. And we must deprive you of Denis, for we need his help over a big building affair. That's how we are, we others, we don't shirk duty."

Constance had also risen. "The carriage must be waiting," said she; "will you take it?"

"No, no, we will go on foot. A walk will clear our heads."

The sky was overcast, and as it grew darker and darker Ambroise, going to the window, exclaimed: "You will get wet."

"Oh! the rain has been threatening ever since this morning, but we shall have time to get to the works."

It was then understood that Constance should take Charlotte with her in the brougham and set her down at the door of the little pavilion adjoining the factory. As for Valentine, she was in no hurry and could quietly return to the Avenue d'Antin, which was close by, as soon as the sky might clear. And with regard to Marianne and Mathieu, they had just yielded to Andree's affectionate entreaties, and had arranged to spend the whole day and dine there, returning to Chantebled by the last train. Thus the fete would be complete, and the young couple were enraptured at the prospect.

The departure of the others was enlivened by a curious incident, a mistake which Constance made, and which seemed very comical amid all the mirth promoted by the copious lunch. She had turned towards Denis, and, looking at him with her pale eyes, she quietly asked him "Blaise, my friend, will you give me my boa? I must have left it in the ante-room."

Everybody began to laugh, but she failed to understand the reason. And it was in the same tranquil way as before that she thanked Denis when he brought her the boa: "I am obliged to you, Blaise; you are very amiable."

Thereupon came an explosion; the others almost choked with laughter, so droll did her quiet assurance seem to them. What was the matter, then? Why did they all laugh at her in that fashion? She ended by suspecting that she had made a mistake, and looked more attentively at the twins.

"Ah, yes, it isn't Blaise, but Denis! But it can't be helped. I am always mistaking them since they have worn their beards trimmed in the same fashion."

Thereupon Marianne, in her obliging way, in order to take any sting away from the laughter, repeated the well-known family story of how she herself, when the twins were children and slept together, had been wont to awake them in order to identify them by the different color of their eyes. The others, Beauchene and Valentine, then intervened and recalled circumstances under which they also had mistaken the twins one for the other, so perfect was their resemblance on certain occasions, in certain lights. And it was amid all this gay animation that the company separated after exchanging all sorts of embraces and handshakes.

Once in the brougham, Constance spoke but seldom to Charlotte, taking as a pretext a violent headache which the prolonged lunch had increased. With a weary air and her eyes half closed she began to reflect. After Rose's death, and when little Christophe likewise had been carried off, a revival of hope had come to her, for all at once she had felt quite young again. But when she consulted Boutan on the matter he dealt her a final blow by informing her that her hopes were quite illusive. Thus, for two months now, her rage and despair had been increasing. That very morning at that christening, and now in that carriage beside that young woman who was again expecting to become a mother, it was this which poisoned her mind, filled her with jealousy and spite, and rendered her capable of any evil deed. The loss of her son, the childlessness to which she was condemned, all threw her into a state of morbid perversity, fraught with dreams of some monstrous vengeance which she dared not even confess to herself. She accused the whole world of being in league to crush her. Her husband was the most cowardly and idiotic of traitors, for he betrayed her by letting some fresh part of the works pass day by day into the hands of that fellow Blaise, whose wife no sooner lost a child than she had another. She, Constance, was enraged also at seeing her husband so gay and happy, since she had left him to his own base courses. He still retained his air of victorious superiority, declaring that he had remained unchanged, and there was truth in this; for though, instead of being an active master as formerly, he now too often showed himself a senile prowler, on the high road to paralysis, he yet continued to be a practical egotist, one who drew from life the greatest sum of enjoyment possible. He was following his destined road, and if he took to Blaise it was simply because he was delighted to have found an intelligent, hard-working young man who spared him all the cares and worries that were too heavy for his weary shoulders, while still earning for him the money which he needed for his pleasures. Constance knew that something in the way of a partnership arrangement was about to be concluded. Indeed, her husband must have already received a large sum to enable him to make good certain losses and expenses which he had hidden from her. And closing her eyes as the brougham rolled along, she poisoned her mind by ruminating all these things, scarce able to refrain from venting her fury by throwing herself upon that young woman Charlotte, well-loved and fruitful spouse, who sat beside her.

Then the thought of Denis occurred to her. Why was he being taken to the works? Did he also mean to rob her? Yet she knew that he had refused to join his brother, as in his opinion there was not room for two at the establishment of the Boulevard de Grenelle. Indeed, Denis's ambition was to direct some huge works by himself; he possessed an extensive knowledge of mechanics, and this it was that rendered him a valuable adviser whenever a new model of some important agricultural machine had to be prepared at the Beauchene factory. Constance promptly dismissed him from her thoughts; in her estimation there was no reason to fear him; he was a mere passer-by, who on the morrow, perhaps, would establish himself at the other end of France. Then once more the thought of Blaise came back to her, imperative, all-absorbing; and it suddenly occurred to her that if she made haste home she would be able to see Morange alone in his office and ascertain many things from him before the others arrived. It was evident that the accountant must know something of the partnership scheme, even if it were as yet only in a preliminary stage. Thereupon she became impassioned, eager to arrive, certain as she felt of obtaining confidential information from Morange, whom she deemed to be devoted to her.

As the carriage rolled over the Jena bridge she opened her eyes and looked out. "*Mon Dieu!*" said she, "what a time this brougham takes! If the rain would only fall it would, perhaps, relieve my head a little."

She was thinking, however, that a sharp shower would give her more time, as it would compel the three men, Beauchene, Denis, and Blaise, to seek shelter in some doorway. And when the carriage reached the works she hastily stopped the coachman, without even conducting her companion to the little pavilion.

"You will excuse me, won't you, my dear?" said she; "you only have to turn the street corner."

When they had both alighted, Charlotte, smiling and affectionate, took hold of Constance's hand and retained it for a few moments in her own.

"Of course," she replied, "and many thanks. You are too kind. When you see my husband, pray tell him that you left me safe, for he grows anxious at the slightest thing."

Thereupon Constance in her turn had to smile and promise with many professions of friendship that she would duly execute the commission. Then they parted. "Au revoir, till to-morrow"—"Yes, yes, till to-morrow, au revoir."

Eighteen years had now already elapsed since Morange had lost his wife Valerie; and nine had gone by since the death of his daughter Reine. Yet it always seemed as if he were on the morrow of those disasters, for he had retained his black garb, and still led a cloister-like, retired life, giving utterance only to such words as were indispensable. On the other hand, he had again become a good model clerk, a correct painstaking accountant, very punctual in his habits, and rooted as it were to the office chair in which he had taken his seat every morning for thirty years past. The truth was that his wife and his daughter had carried off with them all his will-power, all his ambitious thoughts, all that he had momentarily dreamt of winning for their sakes—a large fortune and a luxurious triumphant life. He, who was now so much alone, who had relapsed into childish timidity and weakness, sought nothing beyond his humble daily task, and was content to die in the shady corner to which he was accustomed. It was suspected, however, that he led a mysterious maniacal life, tinged with anxious jealousy, at home, in that flat of the Boulevard de Grenelle which he had so obstinately refused to quit. His servant had orders to admit nobody, and she herself knew nothing. If he gave her free admittance to the dining- and drawing-rooms, he did not allow her to set foot in his own bedroom, formerly shared by Valerie, nor in that which Reine had occupied. He himself alone entered these chambers, which he regarded as sanctuaries, of which he was the sole priest. Under pretence of sweeping or dusting, he would shut himself up in one or the other of them for hours at a time. It was in vain that the servant tried to glance inside, in vain that she listened at the doors when he spent his holidays at home; she saw nothing and heard nothing. Nobody could have told what relics those chapels contained, nor with what religious cult he honored them. Another cause of surprise was his niggardly, avaricious life, which, as time went on, had become more and more pronounced, in such wise that his only expenses were his rental of sixteen hundred francs, the wages he paid to his servant, and the few pence per day which she with difficulty extracted from him to defray the cost of food and housekeeping. His salary had now risen to eight thousand francs a year, and he certainly did not spend half of it. What became, then, of his big savings, the money which he refused to devote to enjoyment? In what secret hole, and for what purpose, what secret passion, did he conceal it? Nobody could tell. But amid it all he remained very gentle, and, unlike most misers, continued very cleanly in his habits, keeping his beard, which was now white as snow, very carefully tended. And he came to his office every morning with a little smile on his face, in such wise that nothing in this man of regular methodical life revealed the collapse within him, all the ashes and smoldering fire which disaster had left in his heart.

By degrees a link of some intimacy had been formed between Constance and Morange. When, after his daughter's death, she had seen him return to the works quite a wreck, she had been stirred by deep pity, with which some covert personal anxiety confusedly mingled. Maurice was destined to live five years longer, but she was already haunted by apprehensions, and could never meet Morange without experiencing a chilling shudder, for he, as she repeated to herself, had lost his only child. "Ah, God! so such a catastrophe was possible." Then, on being stricken herself, on experiencing the horrible distress, on smarting from the sudden, gaping, incurable wound of her bereavement, she had drawn nearer to that brother in misfortune, treating him with a kindness which she showed to none other. At times she would invite him to spend an evening with her, and the pair of them would chat together, or more often remain silent, face to face, sharing each other's woe. Later on she had profited by this intimacy to obtain information from Morange respecting affairs at the factory, of which her husband avoided speaking. It was more particularly since she had suspected the latter of bad management, blunders and debts, that she endeavored to turn the accountant into a confidant, even a spy, who might aid her to secure as much control of the business as possible. And this was why she was so anxious to return to the factory that day, and profit by the opportunity to see Morange privately, persuaded as she was that she would induce him to speak out in the absence of his superiors.

She scarcely tarried to take off her gloves and her bonnet. She found the accountant in his little office, seated in his wonted place, and leaning over the everlasting ledger which was open before him.

"Why, is the christening finished?" he exclaimed in astonishment.

Forthwith she explained her presence in such a way as to enable her to speak of what she had at heart. "Why, yes. That is to say, I came away because I had such a dreadful headache. The others have remained yonder. And as we are alone here together it occurred to me that it might do me good to have a chat with you. You know how highly I esteem you. Ah! I am not happy, not happy at all."

She had sunk upon a chair overcome by the tears which she had been restraining so long in the presence of the happiness of others. Quite upset at seeing her in this condition, having little strength himself, Morange wished to summon her maid. He almost feared that she might have a fainting fit. But she prevented him.

"I have only you left me, my friend," said she. "Everybody else forsakes me, everybody is against me. I can feel it; I am being ruined; folks are bent on annihilating me, as if I had not already lost everything when I lost my child. And since you alone remain to me, you who know my torments, you who have no daughter left you, pray for heaven's sake help me and tell me the truth! In that wise I shall at least be able to defend myself."

On hearing her speak of his daughter Morange also had begun to weep. And now, therefore, she might question him, it was certain that he would answer and tell her everything, overpowered as he was by the common grief which she had evoked. Thus he informed her that an agreement was indeed on the point of being signed by Blaise and Beauchene, only it was not precisely a deed of partnership. Beauchene having drawn large sums from the strong-box of the establishment for expenses which he could not confess—a horrible story of blackmailing, so it was rumored—had been obliged to make a confidant of Blaise, the trusty and active lieutenant who managed the establishment. And he had even asked him to find somebody willing to lend him some money. Thereupon the young man had offered it himself; but doubtless it was his father, Mathieu Froment, who advanced the cash, well pleased to invest it in the works in his son's name. And now, with the view of putting everything in order, it had been resolved that the property should be divided into six parts, and that one of these parts or shares should be attributed to Blaise as reimbursement for the loan. Thus the young fellow would possess an interest of one sixth in the establishment, unless indeed Beauchene should buy him out again within a stipulated period. The danger was that, instead of freeing himself in this fashion, Beauchene might yield to the temptation of selling the other parts one by one, now that he was gliding down a path of folly and extravagance.

Constance listened to Morange, quivering and quite pale. "Is this signed?" she asked.

"No, not yet. But the papers are ready and will be signed shortly. Moreover, it is a reasonable and necessary solution of the difficulty."

She was evidently of another opinion. A feeling of revolt possessed her, and she strove to think of some decisive means of preventing the ruin and shame which in her opinion threatened her. "My God, what am I to do? How can I act?" she gasped; and then, in her rage at finding no device, at being powerless, this cry escaped her: "Ah! that scoundrel Blaise!"

Worthy Morange was quite moved by it. Still he had not fully understood. And so, in his quiet way, he endeavored to calm Constance, explaining that Blaise had a very good heart, and that in the circumstances in question he had behaved in the best way possible, doing all that he could to stifle scandal, and even displaying great disinterestedness. And as Constance had risen, satisfied with knowing the truth, and anxious that the three men might not find her there on their arrival, the accountant likewise quitted his chair, and accompanied her along the gallery which she had to follow in order to return to her house.

"I give you my word of honor, madame," said Morange, "that the young man has made no base calculations in the matter. All the papers pass through my hands, and nobody could know more than I know myself. Besides, if I had entertained the slightest doubt of any machination, I should have endeavored to requite your kindness by warning you."

She no longer listened to him, however; in fact, she was anxious to get rid of him, for all at once the long-threatening rain had begun to fall violently, lashing the glass roof. So dark a mass of clouds had overspread the sky that it was almost night in the gallery, though four o'clock had scarcely struck. And it occurred to Constance that in presence of such a deluge the three men would certainly take a cab. So she hastened her steps, still followed, however, by the accountant.

"For instance," he continued, "when it was a question of drawing up the agreement—"

But he suddenly paused, gave vent to a hoarse exclamation, and stopped her, pulling her back as if in terror.

"Take care!" he gasped.

There was a great cavity before them. Here, at the end of the gallery, before reaching the corridor which communicated with the private house, there was a steam lift of great power, which was principally used for lowering heavy articles to the packing room. It only worked as a rule on certain days; on all others the huge trap remained closed. When the appliance was working a watchman was always stationed there to superintend the operations.

"Take care! take care!" Morange repeated, shuddering with terror.

The trap was open, and the huge cavity gaped before them; there was no barrier, nothing to warn them and prevent them from making a fearful plunge. The rain still pelted on the glass roof, and the darkness had become so complete in the gallery that they had walked on without seeing anything before them. Another step would have hurled them to destruction. It was little short of miraculous that the accountant should have become anxious in presence of the increasing gloom in that corner, where he had divined rather than perceived the abyss.

Constance, however, still failing to understand her companion, sought to free herself from his wild grasp.

"But look!" he cried.

And he bent forward and compelled her also to stoop over the cavity. It descended through three floors to the very lowest basement, like a well of darkness. A damp odor arose: one could scarce distinguish the vague outlines of thick ironwork; alone, right at the bottom, burnt a lantern, a distant speck of light, as if the better to indicate the depth and horror of the gulf. Morange and Constance drew back again blanching.

And now Morange burst into a temper. "It is idiotic!" he exclaimed. "Why don't they obey the regulations! As a rule there is a man here, a man expressly told off for this duty, who ought not to stir from his post so long as the trap has not come up again. Where is he? What on earth can the rascal be up to?"

The accountant again approached the hole, and shouted down it in a fury: "Bonnard!"

No reply came: the pit remained bottomless, black and void.

"Bonnard! Bonnard!"

ÉMILE ZOLA

And still nothing was heard, not a sound; the damp breath of the darkness alone ascended as from the deep silence of the tomb.

Thereupon Morange resorted to action. "I must go down; I must find Bonnard. Can you picture us falling through that hole to the very bottom? No, no, this cannot be allowed. Either he must close this trap or return to his post. What can he be doing? Where can he be?"

Morange had already betaken himself to a little winding staircase, by which one reached every floor beside the lift, when in a voice which gradually grew more indistinct, he again called: "I beg you, madame, pray wait for me; remain there to warn anybody who might pass."

Constance was alone. The dull rattle of the rain on the glass above her continued, but a little livid light was appearing as a gust of wind carried off the clouds. And in that pale light Blaise suddenly appeared at the end of the gallery. He had just returned to the factory with Denis and Beauchene, and had left his companions together for a moment, in order to go to the workshops to procure some information they required. Preoccupied, absorbed once more in his work, he came along with an easy step, his head somewhat bent. And when Constance saw him thus appear, all that she felt in her heart was the smart of rancor, a renewal of her anger at what she had learnt of that agreement which was to be signed on the morrow and which would despoil her. That enemy who was in her home and worked against her, a revolt of her whole being urged her to exterminate him, and thrust him out like some usurper, all craft and falsehood.

He drew nearer. She was in the dense shadow near the wall, so that he could not see her. But on her side, as he softly approached steeped in a grayish light, she could see him with singular distinctness. Never before had she so plainly divined the power of his lofty brow, the intelligence of his eyes, the firm will of his mouth. And all at once she was struck with fulgural certainty; he was coming towards the cavity without seeing it and he would assuredly plunge into the depths unless she should stop him as he passed. But a little while before, she, like himself, had come from yonder, and would have fallen unless a friendly hand had restrained her; and the frightful shudder of that moment yet palpitated in her veins; she could still and ever see the damp black pit with the little lantern far below. The whole horror of it flashed before her eyes—the ground failing one, the sudden drop with a great shriek, and the smash a moment afterwards.

Blaise drew yet nearer. But certainly such a thing was impossible; she would prevent it, since a little motion of her hand would suffice.

Would she not always have time to stretch out her arms when he was there before her? And yet from the recesses of her being a very clear and frigid voice seemed to ascend, articulating brief words which rang in her ears as if repeated by a trumpet blast. If he should die it would be all over, the factory would never belong to him. She who had bitterly lamented that she could devise no obstacle had merely to let this helpful chance take its own course. And this, indeed, was what the voice said, what it repeated with keen insistence, never adding another syllable. After that there would be nothing. After that there would merely remain the shattered remnants of a suppressed man, and a pit of darkness splashed with blood, in which she discerned, foresaw nothing more. What would happen on the morrow? She did not wish to know; indeed there would be no morrow. It was solely the brutal immediate fact which the imperious voice demanded. He dead, it would be all over, he would never possess the works.

He drew nearer still. And within her now there raged a frightful battle. How long did it last—days? years? Doubtless but a few seconds. She was still resolved that she would stop him as he passed, certain as she felt that she would conquer her horrible thoughts when the moment came for the decisive gesture. And yet those thoughts invaded her, became materialized within her, like some physical craving, thirst or hunger. She hungered for that finish, hungered to the point of suffering, seized by one of those sudden desperate longings which beget crime; such as when a passer-by is despoiled and throttled at the corner of a street. It seemed to her that if she could not satisfy her craving she herself must lose her life. A consuming passion, a mad desire for that man's annihilation filled her as she saw him approach. She could now see him still more plainly and the sight of him exasperated her. His forehead, his eyes, his lips tortured her like some hateful spectacle. Another step, yet one more, then another, and he would be before her. Yes, yet another step, and she was already stretching out her hand in readiness to stop him as soon as he should brush past.

He came along. What was it that happened? O God! When he was there, so absorbed in his thoughts that he brushed against her without feeling her, she turned to stone. Her hand became icy cold, she could not lift it, it hung too heavily from her arm. And amid her scorching fever a great cold shudder came upon her, immobilizing and stupefying her, while she was deafened by the clamorous voice rising from the depths of her being. All demur was swept away; the craving for that death remained intense, invincible, beneath the imperious stubborn call of the inner voice which robbed her of the power of will and action. He would be dead and he would never possess the works. And therefore, standing stiff and breathless against the wall, she did not stop him. She could hear his light breathing, she could discern his profile, then the nape of his neck. He had passed. Another step, another step! And yet if she had raised a call she might still have changed the course of destiny even at that last moment. She fancied that she had some such intention, but she was clenching her teeth tightly enough to break them. And he, Blaise, took yet a further step, still advancing quietly and confidently over that friendly ground, without even a glance before him, absorbed as he was in thoughts of his work. And the ground failed him, and there was a loud, terrible cry, a sudden gust following the fall, and a dull crash down below in the depths of the black darkness.

Constance did not stir. For a moment she remained as if petrified, still listening, still waiting. But only deep silence arose from the abyss. She could merely hear the rain pelting on the glass roof with renewed rage. And thereupon she fled, turned into the passage, re-entered her drawing-room. There she collected and questioned herself. Had she desired that abominable thing? No, her will had had nought to do with it. Most certainly it had been paralyzed, prevented from acting. If it had been possible for the thing to occur, it had occurred quite apart from her, for assuredly she had been absent. Absent, that word reassured her. Yes, indeed, that was the case, she had been absent. All her past life spread out behind her, faultless, pure of any evil action. Never had she sinned, never until that day had any consciousness of guilt weighed upon her conscience. An honest and virtuous woman, she had remained upright amidst all the excesses of her husband. An impassioned mother, she had been ascending her calvary ever since her son's death. And this recollection of Maurice alone drew her for a moment from her callousness, choked her with a rising sob, as if in that direction lay her madness, the vainly sought explanation of the crime. Vertigo again fell upon her, the thought of her dead son and of the other being master in his place, all her perverted passion for that only son of hers, the despoiled prince, all her poisoned, fermenting rage which had unhinged and maddened her, even to the point of murder. Had that monstrous vegetation growing within her reached her brain then? A rush of blood suffices at times to bedim a conscience. But she obstinately clung to the view that she had been absent; she forced back her tears and remained frigid. No remorse came to her. It was done, and 'twas good that it should be done. It was necessary. She had not pushed him, he himself had fallen. Had she not been there he would have fallen just the same. And so since she had not been there, since both her brain and her heart had been absent, it did not concern her. And ever and ever resounded the words which absolved her and chanted her victory; he was dead, and would never possess the works.

Erect in the middle of the drawing-room, Constance listened, straining her ears. Why was it that she heard nothing? How long they were in going down to pick him up! Anxiously waiting for the tumult which she expected, the clamor of horror which would assuredly rise from the works, the heavy footsteps, the loud calls, she held her breath, quivering at the slightest, faintest sound. Several minutes still elapsed, and the cosey quietude of her drawing-room pleased her. That room was like an asylum of bourgeois rectitude, luxurious dignity, in which she felt protected, saved. Some little objects on which her eyes lighted, a pocket scent-bottle ornamented with an opal, a paper-knife of burnished silver left inside a book, fully reassured her. She was moved, almost surprised at the sight of them, as if they had acquired some new and particular meaning. Then she shivered slightly and perceived that her hands were icy cold. She rubbed them together gently, wishing to warm them a little. Why was it, too, that she now felt so tired? It seemed to her as if she had just returned from some long walk, from some accident, from some affray in which she had been bruised. She felt within her also a tendency to somnolence, the somnolence of satiety, as if she had feasted too copiously off some spicy dish, after too great a hunger. Amid the fatigue which benumbed her limbs she desired nothing more; apart from her sleepiness all that she felt was a kind of astonishment that things should be as they were. However, she had again begun to listen, repeating that if that frightful silence continued, she would certainly sink upon a chair, close her eyes, and sleep. And at last it seemed to her that she detected a faint sound, scarcely a breath, far away.

What was it? No, there was nothing yet. Perhaps she had dreamt that horrible scene, perhaps it had all been a nightmare; that man marching on, that black pit, that loud cry of terror! Since she heard nothing, perhaps nothing had really happened. Were it true a clamor would have ascended from below in a growing wave of sound, and a distracted rush up the staircase and along the passages would have brought her the news. Then again she detected the faint distant sound, which seemed to draw a little nearer. It was not the tramping of a crowd; it seemed to be a mere footfall, perhaps that of some pedestrian on the quay. Yet no; it came from the works, and now it was quite distinct; it ascended steps and then sped along a passage. And the steps became quicker, and a panting could be heard, so tragical that she at last divined that the horror was at hand. All at once the door was violently flung open. Morange entered. He was alone, beside himself, with livid face and scarce able to stammer.

"He still breathes, but his head is smashed; it is all over."

"What ails you?" she asked. "What is the matter?"

He looked at her, agape. He had hastened upstairs at a run to ask her for an explanation, for he had quite lost his poor head over that unaccountable catastrophe. And the apparent ignorance and tranquillity in which he found Constance completed his dismay.

"But I left you near the trap," said he.

"Near the trap, yes. You went down, and I immediately came up here."

"But before I went down," he resumed with despairing violence, "I begged you to wait for me and keep a watch on the hole, so that nobody might fall through it."

"Oh! dear no. You said nothing to me, or, at all events, I heard nothing, understood nothing of that kind."

In his terror he peered into her eyes. Assuredly she was lying. Calm as she might appear, he could detect her voice trembling. Besides, it was evident she must still have been there, since he had not even had time to get below before it happened. And all at once he recalled their conversation, the questions she had asked him and her cry of hatred against the unfortunate young fellow who had now been picked up, covered with blood, in the depths of that abyss. Beneath the gust of horror which chilled him, Morange could only find these words: "Well, madame, poor Blaise came just behind you and broke his skull."

Her demeanor was perfect; her hands quivered as she raised them, and it was in a halting voice that she exclaimed: "Good Lord! good Lord, what a frightful misfortune."

But at that moment an uproar arose through the house. The drawing-room door had remained open, and the voices and footsteps of a number of people drew nearer, became each moment more distinct. Orders were being given on the stairs, men were straining and drawing breath, there were all the signs of the approach of some cumbrous burden, carried as gently as possible.

"What! is he being brought up here to me?" exclaimed Constance turning pale, and her involuntary cry would have sufficed to enlighten the accountant had he needed it. "He is being brought to me here!"

It was not Morange who answered; he was stupefied by the blow. But Beauchene abruptly appeared preceding the body, and he likewise was livid and beside himself, to such a degree did this sudden visit of death thrill him with fear, in his need of happy life.

"Morange will have told you of the frightful catastrophe, my dear," said he. "Fortunately Denis was there, for the question of responsibility towards his family. And it was Denis, too, who, just as we were about to carry the poor fellow home to the pavilion, opposed it, saying that, given his wife's condition, we should kill her if we carried him to her in this dying state. And so the only course was to bring him here, was it not?"

Then he quitted his wife with a gesture of bewilderment, and returned to the landing, where one could hear him repeating in a quivering voice: "Gently, gently, take care of the balusters."

The lugubrious train entered the drawing-room. Blaise had been laid on a stretcher provided with a mattress. Denis, as pale as linen, followed, supporting the pillow on which rested his brother's head. A little streamlet of blood coursed over the dying man's brow, his eyes were closed. And four factory hands held the shafts of the stretcher. Their heavy shoes crushed down the carpet, and fragile articles of furniture were thrust aside anyhow to open a passage for this invasion of horror and of fright.

Amid his bewilderment, an idea occurred to Beauchene, who continued to direct the operation.

"No, no, don't leave him there. There is a bed in the next room. We will take him up very gently with the mattress, and lay him with it on the bed."

It was Maurice's room; it was the bed in which Maurice had died, and which Constance with maternal piety had kept unchanged, consecrating the room to her son's memory. But what could she say? How could she prevent Blaise from dying there in his turn, killed by her?

The abomination of it all, the vengeance of destiny which exacted this sacrilege, filled her with such a feeling of revolt that at the moment when vertigo was about to seize her and the flooring began to flee from beneath her feet, she was lashed by it and kept erect. And then she displayed extraordinary strength, will, and insolent courage. When the stricken man passed before her, her puny little frame stiffened and grew. She looked at him, and her yellow face remained motionless, save for a flutter of her eyelids and an involuntary nervous twinge on the left side of her mouth, which forced a slight grimace. But that was all, and again she became perfect both in words and gesture, doing and saying what was necessary without lavishness, but like one simply thunderstruck by the suddenness of the catastrophe.

However, the orders had been carried out in the bedroom, and the bearers withdrew greatly upset. Down below, directly the accident had been discovered, old Moineaud had been told to take a cab and hasten to Dr. Boutan's to bring him back with a surgeon, if one could be found on the way.

"All the same, I prefer to have him here rather than in the basement," Beauchene repeated mechanically as he stood before the bed. "He still breathes. There! see, it is quite apparent. Who knows? Perhaps Boutan may be able to pull him through, after all."

Denis, however, entertained no illusions. He had taken one of his brother's cold yielding hands in his own and he could feel that it was again becoming a mere thing, as if broken, wrenched away from life in that great fall. For a moment he remained motionless beside the death-bed, with the mad hope they he might, perhaps, by his clasp infuse a little of the blood in his own heart into the veins of the dying man. Was not that blood common to them both? Had not their twin brotherhood drunk life from the same source? It was the other half of himself that was about to die. Down below, after raising a loud cry of heartrending distress, he had said nothing. Now all at once he spoke.

"One must go to Ambroise's to warn my mother and father. Since he still breathes, perhaps they will arrive soon enough to embrace him."

"Shall I go to fetch them?" Beauchene good-naturedly inquired.

"No, no! thanks. I did at first think of asking that service of you, but I have reflected. Nobody but myself can break this horrible news to mamma. And nothing must be done as yet with regard to Charlotte. We will see about that by and by, when I come back. I only hope that death will have a little patience, so that I may find my poor brother still alive."

He leant forward and kissed Blaise, who with his eyes closed remained motionless, still breathing faintly. Then distractedly Denis printed another kiss upon his hand and hurried off.

Constance meantime was busying herself, calling the maid, and requesting her to bring some warm water in order that they might wash the sufferer's blood-stained brow. It was impossible to think of taking off his jacket; they had to content themselves with doing the little they could to improve his appearance pending the arrival of the doctor. And during these preparations, Beauchene, haunted, worried by the accident, again began to speak of it.

"It is incomprehensible. One can hardly believe such a stupid mischance to be possible. Down below the transmission gearing gets out of order, and this prevents the mechanician from sending the trap up again. Then, up above, Bonnard gets angry, calls, and at last decides to go down in a fury when he finds that nobody answers him. Then Morange arrives, flies into a temper, and goes down in his turn, exasperated at receiving no answer to his calls for Bonnard. Poor Bonnard! he's sobbing; he wanted to kill himself when he saw the fine result of his absence."

At this point Beauchene abruptly broke off and turned to Constance. "But what about you?" he asked. "Morange told me that he had left you up above near the trap."

She was standing in front of her husband, in the full light which came through the window. And again did her eyelids beat while a little nervous twinge slightly twisted her mouth on the left side. That was all.

"I? Why I had gone down the passage. I came back here at once, as Morange knows very well."

A moment previously, Morange, annihilated, his legs failing him, had sunk upon a chair. Incapable of rendering any help, he sat there silent, awaiting the end. When he heard Constance lie in that quiet fashion, he looked at her. The assassin was herself, he no longer doubted it. And at that moment he felt a craving to proclaim it, to cry it aloud.

"Why, he thought that he had begged you to remain there on the watch," Beauchene resumed, addressing his wife.

"At all events his words never reached me," Constance duly answered. "Should I have moved if he had asked me to do that?" And turning towards the accountant she, in her turn, had the courage to fix her pale eyes upon him. "Just remember, Morange, you rushed down like a madman, you said nothing to me, and I went on my way."

Beneath those pale eyes, keen as steel, which dived into his own, Morange was seized with abject fear. All his weakness, his cowardice of heart returned. Could he accuse her of such an atrocious crime? He pictured the consequences. And then, too, he no longer knew if he were right or not; his poor maniacal mind was lost.

"It is possible," he stammered, "I may simply have thought I spoke. And it must be so since it can't be otherwise."

Then he relapsed into silence with a gesture of utter lassitude. The complicity demanded was accepted. For a moment he thought of rising to see if Blaise still breathed; but he did not dare. Deep peacefulness fell upon the room.

Ah! how great was the anguish, the torture in the cab, when Blaise brought Mathieu and Marianne back with him. He had at first spoken to them simply of an accident, a rather serious fall. But as the vehicle rolled along he had lost his self-possession, weeping and confessing the truth in response to their despairing questions. Thus, when they at last reached the factory, they doubted no longer, their child was dead. Work had just been stopped, and they recalled their visit to the place on the morrow of Maurice's death. They were returning to the same stillness, the same grave-like silence. All the rumbling life had suddenly ceased, the machines were cold and mute, the workshops darkened and deserted. Not a sound remained, not a soul, not a puff of that steam which was like the very breath of the place. He who had watched over its work was dead, and it was dead like him. Then their affright increased when they passed from the factory to the house amid that absolute solitude, the gallery steeped in slumber, the staircase quivering, all the doors upstairs open, as in some uninhabited place long since deserted. In the ante-room they found no servant. And it was indeed in the same tragedy of sudden death that they again participated, only this time it was their own son whom they were to find in the same room, on the same bed, frigid, pale, and lifeless.

Blaise had just expired. Boutan was there at the head of the bed, holding the inanimate hand in which the final pulsation of blood was dying away. And when he saw Mathieu and Marianne, who had instinctively crossed the disorderly drawing-room, rushing into that bedchamber whose odor of nihility they recognized, he could but murmur in a voice full of sobs:

"My poor friends, embrace him; you will yet have a little of his last breath."

That breath had scarce ceased, and the unhappy mother, the unhappy father, had already sprung forward, kissing those lips that exhaled the final quiver of life, and sobbing and crying their distress aloud. Their Blaise was dead. Like Rose, he had died suddenly, a year later, on a day of festivity. Their heart wound, scarce closed as yet, opened afresh with a tragic rending. Amid their long felicity this was the second time that they were thus terribly recalled to human wretchedness; this was the second hatchet stroke which fell on the flourishing, healthy, happy family. And their fright increased. Had they not yet finished paying their accumulated debt to misfortune? Was slow destruction now arriving with blow following blow? Already since Rose had quitted them, her bier strewn with flowers, they had feared to see their prosperity and fruitfulness checked and interrupted now that there was an open breach. And to-day, through that bloody breach, their Blaise departed in the most frightful of fashions, crushed as it were by the jealous anger of destiny. And now what other of their children would be torn away from them on the morrow to pay in turn the ransom of their happiness?

Mathieu and Marianne long remained sobbing on their knees beside the bed. Constance stood a few paces away, silent, with an air of quivering desolation. Beauchene, as if to combat that fear of death which made him shiver, had a moment previously seated himself at the little writing-table formerly used by Maurice, which had been left in the drawing-room like a souvenir. And he then strove to draw up a notice to his workpeople, to inform them that the factory would remain closed until the day after the funeral. He was vainly seeking words when he perceived Denis coming out of the bedroom, where he had wept all his tears and set his whole heart in the last kiss which he had bestowed on his departed brother. Beauchene called him, as if desirous of diverting him from his gloomy thoughts. "There, sit down here and continue this," said he.

Constance, in her turn entering the drawing-room, heard those words. They were virtually the same as the words which her husband had pronounced when making Blaise seat himself at that same table of Maurice's, on the day when he had given him the place of that poor boy, whose body almost seemed to be still lying on the bed in the adjoining room. And she recoiled with fright on seeing Denis seated there and writing. Had not Blaise resuscitated? Even as she had mistaken the twins one for the other that very afternoon on rising from the gay baptismal lunch, so now again she saw Blaise in Denis, the pair of them so similar physically that in former times their parents had only been able to distinguish them by the different color of their eyes. And thus it was as if Blaise returned and resumed his place; Blaise, who would possess the works although she had killed him. She had made a mistake; dead as he was, he would nevertheless have the works. She had killed one of those Froments, but behold another was born. When one died his brother filled up the breach. And her crime then appeared to her such a useless one, such a stupid one, that she was aghast at it, the hair on the nape of her neck standing up, while she burst into a cold sweat of fear, and recoiled as from a spectre.

"It is a notice for the workpeople," Beauchene repeated. "We will have it posted at the entrance."

She wished to be brave, and, approaching her husband, she said to him: "Draw it up yourself. Why give Blaise the trouble at such a moment as this?"

She had said "Blaise"; and once more an icy sensation of horror came over her. Unconsciously she had heard herself saying yonder, in the ante-room: "Blaise, where did I put my boa?" And it was Denis who had brought it to her. Of what use had it been for her to kill Blaise, since Denis was there? When death mows down a soldier of life, another is always ready to take the vacant post of combat.

But a last defeat awaited her. Mathieu and Marianne reappeared, while Morange, seized with a need of motion, came and went with an air of stupefaction, quite losing his wits amid his dreadful sufferings, those awful things which could but unhinge his narrow mind.

"I am going down," stammered Marianne, trying to wipe away her tears and to remain erect. "I wish to see Charlotte, and prepare and tell her of the misfortune. I alone can find the words to say, so that she may not die of the shock, circumstanced as she is."

But Mathieu, full of anxiety, sought to detain his wife, and spare her this fresh trial. "No, I beg you," he said; "Denis will go, or I will go myself."

With gentle obstinacy, however, she still went towards the stairs. "I am the only one who can tell her of it, I assure you—I shall have strength—"

But all at once she staggered and fainted. It became necessary to lay her on a sofa in the drawing-room. And when she recovered consciousness, her face remained quite white and distorted, and an attack of nausea came upon her. Then, as Constance, with an air of anxious solicitude, rang for her maid and sent for her little medicine-chest, Mathieu confessed the truth, which hitherto had been kept secret; Marianne, like Charlotte, was *enceinte*. It confused her a little, he said, since she was now three-and-forty years old; and so they had not mentioned it. "Ah! poor brave wife!" he added. "She wished to spare our daughter-in-law too great a shock; I trust that she herself will not be struck down by it."

Enceinte, good heavens! As Constance heard this, it seemed as if a bludgeon were falling on her to make her defeat complete. And so, even if she should now let Denis, in his turn, kill himself, another Froment was coming who would replace him. There was ever another and another of that race—a swarming of strength, an endless fountain of life, against which it became impossible to battle. Amid her stupefaction at finding the breach repaired when scarce opened, Constance realized her powerlessness and nothingness, childless as she was fated to remain. And she felt vanquished, overcome with awe, swept away as it were herself; thrust aside by the victorious flow of everlasting Fruitfulness.

XVIII

Fourteen months later there was a festival at Chantebled. Denis, who had taken Blaise's place at the factory, was married to Marthe Desvignes. And after all the grievous mourning this was the first smile, the bright warm sun of springtime, so to say, following severe winter. Mathieu and Marianne, hitherto grief-stricken and clad in black, displayed a gayety tinged with soft emotion in presence of the sempiternal renewal of life. The mother had been willing to don less gloomy a gown, and the father had agreed to defer no longer a marriage that had long since been resolved upon, and was necessitated by all sorts of considerations. For more than two years now Rose had been sleeping in the little cemetery of Janville, and for more than a year Blaise had joined her there, beneath flowers which were ever fresh. And the souvenir of the dear dead ones, whom they all visited, and who had remained alive in all their hearts, was to participate in the coming festival. It was as if they themselves had decided with their parents that the hour for the espousals had struck, and that regret for their loss ought no longer to bar the joy of growth and increase.

Denis's installation at the Beauchene works in his brother's place had come about quite naturally. If he had not gone thither on leaving the science school where he had spent three years, it was simply because the position was at that time already held by Blaise. All his technical studies marked him out for the post. In a single day he had fitted himself for it, and he simply had to take up his quarters in the little pavilion, Charlotte having fled to Chantebled with her little Berthe directly after the horrible catastrophe. It should be added that Denis' entry into the establishment offered a convenient solution with regard to the large sum of money lent to Beauchene, which, it had been arranged, should be reimbursed by a sixth share in the factory. That money came from the family, and one brother simply took the place of the other, signing the agreement which the deceased would have signed. With a delicate rectitude, however, Denis insisted that out of his share of the profits an annuity should be assigned to Charlotte, his brother's widow.

Thus matters were settled in a week, in the manner that circumstances logically demanded, and without possibility of discussion. Constance, bewildered and overwhelmed, was not even able to struggle. Her husband reduced her to silence by repeating: "What would you have me do? I must have somebody to help me, and it is just as well to take Denis as a stranger. Besides, if he worries me I will buy him out within a year and give him his dismissal!"

At this Constance remained silent to avoid casting his ignominy in his face, amid her despair at feeling the walls of the house crumble and fall, bit by bit, upon her.

Once installed at the works, Denis considered that the time had come to carry out the matrimonial plans which he had long since arranged with Marthe Desvignes. The latter, Charlotte's younger sister and at one time the inseparable friend of Rose, had been waiting for him for nearly three years now, with her bright smile and air of affectionate good sense. They had known one another since childhood, and had exchanged many a vow along the lonely paths of Janville. But they had said to one another that they would do nothing prematurely, that for the happiness of a whole lifetime one might well wait until one was old enough and strong enough to undertake family duties. Some people were greatly astonished that a young man whose future was so promising, and whose position at twenty-six years of age was already a superb one, should thus obstinately espouse a penniless girl. Mathieu and Marianne smiled, however, and consented, knowing their son's good reasons. He had no desire to marry a rich girl who would cost him more than she brought, and he was delighted at having discovered a pretty, healthy, and very sensible and skilful young woman, who would be at all times his companion, helpmate, and consoler. He feared no surprises with her, for he had studied her; she united charm and good sense with kindliness, all that was requisite for the happiness of a household. And he himself was very good-natured, prudent, and sensible, and she knew it and willingly took his arm to tread life's path with him, certain as she felt that they would thus walk on together until life's end should be reached, ever advancing with the same tranquil step under the divine and limpid sun of reason merged in love.

Great preparations were made at Chantebled on the day before the wedding. Nevertheless, the ceremony was to remain of an intimate character, on account of the recent mourning. The only guests, apart from members of the family, were the Seguins and the Beauchenes, and even the latter were cousins. So there would scarcely be more than a score of them altogether, and only a lunch was to be given. One matter which gave them some brief concern was to decide where to set the table, and how to decorate it. Those early days of July were so bright and warm that they resolved to place it out of doors under the trees. There was a fitting and delightful spot in front of the old shooting-box, the primitive pavilion, which had been their first residence on their arrival in the Janville district. That pavilion was indeed like the family nest, the hearth whence it had radiated over the surrounding region. As the pavilion had threatened ruin, Mathieu had repaired and enlarged it with the idea of retiring thither with Marianne, and Charlotte and her children, as soon as he should cede the farm to his son Gervais, that being his intention. He was, indeed, pleased with the idea of living in retirement like a patriarch, like a king who had willingly abdicated, but whose wise counsel was still sought and accepted. In place of the former wild garden a large lawn now stretched before the pavilion, surrounded by some beautiful trees, elms and hornbeams. These Mathieu had planted, and he had watched them grow; thus they seemed to him to be almost part of his flesh. But his real favorite was an oak tree, nearly twenty years of age and already sturdy, which stood in the centre of the lawn, where he had planted it with Marianne, who had held the slender sapling in position while he plied his spade on the day when they had founded their domain of Chantebled. And near this oak, which thus belonged to their robust family, there was a basin of living water, fed by the captured springs of the plateau—water whose crystalline song made the spot one of continual joy.

It was here then that a council was held on the day before the wedding. Mathieu and Marianne repaired thither to see what preparations would be necessary, and they found Charlotte with a sketch-book on her knees, rapidly finishing an impression of the oak tree.

"What is that—a surprise?" they asked.

She smiled with some confusion. "Yes, yes, a surprise; you will see."

Then she confessed that for a fortnight past she had been designing in water colors a series of menu cards for the wedding feast. And, prettily and lovingly enough, her idea had been to depict children's games and children's heads; indeed, all the members of the family in their childish days. She had taken their likenesses from old photographs, and her sketch of the oak tree was to serve as a background for the portraits of the two youngest scions of the house—little Benjamin and little Guillaume.

Mathieu and Marianne were delighted with that fleet procession of little faces all white and pink which they perfectly recognized as they saw them pass before their eyes. There were the twins nestling in their cradle, locked in one another's arms; there was Rose, the dear lost one, in her little shift; there were Ambroise and Gervais, bare, and wrestling on a patch of grass; there were Gregoire and Nicolas birdnesting; there were Claire and the three other girls, Louise, Madeleine, and Marguerite, romping about the farm, quarrelling with the fowls, springing upon the horses' backs. But what particularly touched Marianne was the sketch of her last-born, little Benjamin, now nine months old, whom Charlotte had depicted reclining under the oak tree in the same little carriage as her own son Guillaume, who was virtually of the same age, having been born but eight days later.

"The uncle and the nephew," said Mathieu jestingly. "All the same, the uncle is the elder by a week."

As Marianne stood there smiling, soft tears came into her eyes, and the sketch shook in her happy hands.

"The dears!" said she; "my son and grandson. With those dear little ones I am once again a mother and a grandmother. Ah, yes! those two are the supreme consolation; they have helped to heal the wound; it is they who have brought us back hope and courage."

This was true. How overwhelming had been the mourning and sadness of the early days when Charlotte, fleeing the factory, had sought refuge at the farm! The tragedy by which Blaise had been carried off had nearly killed her. Her first solace was to see that her daughter Berthe, who had been rather sickly in Paris, regained bright rosy cheeks amid the open air of Chantebled. Moreover, she had settled her life: she would spend her remaining years, in that hospitable house, devoting herself to her two children, and happy in having so affectionate a grandmother and grandfather to help and sustain her. She had always shown herself to be somewhat apart from life, possessed of a dreamy nature, only asking to love and to be loved in return.

So by degrees she settled down once more, installed beside her grandparents in the old pavilion, which Mathieu fitted up for the three of them. And wishing to occupy herself, irrespective of her income from the factory, she even set to work again and painted miniatures, which a dealer in Paris readily purchased. But her grief was mostly healed by her little Guillaume, that child bequeathed to her by her dead husband, in whom he resuscitated. And it was much the same with Marianne since the birth of Benjamin. A new son had replaced the one she had lost, and helped to fill the void in her heart. The two women, the two mothers, found infinite solace in nursing those babes. For them they forgot themselves; they reared them together, watching them grow side by side; they gave them the breast at the same hours, and it was their desire to see them both become very strong, very handsome, and very good. Although one mother was almost twice as old as the other, they became, as it were, sisters. The same nourishing milk flowed from both their fruitful bosoms. And gleams of light penetrated their mourning: they began to laugh when they saw those little cherubs laugh, and nothing could have been gayer than the sight of that mother-in-law and that daughter-in-law side by side, almost mingling, having but one cradle between them, amid an unceasing florescence of maternity.

"Be careful," Mathieu suddenly said to Charlotte; "hide your drawings, here are Gervais and Claire coming about the table."

Gervais at nineteen years of age was quite a colossus, the tallest and the strongest of the family, with short, curly black hair, large bright eyes, and a full broad-featured face. He had remained his father's favorite son, the son of the fertile earth, the one in whom Mathieu fostered a love for the estate, a passion for skilful agriculture, in order that later on the young man might continue the good work which had been begun. Mathieu already disburdened himself on Gervais of a part of his duties, and was only waiting to see him married to give him the control of the whole farm. And he often thought of adjoining to him Claire when she found a husband in some worthy, sturdy fellow who would assume part of the labor. Two men agreeing well would be none too many for an enterprise which was increasing in importance every day. Since Marianne had again been nursing, Claire had been attending to her work. Though she had no beauty, she was of vigorous health and quite strong for her seventeen years. She busied herself more particularly with cookery and household affairs, but she also kept the accounts, being shrewd-witted and very economically inclined, on which account the prodigals of the family often made fun of her.

"And so it's here that the table is to be set," said Gervais; "I shall have to see that the lawn is mowed then."

On her side Claire inquired what number of people there would be at table and how she had better place them. Then, Gervais having called to Frederic to bring a scythe, the three of them went on discussing the arrangements. After Rose's death, Frederic, her betrothed, had continued working beside Gervais, becoming his most active and intelligent comrade and helper. For some months, too, Marianne and Mathieu had noticed that he was revolving around Claire, as though, since he had lost the elder girl, he were willing to content himself with the younger one, who was far less beautiful no doubt, but withal a good and sturdy housewife. This had at first saddened the parents. Was it possible to forget their dear daughter? Then, however, they felt moved, for the thought came to them that the family ties would be drawn yet closer, that the young fellow's heart would not roam in search of love elsewhere, but would remain with them. So closing their eyes to what went on, they smiled, for in Frederic, when Claire should be old enough to marry, Gervais would find the brother-in-law and partner that he needed.

The question of the table had just been settled when a sudden invasion burst through the tall grass around the oak tree; skirts flew about, and loose hair waved in the sunshine.

"Oh!" cried Louise, "there are no roses."

"No," repeated Madeleine, "not a single white rose."

"And," added Marguerite, "we have inspected all the bushes. There are no white roses, only red ones."

Thirteen, eleven, and nine, such were their respective ages. Louise, plump and gay, already looked a little woman; Madeleine, slim and pretty, spent hours at her piano, her eyes full of dreaminess; Marguerite, whose nose was rather too large and whose lips were thick, had beautiful golden hair. She would pick up little birds at winter time and warm them with her hands. And the three of, them, after scouring the back garden, where flowers mingled with vegetables, had now rushed up in despair at their vain search. No white roses for a wedding! That was the end of everything! What could they offer to the bride? And what could they set upon the table?

Behind the three girls, however, appeared Gregoire, with jeering mien, and his hands in his pockets. At fifteen he was very malicious, the most turbulent, worrying member of the family, a lad inclined to the most diabolical devices. His pointed nose and his thin lips denoted also his adventurous spirit, his will power, and his skill in effecting his object. And, apparently much amused by his sisters' disappointment, he forgot himself and exclaimed, by way of teasing them: "Why, I know where there are some white roses, and fine ones, too."

"Where is that?" asked Mathieu.

"Why, at the mill, near the wheel, in the little enclosure. There are three big bushes which are quite white, with roses as big as cabbages."

Then he flushed and became confused, for his father was eyeing him severely.

"What! do you still prowl round the mill?" said Mathieu. "I had forbidden you to do so. As you know that there are white roses in the enclosure you must have gone in, eh?"

"No; I looked over the wall."

"You climbed up the wall, that's the finishing touch! So you want to land me in trouble with those Lepailleurs, who are decidedly very foolish and very malicious people. There is really a devil in you, my boy."

That which Gregoire left unsaid was that he repaired to the enclosure in order that he might there join Therese, the miller's fair-haired daughter with the droll, laughing face, who was also a terribly adventurous damsel for her thirteen years. True, their meetings were but childish play, but at the end of the enclosure, under the apple trees, there was a delightful nook where one could laugh and chat and amuse oneself at one's ease.

"Well, just listen to me," Mathieu resumed. "I won't have you going to play with Therese again. She is a pretty little girl, no doubt. But that house is not a place for you to go to. It seems that they fight one another there now."

This was a fact. When that young scamp Antonin had recovered his health, he had been tormented by a longing to return to Paris, and had done all he could with that object, in view of resuming a life of idleness and dissipation. Lepailleur, greatly irritated at having been duped by his son, had at first violently opposed his plans. But what could he do in the country with that idle fellow, whom he himself had taught to hate the earth and to sneer at the old rotting mill. Besides, he now had his wife against him. She was ever admiring her son's learning, and so stubborn was her faith in him that she was convinced that he would this time secure a good position in the capital. Thus the father had been obliged to give way, and Antonin was now finally wrecking his life while filling some petty employment at a merchant's in the Rue du Mail. But, on the other hand, the quarrelling increased in the home, particularly whenever Lepailleur suspected his wife of robbing him in order to send money to that big lazybones, their son. From the bridge over the Yeuse on certain days one could hear oaths and blows flying about. And here again was family life destroyed, strength wasted, and happiness spoilt.

Carried off by perfect anger, Mathieu continued: "To think of it; people who had everything needful to be happy! How can one be so stupid? How can one seek wretchedness for oneself with such obstinacy?

As for that idea of theirs of an only son, and their vanity in wanting to make a gentleman of him, ah! well, they have succeeded finely! They must be extremely pleased to-day! It is just like Lepailleur's hatred of the earth, his old-fashioned system of cultivation, his obstinacy in leaving his bit of moorland barren and refusing to sell it to me, no doubt by way of protesting against our success! Can you imagine anything so stupid? And it's just like his mill; all folly and idleness he stands still, looking at it fall into ruins. He at least had a reason for that in former times; he used to say that as the region had almost renounced corn-growing, the peasants did not bring him enough grain to set his mill-stones working. But nowadays when, thanks to us, corn overflows on all sides, surely he ought to have pulled down his old wheel and have replaced it by a good engine. Ah! if I were in his place I would already have a new and bigger mill there, making all use of the water of the Yeuse, and connecting it with Janville railway station by a line of rails, which would not cost so much to lay down."

Gregoire stood listening, well pleased that the storm should fall on another than himself. And Marianne, seeing that her three daughters were still greatly grieved at having no white roses, consoled them, saying: "Well, for the table to-morrow morning you must gather those which are the lightest in color—the pale pink ones; they will do very well."

Thereupon Mathieu, calming down, made the children laugh, by adding gayly: "Gather the red ones too, the reddest you find. They will symbolize the blood of life!"

Marianne and Charlotte were still lingering there talking of all the preparations, when other little feet came tripping through the grass. Nicolas, quite proud of his seven years, was leading his niece Berthe, a big girl of six. They agreed very well together. That day they had remained indoors playing at "fathers and mothers" near the cradle occupied by Benjamin and Guillaume, whom they called their babies. But all at once the infants had awoke, clamoring for nourishment. And Nicolas and Berthe, quite alarmed, had thereupon run off to fetch the two mothers.

"Mamma!" called Nicolas, "Benjamin's asking for you. He's thirsty."

"Mamma, mamma!" repeated Berthe, "Guillaume's thirsty. Come quick, he's in a hurry."

Marianne and Charlotte laughed. True enough, the morrow's wedding had made them forget their pets; and so they hastily returned to the house.

On the following day those happy nuptials were celebrated in affectionate intimacy. There were but one-and-twenty at table under the oak tree in the middle of the lawn, which, girt with elms and hornbeams, seemed like a hall of verdure. The whole family was present: first those of the farm, then Denis the bridegroom, next Ambroise and his wife Andree, who had brought their little Leonce with them. And apart from the family proper, there were only the few invited relatives, Beauchene and Constance, Seguin and Valentine, with, of course, Madame Desvignes, the bride's mother. There were twenty-one at table, as has been said; but besides those one-and-twenty there were three very little ones present: Leonce, who at fifteen months had just been weaned, and Benjamin and Guillaume, who still took the breast. Their little carriages had been drawn up near, so that they also belonged to the party, which was thus a round two dozen. And the table, flowery with roses, sent forth a delightful perfume under the rain of summer sunbeams which flecked it with gold athwart the cool shady foliage. From one horizon to the other stretched the wondrous tent of azure of the triumphant July sky. And Marthe's white bridal gown, and the bright dresses of the girls, big and little; all those gay frocks, and all that fine youthful health, seemed like the very florescence of that green nook of happiness. They lunched joyously, and ended by clinking glasses in country fashion, while wishing all sorts of prosperity to the bridal pair and to everybody present.

Then, while the servants were removing the cloth, Seguin, who affected an interest in horse-breeding and cattle-raising, wished Mathieu to show him his stables. He had talked nothing but horseflesh during the meal, and was particularly desirous of seeing some big farm-horses, whose great strength had been praised by his host. He persuaded Beauchene to join him in the inspection, and the three men were starting, when Constance and Valentine, somewhat inquisitive with respect to that farm, the great growth of which still filled them with stupefaction, decided to follow, leaving the rest of the family installed under the trees, amid the smiling peacefulness of that fine afternoon.

The cow-houses and stables were on the right hand. But in order to reach them one had to cross the great yard, whence the entire estate could be seen. And here there was a halt, a sudden stopping inspired by admiration, so grandly did the work accomplished show forth under the sun. They had known that land dry and sterile, covered with mere scrub; they beheld it now one sea of waving corn, of crops whose growth increased at each successive season. Up yonder, on the old marshy plateau, the fertility was such, thanks to the humus amassed during long centuries, that Mathieu did not even manure the ground as yet. Then, to right and to left, the former sandy slopes spread out all greenery, fertilized by the springs which ever brought them increase of fruitfulness. And the very woods afar off, skilfully arranged, aired by broad clearings, seemed to possess more sap, as if all the surrounding growth of life had instilled additional vigor into them. With this vigor, this power, indeed, the whole domain was instinct; it was creation, man's labor fertilizing sterile soil, and drawing from it a wealth of nourishment for expanding humanity, the conqueror of the world.

There was a long spell of silence. At last Seguin, in his dry shrill voice, with a tinge of bitterness born of his own ruin, remarked: "You have done a good stroke of business. I should never have believed it possible."

Then they walked on again. But in the sheds, the cow-houses, the sheep-cotes, and all round, the sensation of strength and power yet increased. Creation was there continuing; the cattle, the sheep, the fowls, the rabbits, all that dwelt and swarmed there were incessantly increasing and multiplying. Each year the ark became too small, and fresh pens and fresh buildings were required. Life increased life; on all sides there were fresh broods, fresh flocks, fresh herds; all the conquering wealth of inexhaustible fruitfulness.

When they reached the stables Seguin greatly admired the big draught horses, and praised them with the expressions of a connoisseur. Then he returned to the subject of breeding, and cited some extraordinary results that one of his friends obtained by certain crosses. So far as the animal kingdom was concerned his ideas were sound enough, but when he came to the consideration of human kind he was as erratic as ever. As they walked back from the stables he began to descant on the population question, denouncing the century, and repeating all his old theories. Perhaps it was jealous rancor that impelled him to protest against the victory of life which the whole farm around him proclaimed so loudly. Depopulation! why, it did not extend fast enough. Paris, which wished to die, so people said, was really taking its time about it. All the same, he noticed some good symptoms, for bankruptcy was increasing on all sides—in science, politics, literature, and even art. Liberty was already dead. Democracy, by exasperating ambitious instincts and setting classes in conflict for power, was rapidly leading to a social collapse. Only the poor still had large families; the elite, the people of wealth and intelligence, had fewer and fewer children, so that, before final annihilation came, there might still be a last period of acceptable civilization, in which there would remain only a few men and women of supreme refinement, content with perfumes for sustenance and mere breath for enjoyment. He, however, was disgusted, for he now felt certain that he would not see that period since it was so slow in coming.

"If only Christianity would return to the primitive faith," he continued, "and condemn woman as an impure, diabolical, and harmful creature, we might go and lead holy lives in the desert, and in that way bring the world to an end much sooner. But the political Catholicism of nowadays, anxious to keep alive itself, allows and regulates marriage, with the view of maintaining things as they are. Oh! you will say, of course, that I myself married and that I have children, which is true; but I am pleased to think that they will redeem my fault. Gaston says that a soldier's only wife ought to be his sword, and so he intends to remain single; and as Lucie, on her side, has taken the veil at the Ursulines, I feel quite at ease. My race is, so to say, already extinct, and that delights me."

Mathieu listened with a smile. He was acquainted with that more or less literary form of pessimism. In former days all such views, as, for instance, the struggle of civilization against the birth-rate, and the relative childlessness of the most intelligent and able members of the community, had disturbed him. But since he had fought the cause of love he had found another faith. Thus he contented himself with saying rather maliciously: "But you forget your daughter Andree and her little boy Leonce."

"Oh! Andree!" replied Seguin, waving his hand as if she did not belong to him.

Valentine, however, had stopped short, gazing at him fixedly. Since their household had been wrecked and they had been leading lives apart, she no longer tolerated his sudden attacks of insane brutality and jealousy. By reason also of the squandering of their fortune she had a hold on him, for he feared that she might ask for certain accounts to be rendered her.

"Yes," he granted, "there is Andree; but then girls don't count."

They were walking on again when Beauchene, who had hitherto contented himself with puffing and chewing his cigar, for reserve was imposed upon him by the frightful drama of his own family life, was unable to remain silent any longer. Forgetful, relapsing into the extraordinary unconsciousness which always set him erect, like a victorious superior man, he spoke out loudly and boldly:

"I don't belong to Seguin's school, but, all the same, he says some true things. That population question greatly interests me even now, and I can flatter myself that I know it fully. Well, it is evident that Malthus was right. It is not allowable for people to have families without knowing how they will be able to nourish them. If the poor die of starvation it is their fault, and not ours."

Then he reverted to his usual lecture on the subject. The governing classes alone were reasonable in keeping to small families. A country could only produce a certain supply of food, and was therefore restricted to a certain population. People talked of the faulty division of wealth; but it was madness to dream of an Utopia, where there would be no more masters but only so many brothers, equal workers and sharers, who would apportion happiness among themselves like a birthday-cake. All the evil then came from the lack of foresight among the poor, though with brutal frankness he admitted that employers readily availed themselves of the circumstance that there was a surplus of children to hire labor at reduced rates.

Then, losing all recollection of the past, infatuated, intoxicated with his own ideas, he went on talking of himself. "People pretend that we are not patriots because we don't leave troops of children behind us. But that is simply ridiculous; each serves the country in his own way. If the poor folks give it soldiers, we give it our capital—all the proceeds of our commerce and industry. A fine lot of good would it do the country if we were to ruin ourselves with big families, which would hamper us, prevent us from getting rich, and afterwards destroy whatever we create by subdividing it. With our laws and customs there can be no substantial fortune unless a family is limited to one son. And yes, that is necessary; but one son—an only son—that is the only wise course; therein lies the only possible happiness."

It became so painful to hear him, in his position, speaking in that fashion, that the others remained silent, full of embarrassment. And he, thinking that he was convincing them, went on triumphantly: "Thus, I myself—"

But at this moment Constance interrupted him. She had hitherto walked on with bowed head amid that flow of chatter which brought her so much torture and shame, an aggravation, as it were, of her defeat. But now she raised her face, down which two big tears were trickling.

"Alexandre!" she said.

"What is it, my dear?"

He did not yet understand. But on seeing her tears, he ended by feeling disturbed, in spite of all his fine assurance. He looked at the others, and wishing to have the last word, he added: "Ah, yes! our poor child. But particular cases have nothing to do with general theories; ideas are still ideas."

Silence fell between them. They were now near the lawn where the family had remained. And for the last moment Mathieu had been thinking of Morange, whom he had also invited to the wedding, but who had excused himself from attending, as if he were terrified at the idea of gazing on the joy of others, and dreaded, too, lest some sacrilegious attempt should be made in his absence on the mysterious sanctuary where he worshipped. Would he, Morange—so Mathieu wondered—have clung like Beauchene to his former ideas? Would he still have defended the theory of the only child; that hateful, calculating theory which had cost him both his wife and his daughter? Mathieu could picture him flitting past, pale and distracted, with the step of a maniac hastening to some mysterious end, in which insanity would doubtless have its place. But the lugubrious vision vanished, and then again before Mathieu's eyes the lawn spread out under the joyous sun, offering between its belt of foliage such a picture of happy health and triumphant beauty, that he felt impelled to break the mournful silence and exclaim:

"Look there! look there! Isn't that gay; isn't that a delightful scene— all those dear women and dear children in that setting of verdure? It ought to be painted to show people how healthy and beautiful life is!"

Time had not been lost on the lawn since the Beauchenes and Seguins had gone off to visit the stables. First of all there had been a distribution of the menu cards, which Charlotte had adorned with such delicate water-color sketches. This surprise of hers had enraptured them all at lunch, and they still laughed at the sight of those pretty children's heads. Then, while the servants cleared the table, Gregoire achieved a great success by offering the bride a bouquet of splendid white roses, which he drew out of a bush where he had hitherto kept it hidden. He had doubtless been waiting for some absence of his father's. They were the roses of the mill; with Therese's assistance he must have pillaged the bushes in the enclosure. Marianne, recognizing how serious was the transgression, wished to scold him. But what superb white roses they were, as big as cabbages, as he himself had said! And he was entitled to triumph over them, for they were the only white roses there, and had been secured by himself, like the wandering urchin he was with a spice of knight-errantry in his composition, quite ready to jump over walls and cajole damsels in order to deck a bride with snowy blooms.

"Oh! papa won't say anything," he declared, with no little self-assurance; "they are far too beautiful."

This made the others laugh; but fresh emotion ensued, for Benjamin and Guillaume awoke and screamed their hunger aloud. It was gayly remarked, however, that they were quite entitled to their turn of feasting. And as it was simply a family gathering there was no embarrassment on the part of the mothers. Marianne took Benjamin on her knees in the shade of the oak tree, and Charlotte placed herself with Guillaume on her right hand; while, on her left, Andree seated herself with little Leonce, who had been weaned a week previously, but was still very fond of caresses.

It was at this moment that the Beauchenes and the Seguins reappeared with Mathieu, and stopped short, struck by the charm of the spectacle before them. Between a framework of tall trees, under the patriarchal oak, on the thick grass of the lawn the whole vigorous family was gathered in a group, instinct with gayety, beauty, and strength. Gervais and Claire, ever active, were, with Frederic, hurrying on the servants, who made no end of serving the coffee on the table which had just been cleared. For this table the three younger girls, half buried in a heap of flowers, tea and blush and crimson roses, were now, with the help of knight Gregoire, devising new decorations. Then, a few paces away, the bridal pair, Denis and Marthe, were conversing in undertones; while the bride's mother, Madame Desvignes, sat listening to them with a discreet and infinitely gentle smile upon her lips. And it was in the midst of all this that Marianne, radiant, white of skin, still fresh, ever beautiful, with serene strength, was giving the breast to her twelfth child, her Benjamin, and smiling at him as he sucked away; while surrendering her other knee to little Nicolas, who was jealous of his younger brother. And her two daughters-in-law seemed like a continuation of herself. There was Andree on the left with Ambroise, who had stepped up to tease his little Léonce; and Charlotte on the right with her two children, Guillaume, who hung on her breast, and Berthe, who had sought a place among her skirts. And here, faith in life had yielded prosperity, ever-increasing, overflowing wealth, all the sovereign florescence of happy fruitfulness.

Seguin, addressing himself to Marianne, asked her jestingly: "And so that little gentleman is the fourteenth you have nursed?"

She likewise laughed. "No; I mustn't tell fibs! I have nursed twelve, including this one; that is the exact number."

Beauchene, who had recovered his self-possession, could not refrain from intervening once more: "A full dozen, eh! It is madness!"

"I share your opinion," said Mathieu, laughing in his turn. "At all events, if it is not madness it is extravagance, as we admit, my wife and I, when we are alone. And we certainly don't think that all people ought to have such large families as ours. But, given the situation in France nowadays, with our population dwindling and that of nearly every other country increasing, it is hardly possible to complain of even the largest family. Thus, even if our example be exaggerated, it remains an example, I think, for others to think over."

Marianne listened, still smiling, but with tears standing in her eyes. A feeling of gentle sadness was penetrating her; her heart-wound had reopened even amid all her joy at seeing her children assembled around her. "Yes," said she in a trembling voice, "there have been twelve, but I have only ten left. Two are already sleeping yonder, waiting for us underground."

There was no sign of dread, however, in that evocation of the peaceful little cemetery of Janville and the family grave in which all the children hoped some day to be laid, one after the other, side by side. Rather did that evocation, coming amid that gay wedding assembly, seem like a promise of future blessed peace. The memory of the dear departed ones remained alive, and lent to one and all a kind of loving gravity even amid their mirth. Was it not impossible to accept life without accepting death. Each came here to perform his task, and then, his work ended, went to join his elders in that slumber of eternity where the great fraternity of humankind was fulfilled.

But in presence of those jesters, Beauchene and Seguin, quite a flood of words rose to Mathieu's lips. He would have liked to answer them; he would have liked to triumph over the mendacious theories which they still dared to assert even in their hour of defeat. To fear that the earth might become over-populated, that excess of life might produce famine, was this not idiotic? Others only had to do as he had done: create the necessary subsistence each time that a child was born to them. And he would have pointed to Chantebled, his work, and to all the corn growing up under the sun, even as his children grew. They could not be charged with having come to consume the share of others, since each was born with his bread before him. And millions of new beings might follow, for the earth was vast: more than two-thirds of it still remained to be placed under cultivation, and therein lay endless fertility for unlimited humanity. Besides, had not every civilization, every progress, been due to the impulse of numbers? The improvidence of the poor had alone urged revolutionary multitudes to the conquest of truth, justice, and happiness. And with each succeeding day the human torrent would require more kindliness, more equity, the logical division of wealth by just laws regulating universal labor. If it were true, too, that civilization was a check to excessive natality, this phenomenon itself might make one hope in final equilibrium in the far-off ages, when the earth should be entirely populated and wise enough to live in a sort of divine immobility. But all this was pure speculation beside the needs of the hour, the nations which must be built up afresh and incessantly enlarged, pending the eventual definitive federation of mankind. And it was really an example, a brave and a necessary one, that Marianne and he were giving, in order that manners and customs, and the idea of morality and the idea of beauty might be changed.

Full of these thoughts Mathieu was already opening his mouth to speak. But all at once he felt how futile discussion would be in presence of that admirable scene; that mother surrounded by such a florescence of vigorous children; that mother nursing yet another child, under the big oak which she had planted. She was bravely accomplishing her task— that of perpetuating the world. And hers was the sovereign beauty.

Mathieu could think of only one thing that would express everything, and that was to kiss her with all his heart before the whole assembly.

"There, dear wife! You are the most beautiful and the best! May all the others do as you have done."

Then, when Marianne had gloriously returned his kiss, there arose an acclamation, a tempest of merry laughter. They were both of heroic mould; it was with a great dash of heroism that they had steered their bark onward, thanks to their full faith in life, their will of action, and the force of their love. And Constance was at last conscious of it: she could realize the conquering power of fruitfulness; she could already see the Froments masters of the factory through their son Denis; masters of Seguin's mansion through their son Ambroise; masters, too, of all the countryside through their other children. Numbers spelt victory. And shrinking, consumed with a love which she could never more satisfy, full of the bitterness of her defeat, though she yet hoped for some abominable revenge of destiny, she—who never wept!—turned aside to hide the big hot tears which now burnt her withered cheeks.

Meantime Benjamin and Guillaume were enjoying themselves like greedy little men whom nothing could disturb. Had there been less laughter one might have heard the trickling of their mothers' milk: that little stream flowing forth amid the torrent of sap which upraised the earth and made the big trees quiver in the powerful July blaze. On every side fruitful life was conveying germs, creating and nourishing. And for its eternal work an eternal river of milk flowed through the world.

XIX

One Sunday morning Norine and Cecile—who, though it was rightly a day of rest, were, nevertheless, working on either side of their little table, pressed as they were to deliver boxes for the approaching New Year season—received a visit which left them pale with stupor and fright.

Their unknown hidden life had hitherto followed a peaceful course, the only battle being to make both ends meet every week, and to put by the rent money for payment every quarter. During the eight years that the sisters had been living together in the Rue de la Federation near the Champ de Mars, occupying the same big room with cheerful windows, a room whose coquettish cleanliness made them feel quite proud, Norine's child had grown up steadily between his two affectionate mothers. For he had ended by confounding them together: there was Mamma Norine and there was Mamma Cecile; and he did not exactly know whether one of the two was more his mother than the other. It was for him alone that they both lived and toiled, the one still a fine, good-looking woman at forty years of age, the other yet girlish at thirty.

Now, at about ten o'clock that Sunday, there came in succession two loud knocks at the door. When the latter was opened a short, thick-set fellow, about eighteen, stepped in. He was dark-haired, with a square face, a hard prominent jaw, and eyes of a pale gray. And he wore a ragged old jacket and a gray cloth cap, discolored by long usage.

"Excuse me," said he; "but isn't it here that live Mesdames Moineaud, who make cardboard boxes?"

Norine stood there looking at him with sudden uneasiness. Her heart had contracted as if she were menaced. She had certainly seen that face somewhere before; but she could only recall one old-time danger, which suddenly seemed to revive, more formidable than ever, as if threatening to spoil her quiet life.

"Yes, it is here," she answered.

Without any haste the young man glanced around the room. He must have expected more signs of means than he found, for he pouted slightly. Then his eyes rested on the child, who, like a well-behaved little boy, had been amusing himself with reading, and had now raised his face to examine the newcomer. And the latter concluded his examination by directing a brief glance at the other woman who was present, a slight, sickly creature who likewise felt anxious in presence of that sudden apparition of the unknown.

"I was told the left-hand door on the fourth floor," the young man resumed. "But, all the same, I was afraid of making a mistake, for the things I have to say can't be said to everybody. It isn't an easy matter, and, of course, I thought it well over before I came here."

He spoke slowly in a drawling way, and after again making sure that the other woman was too young to be the one he sought, he kept his pale eyes steadily fixed on Norine. The growing anguish with which he saw her quivering, the appeal that she was evidently making to her memory, induced him to prolong things for another moment. Then he spoke out: "I am the child who was put to nurse at Rougemont; my name is Alexandre-Honore."

There was no need for him to say anything more. The unhappy Norine began to tremble from head to foot, clasped and wrung her hands, while an ashen hue came over her distorted features. Good heavens—Beauchene! Yes, it was Beauchene whom he resembled, and in so striking a manner, with his eyes of prey, his big jaw which proclaimed an enjoyer consumed by base voracity, that she was now astonished that she had not been able to name him at her first glance. Her legs failed her, and she had to sit down.

"So it's you," said Alexandre.

As she continued shivering, confessing the truth by her manner, but unable to articulate a word, to such a point did despair and fright clutch her at the throat, he felt the need of reassuring her a little, particularly if he was to keep that door open to him.

"You must not upset yourself like that," said he; "you have nothing to fear from me; it isn't my intention to give you any trouble. Only when I learnt at last where you were I wished to know you, and that was natural, wasn't it? I even fancied that perhaps you might be pleased to see me. . . Then, too, the truth is that I'm precious badly off. Three years ago I was silly enough to come back to Paris, where I do little more than starve. And on the days when one hasn't breakfasted, one feels inclined to look up one's parents, even though they may have turned one into the street, for, all the same, they can hardly be so hard-hearted as to refuse one a plateful of soup."

Tears rose to Norine's eyes. This was the finishing stroke, the return of that wretched cast-off son, that big suspicious-looking fellow who accused her and complained of starving. Annoyed at being unable to elicit from her any response but shivers and sobs, Alexandre turned to Cecile: "You are her sister, I know," said he; "tell her that it's stupid of her to go on like that. I haven't come to murder her. It's funny how pleased she is to see me! Yet I don't make any noise, and I said nothing whatever to the door-porter downstairs, I assure you."

Then as Cecile, without answering him, rose to go and comfort Norine, he again became interested in the child, who likewise felt frightened and turned pale on seeing the grief of his two mammas.

"So that lad is my brother?"

Thereupon Norine suddenly sprang to her feet and set herself between the child and him. A mad fear had come to her of some catastrophe, some great collapse which would crush them all. Yet she did not wish to be harsh, she even sought kind words, but amid it all she lost her head, carried away by feelings of revolt, rancor, instinctive hostility.

"You came, I can understand it. But it is so cruel. What can I do? After so many years one doesn't know one another, one has nothing to say. And, besides, as you can see for yourself, I'm not rich."

Alexandre glanced round the room for the second time. "Yes, I see," he answered; "and my father, can't you tell me his name?"

She remained thunderstruck by this question and turned yet paler, while he continued: "Because if my father should have any money I should know very well how to make him give me some. People have no right to fling children into the gutter like that."

All at once Norine had seen the past rise up before her: Beauchene, the works, and her father, who now had just quitted them owing to his infirmities, leaving his son Victor behind him.

And a sort of instinctive prudence came to her at the thought that if she were to give up Beauchene's name she might compromise all her happy life, since terrible complications might ensue. The dread she felt of that suspicious-looking lad, who reeked of idleness and vice, inspired her with an idea: "Your father? He has long been dead," said she.

He could have known nothing, have learnt nothing on that point, for, in presence of the energy of her answer, he expressed no doubt whatever of her veracity, but contented himself with making a rough gesture which indicated how angry he felt at seeing his hungry hopes thus destroyed.

"So I've got to starve!" he growled.

Norine, utterly distracted, was possessed by one painful desire—a desire that he might take himself away, and cease torturing her by his presence, to such a degree did remorse, and pity, and fright, and horror now wring her bleeding heart. She opened a drawer and took from it a ten-franc piece, her savings for the last three months, with which she had intended to buy a New Year's present for her little boy. And giving those ten francs to Alexandre, she said: "Listen, I can do nothing for you. We live all three in this one room, and we scarcely earn our bread. It grieves me very much to know that you are so unfortunately circumstanced. But you mustn't rely on me. Do as we do—work."

He pocketed the ten francs, and remained there for another moment swaying about, and saying that he had not come for money, and that he could very well understand things. For his part he always behaved properly with people when people behaved properly with him. And he repeated that since she showed herself good-natured he had no idea of creating any scandal. A mother who did what she could performed her duty, even though she might only give a ten-sous piece. Then, as he was at last going off, he inquired: "Won't you kiss me?"

She kissed him, but with cold lips and lifeless heart, and the two smacking kisses which, with noisy affectation, he gave her in return, left her cheeks quivering.

"And au revoir, eh?" said he. "Although one may be poor and unable to keep together, each knows now that the other's in the land of the living. And there is no reason why I shouldn't come up just now and again to wish you good day when I'm passing."

When he had at last disappeared long silence fell amid the infinite distress which his short stay had brought there. Norine had again sunk upon a chair, as if overwhelmed by this catastrophe. Cecile had been obliged to sit down in front of her, for she also was overcome. And it was she who, amid the mournfulness of that room, which but a little while ago had held all their happiness, spoke out the first to complain and express her astonishment.

"But you did not ask him anything; we know nothing about him," said she. "Where has he come from? What is he doing? What does he want? And, in particular, how did he manage to discover you? These were the interesting things to learn."

"Oh! what would you have!" replied Norine. "When he told me his name he knocked all the strength out of me; I felt as cold as ice! Oh! it's he, there's no doubt of it. You recognized his likeness to his father, didn't you? But you are right; we know nothing, and now we shall always be living with that threat over our heads, in fear that everything will crumble down upon us."

All her strength, all her courage was gone, and she began to sob, stammering indistinctly: "To think of it! a big fellow of eighteen falling on one like that without a word of warning! And it's quite true that I don't love him, since I don't even know him. When he kissed me I felt nothing. I was icy cold, as if my heart were frozen. O God! O God! what trouble to be sure, and how horrid and cruel it all is!"

Then, as her little boy, on seeing her weep, ran up and flung himself, frightened and tearful, against her bosom, she wildly caught him in her arms. "My poor little one! my poor little one! if only you don't suffer by it; if only my sin doesn't fall on you! Ah! that would be a terrible punishment. Really the best course is for folks to behave properly in life if they don't want to have a lot of trouble afterwards!"

In the evening the sisters, having grown somewhat calmer, decided that their best course would be to write to Mathieu. Norine remembered that he had called on her a few years previously to ask if Alexandre had not been to see her. He alone knew all the particulars of the business, and where to obtain information. And, indeed, as soon as the sisters' letter reached him Mathieu made haste to call on them in the Rue de la Federation, for he was anxious with respect to the effect which any scandal might have at the works, where Beauchene's position was becoming worse every day. After questioning Norine at length, he guessed that Alexandre must have learnt her address through La Couteau, though he could not say precisely how this had come about. At last, after a long month of discreet researches, conversations with Madame Menoux, Celeste, and La Couteau herself, he was able in some measure to explain things. The alert had certainly come from the inquiry intrusted to the nurse-agent at Rougemont, that visit which she had made to the hamlet of Saint-Pierre in quest of information respecting the lad who was supposed to be in apprenticeship with Montoir the wheelwright. She had talked too much, said too much, particularly to the other apprentice, that Richard, another foundling, and one of such bad instincts, too, that seven months later he had taken flight, like Alexandre, after purloining some money from his master. Then years elapsed, and all trace of them was lost. But later on, most assuredly they had met one another on the Paris pavement, in such wise that the big carroty lad had told the little dark fellow the whole story how his relatives had caused a search to be made for him, and perhaps, too, who his mother was, the whole interspersed with tittle-tattle and ridiculous inventions. Still this did not explain everything, and to understand how Alexandre had procured his mother's actual address, Mathieu had to presume that he had secured it from La Couteau, whom Celeste had acquainted with so many things. Indeed, he learnt at Broquette's nurse-agency that a short, thickset young man with pronounced jaw-bones had come there twice to speak to La Couteau. Nevertheless, many points remained unexplained; the whole affair had taken place amid the tragic, murky gloom of Parisian low life, whose mire it is not healthy to stir. Mathieu ended by resting content with a general notion of the business, for he himself felt frightened at the charges already hanging over those two young bandits, who lived so precariously, dragging their idleness and their vices over the pavement of the great city. And thus all his researches had resulted in but one consoling certainty, which was that even if Norine the mother was known, the father's name and position were certainly not suspected by anybody.

When Mathieu saw Norine again on the subject he terrified her by the few particulars which he was obliged to give her.

"Oh! I beg you, I beg you, do not let him come again," she pleaded. "Find some means; prevent him from coming here. It upsets me too dreadfully to see him."

Mathieu, of course, could do nothing in this respect. After mature reflection he realized that the great object of his efforts must be to prevent Alexandre from discovering Beauchene. What he had learnt of the young man was so bad, so dreadful, that he wished to spare Constance the pain and scandal of being blackmailed. He could see her blanching at the thought of the ignominy of that lad whom she had so passionately desired to find, and he felt ashamed for her sake, and deemed it more compassionate and even necessary to bury the secret in the silence of the grave. Still, it was only after a long fight with himself that he came to this decision, for he felt that it was hard to have to abandon the unhappy youth in the streets. Was it still possible to save him? He doubted it. And besides, who would undertake the task, who would know how to instil honest principles into that waif by teaching him to work? It all meant yet another man cast overboard, forsaken amid the tempest, and Mathieu's heart bled at the thought of condemning him, though he could think of no reasonable means of salvation.

"My opinion," he said to Norine, "is that you should keep his father's name from him for the present. Later on we will see. But just now I should fear worry for everybody."

She eagerly acquiesced. "Oh! you need not be anxious," she responded. "I have already told him that his father is dead. If I were to speak out everything would fall on my shoulders, and my great desire is to be left in peace in my corner with my little one."

With sorrowful mien Mathieu continued reflecting, unable to make up his mind to utterly abandon the young man. "If he would only work, I would find him some employment. And I would even take him on at the farm later, when I should no longer have cause to fear that he might contaminate my people. However, I will see what can be done; I know a wheelwright who would doubtless employ him, and I will write to you in order that you may tell him where to apply, when he comes back to see you."

"What? When he comes back!" she cried in despair. "So you think that he will come back. O God! O God! I shall never be happy again."

He did, indeed, come back. But when she gave him the wheelwright's address he sneered and shrugged his shoulders. He knew all about the Paris wheelwrights! A set of sweaters, a parcel of lazy rogues, who made poor people toil and moil for them. Besides, he had never finished his apprenticeship; he was only fit for running errands, in which capacity he was willing to accept a post in a large shop. When Mathieu had procured him such a situation, he did not remain in it a fortnight. One fine evening he disappeared with the parcels of goods which he had been told to deliver. In turn he tried to learn a baker's calling, became a mason's hodman, secured work at the markets, but without ever fixing himself anywhere. He simply discouraged his protector, and left all sorts of roguery behind him for others to liquidate. It became necessary to renounce the hope of saving him. When he turned up, as he did periodically, emaciated, hungry, and in rags, they had to limit themselves to providing him with the means to buy a jacket and some bread.

Thus Norine lived on in a state of mortal disquietude. For long weeks Alexandre seemed to be dead, but she, nevertheless, started at the slightest sound that she heard on the landing. She always felt him to be there, and whenever he suddenly rapped on the door she recognized his heavy knock and began to tremble as if he had come to beat her. He had noticed how his presence reduced the unhappy woman to a state of abject terror, and he profited by this to extract from her whatever little sums she hid away. When she had handed him the five-franc piece which Mathieu, as a rule, left with her for this purpose, the young rascal was not content, but began searching for more. At times he made his appearance in a wild, haggard state, declaring that he should certainly be sent to prison that evening if he did not secure ten francs, and talking the while of smashing everything in the room or else of carrying off the little clock in order to sell it. And it was then necessary for Cecile to intervene and turn him out of the place; for, however puny she might be, she had a brave heart. But if he went off it was only to return a few days later with fresh demands, threatening that he would shout his story to everybody on the stairs if the ten francs were not given to him. One day, when his mother had no money in the place and began to weep, he talked of ripping up the mattress, where, said he, she probably kept her hoard. Briefly, the sisters' little home was becoming a perfect hell.

The greatest misfortune of all, however, was that in the Rue de la Federation Alexandre made the acquaintance of Alfred, Norine's youngest brother, the last born of the Moineaud family. He was then twenty, and thus two years the senior of his nephew. No worse prowler than he existed. He was the genuine rough, with pale, beardless face, blinking eyes, and twisted mouth, the real gutter-weed that sprouts up amid the Parisian manure-heaps. At seven years of age he robbed his sisters, beating Cecile every Saturday in order to tear her earnings from her. Mother Moineaud, worn out with hard work and unable to exercise a constant watch over him, had never managed to make him attend school regularly, or to keep him in apprenticeship. He exasperated her to such a degree that she herself ended by turning him into the streets in order to secure a little peace and quietness at home. His big brothers kicked him about, his father was at work from morning till evening, and the child, thus morally a waif, grew up out of doors for a career of vice and crime among the swarms of lads and girls of his age, who all rotted there together like apples fallen on the ground. And as Alfred grew he became yet more corrupt; he was like the sacrificed surplus of a poor man's family, the surplus poured into the gutter, the spoilt fruit which spoils all that comes into contact with it.

Like Alexandre, too, he nowadays only lived chancewise, and it was not even known where he had been sleeping, since Mother Moineaud had died at a hospital exhausted by her long life of wretchedness and family cares which had proved far too heavy for her. She was only sixty at the time of her death, but was as bent and as worn out as a centenarian. Moineaud, two years older, bent like herself, his legs twisted by paralysis, a lamentable wreck after fifty years of unjust toil, had been obliged to quit the factory, and thus the home was empty, and its few poor sticks had been cast to the four winds of heaven.

Moineaud fortunately received a little pension, for which he was indebted to Denis's compassionate initiative. But he was sinking into second childhood, worn out by his long and constant efforts, and not only did he squander his few coppers in drink, but he could not be left alone, for his feet were lifeless, and his hands shook to such a degree that he ran the risk of setting all about him on fire whenever he tried to light his pipe. At last he found himself stranded in the home of his daughters, Norine and Cecile, the only two who had heart enough to take him in. They rented a little closet for him, on the fifth floor of the house, over their own room, and they nursed him and bought him food and clothes with his pension-money, to which they added a good deal of their own. As they remarked in their gay, courageous way, they now had two children, a little one and a very old one, which was a heavy burden for two women who earned but five francs a day, although they were ever making boxes from morn till night, There was a touch of soft irony in the circumstance that old Moineaud should have been unable to find any other refuge than the home of his daughter Norine— that daughter whom he had formerly turned away and cursed for her misconduct, that hussy who had dishonored him, but whose very hands he now kissed when, for fear lest he should set the tip of his nose ablaze, she helped him to light his pipe.

All the same, the shaky old nest of the Moineauds was destroyed, and the whole family had flown off, dispersed chancewise. Irma alone, thanks to her fine marriage with a clerk, lived happily, playing the part of a lady, and so full of vanity that she no longer condescended to see her brothers and sisters. Victor, meantime, was leading at the factory much the same life as his father had led, working at the same mill as the other, and in the same blind, stubborn way. He had married, and though he was under six-and-thirty, he already had six children, three boys and three girls, so that his wife seemed fated to much the same existence as his mother La Moineaude. Both of them would finish broken down, and their children in their turn would unconsciously perpetuate the swarming and accursed starveling race.

At Euphrasie's, destiny the inevitable showed itself more tragic still. The wretched woman had not been lucky enough to die. She had gradually become bedridden, quite unable to move, though she lived on and could hear and see and understand things. From that open grave, her bed, she had beheld the final break-up of what remained of her sorry home. She was nothing more than a thing, insulted by her husband and tortured by Madame Joseph, who would leave her for days together without water, and fling her occasional crusts much as they might be flung to a sick animal whose litter is not even changed. Terror-stricken, and full of humility amid her downfall, Euphrasie resigned herself to everything; but the worst was that her three children, her twin daughters and her son, being abandoned to themselves, sank into vice, the all-corrupting life of the streets. Benard, tired out, distracted by the wreck of his home, had taken to drinking with Madame Joseph; and afterwards they would fight together, break the furniture, and drive off the children, who came home muddy, in rags, and with their pockets full of stolen things. On two occasions Benard disappeared for a week at a time. On the third he did not come back at all. When the rent fell due, Madame Joseph in her turn took herself off. And then came the end. Euphrasie had to be removed to the hospital of La Salpetriere, the last refuge of the aged and the infirm; while the children, henceforth without a home in name, were driven into the gutter. The boy never turned up again; it was as if he had been swallowed by some sewer. One of the twin girls, found in the streets, died in a hospital during the ensuing year; and the other, Toinette, a fair-haired scraggy hussy, who, however puny she might look, was a terrible little creature with the eyes and the teeth of a wolf, lived under the bridges, in the depths of the stone quarries, in the dingy garrets of haunts of vice, so that at sixteen she was already an expert thief. Her fate was similar to Alfred's; here was a girl morally abandoned, then contaminated by the life of the streets, and carried off to a criminal career. And, indeed, the uncle and the niece having met by chance, ended by consorting together, their favorite refuge, it was thought, being the limekilns in the direction of Les Moulineaux.

One day then it happened that Alexandre upon calling at Norine's there encountered Alfred, who came at times to try to extract a half-franc from old Moineaud, his father. The two young bandits went off together, chatted, and met again. And from that chance encounter there sprang a band. Alexandre was living with Richard, and Alfred brought

Toinette to them. Thus they were four in number, and the customary developments followed: begging at first, the girl putting out her hand at the instigation of the three prowlers, who remained on the watch and drew alms by force at nighttime from belated bourgeois encountered in dark corners; next came vulgar vice and its wonted attendant, blackmail; and then theft, petty larceny to begin with, the pilfering of things displayed for sale by shopkeepers, and afterwards more serious affairs, premeditated expeditions, mapped out like real war plans.

The band slept wherever it could; now in suspicious dingy doss-houses, now on waste ground. In summer time there were endless saunters through the woods of the environs, pending the arrival of night, which handed Paris over to their predatory designs. They found themselves at the Central Markets, among the crowds on the boulevards, in the low taverns, along the deserted avenues—indeed, wherever they sniffed the possibility of a stroke of luck, the chance of snatching the bread of idleness, or the pleasures of vice. They were like a little clan of savages on the war-path athwart civilization, living outside the pale of the laws. They suggested young wild beasts beating the ancestral forest; they typified the human animal relapsing into barbarism, forsaken since birth, and evincing the ancient instincts of pillage and carnage. And like noxious weeds they grew up sturdily, becoming bolder and bolder each day, exacting a bigger and bigger ransom from the fools who toiled and moiled, ever extending their thefts and marching along the road to murder.

Never should it be forgotten that the child, born chancewise, and then cast upon the pavement, without supervision, without prop or help, rots there and becomes a terrible ferment of social decomposition. All those little ones thrown to the gutter, like superfluous kittens are flung into some sewer, all those forsaken ones, those wanderers of the pavement who beg, and thieve, and indulge in vice, form the dung-heap in which the worst crimes germinate. Childhood left to wretchedness breeds a fearful nucleus of infection in the tragic gloom of the depths of Paris. Those who are thus imprudently cast into the streets yield a harvest of brigandage—that frightful harvest of evil which makes all society totter.

When Norine, through the boasting of Alexandre and Alfred, who took pleasure in astonishing her, began to suspect the exploits of the band, she felt so frightened that she had a strong bolt placed upon her door. And when night had fallen she no longer admitted any visitor until she knew his name. Her torture had been lasting for nearly two years; she was ever quivering with alarm at the thought of Alexandre rushing in upon her some dark night. He was twenty now; he spoke authoritatively, and threatened her with atrocious revenge whenever he had to retire with empty hands. One day, in spite of Cecile, he threw himself upon the wardrobe and carried off a bundle of linen, handkerchiefs, towels, napkins, and sheets, intending to sell them. And the sisters did not dare to pursue him down the stairs. Despairing, weeping, overwhelmed by it all, they had sunk down upon their chairs.

That winter proved a very severe one; and the two poor workwomen, pillaged in this fashion, would have perished in their sorry home of cold and starvation, together with the dear child for whom they still did their best, had it not been for the help which their old friend, Madame Angelin, regularly brought them. She was still a lady-delegate of the Poor Relief Service, and continued to watch over the children of unhappy mothers in that terrible district of Grenelle, whose poverty is so great. But for a long time past she had been unable to do anything officially for Norine. If she still brought her a twenty-franc piece every month, it was because charitable people intrusted her with fairly large amounts, knowing that she could distribute them to advantage in the dreadful inferno which her functions compelled her to frequent. She set her last joy and found the great consolation of her desolate, childless life in thus remitting alms to poor mothers whose little ones laughed at her joyously as soon as they saw her arrive with her hands full of good things.

One day when the weather was frightful, all rain and wind, Madame Angelin lingered for a little while in Norine's room. It was barely two o'clock in the afternoon, and she was just beginning her round. On her lap lay her little bag, bulging out with the gold and the silver which she had to distribute. Old Moineaud was there, installed on a chair and smoking his pipe, in front of her. And she felt concerned about his needs, and explained that she would have greatly liked to obtain a monthly relief allowance for him.

"But if you only knew," she added, "what suffering there is among the poor during these winter months. We are quite swamped, we cannot give to everybody, there are too many. And after all you are among the fortunate ones. I find some lying like dogs on the tiled floors of their rooms, without a scrap of coal to make a fire or even a potato to eat. And the poor children, too, good Heavens! Children in heaps among vermin, without shoes, without clothes, all growing up as if destined for prison or the scaffold, unless consumption should carry them off."

Madame Angelin quivered and closed her eyes as if to escape the spectacle of all the terrifying things that she evoked, the wretchedness, the shame, the crimes that she elbowed during her continual perambulations through that hell of poverty, vice, and hunger. She often returned home pale and silent, having reached the uttermost depths of human abomination, and never daring to say all. At times she trembled and raised her eyes to Heaven, wondering what vengeful cataclysm would swallow up that accursed city of Paris.

"Ah!" she murmured once more; "their sufferings are so great, may their sins be forgiven them."

Moineaud listened to her in a state of stupor, as if he were unable to understand. At last with difficulty he succeeded in taking his pipe from his mouth. It was, indeed, quite an effort now for him to do such a thing, and yet for fifty years he had wrestled with iron—iron in the vice or on the anvil.

"There is nothing like good conduct," he stammered huskily. "When a man works he's rewarded."

Then he wished to set his pipe between his lips once more, but was unable to do so. His hand, deformed by the constant use of tools, trembled too violently. So it became necessary for Norine to rise from her chair and help him.

"Poor father!" exclaimed Cecile, who had not ceased working, cutting out the cardboard for the little boxes she made: "What would have become of him if we had not given him shelter? It isn't Irma, with her stylish hats and her silk dresses who would have cared to have him at her place."

Meantime Norine's little boy had taken his stand in front of Madame Angelin, for he knew very well that, on the days when the good lady called, there was some dessert at supper in the evening. He smiled at her with the bright eyes which lit up his pretty fair face, crowned with tumbled sunshiny hair. And when she noticed with what a merry glance he was waiting for her to open her little bag, she felt quite moved.

"Come and kiss me, my little friend," said she.

She knew no sweeter reward for all that she did than the kisses of the children in the poor homes whither she brought a little joy. When the youngster had boldly thrown his arms round her neck, her eyes filled with tears; and, addressing herself to his mother, she repeated:

"No, no, you must not complain; there are others who are more unhappy than you. I know one who if this pretty little fellow could only be her own would willingly accept your poverty, and paste boxes together from morning till night and lead a recluse's life in this one room, which he suffices to fill with sunshine. Ah! good Heavens, if you were only willing, if we could only change."

For a moment she became silent, afraid that she might burst into sobs. The wound dealt her by her childlessness had always remained open. She and her husband were now growing old in bitter solitude in three little rooms overlooking a courtyard in the Rue de Lille. In this retirement they subsisted on the salary which she, the wife, received as a lady-delegate, joined to what they had been able to save of their original fortune. The former fan-painter of triumphant mien was now completely blind, a mere thing, a poor suffering thing, whom his wife seated every morning in an armchair where she still found him in the evening when she returned home from her incessant peregrinations through the frightful misery of guilty mothers and martyred children. He could no longer eat, he could no longer go to bed without her help, he had only her left him, he was her child as he would say at times with a despairing irony which made them both weep.

A child? Ah, yes! she had ended by having one, and it was he! An old child, born of disaster; one who appeared to be eighty though he was less than fifty years old, and who amid his black and ceaseless night ever dreamt of sunshine during the long hours which he was compelled to spend alone. And Madame Angelin did not only envy that poor workwoman her little boy, she also envied her that old man smoking his pipe yonder, that infirm relic of labor who at all events saw clearly and still lived.

"Don't worry the lady," said Norine to her son; for she felt anxious, quite moved indeed, at seeing the other so disturbed, with her heart so full. "Run away and play."

She had learnt a little of Madame Angelin's sad story from Mathieu. And with the deep gratitude which she felt towards her benefactress was blended a sort of impassioned respect, which rendered her timid and deferent each time that she saw her arrive, tall and distinguished, ever clad in black, and showing the remnants of her former beauty which sorrow had wrecked already, though she was barely six-and-forty years of age. For Norine, the lady-delegate was like some queen who had fallen from her throne amid frightful and undeserved sufferings.

"Run away, go and play, my darling," Norine repeated to her boy: "you are tiring madame."

"Tiring me, oh no!" exclaimed Madame Angelin, conquering her emotion. "On the contrary, he does me good. Kiss me, kiss me again, my pretty fellow."

Then she began to bestir and collect herself.

"Well, it is getting late, and I have so many places to go to between now and this evening! This is what I can do for you."

She was at last taking a gold coin from her little bag, but at that very moment a heavy blow, as if dealt by a fist, resounded on the door. And Norine turned ghastly pale, for she had recognized Alexandre's brutal knock. What could she do? If she did not open the door, the bandit would go on knocking, and raise a scandal. She was obliged to open it, but things did not take the violent tragical turn which she had feared. Surprised at seeing a lady there, Alexandre did not even open his mouth. He simply slipped inside, and stationed himself bolt upright against the wall. The lady-delegate had raised her eyes and then carried them elsewhere, understanding that this young fellow must be some friend, probably some relative. And without thought of concealment, she went on:

"Here are twenty francs, I can't do more. Only I promise you that I will try to double the amount next month. It will be the rent month, and I've already applied for help on all sides, and people have promised to give me the utmost they can. But shall I ever have enough? So many applications are made to me."

Her little bag had remained open on her knees, and Alexandre, with his glittering eyes, was searching it, weighing in fancy all the treasure of the poor that it contained, all the gold and silver and even the copper money that distended its sides. Still in silence, he watched Madame Angelin as she closed it, slipped its little chain round her wrist, and then finally rose from her chair.

"Well, au revoir, till next month then," she resumed. "I shall certainly call on the 5th; and in all probability I shall begin my round with you. But it's possible that it may be rather late in the afternoon, for it happens to be my poor husband's name-day. And so be brave and work well."

Norine and Cecile had likewise risen, in order to escort her to the door. Here again there was an outpouring of gratitude, and the child once more kissed the good lady on both cheeks with all his little heart. The sisters, so terrified by Alexandre's arrival, at last began to breathe again.

In point of fact the incident terminated fairly well, for the young man showed himself accommodating. When Cecile returned from obtaining change for the gold, he contented himself with taking one of the four five-franc pieces which she brought up with her. And he did not tarry to torture them as was his wont, but immediately went off with the money he had levied, whistling the while the air of a hunting-song.

The 5th of the ensuing month, a Saturday, was one of the gloomiest, most rainy days of that wretched, mournful winter. Darkness fell rapidly already at three o'clock in the afternoon, and it became almost night. At the deserted end of Rue de la Federation there was an expanse of waste ground, a building site, for long years enclosed by a fence, which dampness had ended by rotting. Some of the boards were missing, and at one part there was quite a breach. All through that afternoon, in spite of the constantly recurring downpours, a scraggy girl remained stationed near that breach, wrapped to her eyes in the ragged remnants of an old shawl, doubtless for protection against the cold. She seemed to be waiting for some chance meeting, the advent it might be of some charitably disposed wayfarer. And her impatience was manifest, for while keeping close to the fence like some animal lying in wait, she continually peered through the breach, thrusting out her tapering weasel's head and watching yonder, in the direction of the Champ de Mars.

Hours went by, three o'clock struck, and then such dark clouds rolled over the livid sky, that the girl herself became blurred, obscured, as if she were some mere piece of wreckage cast into the darkness. At times she raised her head and watched the sky darken, with eyes that glittered as if to thank it for throwing so dense a gloom over that deserted corner, that spot so fit for an ambuscade. And just as the rain had once more begun to fall, a lady could be seen approaching, a lady clad in black, quite black, under an open umbrella. While seeking to avoid the puddles in her path, she walked on quickly, like one in a hurry, who goes about her business on foot in order to save herself the expense of a cab.

From some precise description which she had obtained, Toinette, the girl, appeared to recognize this lady from afar off. She was indeed none other than Madame Angelin, coming quickly from the Rue de Lille, on her way to the homes of her poor, with the little chain of her little bag encircling her wrist. And when the girl espied the gleaming steel of that little chain, she no longer had any doubts, but whistled softly. And forthwith cries and moans arose from a dim corner of the vacant ground, while she herself began to wail and call distressfully.

Astonished, disturbed by it all, Madame Angelin stopped short.

"What is the matter, my girl?" she asked.

"Oh! madame, my brother has fallen yonder and broken his leg."

"What, fallen? What has he fallen from?"

"Oh! madame, there's a shed yonder where we sleep, because we haven't any home, and he was using an old ladder to try to prevent the rain from pouring in on us, and he fell and broke his leg."

Thereupon the girl burst into sobs, asking what was to become of them, stammering that she had been standing there in despair for the last ten minutes, but could see nobody to help them, which was not surprising with that terrible rain falling and the cold so bitter. And while she stammered all this, the calls for help and the cries of pain became louder in the depths of the waste ground.

Though Madame Angelin was terribly upset, she nevertheless hesitated, as if distrustful.

"You must run to get a doctor, my poor child," said she, "I can do nothing."

"Oh! but you can, madame; come with me, I pray you. I don't know where there's a doctor to be found. Come with me, and we will pick him up, for I can't manage it by myself; and at all events we can lay him in the shed, so that the rain sha'n't pour down on him."

This time the good woman consented, so truthful did the girl's accents seem to be. Constant visits to the vilest dens, where crime sprouted from the dunghill of poverty, had made Madame Angelin brave. She was obliged to close her umbrella when she glided through the breach in the fence in the wake of the girl, who, slim and supple like a cat, glided on in front, bareheaded, in her ragged shawl.

"Give me your hand, madame," said she. "Take care, for there are some trenches. . . It's over yonder at the end. Can you hear how he's moaning, poor brother? . . . Ah! here we are!"

Then came swift and overwhelming savagery. The three bandits, Alexandre, Richard, and Alfred, who had been crouching low, sprang forward and threw themselves upon Madame Angelin with such hungry, wolfish violence that she was thrown to the ground. Alfred, however, being a coward, then left her to the two others, and hastened with Toinette to the breach in order to keep watch. Alexandre, who had a handkerchief rolled up, all ready, thrust it into the poor lady's mouth to stifle her cries. Their intention was to stun her only and then make off with her little bag.

But the handkerchief must have slipped out, for she suddenly raised a shriek, a loud and terrible shriek. And at that moment the others near the breach gave the alarm whistle: some people were, doubtless, drawing near. It was necessary to finish. Alexandre knotted the handkerchief round the unhappy woman's neck, while Richard with his fist forced her shriek back into her throat. Red madness fell upon them, they both began to twist and tighten the handkerchief, and dragged the poor creature over the muddy ground until she stirred no more. Then, as the whistle sounded again, they took the bag, left the body there with the handkerchief around the neck, and galloped, all four of them, as far as the Grenelle bridge, whence they flung the bag into the Seine, after greedily thrusting the coppers, and the white silver, and the yellow gold into their pockets.

When Mathieu read the particulars of the crime in the newspapers, he was seized with fright and hastened to the Rue de la Federation. The murdered woman had been promptly identified, and the circumstance that the crime had been committed on that plot of vacant ground but a hundred yards or so from the house where Norine and Cecile lived upset him, filled him with a terrible presentiment. And he immediately realized that his fears were justified when he had to knock three times at Norine's door before Cecile, having recognized his voice, removed the articles with which it had been barricaded, and admitted him inside. Norine was in bed, quite ill, and as white as her sheets. She began to sob and shuddered repeatedly as she told him the story: Madame Angelin's visit the previous month, and the sudden arrival of Alexandre, who had seen the bag and had heard the promise of further help, at a certain hour on a certain date. Besides, Norine could have no doubts, for the handkerchief found round the victim's neck was one of hers which Alexandre had stolen: a handkerchief embroidered with the initial letters of her Christian name, one of those cheap fancy things which are sold by thousands at the big linendrapery establishments. That handkerchief, too, was the only clew to the murderers, and it was such a very vague one that the police were still vainly seeking the culprits, quite lost amid a variety of scents and despairing of success.

Mathieu sat near the bed listening to Norine and feeling icy cold. Good God! that poor, unfortunate Madame Angelin! He could picture her in her younger days, so gay and bright over yonder at Janville, roaming the woods there in the company of her husband, the pair of them losing themselves among the deserted paths, and lingering in the discreet shade of the pollard willows beside the Yeuse, where their love kisses sounded beneath the branches like the twittering of song birds. And he could picture her at a later date, already too severely punished for her lack of foresight, in despair at remaining childless, and bowed down with grief as by slow degrees her husband became blind, and night fell upon the little happiness yet left to them. And all at once Mathieu also pictured that wretched blind man, on the evening when he vainly awaited the return of his wife, in order that she might feed him and put him to bed, old child that he was, now motherless, forsaken, forever alone in his dark night, in which he could only see the bloody spectre of his murdered helpmate. Ah! to think of it, so bright a promise of radiant life, followed by such destiny, such death!

"We did right," muttered Mathieu, as his thoughts turned to Constance, "we did right to keep that ruffian in ignorance of his father's name. What a terrible thing! We must bury the secret as deeply as possible within us."

Norine shuddered once more.

"Oh! have no fear," she answered, "I would die rather than speak."

Months, years, flowed by; and never did the police discover the murderers of the lady with the little bag. For years, too, Norine shuddered every time that anybody knocked too roughly at her door. But Alexandre did not reappear there. He doubtless feared that corner of the Rue de la Federation, and remained as it were submerged in the dim unsoundable depths of the ocean of Paris.

XX

During the ten years which followed, the vigorous sprouting of the Froments, suggestive of some healthy vegetation of joy and strength, continued in and around the ever and ever richer domain of Chantebled. As the sons and the daughters grew up there came fresh marriages, and more and more children, all the promised crop, all the promised swarming of a race of conquerors.

First it was Gervais who married Caroline Boucher, daughter of a big farmer of the region, a fair, fine-featured, gay, strong girl, one of those superior women born to rule over a little army of servants. On leaving a Parisian boarding-school she had been sensible enough to feel no shame of her family's connection with the soil. Indeed she loved the earth and had set herself to win from it all the sterling happiness of her life. By way of dowry she brought an expanse of meadow-land in the direction of Lillebonne, which enlarged the estate by some seventy acres. But she more particularly brought her good humor, her health, her courage in rising early, in watching over the farmyard, the dairy, the whole home, like an energetic active housewife, who was ever bustling about, and always the last to bed.

Then came the turn of Claire, whose marriage with Frederic Berthaud, long since foreseen, ended by taking place. There were tears of soft emotion, for the memory of her whom Berthaud had loved and whom he was to have married disturbed several hearts on the wedding day when the family skirted the little cemetery of Janville as it returned to the farm from the municipal offices. But, after all, did not that love of former days, that faithful fellow's long affection, which in time had become transferred to the younger sister, constitute as it were another link in the ties which bound him to the Froments? He had no fortune, he brought with him only his constant faithfulness, and the fraternity which had sprung up between himself and Gervais during the many seasons when they had ploughed the estate like a span of tireless oxen drawing the same plough. His heart was one that could never be doubted, he was the helper who had become indispensable, the husband whose advent would mean the best of all understandings and absolute certainty of happiness.

From the day of that wedding the government of the farm was finally settled. Though Mathieu was barely five-and-fifty he abdicated, and transferred his authority to Gervais, that son of the earth as with a laugh he often called him, the first of his children born at Chantebled, the one who had never left the farm, and who had at all times given him the support of his arm and his brain and his heart. And now Frederic in turn would think and strive as Gervais's devoted lieutenant, in the great common task. Between them henceforth they would continue the father's work, and perfect the system of culture, procuring appliances of new design from the Beauchene works, now ruled by Denis, and ever drawing from the soil the largest crops that it could be induced to yield. Their wives had likewise divided their share of authority; Claire surrendered the duties of supervision to Caroline, who was stronger and more active than herself, and was content to attend to the accounts, the turnover of considerable sums of money, all that was paid away and all that was received. The two couples seemed to have been expressly and cleverly selected to complete one another and to accomplish the greatest sum of work without ever the slightest fear of conflict. And, indeed, they lived in perfect union, with only one will among them, one purpose which was ever more and more skilfully effected—the continual increase of the happiness and wealth of Chantebled under the beneficent sun.

At the same time, if Mathieu had renounced the actual exercise of authority, he none the less remained the creator, the oracle who was consulted, listened to, and obeyed. He dwelt with Marianne in the old shooting-box which had been transformed and enlarged into a very comfortable house. Here they lived like the founders of a dynasty who had retired in full glory, setting their only delight in beholding around them the development and expansion of their race, the birth and growth of their children's children. Leaving Claire and Gervais on one side, there were as yet only Denis and Ambroise—the first to wing their flight abroad—engaged in building up their fortunes in Paris. The three girls, Louise, Madeleine, and Marguerite, who would soon be old enough to marry, still dwelt in the happy home beside their parents, as well as the three youngest boys, Gregoire, the free lance, Nicolas, the most stubborn and determined of the brood, and Benjamin, who was of a dreamy nature. All these finished growing up at the edge of the nest, so to say, with the window of life open before them, ready for the day when they likewise would take wing.

With them dwelt Charlotte, Blaise's widow, and her two children, Berthe and Guillaume, the three of them occupying an upper floor of the house where the mother had installed her studio. She was becoming rich since her little share in the factory profits, stipulated by Denis, had been increasing year by year; but nevertheless, she continued working for her dealer in miniatures. This work brought her pocket-money, she gayly said, and would enable her to make her children a present whenever they might marry. There was, indeed, already some thought of Berthe marrying; and assuredly she would be the first of Mathieu and Marianne's grandchildren to enter into the state of matrimony. They smiled softly at the idea of becoming great-grandparents before very long perhaps.

After the lapse of four years, Gregoire, first of the younger children, flew away. There was a great deal of trouble, quite a little drama in connection with the affair, which Mathieu and Marianne had for some time been anticipating. Gregoire was anything but reasonable. Short, but robust, with a pert face in which glittered the brightest of eyes, he had always been the turbulent member of the family, the one who caused the most anxiety. His childhood had been spent in playing truant in the woods of Janville, and he had afterwards made a mere pretence of studying in Paris, returning home full of health and spirits, but unable or unwilling to make up his mind with respect to any particular trade or profession. Already four-and-twenty, he knew little more than how to shoot and fish, and trot about the country on horseback. He was certainly not more stupid or less active than another, but he seemed bent on living and amusing himself according to his fancy. The worst was that for some months past all the gossips of Janville had been relating that he had renewed his former boyish friendship with Therese Lepailleur, the miller's daughter, and that they were to be met of an evening in shady nooks under the pollard-willows by the Yeuse.

One morning Mathieu, wishing to ascertain if the young coveys of partridges were plentiful in the direction of Mareuil, took Gregoire with him; and when they found themselves alone among the plantations of the plateau, he began to talk to him seriously.

"You know I'm not pleased with you, my lad," said he. "I really cannot understand the idle life which you lead here, while all the rest of us are hard at work. I shall wait till October since you have positively promised me that you will then come to a decision and choose the calling which you most fancy. But what is all this tittle-tattle which I hear about appointments which you keep with the daughter of the Lepailleurs? Do you wish to cause us serious worry?"

Gregoire quietly began to laugh.

"Oh, father! You are surely not going to scold a son of yours because he happens to be on friendly terms with a pretty girl! Why, as you may remember, it was I who gave her her first bicycle lesson nearly ten years ago. And you will recollect the fine white roses which she helped me to secure in the enclosure by the mill for Denis' wedding."

Gregoire still laughed at the memory of that incident, and lived afresh through all his old time sweethearting—the escapades with Therese along the river banks, and the banquets of blackberries in undiscoverable hiding-places, deep in the woods. And it seemed, too, that the love of childhood had revived, and was now bursting into consuming fire, so vividly did his cheeks glow, and so hotly did his eyes blaze as he thus recalled those distant times.

"Poor Therese! We had been at daggers drawn for years, and all because one evening, on coming back from the fair at Vieux-Bourg, I pushed her into a pool of water where she dirtied her frock. It's true that last spring we made it up again on finding ourselves face to face in the little wood at Monval over yonder. But come, father, do you mean to say that it's a crime if we take a little pleasure in speaking to one another when we meet?"

Rendered the more anxious by the fire with which Gregoire sought to defend the girl, Mathieu spoke out plainly.

"A crime? No, if you just wish one another good day and good evening. Only folks relate that you are to be seen at dusk with your arms round each other's waist, and that you go stargazing through the grass alongside the Yeuse."

Then, as Gregoire this time without replying laughed yet more loudly, with the merry laugh of youth, his father gravely resumed:

"Listen, my lad, it is not at all to my taste to play the gendarme behind my sons. But I won't have you drawing some unpleasant business with the Lepailleurs on us all. You know the position, they would be delighted to give us trouble. So don't give them occasion for complaining, leave their daughter alone."

"Oh! I take plenty of care," cried the young man, thus suddenly confessing the truth. "Poor girl! She has already had her ears boxed because somebody told her father that I had been met with her. He answered that rather than give her to me he would throw her into the river."

"Ah! you see," concluded Mathieu. "It is understood, is it not? I shall rely on your good behavior."

Thereupon they went their way, scouring the fields as far as the road to Mareuil. Coveys of young partridges, still weak on the wing, started up both to the right and to the left. The shooting would be good. Then as the father and the son turned homeward, slackening their pace, a long spell of silence fell between them. They were both reflecting.

"I don't wish that there should be any misunderstanding between us," Mathieu suddenly resumed; "you must not imagine that I shall prevent you from marrying according to your tastes and that I shall require you to take an heiress. Our poor Blaise married a portionless girl. And it was the same with Denis; besides which I gave your sister, Claire, in marriage to Frederic, who was simply one of our farm hands. So I don't look down on Therese. On the contrary, I think her charming. She's one of the prettiest girls of the district—not tall, certainly, but so alert and determined, with her little pink face shining under such a wild crop of fair hair, that one might think her powdered with all the flour in the mill."

"Yes, isn't that so, father?" interrupted Gregoire enthusiastically. "And if you only knew how affectionate and courageous she is! She's worth a man any day. It's wrong of them to smack her, for she will never put up with it. Whenever she sets her mind on anything she's bound to do it, and it isn't I who can prevent her."

Absorbed in some reflections of his own, Mathieu scarcely heard his son.

"No, no," he resumed; "I certainly don't look down on their mill. If it were not for Lepailleur's stupid obstinacy he would be drawing a fortune from that mill nowadays. Since corn-growing has again been taken up all over the district, thanks to our victory, he might have got a good pile of crowns together if he had simply changed the old mechanism of his wheel which he leaves rotting under the moss. And better still, I should like to see a good engine there, and a bit of a light railway line connecting the mill with Janville station."

In this fashion he continued explaining his ideas while Gregoire listened, again quite lively and taking things in a jesting way.

"Well, father," the young man ended by saying, "as you wish that I should have a calling, it's settled. If I marry Therese, I'll be a miller."

Mathieu protested in surprise: "No, no, I was merely talking. And besides, you have promised me, my lad, that you will be reasonable. So once again, for the sake of the peace and quietness of all of us, leave Therese alone, for we can only expect to reap worry with the Lepailleurs."

The conversation ceased and they returned to the farm. That evening, however, the father told the mother of the young man's confession, and she, who already entertained various misgivings, felt more anxious than ever. Still a month went by without anything serious happening.

Then, one morning Marianne was astounded at finding Gregoire's bedroom empty. As a rule he came to kiss her. Perhaps he had risen early, and had gone on some excursion in the environs. But she trembled slightly when she remembered how lovingly he had twice caught her in his arms on the previous night when they were all retiring to bed. And as she looked inquisitively round the room she noticed on the mantelshelf a letter addressed to her—a prettily worded letter in which the young fellow begged her to forgive him for causing her grief, and asked her to excuse him with his father, for it was necessary that he should leave them for a time. Of his reasons for doing so and his purpose, however, no particulars were given.

This family rending, this bad conduct on the part of the son who had been the most spoilt of all, and who, in a fit of sudden folly was the first to break the ties which united the household together, was a very painful blow for Marianne and Mathieu. They were the more terrified since they divined that Gregoire had not gone off alone. They pieced together the incidents of the deplorable affair. Charlotte remembered that she had heard Gregoire go downstairs again, almost immediately after entering his bedroom, and before the servants had even bolted the house-doors for the night. He had certainly rushed off to join Therese in some coppice, whence they must have hurried away to Vieux-Bourg station which the last train to Paris quitted at five-and-twenty minutes past midnight. And it was indeed this which had taken place. At noon the Froments already learnt that Lepailleur was creating a terrible scandal about the flight of Therese. He had immediately gone to the gendarmes to shout the story to them, and demand that they should bring the guilty hussy back, chained to her accomplice, and both of them with gyves about their wrists.

He on his side had found a letter in his daughter's bedroom, a plucky letter in which she plainly said that as she had been struck again the previous day, she had had enough of it, and was going off of her own free will. Indeed, she added that she was taking Gregoire with her, and was quite big and old enough, now that she was two-and-twenty, to know what she was about. Lepailleur's fury was largely due to this letter which he did not dare to show abroad; besides which, his wife, ever at

ÉMILE ZOLA

war with him respecting their son Antonin, not only roundly abused Therese, but sneeringly declared that it might all have been expected, and that he, the father, was the cause of the gad-about's misconduct. After that, they engaged in fisticuffs; and for a whole week the district did nothing but talk about the flight of one of the Chantebled lads with the girl of the mill, to the despair of Mathieu and Marianne, the latter of whom in particular grieved over the sorry business.

Five days later, a Sunday, matters became even worse. As the search for the runaways remained fruitless Lepailleur, boiling over with rancor, went up to the farm, and from the middle of the road—for he did not venture inside—poured forth a flood of ignoble insults. It so happened that Mathieu was absent; and Marianne had great trouble to restrain Gervais as well as Frederic, both of whom wished to thrust the miller's scurrilous language back into his throat. When Mathieu came home in the evening he was extremely vexed to hear of what had happened.

"It is impossible for this state of things to continue," he said to his wife, as they were retiring to rest. "It looks as if we were hiding, as if we were guilty in the matter. I will go to see that man in the morning. There is only one thing, and a very simple one, to be done, those unhappy children must be married. For our part we consent, is it not so? And it is to that man's advantage to consent also. To-morrow the matter must be settled."

On the following day, Monday, at two o'clock in the afternoon, Mathieu set out for the mill. But certain complications, a tragic drama, which he could not possibly foresee, awaited him there. For years now a stubborn struggle had been going on between Lepailleur and his wife with respect to Antonin. While the farmer had grown more and more exasperated with his son's idleness and life of low debauchery in Paris, the latter had supported her boy with all the obstinacy of an illiterate woman, who was possessed of a blind faith in his fine handwriting, and felt convinced that if he did not succeed in life it was simply because he was refused the money necessary for that purpose. In spite of her sordid avarice in some matters, the old woman continued bleeding herself for her son, and even robbed the house, promptly thrusting out her claws and setting her teeth ready to bite whenever she was caught in the act, and had to defend some twenty-franc piece or other, which she had been on the point of sending away. And each time the battle began afresh, to such a point indeed that it seemed as if the shaky old mill would some day end by falling on their heads.

Then, all at once, Antonin, a perfect wreck at thirty-six years of age, fell seriously ill. Lepailleur forthwith declared that if the scamp had the audacity to come home he would pitch him over the wheel into the water. Antonin, however, had no desire to return home; he held the country in horror and feared, too, that his father might chain him up like a dog. So his mother placed him with some people of Batignolles, paying for his board and for the attendance of a doctor of the district. This had been going on for three months or so, and every fortnight La Lepailleur went to see her son. She had done so the previous Thursday, and on the Sunday evening she received a telegram summoning her to Batignolles again. Thus, on the morning of the day when Mathieu repaired to the mill, she had once more gone to Paris after a frightful quarrel with her husband, who asked if their good-for-nothing son ever meant to cease fooling them and spending their money, when he had not the courage even to turn a spit of earth.

Alone in the mill that morning Lepailleur did not cease storming. At the slightest provocation he would have hammered his plough to pieces, or have rushed, axe in hand, and mad with hatred, on the old wheel by way of avenging his misfortunes. When he saw Mathieu come in he believed in some act of bravado, and almost choked.

"Come, neighbor," said the master of Chantebled cordially, "let us both try to be reasonable. I've come to return your visit, since you called upon me yesterday. Only, bad words never did good work, and the best course, since this misfortune has happened, is to repair it as speedily as possible. When would you have us marry off those bad children?"

Thunderstruck by the quiet good nature of this frontal attack, Lepailleur did not immediately reply. He had shouted over the house roofs that he would have no marriage at all, but rather a good lawsuit by way of sending all the Froments to prison. Nevertheless, when it came to reflection, a son of the big farmer of Chantebled was not to be disdained as a son-in-law.

"Marry them, marry them," he stammered at the first moment. "Yes, by fastening a big stone to both their necks and throwing them together into the river. Ah! the wretches! I'll skin them, I will, her as well as him."

At last, however, the miller grew calmer and was even showing a disposition to discuss matters, when all at once an urchin of Janville came running across the yard.

"What do you want, eh?" called the master of the premises.

"Please, Monsieur Lepailleur, it's a telegram."

"All right, give it here."

The lad, well pleased with the copper he received as a gratuity, had already gone off, and still the miller, instead of opening the telegram, stood examining the address on it with the distrustful air of a man who does not often receive such communications. However, he at last had to tear it open. It contained but three words: "Your son dead"; and in that brutal brevity, that prompt, hasty bludgeon-blow, one could detect the mother's cold rage and eager craving to crush without delay the man, the father yonder, whom she accused of having caused her son's death, even as she had accused him of being responsible for her daughter's flight. He felt this full well, and staggered beneath the shock, stunned by the words that appeared on that strip of blue paper, reading them again and again till he ended by understanding them. Then his hands began to tremble and he burst into oaths.

"Thunder and blazes! What again is this? Here's the boy dying now! Everything's going to the devil!"

But his heart dilated and tears appeared in his eyes. Unable to remain standing, he sank upon a chair and again obstinately read the telegram; "Your son dead—Your son dead," as if seeking something else, the particulars, indeed, which the message did not contain. Perhaps the boy had died before his mother's arrival. Or perhaps she had arrived just before he died. Such were his stammered comments. And he repeated a score of times that she had taken the train at ten minutes past eleven and must have reached Batignolles about half-past twelve. As she had handed in the telegram at twenty minutes past one it seemed more likely that she had found the lad already dead.

"Curse it! curse it!" he shouted; "a cursed telegram, it tells you nothing, and it murders you! She might, at all events, have sent somebody. I shall have to go there. Ah the whole thing's complete, it's more than a man can bear!"

Lepailleur shouted those words in such accents of rageful despair that Mathieu, full of compassion, made bold to intervene. The sudden shock of the tragedy had staggered him, and he had hitherto waited in silence. But now he offered his services and spoke of accompanying the other to Paris. He had to retreat, however, for the miller rose to his feet, seized with wild exasperation at perceiving him still there in his house.

"Ah! yes, you came; and what was it you were saying to me? That we ought to marry off those wretched children? Well, you can see that I'm in proper trim for a wedding! My boy's dead! You've chosen your day well. Be off with you, be off with you, I say, if you don't want me to do something dreadful!"

He raised his fists, quite maddened as he was by the presence of Mathieu at that moment when his whole life was wrecked. It was terrible indeed that this bourgeois who had made a fortune by turning himself into a peasant should be there at the moment when he so suddenly learnt the death of Antonin, that son whom he had dreamt of turning into a Monsieur by filling his mind with disgust of the soil and sending him to rot of idleness and vice in Paris! It enraged him to find that he had erred, that the earth whom he had slandered, whom he had taxed with decrepitude and barrenness was really a living, youthful, and fruitful spouse to the man who knew how to love her! And nought but ruin remained around him, thanks to his imbecile resolve to limit his family: a foul life had killed his only son, and his only daughter had gone off with a scion of the triumphant farm, while he was now utterly alone, weeping and howling in his deserted mill, that mill which he had likewise disdained and which was crumbling around him with old age.

"You hear me!" he shouted. "Therese may drag herself at my feet; but I will never, never give her to your thief of a son! You'd like it, wouldn't you? so that folks might mock me all over the district, and so that you might eat me up as you have eaten up all the others!"

This finish to it all had doubtless appeared to him, confusedly, in a sudden threatening vision: Antonin being dead, it was Gregoire who would possess the mill, if he should marry Therese. And he would possess the moorland also, that enclosure, hitherto left barren with such savage delight, and so passionately coveted by the farm. And doubtless he would cede it to the farm as soon as he should be the master. The thought that Chantebled might yet be increased by the fields which he, Lepailleur, had withheld from it brought the miller's delirious rage to a climax.

"Your son, I'll send him to the galleys! And you, if you don't go, I'll throw you out! Be off with you, be off!"

Mathieu, who was very pale, slowly retired before this furious madman. But as he went off he calmly said: "You are an unhappy man. I forgive you, for you are in great grief. Besides, I am quite easy, sensible things always end by taking place."

Again, a month went by. Then, one rainy morning in October, Madame Lepailleur was found hanging in the mill stable. There were folks at Janville who related that Lepailleur had hung her there. The truth was that she had given signs of melancholia ever since the death of Antonin. Moreover, the life led at the mill was no longer bearable; day by day the husband and wife reproached one another for their son's death and their daughter's flight, battling ragefully together like two abandoned beasts shut up in the same cage. Folks were merely astonished that such a harsh, avaricious woman should have been willing to quit this life without taking her goods and chattels with her.

As soon as Therese heard of her mother's death she hastened home, repentant, and took her place beside her father again, unwilling as she was that he should remain alone in his two-fold bereavement. At first it proved a terrible time for her in the company of that brutal old man who was exasperated by what he termed his bad luck. But she was a girl of sterling courage and prompt decision; and thus, after a few weeks, she had made her father consent to her marriage with Gregoire, which, as Mathieu had said, was the only sensible course. The news gave great relief at the farm whither the prodigal son had not yet dared to return. It was believed that the young couple, after eloping together, had lived in some out of the way district of Paris, and it was even suspected that Ambroise, who was liberally minded, had, in a brotherly way, helped them with his purse. And if, on the one hand, Lepailleur consented to the marriage in a churlish, distrustful manner—like one who deemed himself robbed, and was simply influenced by the egotistical dread of some day finding himself quite alone again in his gloomy house— Mathieu and Marianne, on the other side, were delighted with an arrangement which put an end to an equivocal situation that had caused them the greatest suffering, grieved as they were by the rebellion of one of their children.

Curiously enough, it came to pass that Gregoire, once married and installed at the mill in accordance with his wife's desire, agreed with his father-in-law far better than had been anticipated. This resulted in particular from a certain discussion during which Lepailleur had wished to make Gregoire swear, that, after his death, he would never dispose of the moorland enclosure, hitherto kept uncultivated with peasant stubbornness, to any of his brothers or sisters of the farm. Gregoire took no oath on the subject, but gayly declared that he was not such a fool as to despoil his wife of the best part of her inheritance, particularly as he proposed to cultivate those moors and, within two or three years' time, make them the most fertile land in the district. That which belonged to him did not belong to others, and people would soon see that he was well able to defend the property which had fallen to his lot. Things took a similar course with respect to the mill, where Gregoire at first contented himself with repairing the old mechanism, for he was unwilling to upset the miller's habits all at once, and therefore postponed until some future time the installation of an engine, and the laying down of a line of rails to Janville station—all those ideas formerly propounded by Mathieu which henceforth fermented in his audacious young mind.

In this wise, then, people found themselves in presence of a new Gregoire. The madcap had become wise, only retaining of his youthful follies the audacity which is needful for successful enterprise. And it must be said that he was admirably seconded by the fair and energetic Therese. They were both enraptured at now being free to love each other in the romantic old mill, garlanded with ivy, pending the time when they would resolutely fling it to the ground to install in its place the great white meal stores and huge new mill-stones, which, with their conquering ambition, they often dreamt of.

During the years that followed, Mathieu and Marianne witnessed other departures. The three daughters, Louise, Madeleine, and Marguerite, in turn took their flight from the family nest. All three found husbands in the district. Louise, a plump brunette, all gayety and health, with abundant hair and large laughing eyes, married notary Mazaud of Janville, a quiet, pensive little man, whose occasional silent smiles alone denoted the perfect satisfaction which he felt at having found a wife of such joyous disposition. Then Madeleine, whose chestnut tresses were tinged with gleaming gold, and who was slimmer than her sister, and of a more dreamy style of beauty, her character and disposition refined by her musical tastes, made a love match which was quite a romance. Herbette, the architect, who became her husband, was a handsome, elegant man, already celebrated; he owned near Monvel a park-like estate, where he came to rest at times from the fatigue of his labors in Paris.

At last, Marguerite, the least pretty of the girls—indeed, she was quite plain, but derived a charm from her infinite goodness of heart— was chosen in marriage by Dr. Chambouvet, a big, genial, kindly fellow, who had inherited his father's practice at Vieux-Bourg, where he lived in a large white house, which had become the resort of the poor. And thus the three girls being married, the only ones who remained with Mathieu and Marianne in the slowly emptying nest were their two last boys, Nicolas and Benjamin.

At the same time, however, as the youngsters flew away and installed themselves elsewhere, there came other little ones, a constant swarming due to the many family marriages. In eight years, Denis, who reigned at the factory in Paris, had been presented by his wife with three children, two boys, Lucien and Paul, and a girl, Hortense. Then Leonce, the son of Ambroise, who was conquering such a high position in the commercial world, now had a brother, Charles, and two little sisters, Pauline and Sophie. At the farm, moreover, Gervais was already the father of two boys, Leon and Henri, while Claire, his sister, could count three children, a boy, Joseph, and two daughters, Lucile and Angele. There was also Gregoire, at the mill, with a big boy who had received the name of Robert; and there were also the three last married daughters—Louise, with a girl two years old; Madeleine, with a boy six months of age; and Marguerite, who in anticipation of a happy event, had decided to call her child Stanislas, if it were a boy, and Christine, if it should be a girl.

Thus upon every side the family oak spread out its branches, its trunk forking and multiplying, and boughs sprouting from boughs at each successive season. And withal Mathieu was not yet sixty, and Marianne not yet fifty-seven. Both still possessed flourishing health, and strength, and gayety, and were ever in delight at seeing the family, which had sprung from them, thus growing and spreading, invading all the country around, even like a forest born from a single tree.

But the great and glorious festival of Chantebled at that period was the birth of Mathieu and Marianne's first great-grandchild—a girl, called Angeline, daughter of their granddaughter, Berthe. In this little girl, all pink and white, the ever-regretted Blaise seemed to live again. So closely did she resemble him that Charlotte, his widow, already a grandmother in her forty-second year, wept with emotion at the sight of her. Madame Desvignes had died six months previously, passing away, even as she had lived, gently and discreetly, at the termination of her task, which had chiefly consisted in rearing her two daughters on the scanty means at her disposal. Still it was she, who, before quitting the scene, had found a husband for her granddaughter, Berthe, in the person of Philippe Havard, a young engineer who had recently been appointed assistant-manager at a State factory near Mareuil. It was at Chantebled, however, that Berthe's little Angeline was born; and on the day of the churching, the whole family assembled together there once more to glorify the great-grandfather and great-grandmother.

"Ah! well," said Marianne gayly, as she stood beside the babe's cradle, "if the young ones fly away there are others born, and so the nest will never be empty."

"Never, never!" repeated Mathieu with emotion, proud as he felt of that continual victory over solitude and death. "We shall never be left alone!"

Yet there came another departure which brought them many tears. Nicolas, the youngest but one of their boys, who was approaching his twentieth birthday, and thus nigh the cross-roads of life, had not yet decided which one he would follow. He was a dark, sturdy young man, with an open, laughing face. As a child, he had adored tales of travel and far-away adventure, and had always evinced great courage and endurance, returning home enraptured from interminable rambles, and never uttering complaints, however badly his feet might be blistered. And withal he possessed a most orderly mind, ever carefully arranging and classifying his little belongings in his drawers, and looking down with contempt on the haphazard way in which his sisters kept their things.

Later on, as he grew up, he became thoughtful, as if he were vainly seeking around him some means of realizing his two-fold craving, that of discovering some new land and organizing it properly. One of the last-born of a numerous family, he no longer found space enough for the amplitude and force of his desires. His brothers and sisters had already taken all the surrounding lands, and he stifled, threatened also, as it were, with famine, and ever sought the broad expanse that he dreamt of, where he might grow and reap his bread. No more room, no more food! At first he knew not in which direction to turn, but groped and hesitated for some months. Nevertheless, his hearty laughter continued to gladden the house; he wearied neither his father nor his mother with the care of his destiny, for he knew that he was already strong enough to fix it himself.

There was no corner left for him at the farm where Gervais and Claire took up all the room. At the Beauchene works Denis was all sufficient, reigning there like a conscientious toiler, and nothing justified a younger brother in claiming a share beside him. At the mill, too, Gregoire was as yet barely established, and his kingdom was so small that he could not possibly cede half of it. Thus an opening was only possible with Ambroise, and Nicolas ended by accepting an obliging offer which the latter made to take him on trial for a few months, by way of initiating him into the higher branches of commerce. Ambroise's fortune was becoming prodigious since old uncle Du Hordel had died, leaving him his commission business. Year by year the new master increased his trade with all the countries of the world. Thanks to his lucky audacity and broad international views, he was enriching himself with the spoils of the earth. And though Nicolas again began to stifle in Ambroise's huge store-houses, where the riches of distant countries, the most varied climes, were collected together, it was there that his real vocation came to him; for a voice suddenly arose, calling him away yonder to dim, unknown regions, vast stretches of country yet sterile, which needed to be populated, and cleared and sowed with the crops of the future.

For two months Nicolas kept silent respecting the designs which he was now maturing. He was extremely discreet, as are all men of great energy, who reflect before they act. He must go, that was certain, since neither space nor sufficiency of sunlight remained for him in the cradle of his birth; but if he went off alone, would that not be going in an imperfect state, deficient in the means needed for the heroic task of populating and clearing a new land? He knew a girl of Janville, one Lisbeth Moreau, who was tall and strong, and whose robust health, seriousness, and activity had charmed him. She was nineteen years of age, and, like Nicolas, she stifled in the little nook to which destiny had confined her; for she craved for the free and open air, yonder, afar off. An orphan, and long dependent on an aunt, who was simply a little village haberdasher, she had hitherto, from feelings of affection, remained cloistered in a small and gloomy shop. But her aunt had lately died, leaving her some ten thousand francs, and her dream was to sell the little business, and go away and really live at last. One October evening, when Nicolas and Lisbeth told one another things that they had never previously told anybody, they came to an understanding. They resolutely took each other's hand and plighted their troth for life, for the hard battle of creating a new world, a new family, somewhere on the earth's broad surface, in those mysterious, far away climes of which they knew so little. 'Twas a delightful betrothal, full of courage and faith.

Only then, everything having been settled, did Nicolas speak out, announcing his departure to his father and mother. It was an autumn evening, still mild, but fraught with winter's first shiver, and the twilight was falling. Intense grief wrung the parents' hearts as soon as they understood their son. This time it was not simply a young one flying from the family nest to build his own on some neighboring tree of the common forest; it was flight across the seas forever, severance without hope of return. They would see their other children again, but this one was breathing an eternal farewell. Their consent would be the share of cruel sacrifice, that life demands, their supreme gift to life, the tithe levied by life on their affection and their blood. To pursue its victory, life, the perpetual conqueror, demanded this portion of their flesh, this overplus of the numerous family, which was overflowing, spreading, peopling the world. And what could they answer, how could they refuse? The son who was unprovided for took himself off; nothing could be more logical or more sensible. Far beyond the fatherland there were vast continents yet uninhabited, and the seed which is scattered by the breezes of heaven knows no frontiers. Beyond the race there is mankind with that endless spreading of humanity that is leading us to the one fraternal people of the accomplished times, when the whole earth shall be but one sole city of truth and justice.

Moreover, quite apart from the great dream of those seers, the poets, Nicolas, like a practical man, whatever his enthusiasm, gayly gave his reasons for departing. He did not wish to be a parasite; he was setting off to the conquest of another land, where he would grow the bread he needed, since his own country had no field left for him. Besides, he took his country with him in his blood; she it was that he wished to enlarge afar off with unlimited increase of wealth and strength. It was ancient Africa, the mysterious, now explored, traversed from end to end, that attracted him. In the first instance he intended to repair to Senegal, whence he would doubtless push on to the Soudan, to the very heart of the virgin lands where he dreamt of a new France, an immense colonial empire, which would rejuvenate the old Gallic race by endowing it with its due share of the earth. And it was there that he had the ambition of carving out a kingdom for himself, and of founding with Lisbeth another dynasty of Froments, and a new Chantebled, covering under the hot sun a tract ten times as extensive as the old one, and peopled with the people of his own children. And he spoke of all this with such joyous courage that Mathieu and Marianne ended by smiling amid their tears, despite the rending of their poor hearts.

"Go, my lad, we cannot keep you back. Go wherever life calls you, wherever you may live with more health and joy and strength. All that may spring from you yonder will still be health and joy and strength derived from us, of which we shall be proud. You are right, one must not weep, your departure must be a fete, for the family does not separate, it simply extends, invades, and conquers the world."

Nevertheless, on the day of farewell, after the marriage of Nicolas and Lisbeth there was an hour of painful emotion at Chantebled. The family had met to share a last meal all together, and when the time came for the young and adventurous couple to tear themselves from the maternal soil there were those who sobbed although they had vowed to be very brave. Nicolas and Lisbeth were going off with little means, but rich in hopes. Apart from the ten thousand francs of the wife's dowry they had only been willing to take another ten thousand, just enough to provide for the first difficulties. Might courage and labor therefore prove sturdy artisans of conquest.

Young Benjamin, the last born of the brothers Froment, was particularly upset by this departure. He was a delicate, good-looking child not yet twelve years old, whom his parents greatly spoiled, thinking that he was weak. And they were quite determined that they would at all events keep him with them, so handsome did they find him with his soft limpid eyes and beautiful curly hair. He was growing up in a languid way, dreamy, petted, idle among his mother's skirts, like the one charming weakling of that strong, hardworking family.

"Let me kiss you again, my good Nicolas," said he to his departing brother. "When will you come back?"

"Never, my little Benjamin."

The boy shuddered.

"Never, never!" he repeated. "Oh! that's too long. Come back, come back some day, so that I may kiss you again."

"Never," repeated Nicolas, turning pale himself. "Never, never."

He had lifted up the lad, whose tears were raining fast; and then for all came the supreme grief, the frightful moment of the hatchet-stroke, of the separation which was to be eternal.

"Good-by, little brother! Good-by, good-by, all of you!"

While Mathieu accompanied the future conqueror to the door for the last time wishing him victory, Benjamin in wild grief sought a refuge beside his mother who was blinded by her tears. And she caught him up with a passionate clasp, as if seized with fear that he also might leave her. He was the only one now left to them in the family nest.

XXI

At the factory, in her luxurious house on the quay, where she had long reigned as sovereign mistress, Constance for twelve years already had been waiting for destiny, remaining rigid and stubborn amid the continual crumbling of her life and hopes.

During those twelve years Beauchene had pursued a downward course, the descent of which was fatal. He was right at the bottom now, in the last state of degradation. After beginning simply as a roving husband, festively inclined, he had ended by living entirely away from his home, principally in the company of two women, aunt and niece. He was now but a pitiful human rag, fast approaching some shameful death. And large as his fortune had been, it had not sufficed him; as he grew older he had squandered money yet more and more lavishly, immense sums being swallowed up in disreputable adventures, the scandal of which it had been necessary to stifle. Thus he at last found himself poor, receiving but a small portion of the ever-increasing profits of the works, which were in full prosperity.

This was the disaster which brought so much suffering to Constance in her incurable pride. Beauchene, since the death of his son, had quite abandoned himself to a dissolute life, thinking of nothing but his pleasures, and taking no further interest in his establishment. What was the use of defending it, since there was no longer an heir to whom it might be transmitted, enlarged and enriched? And thus he had surrendered it, bit by bit, to Denis, his partner, whom, by degrees, he allowed to become the sole master. On arriving at the works, Denis had possessed but one of the six shares which represented the totality of the property according to the agreement. And Beauchene had even reserved to himself the right of repurchasing that share within a certain period. But far from being in a position to do so before the appointed date was passed, he had been obliged to cede yet another share to the young man, in order to free himself of debts which he could not confess.

From that time forward it became a habit with Beauchene to cede Denis a fresh share every two years. A third followed the second, then came the turn of the fourth and the fifth, in such wise, indeed, that after a final arrangement, he had not even kept a whole share for himself; but simply some portion of the sixth. And even that was really fictitious, for Denis had only acknowledged it in order to have a pretext for providing

ÉMILE ZOLA

him with a certain income, which, by the way, he subdivided, handing half of it to Constance every month.

She, therefore, was ignorant of nothing. She knew that, as a matter of fact, the works would belong to that son of the hated Froments, whenever he might choose to close the doors on their old master, who, as it happened, was never seen now in the workshops. True, there was a clause in the covenant which admitted, so long as that covenant should not be broken, the possibility of repurchasing all the shares at one and the same time. Was it, then, some mad hope of doing this, a fervent belief in a miracle, in the possibility of some saviour descending from Heaven, that kept Constance thus rigid and stubborn, awaiting destiny? Those twelve years of vain waiting—and increasing decline did not seem to have diminished her conviction that in spite of everything she would some day triumph. No doubt her tears had gushed forth at Chantebled in presence of the victory of Mathieu and Marianne; but she soon recovered her self-possession, and lived on in the hope that some unexpected occurrence would at last prove that she, the childless woman, was in the right.

She could not have said precisely what it was she wished; she was simply bent on remaining alive until misfortune should fall upon the over-numerous family, to exculpate her for what had happened in her own home, the loss of her son who was in the grave, and the downfall of her husband who was in the gutter—all the abomination, indeed, which had been so largely wrought by herself, but which filled her with agony. However much her heart might bleed over her losses, her vanity as an honest bourgeoise filled her with rebellious thoughts, for she could not admit that she had been in the wrong. And thus she awaited the revenge of destiny in that luxurious house, which was far too large now that she alone inhabited it. She only occupied the rooms on the first floor, where she shut herself up for days together with an old serving woman, the sole domestic that she had retained. Gowned in black, as if bent on wearing eternal mourning for Maurice, always erect, stiff, and haughtily silent, she never complained, although her covert exasperation had greatly affected her heart, in such wise that she experienced at times most terrible attacks of stifling. These she kept as secret as possible, and one day when the old servant ventured to go for Doctor Boutan she threatened her with dismissal. She would not even answer the doctor, and she refused to take any remedies, certain as she felt that she would last as long as the hope which buoyed her up.

Yet what anguish it was when she suddenly began to stifle, all alone in the empty house, without son or husband near her! She called nobody since she knew that nobody would come. And the attack over, with what unconquerable obstinacy did she rise erect again, repeating that her presence sufficed to prevent Denis from being the master, from reigning alone in full sovereignty, and that in any case he would not have the house and install himself in it like a conqueror, so long as she had not sunk to death under the final collapse of the ceilings.

Amid this retired life, Constance, haunted as she was by her fixed idea, had no other occupation than that of watching the factory, and ascertaining what went on there day by day. Morange, whom she had made her confidant, gave her information in all simplicity almost every evening, when he came to speak to her for a moment after leaving his office. She learnt everything from his lips—the successive sales of the shares into which the property had been divided, their gradual acquisition by Denis, and the fact that Beauchene and herself were henceforth living on the new master's liberality. Moreover, she so organized her system of espionage as to make the old accountant tell her unwittingly all that he knew of the private life led by Denis, his wife Marthe, and their children, Lucien, Paul, and Hortense all, indeed, that was done and said in the modest little pavilion where the young people, in spite of their increasing fortune, were still residing, evincing no ambitious haste to occupy the large house on the quay. They did not even seem to notice what scanty accommodation they had in that pavilion, while she alone dwelt in the gloomy mansion, which was so spacious that she seemed quite lost in it. And she was enraged, too, by their deference, by the tranquil way in which they waited for her to be no more; for she had been unable to make them quarrel with her, and was obliged to show herself grateful for the means they gave her, and to kiss their children, whom she hated, when they brought her flowers.

Thus, months and years went by, and almost every evening when Morange for a moment called on Constance, he found her in the same little silent salon, gowned in the same black dress, and stiffened into a posture of obstinate expectancy. Though no sign was given of destiny's revenge, of the patiently hoped-for fall of misfortune upon others, she never seemed to doubt of her ultimate victory. On the contrary, when things fell more and more heavily upon her, she drew herself yet more erect, defying fate, buoyed up by the conviction that it would at last be forced to prove that she was right. Thus, she remained immutable, superior to fatigue, and ever relying on a prodigy.

Each evening, when Morange called during those twelve years, the conversation invariably began in the same way.

"Nothing fresh since yesterday, dear madame?"

"No, my friend, nothing."

"Well, the chief thing is to enjoy good health. One can wait for better days."

"Oh! nobody enjoys good health; still one waits all the same."

And now one evening, at the end of the twelve years, as Morange went in to see her, he detected that the atmosphere of the little drawing-room was changed, quivering as it were with restrained delight amid the eternal silence.

"Nothing fresh since yesterday, dear madame?"

"Yes, my friend, there's something fresh."

"Something favorable I hope, then; something pleasant that you have been waiting for?"

"Something that I have been waiting for—yes! What one knows how to wait for always comes."

He looked at her in surprise, feeling almost anxious when he saw how altered she was, with glittering eyes and quick gestures. What fulfilment of her desires, after so many years of immutable mourning, could have resuscitated her like that? She smiled, she breathed vigorously, as if she were relieved of the enormous weight which had so long crushed and immured her. But when he asked the cause of her great happiness she said:

"I will not tell you yet, my friend. Perhaps I do wrong to rejoice; for everything is still very vague and doubtful. Only somebody told me this morning certain things, which I must make sure of, and think over. When I have done so I shall confide in you, you may rely on it, for I tell you everything; besides which, I shall no doubt need your help. So have a little patience, some evening you shall come to dinner with me here, and we shall have the whole evening before us to chat at our ease. But ah! *mon Dieu!* if it were only true, if it were only the miracle at last!"

More than three weeks elapsed before Morange heard anything further. He saw that Constance was very thoughtful and very feverish, but he did not even question her, absorbed as he himself was in the solitary, not to say automatic, life which he had made for himself. He had lately completed his sixty-ninth year; thirty years had gone by since the death of his wife Valerie, more than twenty since his daughter Reine had joined her, and he still ever lived on in his methodical, punctual manner, amid the downfall of his existence. Never had man suffered more than he, passed through greater tragedies, experienced keener remorse, and withal he came and went in a careful, correct way, ever and ever prolonging his career of mediocrity, like one whom many may have forgotten, but whom keenness of grief has preserved.

Nevertheless Morange had evidently sustained some internal damage of a nature to cause anxiety. He was lapsing into the most singular manias. While obstinately retaining possession of the over-large flat which he had formerly occupied with his wife and daughter, he now lived there absolutely alone; for he had dismissed his servant, and did his own marketing, cooking, and cleaning. For ten years nobody but himself had been inside his rooms, and the most filthy neglect was suspected there. But in vain did the landlord speak of repairs, he was not allowed even to cross the threshold. Moreover, although the old accountant, who was now white as snow, with a long, streaming beard, remained scrupulously clean of person, he wore a most wretched threadbare coat, which he must have spent his evenings in repairing. Such, too, was his maniacal, sordid avarice that he no longer spent a farthing on himself apart from the money which he paid for his bread—bread of the commonest kind, which he purchased every four days and ate when it was stale, in order that he might make it last the longer. This greatly puzzled the people who were acquainted with him, and never a week went by without the house-porter propounding the question: "When a gentleman of such quiet habits earns eight thousand francs a year at his office and never spends a cent, what can he do with his money?" Some folks even tried to reckon up the amount which Morange must be piling in some corner, and thought that it might perhaps run to some hundreds of thousands of francs.

But more serious trouble declared itself. He was twice snatched away from certain death. One day, when Denis was returning homewards across the Grenelle bridge he perceived Morange leaning far over the parapet, watching the flow of the water, and all ready to make a plunge if he had not been grasped by his coat-tails. The poor man, on recovering his self-possession, began to laugh in his gentle way, and talked of having felt giddy. Then, on another occasion, at the works, Victor Moineaud pushed him away from some machinery in motion at the very moment when, as if hypnotized, he was about to surrender himself to its devouring clutches. Then he again smiled, and acknowledged that he had done wrong in passing so near to the wheels. After this he was watched, for people came to the conclusion that he occasionally lost his head. If Denis retained him as chief accountant, this was, firstly, from a feeling of gratitude for his long services; but, apart from that matter, the extraordinary thing was that Morange had never discharged his duties more ably, obstinately tracing every doubtful centime in his books, and displaying the greatest accuracy over the longest additions. Always showing a calm and restful face, as though no tempest had ever assailed his heart, he clung tightly to his mechanical life, like a discreet maniac, who, though people might not know it, ought, perhaps, to have been placed under restraint.

At the same time, it should be mentioned that for some few years already there had been quite a big affair in Morange's life. Although he was Constance's confidant, although she had made him her creature by the force of her despotic will, he had gradually conceived the greatest affection for Denis's daughter, Hortense. As this child grew up, he fancied that he found in her his own long-mourned daughter, Reine. She had recently completed her ninth year, and each time that Morange met her he was thrown into a state of emotion and adoration, the more touching since it was all a divine illusion on his part, for the two girls in no wise resembled each other, the one having been extremely dark, and the other being nearly fair. In spite of his terrible avarice, the accountant loaded Hortense with dolls and sweetmeats on every possible occasion; and at last his affection for the child absorbed him to such a degree that Constance felt offended by it. She thereupon gave him to understand that whosoever was not entirely on her side was, in reality, against her.

To all appearance, he made his submission; in reality, he only loved the child the more for the thwarting of his passion, and he watched for her in order to kiss her in secret. In his daily intercourse with Constance, in showing apparent fidelity to the former mistress of the works, he now simply yielded to fear, like the poor weak being he was, one whom Constance had ever bent beneath her stern hand. The pact between them was an old one, it dated from that monstrous thing which they alone knew, that complicity of which they never spoke, but which bound them so closely together.

He, with his weak, good nature, seemed from that day to have remained annihilated, tamed, cowed like a frightened animal. Since that day, too, he had learnt many other things, and now no secret of the house remained unknown to him. This was not surprising. He had been living there so many years. He had so often walked to and fro with his short, discreet, maniacal step, hearing, seeing, and surprising everything! However, this madman, who knew the truth and who remained silent—this madman, left free amid the mysterious drama enacted in the Beauchenes' home, was gradually coming to a rebellious mood, particularly since he was compelled to hide himself to kiss his little friend Hortense. His heart growled at the thought of it, and he felt ready to explode should his passion be interfered with.

All at once, one evening, Constance kept him to dinner. And he suspected that the hour of her revelations had come, on seeing how she quivered and how erectly she carried her little figure, like a fighter henceforth certain of victory. Nevertheless, although the servant left them alone after bringing in at one journey the whole of the frugal repast, she did not broach the great affair at table. She spoke of the factory and then of Denis and his wife Marthe, whom she criticised, and she was even so foolish as to declare that Hortense was badly behaved, ugly, and destitute of grace. The accountant, like the coward he was, listened to her, never daring to protest in spite of the irritation and rebellion of his whole being.

"Well, we shall see," she said at last, "when one and all are put back into their proper places."

Then she waited until they returned to the little drawing-room, and the doors were shut behind them; and it was only then, near the fire, amid the deep silence of the winter evening, that she spoke out on the subject which she had at heart:

"As I think I have already told you, my friend, I have need of you. You must obtain employment at the works for a young man in whom I am interested. And if you desire to please me, you will even take him into your own office."

Morange, who was seated in front of her on the other side of the chimney-piece, gave her a look of surprise.

"But I am not the master," he replied; "apply to the master, he will certainly do whatever you ask."

"No, I do not wish to be indebted to Denis in any way. Besides, that would not suit my plans. You yourself must recommend the young man, and take him as an assistant, coaching him and giving him a post under you. Come, you surely have the power to choose a clerk. Besides, I insist on it."

She spoke like a sovereign, and he bowed his back, for he had obeyed people all his life; first his wife, then his daughter, and now that dethroned old queen who terrified him in spite of the dim feeling of rebellion which had been growing within him for some time past.

ÉMILE ZOLA

"No doubt, I might take the young man on," he said, "but who is he?"

Constance did not immediately reply. She had turned towards the fire, apparently for the purpose of raising a log of wood with the tongs, but in reality to give herself time for further reflection. What good would it do to tell him everything at once? She would some day be forced to tell it him, if she wished to have him entirely on her side; but there was no hurry, and she fancied that it would be skilful policy if at present she merely prepared the ground.

"He is a young man whose position has touched me, on account of certain recollections," she replied. "Perhaps you remember a girl who worked here—oh! a very long time ago, some thirty years at the least—a certain Norine Moineaud, one of old Moineaud's daughters."

Morange had hastily raised his head, and as sudden light flashed on his memory he looked at Constance with dilated eyes. Before he could even weigh his words he let everything escape him in a cry of surprise: "Alexandre-Honore, Norine's son, the child of Rougemont!"

Quite thunderstruck by those words, Constance dropped the tongs she was holding, and gazed into the old man's eyes, diving to the very depths of his soul.

"Ah! you know, then!" she said. "What is it you know? You must tell me; hide nothing. Speak! I insist on it!"

What he knew? Why, he knew everything. He spoke slowly and at length, as from the depths of a dream. He had witnessed everything, learnt everything—Norine's trouble, the money given by Beauchene to provide for her at Madame Bourdieu's, the child carried to the Foundling Hospital and then put out to nurse at Rougemont, whence he had fled after stealing three hundred francs. And the old accountant was even aware that the young scamp, after stranding on the pavement of Paris, had led the vilest of lives there.

"But who told you all that? How do you know all that?" cried Constance, who felt full of anxiety.

He waved his arm with a vague, sweeping gesture, as if to take in all the surrounding atmosphere, the whole house. He knew those things because they were things pertaining to the place, which people had told him of, or which he had guessed. He could no longer remember exactly how they had reached him. But he knew them well.

"You understand," said he, "when one has been in a place for more than thirty years, things end by coming to one naturally. I know everything, everything."

Constance started and deep silence fell. He, with his eyes fixed on the embers, had sunk back into the dolorous past. She reflected that it was, after all, preferable that the position should be perfectly plain. Since he was acquainted with everything, it was only needful that she, with all determination and bravery, should utilize him as her docile instrument.

"Alexandre-Honore, the child of Rougemont," she said. "Yes! that is the young man whom I have at last found again. But are you also aware of the steps which I took twelve years ago, when I despaired of finding him, and actually thought him dead?"

Morange nodded affirmatively, and she again went on speaking, relating that she had long since renounced her old plans, when all at once destiny had revealed itself to her.

"Imagine a flash of lightning!" she exclaimed. "It was on the morning of the day when you found me so moved! My sister-in-law, Seraphine, who does not call on me four times a year, came here, to my great surprise, at ten o'clock. She has become very strange, as you are aware, and I did not at first pay any attention to the story which she began to relate to me—the story of a young man whom she had become acquainted with through some lady—an unfortunate young man who had been spoilt by bad company, and whom one might save by a little help. Then what a blow it was, my friend, when she all at once spoke out plainly, and told me of the discovery which she had made by chance. I tell you, it is destiny awaking and striking!"

The story was indeed curious. Prematurely aged though she was, Seraphine, amid her growing insanity, continued to lead a wild, rackety life, and the strangest stories were related of her. A singular caprice of hers, given her own viciousness, was to join, as a lady patroness, a society whose purpose was to succor and moralize young offenders on their release from prison. And it was in this wise that she had become acquainted with Alexandre-Honore, now a big fellow of two-and-thirty, who had just completed a term of six years' imprisonment. He had ended by telling her his true story, speaking of Rougemont, naming Norine his mother, and relating the fruitless efforts that he had made in former years to discover his father, who was some immensely wealthy man. In the midst of it, Seraphine suddenly understood everything, and in particular why it was that his face had seemed so familiar to her. His striking resemblance to Beauchene sufficed to throw a vivid light upon the question of his parentage. For fear of worry, she herself told him nothing, but as she remembered how passionately Constance had at one time striven to find him, she went to her and acquainted her with her discovery.

"He knows nothing as yet," Constance explained to Morange. "My sister-in-law will simply send him here as if to a lady friend who will find him a good situation. It appears that he now asks nothing better than to work. If he has misconducted himself, the unhappy fellow, there have been many excuses for it! And, besides, I will answer for him as soon as he is in my hands; he will then only do as I tell him."

All that Constance knew respecting Alexandre's recent years was a story which he had concocted and retailed to Seraphine—a story to the effect that he owed his long term of imprisonment to a woman, the real culprit, who had been his mistress and whom he had refused to denounce. Of course that imprisonment, whatever its cause, only accounted for six out of the twelve years which had elapsed since his disappearance, and the six others, of which he said nothing, might conceal many an act of ignominy and crime. On the other hand, imprisonment at least seemed to have had a restful effect on him; he had emerged from his long confinement, calmer and keener-witted, with the intention of spoiling his life no longer. And cleansed, clad, and schooled by Seraphine, he had almost become a presentable young man.

Morange at last looked up from the glowing embers, at which he had been staring so fixedly.

"Well, what do you want to do with him?" he inquired. "Does he write a decent hand?"

"Yes, his handwriting is good. No doubt, however, he knows very little. It is for that reason that I wish to intrust him to you. You will polish him up for me and make him conversant with everything. My desire is that in a year or two he should know everything about the factory, like a master."

At that last word which enlightened him, the accountant's good sense suddenly awoke. Amid the manias which were wrecking his mind, he had remained a man of figures with a passion for arithmetical accuracy, and he protested.

"Well, madame, since you wish me to assist you, pray tell me everything; tell me in what work we can employ this young man here. Really now, you surely cannot hope through him to regain possession of the factory, re-purchase the shares, and become sole owner of the place?"

Then, with the greatest logic and clearness, he showed how foolish such a dream would be, enumerating figures and fully setting forth how large a sum of money would be needed to indemnify Denis, who was installed in the place like a conqueror.

"Besides, dear madame, I don't understand why you should take that young man rather than another. He has no legal rights, as you must be aware. He could never be anything but a stranger here, and I should prefer an intelligent, honest man, acquainted with our line of business."

Constance had set to work poking the fire logs with the tongs. When she at last looked up she thrust her face towards the other's, and said in a low voice, but violently: "Alexandre is my husband's son, he is the heir. He is not the stranger. The stranger is that Denis, that son of the Froments, who has robbed us of our property! You rend my heart; you make it bleed, my friend, by forcing me to tell you this."

The answer she thus gave was the answer of a conservative bourgeoise, who held that it would be more just if the inheritance should go to an illegitimate scion of the house rather than to a stranger. Doubtless the woman, the wife, the mother within her, bled even as she herself acknowledged, but she sacrificed everything to her rancor; she would drive the stranger away even if in doing so her own flesh should be lacerated. Then, too, it vaguely seemed to her that her husband's son must be in some degree her own, since his father was likewise the father of the son to whom she had given birth, and who was dead. Besides, she would make that young fellow her son; she would direct him, she would compel him to be hers, to work through her and for her.

"You wish to know how I shall employ him in the place," she resumed. "I myself don't know. It is evident that I shall not easily find the hundreds of thousands of francs which may be required. Your figures are accurate, and it is possible that we may never have the money to buy back the property. But, all the same, why not fight, why not try? And, besides—I will admit it—suppose we are vanquished, well then, so much the worse for the other. For I assure you that if this young man will only listen to me, he will then become the agent of destruction, the avenger and punisher, implanted in the factory to wreck it!"

With a gesture which summoned ruin athwart the walls, she finished expressing her abominable hopes. Among her vague plans, reared upon hate, was that of employing the wretched Alexandre as a destructive weapon, whose ravages would bring her some relief. Should she lose all other battles, that would assuredly be the final one. And she had attained to this pitch of madness through the boundless despair in which the loss of her only son had plunged her, withered, consumed by a love which she could not content, then demented, perverted to the point of crime.

Morange shuddered when, with her stubborn fierceness, she concluded: "For twelve years past I have been waiting for a stroke of destiny, and here it is! I would rather perish than not draw from it the last chance of good fortune which it brings me!"

This meant that Denis's ruin was decided on, and would be effected if destiny were willing. And the old accountant could picture the disaster: innocent children struck down in the person of their father, a great and most unjust catastrophe, which made his kindly heart rise in rebellion. Would he allow that fresh crime to be committed without shouting aloud all that he knew? Doubtless the memory of the other crime, the first one, the monstrous buried crime about which they both kept silence, returned at that horrible moment and shone out disturbingly in his eyes, for she herself shuddered as if she could see it there, while with the view of mastering him she gazed at him fixedly. For a moment, as they peered into one another's eyes, they lived once more beside the murderous trap, and shivered in the cold gust which rose from the abyss. And this time again Morange, like a poor weak man overpowered by a woman's will, was vanquished, and did not speak.

"So it is agreed, my friend," she softly resumed. "I rely on you to take Alexandre, in the first place, as a clerk. You can see him here one evening at five o'clock, after dusk, for I do not wish him to know at first what interest I take in him. Shall we say the day after to-morrow?"

"Yes, the evening of the day after to-morrow, if it pleases you, dear madame."

On the morrow Morange displayed so much agitation that the wife of the door-porter of the house where he resided, a woman who was ever watching him, imparted her fears to her husband. The old gentleman was certainly going to have an attack, for he had forgotten to put on his slippers when he came downstairs to fetch some water in the morning; and, besides, he went on talking to himself, and looked dreadfully upset. The most extraordinary incident of the day, however, was that after lunch Morange quite forgot himself, and was an hour late in returning to his office, a lack of punctuality which had no precedent, which, in the memory of everybody at the works, had never occurred before.

As a matter of fact, Morange had been carried away as by a storm, and, walking straight before him, had once more found himself on the Grenelle bridge, where Denis had one day saved him from the fascination of the water. And some force, some impulse had carried him again to the very same spot, and made him lean over the same parapet, gazing, in the same way as previously, at the flowing river. Ever since the previous evening he had been repeating the same words, words which he stammered in an undertone, and which haunted and tortured him. "Would he allow that fresh crime to be committed without shouting aloud what he knew?" No doubt it was those words, of which he could not rid himself, that had made him forget to put on his slippers in the morning, and that had just now again dazed him to the point of preventing him from returning to the factory, as if he no longer recognized the entrance as he passed it. And if he were at present leaning over that water, had he not been impelled thither by an unconscious desire to have done with all his troubles, an instinctive hope of drowning the torment into which he was thrown by those stubbornly recurring words? Down below, at the bottom of the river, those words would at last cease; he would no longer repeat them; he would no longer hear them urging him to an act of energy for which he could not find sufficient strength. And the call of the water was very gentle, and it would be so pleasant to have to struggle no longer, to yield to destiny, like a poor soft-hearted weakling who has lived too long.

Morange leant forward more and more, and in fancy could already feel the sonorous river seizing him, when a gay young voice in the rear recalled him to reality.

"What are you looking at, Monsieur Morange? Are there any big fishes there?"

It was Hortense, looking extremely pretty, and tall already for her ten years, whom a maid was conducting on a visit to some little friends at Auteuil. And when the distracted accountant turned round, he remained for a moment with trembling hands, and eyes moist with tears, at the sight of that apparition, that dear angel, who had recalled him from so far.

"What! is it you, my pet!" he exclaimed. "No, no, there are no big fishes. I think that they hide at the bottom because the water is so cold in winter. Are you going on a visit? You look quite beautiful in that fur-trimmed cloak!"

ÉMILE ZOLA

The little girl began to laugh, well pleased at being flattered and loved, for her old friend's voice quivered with adoration.

"Yes, yes, I am very happy; there are to be some private theatricals where I'm going. Oh! it is amusing to feel happy!"

She spoke those words like his own Reine might formerly have spoken them, and he could have gone down on his knees to kiss her little hands like an idol's.

"But it is necessary that you should always be happy," he replied. "You look so beautiful, I must really kiss you."

"Oh! you may, Monsieur Morange, I'm quite willing. Ah! you know the doll you gave me; her name's Margot, and you have no idea how good she is. Come to see her some day."

He had kissed her; and with glowing heart, ready for martyrdom, he watched her as she went off in the pale light of winter. What he had thought of would be too cowardly: besides, that child must be happy!

He slowly quitted the bridge, while within him the haunting words rang out with decisive distinctness, demanding a reply: "Would he allow that fresh crime to be committed without shouting aloud what he knew?" No, no! It was impossible: he would speak, he would act. Nevertheless, his mind remained clouded, befogged. How could he speak, how could he act?

Then, to crown his extravagant conduct, utterly breaking away from the habits of forty years, he no sooner returned to the office than, instead of immediately plunging into his everlasting additions, he began to write a long letter. This letter, which was addressed to Mathieu, recounted the whole affair—Alexandre's resurrection, Constance's plans, and the service which he himself had promised to render her. These things were set down simply as his impulse dictated, like a kind of confession by which he relieved his feelings. He had not yet come to any positive decision as to how he should play the part of a justiciar, which seemed so heavy to his shoulders. His one purpose was to warn Mathieu in order that there might be two of them to decide and act. And he simply finished by asking the other to come to see him on the following evening, though not before six o'clock, as he desired to see Alexandre and learn how the interview passed off, and what Constance might require of the young man.

The ensuing night, the ensuing day, must have been full of abominable torment for Morange. The doorkeeper's wife recounted, later on, that the fourth-floor tenant had heard the old gentleman walking about overhead all through the night. Doors were slammed, and furniture was dragged about as if for a removal. It was even thought that one could detect cries, sobs, and the monologues of a madman addressing phantoms, some mysterious rendering of worship to the dead who haunted him. And at the works during the day which followed Morange gave alarming signs of distress, of the final sinking of his mind into a flood of gloom. Ever darting troubled glances around him, he was tortured by internal combats, which, without the slightest motive, made him descend the stairs a dozen times, linger before the machinery in motion, and then return to his additions up above, with the bewildered, distracted air of one who could not find what he sought so painfully. When the darkness fell, about four o'clock on that gloomy winter day, the two clerks whom he had with him in his office noticed that he altogether ceased working. From that moment, indeed, he waited with his eyes fixed upon the clock. And when five o'clock struck he once more made sure that a certain total was correct, then rose and went out, leaving the ledger open, as if he meant to return to check the next addition.

He followed the gallery which led to the passage connecting the workshops with the private house. The whole factory was at that hour lighted up, electric lamps cast the brightness of daylight over it, while the stir of work ascended and the walls shook amid the rumbling of machinery. And all at once, before reaching the passage, Morange perceived the lift, the terrible cavity, the abyss of murder in which Blaise had met his death fourteen years previously. Subsequent to that catastrophe, and in order to prevent the like of it from ever occurring again, the trap had been surrounded by a balustrade with a gate, in such wise that a fall became impossible unless one should open the gate expressly to take a plunge. At that moment the trap was lowered and the gate was closed, and Morange, yielding to some superior force, bent over the cavity, shuddering. The whole scene of long ago rose up before him; he was again in the depths of that frightful void; he could see the crushed corpse; and he could feel the gust of terror chilling him in the presence of murder, accepted and concealed. Since he suffered so dreadfully, since he could no longer sleep, since he had promised his dear dead ones that he would join them, why should he not make an end of himself? Two days previously, while leaning over the parapet of the Grenelle bridge, a desire to do so had taken possession of him. He merely had to lose his equilibrium and he would be liberated, laid to rest in the peaceful earth between his wife and his daughter. And, all at once, as if the abyss itself suggested to him the frightful solution for which he had been vainly groping, in his growing madness, for two days past, he thought that he could hear a voice calling him from below, the voice of Blaise, which cried: "Come with the other one! Come with the other one!"

He started violently and drew himself erect; decision had fallen on him in a lightning flash. Insane as he was, that appeared to him to be the one sole logical, mathematical, sensible solution, which would settle everything. It seemed to him so simple, too, that he was astonished that he had sought it so long. And from that moment this poor soft-hearted weakling, whose wretched brain was unhinged, gave proof of iron will and sovereign heroism, assisted by the clearest reasoning, the most subtle craft.

In the first place he prepared everything, set the catch to prevent the trap from being sent up again in his absence, and also assured himself that the balustrade door opened and closed easily. He came and went with a light, aerial step, as if carried off his feet, with his eyes ever on the alert, anxious as he was to be neither seen nor heard. At last he extinguished the three electric lamps and plunged the gallery into darkness. From below, through the gaping cavity the stir of the working factory, the rumbling of the machinery ever ascended. And it was only then, everything being ready, that Morange turned into the passage to betake himself to the little drawing room of the mansion.

Constance was there waiting for him with Alexandre. She had given instructions for the latter to call half-an-hour earlier, for she wished to confess him while as yet telling him nothing of the real position which she meant him to take in the house. She was not disposed to place herself all at once at his mercy, and had therefore simply expressed her willingness to give him employment in accordance with the recommendation of her relative, the Baroness de Lowicz. Nevertheless, she studied him with restrained ardor, and was well pleased to find that he was strong, sturdy, and resolute, with a hard face lighted by terrible eyes, which promised her an avenger. She would finish polishing him up, and then he would suit her perfectly. For his part, without plainly understanding the truth, he scented something, divined that his fortune was at hand, and was quite ready to wait awhile for the certain feast, like a young wolf who consents to be domesticated in order that he may, later on, devour the whole flock at his ease.

When Morange went in only one thing struck him, Alexandre's resemblance to Beauchene, that extraordinary resemblance which had already upset Constance, and which now sent an icy chill through the old accountant as if in purposing to carry out his idea he had condemned his old master.

"I was waiting for you, my friend; you are late, you who are so punctual as a rule," said Constance.

"Yes, there was a little work which I wished to finish."

But she had merely been jesting, she felt so happy. And she immediately settled everything: "Well, here is the gentleman whom I spoke about," she said. "You will begin by taking him with you and making him acquainted with the business, even if in the first instance you can merely send him about on commissions for you. It is understood, is it not?"

"Quite so, dear madame, I will take him with me; you may rely on me."

Then, as she gave Alexandre his dismissal, saying that he might come on the morrow, Morange offered to show him out by way of his office and the workshops, which were still open.

"In that way he will form an acquaintance with the works, and can come straight to me to-morrow."

Constance laughed again, so fully did the accountant's obligingness reassure her.

"That is a good idea, my friend," she said. "Thank you. And au revoir, monsieur; we will take charge of your future if you behave sensibly."

At this moment, however, she was thunderstruck by an extravagant and seemingly senseless incident. Morange, having shown Alexandre out of the little salon, in advance of himself, turned round towards her with the sudden grimace of a madman, revealing his insanity by the distortion of his countenance. And in a low, familiar, sneering voice, he stammered in her face: "Ha! ha! Blaise at the bottom of the hole! He speaks, he has spoken to me! Ha! ha! the somersault! you would have the somersault! And you shall have it again, the somersault, the somersault!"

Then he disappeared, following Alexandre.

She had listened to him agape with wonder. It was all so unforeseen, so idiotic, that at first she did not understand it. But afterwards what a flash of light came to her! That which Morange had referred to was the murder yonder—the thing to which they had never referred, the

ÉMILE ZOLA

monstrous thing which they had kept buried for fourteen years past, which their glances only had confessed, but which, all of a sudden, he had cast in her teeth with the grimace of a madman. What was the meaning of the poor fool's diabolical rebellion, the dim threat which she had felt passing like a gust from an abyss? She turned frightfully pale, she intuitively foresaw some frightful revenge of destiny, that destiny which, only a moment previously, she had believed to be her minion. Yes, it was surely that. And she felt herself carried fourteen years backward, and she remained standing, quivering, icy cold, listening to the sounds which arose from the works, waiting for the awful thud of the fall, even as on the distant day when she had listened and waited for the other to be crushed and killed.

Meantime Morange, with his discreet, short step, was leading Alexandre away, and speaking to him in a quiet, good-natured voice.

"I must ask your pardon for going first, but I have to show you the way. Oh! this is a very intricate place, with stairs and passages whose turns and twists never end. The passage now turns to the left, you see."

Then, on reaching the gallery where the darkness was complete, he affected anger in the most natural manner possible.

"Ah! well, that is just their way. They haven't yet lighted up this part. The switch is at the other end. Fortunately I know where to step, for I have been going backwards and forwards here for the last forty years. Mind follow me carefully."

Thereupon, at each successive step, he warned the other what he ought to do, guiding him along in his obliging way without the faintest tremor in his voice.

"Don't let go of me, turn to the left.—Now we merely have to go straight ahead.—Only, wait a moment, a barrier intersects the gallery, and there is a gate.—There we are! I'm opening the gate, you hear?—Follow me, I'll go first."

Morange quietly stepped into the void, amid the darkness. And, without a cry, he fell. Alexandre who was close in the rear, almost touching him so as not to lose him, certainly detected the void and the gust which followed the fall, as with sudden horror the flooring failed beneath them; but force of motion carried him on, he stepped forward in his turn, howled and likewise fell, head over heels. Both were smashed below, both killed at once. True, Morange still breathed for a few seconds. Alexandre, for his part, lay with his skull broken to pieces and his brains scattered on the very spot where Blaise had been picked up.

Horrible was the stupefaction when those bodies were found there. Nobody could explain the catastrophe. Morange carried off his secret, the reason for that savage act of justice which he had accomplished according to the chance suggestions of his dementia. Perhaps he had wished to punish Constance, perhaps he had desired to repair the old wrong: Denis long since stricken in the person of his brother, and now saved for the sake of his daughter Hortense, who would live happily with Margot, the pretty doll who was so good. By suppressing the criminal instrument the old accountant had indeed averted the possibility of a fresh crime. Swayed by his fixed idea, however, he had doubtless never reasoned that cataclysmic deed of justice, which was above reason, and which passed by with the impassive savagery of a death-dealing hurricane.

At the works there was but one opinion, Morange had assuredly been mad; and he alone could have caused the accident, particularly as it was impossible to account, otherwise than by an act of madness, for the extinguishing of the lights, the opening of the balustrade-door, and the plunge into the cavity which he knew to be there, and into which had followed him the unfortunate young man his companion. Moreover, the accountant's madness was no longer doubted by anybody a few days later, when the doorkeeper of his house related his final eccentricities, and a commissary of police went to search his rooms. He had been mad, mad enough to be placed in confinement.

To begin, nobody had ever seen a flat in such an extraordinary condition, the kitchen a perfect stable, the drawing-room in a state of utter abandonment with its Louis XIV furniture gray with dust, and the dining-room all topsy-turvy, the old oak tables and chairs being piled up against the window as if to shut out every ray of light, though nobody could tell why. The only properly kept room was that in which Reine had formerly slept, which was as clean as a sanctuary, with its pitch-pine furniture as bright as if it had been polished every day. But the apartment in which Morange's madness became unmistakably manifest was his own bedchamber, which he had turned into a museum of souvenirs, covering its walls with photographs of his wife and daughter. Above a table there, the wall facing the window quite disappeared from view, for a sort of little chapel had been set up, decked with a multitude of portraits. In the centre were photographs of Valerie and Reine, both of them at twenty years of age, so that they looked like twin sisters; while symmetrically disposed all around was an extraordinary number of other portraits, again showing Valerie and Reine, now as children, now as girls, and now as women, in every sort of position, too, and every kind of toilet. And below them on the table, like an offering on an altar, was found more than one hundred thousand francs, in gold, and silver, and even copper; indeed, the whole fortune which Morange had been saving up for several years by eating only dry bread, like a pauper.

At last, then, one knew what he had done with his savings; he had given them to his dead wife and daughter, who had remained his will, passion, and ambition. Haunted by remorse at having killed them while dreaming of making them rich, he reserved for them that money which they had so keenly desired, and which they would have spent with so much ardor. It was still and ever for them that he earned it, and he took it to them, lavished it upon them, never devoting even a tithe of it to any egotistical pleasure, absorbed as he was in his vision-fraught worship and eager to pacify and cheer their spirits. And the whole neighborhood gossiped endlessly about the old mad gentleman who had let himself die of wretchedness by the side of a perfect treasure, piled coin by coin upon a table, and for twenty years past tendered to the portraits of his wife and daughter, even as flowers might have been offered to their memory.

About six o'clock, when Mathieu reached the works, he found the place terrified by the catastrophe. Ever since the morning he had been rendered anxious by Morange's letter, which had greatly surprised and worried him with that extraordinary story of Alexandre turning up once more, being welcomed by Constance, and introduced by her into the establishment. Plain as was the greater part of the letter, it contained some singularly incoherent passages, and darted from one point to another with incomprehensible suddenness. Mathieu had read it three times, indulging on each occasion in fresh hypotheses of a gloomier and gloomier nature; for the more he reflected, the more did the affair seem to him to be fraught with menace. Then, on reaching the rendezvous appointed by Morange, he found himself in presence of those bleeding bodies which Victor Moineaud had just picked up and laid out side by side! Silent, chilled to his bones, Mathieu listened to his son, Denis, who had hastened up to tell him of the unexplainable misfortune, the two men falling one atop of the other, first the old mad accountant, and then the young fellow whom nobody knew and who seemed to have dropped from heaven.

Mathieu, for his part, had immediately recognized Alexandre, and if, pale and terrified, he kept silent on the subject, it was because he desired to take nobody, not even his son, into his confidence, given the fresh suppositions, the frightful suppositions, which now arose in his mind from out of all the darkness. He listened with growing anxiety to the enumeration of the few points which were certain: the extinguishing of the electric lights in the gallery and the opening of the balustrade door, which was always kept closed and could only have been opened by some habitue, since, to turn the handle, one had to press a secret spring which kept it from moving. And, all at once, as Victor Moineaud pointed out that the old man had certainly been the first to fall, since one of the young man's legs had been stretched across his stomach, Mathieu was carried fourteen years backward. He remembered old Moineaud picking up Blaise on the very spot where Victor, the son, had just picked up Morange and Alexandre. Blaise! At the thought of his dead boy fresh light came to Mathieu, a frightful suspicion blazed up amid the terrible obscurity in which he had been groping and doubting. And, thereupon, leaving Denis to settle everything down below, he decided to see Constance.

Up above, however, when Mathieu was on the point of turning into the communicating passage, he paused once more, this time near the lift. It was there, fourteen years previously, that Morange, finding the trap open, had gone down to warn and chide the workmen, while Constance, according to her own account, had quietly returned into the house, at the very moment when Blaise, coming from the other end of the dim gallery, plunged into the gulf. Everybody had eventually accepted that narrative as being accurate, but Mathieu now felt that it was mendacious. He could recall various glances, various words, various spells of silence; and sudden certainty came upon him, a certainty based on all the petty things which he had not then understood, but which now assumed the most frightful significance. Yes, it was certain, even though round it there hovered the monstrous vagueness of silent crimes, cowardly crimes, over which a shadow of horrible mystery always lurks. Moreover, it explained the sequel, those two bodies lying below, as far, that is, as logical reasoning can explain a madman's action with all its gaps and mysteriousness. Nevertheless, Mathieu still strove to doubt; before anything else he wished to see Constance.

Showing a waxy pallor, she had remained erect, motionless, in the middle of her little drawing-room. The waiting of fourteen years previously had begun once more, lasting on and on, and filling her with such anxiety that she held her breath the better to listen. Nothing, no stir, no sound of footsteps, had yet ascended from the works. What could be happening then? Was the hateful thing, the dreaded thing, merely a nightmare after all? Yet Morange had really sneered in her face, she had fully understood him. Had not a howl, the thud of a fall, just reached her ears? And now, had not the rumbling of the machinery ceased? It was death, the factory silent, chilled and lost for her. All at once her heart ceased beating as she detected a sound of footsteps drawing nearer and nearer with increased rapidity. The door opened, and it was Mathieu who came in.

She recoiled, livid, as at the sight of a ghost. He, O God! Why he? How was it he was there? Of all the messengers of misfortune he was the one whom she had least expected. Had the dead son risen before her she would not have shuddered more dreadfully than she did at this apparition of the father.

She did not speak. He simply said: "They made the plunge, they are both dead—like Blaise."

Then, though she still said nothing, she looked at him. For a moment their eyes met. And in her glance he read everything: the murder was begun afresh, effected, consummated. Over yonder lay the bodies, dead, one atop of the other.

"Wretched woman, to what monstrous perversity have you fallen! And how much blood there is upon you!"

By an effort of supreme pride Constance was able to draw herself up and even increase her stature, still wishing to conquer, and cry aloud that she was indeed the murderess, that she had always thwarted him, and would ever do so. But Mathieu was already overwhelming her with a final revelation.

"You don't know, then, that that ruffian, Alexandre, was one of the murderers of your friend, Madame Angelin, the poor woman who was robbed and strangled one winter afternoon. I compassionately hid that from you. But he would now be at the galleys had I spoken out! And if I were to speak to-day you would be there too!"

That was the hatchet-stroke. She did not speak, but dropped, all of a lump, upon the carpet, like a tree which has been felled. This time her defeat was complete; destiny, which she awaited, had turned against her and thrown her to the ground. A mother the less, perverted by the love which she had set on her one child, a mother duped, robbed, and maddened, who had glided into murder amid the dementia born of inconsolable motherliness! And now she lay there, stretched out, scraggy and withered, poisoned by the affection which she had been unable to bestow.

Mathieu became anxious, and summoned the old servant, who, after procuring assistance, carried her mistress to her bed and then undressed her. Meantime, as Constance gave no sign of life, seized as she was by one of those fainting fits which often left her quite breathless, Mathieu himself went for Boutan, and meeting him just as he was returning home for dinner, was luckily able to bring him back at once.

Boutan, who was now nearly seventy-two, and was quietly spending his last years in serene cheerfulness, born of his hope in life, had virtually ceased practising, only attending a very few old patients, his friends. However, he did not refuse Mathieu's request. When he had examined Constance he made a gesture of hopelessness, the meaning of which was so plain that Mathieu, his anxiety increasing, bethought himself of trying to find Beauchene in order that the latter might, at least, be present if his wife should die. But the old servant, on being questioned, began by raising her arms to heaven. She did not know where Monsieur might be, Monsieur never left any address. At last, feeling frightened herself, she made up her mind to hasten to the abode of the two women, aunt and niece, with whom Beauchene spent the greater part of his time. She knew their address perfectly well, as her mistress had even sent her thither in pressing emergencies. But she learnt that the ladies had gone with Monsieur to Nice for a holiday; whereupon, not desiring to return without some member of the family, she was seized on her way back with the fine idea of calling on Monsieur's sister, the Baroness de Lowicz, whom she brought, almost by force, in her cab.

It was in vain that Boutan attempted treatment. When Constance opened her eyes again, she looked at him fixedly, recognized him, no doubt, and then lowered her eyelids. And from that moment she obstinately refused to reply to any question that was put to her. She must have heard and have known that people were there, trying to succor her. But she would have none of their succor, she was stubbornly intent on dying, on giving no further sign of life. Neither did she raise her eyelids, nor did her lips part again. It was as if she had already quitted the world amid the mute agony of her defeat.

That evening Seraphine's manner was extremely strange. She reeked of ether, for she drank ether now. When she heard of the two-fold "accident," the death of Morange and that of Alexandre, which had brought on Constance's cardiacal attack, she simply gave an insane grin, a kind of involuntary snigger, and stammered: "Ah! that's funny."

Though she removed neither her hat nor her gloves, she installed herself in an armchair, where she sat waiting, with her eyes wide open and staring straight before her—those brown eyes flecked with gold, whose living light was all that she had retained of her massacred beauty. At sixty-two she looked like a centenarian; her bold, insolent face was ravined, as it were, by her stormy life, and the glow of her sun-like hair had been extinguished by a shower of ashes. And time went on, midnight approached, and she was still there, near that death-bed of which she seemed to be ignorant, in that quivering chamber where she forgot herself, similar to a mere thing, apparently no longer even knowing why she had been brought thither.

Mathieu and Boutan had been unwilling to retire. Since Monsieur was at Nice in the company of those ladies, the aunt and the niece, they decided to spend the night there in order that Constance might not be left alone with the old servant. And towards midnight, while they were chatting together in undertones, they were suddenly stupefied at hearing Seraphine raise her voice, after preserving silence for three hours.

"He is dead, you know," said she.

Who was dead? At last they understood that she referred to Dr. Gaude. The celebrated surgeon, had, indeed, been found in his consulting-room struck down by sudden death, the cause of which was not clearly known. In fact, the strangest, the most horrible and tragical stories were current on the subject. According to one of them a patient had wreaked vengeance on the doctor; and Mathieu, full of emotion, recalled that one day, long ago, Seraphine herself had suggested that all Gaude's unhappy patients ought to band themselves together and put an end to him.

When Seraphine perceived that Mathieu was gazing at her, as in a nightmare, moved by the shuddering silence of that death-watch, she once more grinned like a lunatic, and said: "He is dead, we were all there!"

It was insane, improbable, impossible; and yet was it true or was it false? A cold, terrifying quiver swept by, the icy quiver of mystery, of that which one knows not, which one will never know.

Boutan leant towards Mathieu and whispered in his ear: "She will be raving mad and shut up in a padded cell before a week is over." And, indeed, a week later the Baroness de Lowicz was wearing a straight waistcoat. In her case Dr. Gaude's treatment had led to absolute insanity.

Mathieu and Boutan watched beside Constance until daybreak. She never opened her lips, nor raised her eyelids. As the sun rose up, she turned towards the wall, and then she died.

XXII

S till more years passed, and Mathieu was already sixty-eight and Marianne sixty-five, when amid the increasing good fortune which they owed to their faith in life, and their long courageous hopefulness, a last battle, the most dolorous of their existence, almost struck them down and sent them to the grave, despairing and inconsolable.

One evening Marianne went to bed, quivering, utterly distracted. Quite a rending was taking place in the family. A disastrous and hateful quarrel had set the mill, where Gregoire reigned supreme, against the farm which was managed by Gervais and Claire. And Ambroise, on being selected as arbiter, had fanned the flames by judging the affair in a purely business way from his Paris counting-house, without taking into account the various passions which were kindled.

It was on returning from a secret application to Ambroise, prompted by a maternal longing for peace, that Marianne had taken to her bed, wounded to the heart, and terrified by the thought of the future. Ambroise had received her roughly, almost brutally, and she had gone back home in a state of intense anguish, feeling as if her own flesh were lacerated by the quarrelling of her ungrateful sons. And she had kept her bed, begging Mathieu to say nothing, and explaining that a doctor's services would be useless, since she did not suffer from any malady. She was fading away, however, as he could well detect; she was day by day taking leave of him, carried off by her bitter grief. Was it possible that all those loving and well-loved children, who had grown up under their care and their caresses, who had become the joy and pride of their victory, all those children born of their love, united in their fidelity, a sacred brotherly, sisterly battalion gathered close around them, was it possible that they should now disband and desperately seek to destroy one another? If so, it was true, then, that the more a family increases, the greater is the harvest of ingratitude. And still more accurate became the saying, that to judge of any human being's happiness or unhappiness in life, one must wait until he be dead.

"Ah!" said Mathieu, as he sat near Marianne's bed, holding her feverish hand, "to think of it! To have struggled so much, and to have triumphed so much, and then to encounter this supreme grief, which will bring us more pain than all the others. Decidedly it is true that one must continue battling until one's last breath, and that happiness is only to be won by suffering and tears. We must still hope, still triumph, and conquer and live."

Marianne, however, had lost all courage, and seemed to be overwhelmed.

"No," said she, "I have no energy left me, I am vanquished. I was always able to heal the wounds which came from without, but this wound comes from my own blood; my blood pours forth within me and stifles me. All our work is destroyed. Our joy, our health, our strength, have at the last day become mere lies."

Then Mathieu, whom her grievous fears of a disaster gained, went off to weep in the adjoining room, already picturing his wife dead and himself in utter solitude.

It was with reference to Lepailleur's moorland, the plots intersecting the Chantebled estate, that the wretched quarrel had broken out between the mill and the farm. For many years already, the romantic, ivy-covered old mill, with its ancient mossy wheel, had ceased to exist. Gregoire, at last putting his father's ideas into execution, had thrown it down to replace it by a large steam mill, with spacious meal-stores which a light railway-line connected with Janville station. And he himself, since he had been making a big fortune—for all the wheat of the district was now sent to him—had greatly changed, with nothing of his youthful turbulence left save a quick temper, which his wife Therese with her brave, loving heart alone could somewhat calm. On a score of occasions he had almost broken off all relations with his father-in-law, Lepailleur, who certainly abused his seventy years. Though the old miller, in spite of all his prophecies of ruin, had been unable to prevent the building of the new establishment, he none the less sneered and jeered at it, exasperated as he was at having been in the wrong. He had, in fact, been beaten for the second time. Not only did the prodigious crops of Chantebled disprove his theory of the bankruptcy of the earth, that villainous earth in which, like an obstinate peasant weary of toil and eager for speedy fortune, he asserted nothing more would grow; but now that mill of his, which he had so disdained, was born as it were afresh, growing to a gigantic size, and becoming in his son-in-law's hands an instrument of great wealth.

The worst was that Lepailleur so stubbornly lived on, experiencing continual defeats, but never willing to acknowledge that he was beaten. One sole delight remained to him, the promise given and kept by Gregoire that he would not sell the moorland enclosure to the farm.

The old man had even prevailed on him to leave it uncultivated, and the sight of that sterile tract intersecting the wavy greenery of the beautiful estate of Chantebled, like a spot of desolation, well pleased his spiteful nature. He was often to be seen strolling there, like an old king of the stones and the brambles, drawing up his tall, scraggy figure as if he were quite proud of the poverty of that soil. In going thither one of his objects doubtless was to find a pretext for a quarrel; for it was he who in the course of one of these promenades, when he displayed such provoking insolence, discovered an encroachment on the part of the farm—an encroachment which his comments magnified to such a degree that disastrous consequences seemed probable. As it was, all the happiness of the Froments was for a time destroyed.

In business matters Gregoire invariably showed the rough impulsiveness of a man of sanguine temperament, obstinately determined to part with no fraction of his rights. When his father-in-law told him that the farm had impudently cleared some seven acres of his moorland, with the intention no doubt of carrying this fine robbery even further, if it were not promptly stopped, Gregoire at once decided to inquire into the matter, declaring that he would not tolerate any invasion of that sort. The misfortune then was that no boundary stones could be found. Thus, the people of the farm might assert that they had made a mistake in all good faith, or even that they had remained within their limits. But Lepailleur ragefully maintained the contrary, entered into particulars, and traced what he declared to be the proper frontier line with his stick, swearing that within a few inches it was absolutely correct. However, matters went altogether from bad to worse after an interview between the brothers, Gervais and Gregoire, in the course of which the latter lost his temper and indulged in unpardonable language. On the morrow, too, he began an action-at-law, to which Gervais replied by threatening that he would not send another grain of corn to be ground at the mill. And this rupture of business relations meant serious consequences for the mill, which really owed its prosperity to the custom of Chantebled.

From that moment matters grew worse each day, and conciliation soon seemed to be out of the question; for Ambroise, on being solicited to find a basis of agreement, became in his turn impassioned, and even ended by enraging both parties. Thus the hateful ravages of that fratricidal war were increased: there were now three brothers up in arms against one another. And did not this forebode the end of everything;

might not this destructive fury gain the whole family, overwhelming it as with a blast of folly and hatred after so many years of sterling good sense and strong and healthy affection?

Mathieu naturally tried to intervene. But at the very outset he felt that if he should fail, if his paternal authority should be disregarded, the disaster would become irreparable. Without renouncing the struggle, he therefore waited for some opportunity which he might turn to good account. At the same time, each successive day of discord increased his anxiety. It was really all his own life-work, the little people which had sprung from him, the little kingdom which he had founded under the benevolent sun, that was threatened with sudden ruin. A work such as this can only live by force of love. The love which created it can alone perpetuate it; it crumbles as soon as the bond of fraternal solidarity is broken. Thus it seemed to Mathieu that instead of leaving his work behind him in full florescence of kindliness, joy, and vigor, he would see it cast to the ground in fragments, soiled, and dead even before he were dead himself. Yet what a fruitful and prosperous work had hitherto been that estate of Chantebled, whose overflowing fertility increased at each successive harvest; and that mill too, so enlarged and so flourishing, which was the outcome of his own inspiring suggestions, to say nothing of the prodigious fortunes which his conquering sons had acquired in Paris! Yet it was all this admirable work, which faith in life had created, that a fratricidal onslaught upon life was about to destroy!

One evening, in the mournful gloaming of one of the last days of September, the couch on which Marianne lay dying of silent grief was, by her desire, rolled to the window. Charlotte alone nursed her, and of all her sons she had but the last one, Benjamin, beside her in the now over-spacious house which had replaced the old shooting-box. Since the family had been at war she had kept the doors closed, intent on opening them only to her children when they became reconciled, if they should then seek to make her happy by coming to embrace one another beneath her roof. But she virtually despaired of that sole cure for her grief, the only joy that would make her live again.

That evening, as Mathieu came to sit beside her, and they lingered there hand in hand according to their wont, they did not at first speak, but gazed straight before them at the spreading plain; at the estate, whose interminable fields blended with the mist far away; at the mill yonder on the banks of the Yeuse, with its tall, smoking chimney; and at Paris itself on the horizon, where a tawny cloud was rising as from the huge furnace of some forge.

The minutes slowly passed away. During the afternoon Mathieu had taken a long walk in the direction of the farms of Mareuil and Lillebonne, in the hope of quieting his torment by physical fatigue. And in a low voice, as if speaking to himself, he at last said:

"The ploughing could not take place under better conditions. Yonder on the plateau the quality of the soil has been much improved by the recent methods of cultivation; and here, too, on the slopes, the sandy soil has been greatly enriched by the new distribution of the springs which Gervais devised. The estate has almost doubled in value since it has been in his hands and Claire's. There is no break in the prosperity; labor yields unlimited victory."

"What is the good of it if there is no more love?" murmured Marianne.

"Then, too," continued Mathieu, after a pause, "I went down to the Yeuse, and from a distance I saw that Gregoire had received the new machine which Denis has just built for him. It was being unloaded in the yard. It seems that it imparts a certain movement to the mill-stones, which saves a good third of the power needed. With such appliances the earth may produce seas of corn for innumerable nations, they will all have bread. And that mill-engine, with its regular breath and motion, will produce fresh wealth also."

"What use is it if people hate one another?" Marianne exclaimed.

At this Mathieu dropped the subject. But, in accordance with a resolution which he had formed during his walk, he told his wife that he meant to go to Paris on the morrow. And on noticing her surprise, he pretended that he wished to see to a certain business matter, the settlement of an old account. But the truth was, that he could no longer endure the spectacle of his wife's lingering agony, which brought him so much suffering. He wished to act, to make a supreme effort at reconciliation.

At ten o'clock on the following morning, when Mathieu alighted from the train at the Paris terminus, he drove direct to the factory at Grenelle. Before everything else he wished to see Denis, who had hitherto taken no part in the quarrel. For a long time now, indeed ever since Constance's death, Denis had been installed in the house on the quay with his wife Marthe and their three children. This occupation of the luxurious dwelling set apart for the master had been like a final entry into possession, with respect to the whole works. True, Beauchene had lived several years longer, but his name no longer figured in that of the firm. He had surrendered his last shred of interest in the business for an annuity; and at last one evening it was learnt that he had died that day, struck down by an attack of apoplexy after an over-copious lunch, at the residence of his lady-friends, the aunt and the niece. He had previously been sinking into a state of second childhood, the outcome of his life of fast and furious pleasure. And this, then, was the end of the egotistical debauchee, ever going from bad to worse, and finally swept into the gutter.

"Why! what good wind has blown you here?" cried Denis gayly, when he perceived his father. "Have you come to lunch? I'm still a bachelor, you know; for it is only next Monday that I shall go to fetch Marthe and the children from Dieppe, where they have spent a delightful September."

Then, on hearing that his mother was ailing, even in danger, he become serious and anxious.

"Mamma ill, and in danger! You amaze me. I thought she was simply troubled with some little indisposition. But come, father, what is really the matter? Are you hiding something? Is something worrying you?"

Thereupon he listened to the plain and detailed statement which Mathieu felt obliged to make to him. And he was deeply moved by it, as if the dread of the catastrophe which it foreshadowed would henceforth upset his life. "What!" he angrily exclaimed, "my brothers are up to these fine pranks with their idiotic quarrel! I knew that they did not get on well together. I had heard of things which saddened me, but I never imagined that matters had gone so far, and that you and mamma were so affected that you had shut yourselves up and were dying of it all! But things must be set to rights! One must see Ambroise at once. Let us go and lunch with him, and finish the whole business."

Before starting he had a few orders to give, so Mathieu went down to wait for him in the factory yard. And there, during the ten minutes which he spent walking about dreamily, all the distant past arose before his eyes. He could see himself a mere clerk, crossing that courtyard every morning on his arrival from Janville, with thirty sous for his lunch in his pocket. The spot had remained much the same; there was the central building, with its big clock, the workshops and the sheds, quite a little town of gray structures, surmounted by two lofty chimneys, which were ever smoking. True, his son had enlarged this city of toil; the stretch of ground bordered by the Rue de la Federation and the Boulevard de Grenelle had been utilized for the erection of other buildings. And facing the quay there still stood the large brick house with dressings of white stone, of which Constance had been so proud, and where, with the mien of some queen of industry, she had received her friends in her little salon hung with yellow silk. Eight hundred men now worked in the place; the ground quivered with the ceaseless trepidation of machinery; the establishment had grown to be the most important of its kind in Paris, the one whence came the finest agricultural appliances, the most powerful mechanical workers of the soil. And it was his, Mathieu's, son whom fortune had made prince of that branch of industry, and it was his daughter-in-law who, with her three strong, healthy children near her, received her friends in the little salon hung with yellow silk.

As Mathieu, moved by his recollections, glanced towards the right, towards the pavilion where he had dwelt with Marianne, and where Gervais had been born, an old workman who passed, lifted his cap to him, saying, "Good day, Monsieur Froment."

Mathieu thereupon recognized Victor Moineaud, now five-and-fifty years old, and aged, and wrecked by labor to even a greater degree than his father had been at the time when mother Moineaud had come to offer the Monster her children's immature flesh. Entering the works at sixteen years of age, Victor, like his father, had spent forty years between the forge and the anvil. It was iniquitous destiny beginning afresh: the most crushing toil falling upon a beast of burden, the son hebetated after the father, ground to death under the millstones of wretchedness and injustice.

"Good day, Victor," said Mathieu, "are you well?"

"Oh, I'm no longer young, Monsieur Froment," the other replied. "I shall soon have to look somewhere for a hole to lie in. Still, I hope it won't be under an omnibus."

He alluded to the death of his father, who had finally been picked up under an omnibus in the Rue de Grenelle, with his skull split and both legs broken.

"But after all," resumed Victor, "one may as well die that way as any other! It's even quicker. The old man was lucky in having Norine and Cecile to look after him. If it hadn't been for them, it's starvation that would have killed him, not an omnibus."

Mathieu interrupted. "Are Norine and Cecile well?" he asked.

"Yes, Monsieur Froment. Leastways, as far as I know, for, as you can understand, we don't often see one another. Them and me, that's about all that's left out of our lot; for Irma won't have anything more to do with us since she's become one of the toffs. Euphrasie was lucky enough to die, and that brigand Alfred disappeared, which was real relief, I assure you; for I feared that I should be seeing him at the galleys. And I was really pleased when I had some news of Norine and Cecile lately. Norine is older than I am, you know; she will soon be sixty. But she was always strong, and her boy, it seems, looks after her. Both she and Cecile still work; yes, Cecile still lives on, though one used to think that a fillip would have killed her. It's a pretty home, that one of theirs; two mothers for a big lad of whom they've made a decent fellow."

Mathieu nodded approvingly, and then remarked: "But you yourself, Victor, had boys and girls who must now in their turn be fathers and mothers."

The old workman waved his hand vaguely.

"Yes," said he, "I had eight, one more than my father. They've all gone off, and they are fathers and mothers in their turn, as you say, Monsieur Froment. It's all chance, you know; one has to live. There are some of them who certainly don't eat white bread, ah! that they don't. And the question is whether, when my arms fail me, I shall find one to take me in, as Norine and Cecile took my father. But when everything's said, what can you expect? It's all seed of poverty, it can't grow well, or yield anything good."

For a moment he remained silent; then resuming his walk towards the works, with bent, weary back and hanging hands, dented by toil, he said: "Au revoir, Monsieur Froment."

"Au revoir, Victor," Mathieu answered in a kindly tone.

Having given his orders, Denis now came to join his father, and proposed to him that they should go on foot to the Avenue d'Antin. On the way he warned him that they would certainly find Ambroise alone, for his wife and four children were still at Dieppe, where, indeed, the two sisters-in-law, Andree and Marthe, had spent the season together.

In a period of ten years, Ambroise's fortune had increased tenfold. Though he was barely five-and-forty, he reigned over the Paris market. With his spirit of enterprise, he had greatly enlarged the business left him by old Du Hordel, transforming it into a really universal *comptoir*, through which passed merchandise from all parts of the world. Frontiers did not exist for Ambroise, he enriched himself with the spoils of the earth, particularly striving to extract from the colonies all the wealth they were able to yield, and carrying on his operations with such triumphant audacity, such keen perception, that the most hazardous of his campaigns ended victoriously.

A man of this stamp, whose fruitful activity was ever winning battles, was certain to devour the idle, impotent Seguins. In the downfall of their fortune, the dispersal of the home and family, he had carved a share for himself by securing possession of the house in the Avenue d'Antin. Seguin himself had not resided there for years, he had thought it original to live at his club, where he secured accommodation after he and his wife had separated by consent. Two of the children had also gone off; Gaston, now a major in the army, was on duty in a distant garrison town, and Lucie was cloistered in an Ursuline convent. Thus, Valentine, left to herself and feeling very dreary, no longer able, moreover, to keep up the establishment on a proper footing, in her turn quitted the mansion for a cheerful and elegant little flat on the Boulevard Malesherbes, where she finished her life as a very devout old lady, presiding over a society for providing poor mothers with baby-linen, and thus devoting herself to the children of others—she who had not known how to bring up her own. And, in this wise, Ambroise had simply had to take possession of the empty mansion, which was heavily mortgaged, to such an extent, indeed, that when the Seguins died their heirs would certainly be owing him money.

Many were the recollections which awoke when Mathieu, accompanied by Denis, entered that princely mansion of the Avenue d'Antin! There, as at the factory, he could see himself arriving in poverty, as a needy tenant begging his landlord to repair a roof, in order that the rain might no longer pour down on the four children, whom, with culpable improvidence, he already had to provide for. There, facing the avenue, was the sumptuous Renaissance facade with eight lofty windows on each of its upper floors; there, inside, was the hall, all bronze and marble, conducting to the spacious ground-floor reception-rooms which a winter garden prolonged; and there, up above, occupying all the central part of the first floor, was Seguin's former "cabinet," the vast apartment with lofty windows of old stained glass. Mathieu could well remember that room with its profuse and amusing display of "antiquities," old brocades, old goldsmith's ware and old pottery, and its richly bound books, and its famous modern pewters. And he remembered it also at a later date, in the abandonment to which it had fallen, the aspect of ruin which it had assumed, covered, as it was, with gray dust which bespoke the slow crumbling of the home. And now he found it once more superb and cheerful, renovated with healthier and more substantial luxury by Ambroise, who had put masons and joiners and upholsterers into it for a period of three months. The whole mansion now lived afresh, more luxurious than ever, filled at winter-time with sounds of festivity, enlivened by the laughter of four happy children, and the blaze of a living fortune which effort and conquest ever renewed. And it was no longer Seguin, the idler, the artisan of nothingness, whom Mathieu came to see there, it was his own son Ambroise, a man of creative energy, whose victory had been sought by the very forces of life, which had made him triumph there, installed him as the master in the home of the vanquished.

When Mathieu and Denis arrived Ambroise was absent, but was expected home for lunch. They waited for him, and as the former again crossed the ante-room the better to judge of some new arrangements that had been made, he was surprised at being stopped by a lady who was sitting there patiently, and whom he had not previously noticed.

"I see that Monsieur Froment does not recognize me," she said.

Mathieu made a vague gesture. The woman had a tall, plump figure, and was certainly more than sixty years of age; but she evidently took care of her person, and had a smiling mien, with a long, full face and almost venerable white hair. One might have taken her for some worthy, well-to-do provincial bourgeoise in full dress.

"Celeste," said she. "Celeste, Madame Seguin's former maid."

Thereupon he fully recognized her, but hid his stupefaction at finding her so fortunately circumstanced at the close of her career. He had imagined that she was buried in some sewer.

In a gay, placid way she proceeded to recount her happiness: "Oh! I am very pleased," she said; "I had retired to Rougemont, my birth-place, and I ended by there marrying a retired naval officer, who has a very comfortable pension, not to speak of a little fortune which his first wife left him. As he has two big sons, I ventured to recommend the younger one to Monsieur Ambroise, who was kind enough to take him into his counting-house. And so I have profited by my first journey to Paris since then, to come and give Monsieur Ambroise my best thanks."

She did not say how she had managed to marry the retired naval officer; how she had originally been a servant in his household, and how she had hastened his first wife's death in order to marry him. All things considered, however, she rendered him very happy, and even rid

ÉMILE ZOLA

him of his sons, who were in his way, thanks to the relations she had kept up in Paris.

She continued smiling like a worthy woman, whose feelings softened at the recollection of the past. "You can have no idea how pleased I felt when I saw you pass just now, Monsieur Froment," she resumed. "Ah! it was a long time ago that I first had the honor of seeing you here! You remember La Couteau, don't you? She was always complaining, was she not? But she is very well pleased now; she and her husband have retired to a pretty little house of their own, with some little savings which they live on very quietly. She is no longer young, but she has buried a good many in her time, and she'll bury more before she has finished! For instance, Madame Menoux—you must surely remember Madame Menoux, the little haberdasher close by—well, there was a woman now who never had any luck! She lost her second child, and she lost that big fellow, her husband, whom she was so fond of, and she herself died of grief six months afterwards. I did at one time think of taking her to Rougemont, where the air is so good for one's health. There are old folks of ninety living there. Take La Couteau, for instance, she will live as long as she likes! Oh! yes, it is a very pleasant part indeed, a perfect paradise."

At these words the abominable Rougemont, the bloody Rougemont, arose before Mathieu's eyes, rearing its peaceful steeple above the low plain, with its cemetery paved with little Parisians, where wild flowers bloomed and hid the victims of so many murders.

But Celeste was rattling on again, saying: "You remember Madame Bourdieu whom you used to know in the Rue de Miromesnil; she died very near our village on some property where she went to live when she gave up business, a good many years ago. She was luckier than her colleague La Rouche, who was far too good-natured with people. You must have read about her case in the newspapers, she was sent to prison with a medical man named Sarraille."

"La Rouche! Sarraille!" Yes, Mathieu had certainly read the trial of those two social pests, who were fated to meet at last in their work of iniquity. And what an echo did those names awaken in the past: Valerie Morange! Reine Morange! Already in the factory yard Mathieu had fancied that he could see the shadow of Morange gliding past him— the punctual, timid, soft-hearted accountant, whom misfortune and insanity had carried off into the darkness. And suddenly the unhappy man here again appeared to Mathieu, like a wandering phantom, the restless victim of all the imbecile ambition, all the desperate craving for pleasure which animated the period; a poor, weak, mediocre being, so cruelly punished for the crimes of others, that he was doubtless unable to sleep in the tomb into which he had flung himself, bleeding, with broken limbs. And before Mathieu's eyes there likewise passed the spectre of Seraphine, with the fierce and pain-fraught face of one who is racked and killed by insatiate desire.

"Well, excuse me for having ventured to stop you, Monsieur Froment," Celeste concluded; "but I am very, very pleased at having met you again."

He was still looking at her; and as he quitted her he said, with the indulgence born of his optimism: "May you keep happy since you are happy. Happiness must know what it does."

Nevertheless, Mathieu remained disturbed, as he thought of the apparent injustice of impassive nature. The memory of his Marianne, struck down by such deep grief, pining away through the impious quarrels of her sons, returned to him. And as Ambroise at last came in and gayly embraced him, after receiving Celeste's thanks, he felt a thrill of anguish, for the decisive moment which would save or wreck the family was now at hand.

Indeed, Denis, after inviting himself and Mathieu to lunch, promptly plunged into the subject.

"We are not here for the mere pleasure of lunching with you," said he; "mamma is ill, did you know it?"

"Ill?" said Ambroise. "Not seriously ill?"

"Yes, very ill, in danger. And are you aware that she has been ill like this ever since she came to speak to you about the quarrel between Gregoire and Gervais, when it seems that you treated her very roughly."

"I treated her roughly? We simply talked business, and perhaps I spoke to her like a business man, a little bluntly."

Then Ambroise turned towards Mathieu, who was waiting, pale and silent: "Is it true, father, that mamma is ill and causes you anxiety?"

And as his father replied with a long affirmative nod, he gave vent to his emotion, even as Denis had done at the works immediately on learning the truth.

"But dash it all," he said; "this affair is becoming quite idiotic! In my opinion Gregoire is right and Gervais wrong. Only I don't care a fig about that; they must make it up at once, so that poor mamma may not have another moment's suffering. But then, why did you shut yourselves up? Why did you not let us know how grieved you were? Every one would have reflected and understood things."

Then, all at once, Ambroise embraced his father with that promptness of decision which he displayed to such happy effect in business as soon as ever a ray of light illumined his mind.

"After all, father," said he; "you are the cleverest; you understand things and foresee them. Even if Gregoire were within his rights in bringing an action against Gervais, it would be idiotic for him to do so, because far above any petty private interest, there is the interest of all of us, the interest of the family, which is to remain, united, compact, and unattackable, if it desires to continue invincible. Our sovereign strength lies in our union—And so it's simple enough. We will lunch as quickly as possible and take the first train. We shall go, Denis and I, to Chantebled with you. Peace must be concluded this evening. I will see to it."

Laughing, and well pleased to find his own feelings shared by his two sons, Mathieu returned Ambroise's embrace. And while waiting for lunch to be served, they went down to see the winter garden, which was being enlarged for some fetes which Ambroise wished to give. He took pleasure in adding to the magnificence of the mansion, and in reigning there with princely pomp. At lunch he apologized for only offering his father and brother a bachelor's pot-luck, though, truth to tell, the fare was excellent. Indeed, whenever Andree and the children absented themselves, Ambroise still kept a good cook to minister to his needs, for he held the cuisine of restaurants in horror.

"Well, for my part," said Denis, "I go to a restaurant for my meals; for since Marthe and all the others have been at Dieppe, I have virtually shut up the house."

"You are a wise man, you see," Ambroise answered, with quiet frankness. "For my part, as you are aware, I am an enjoyer. Now, make haste and drink your coffee, and we will start."

They reached Janville by the two o'clock train. Their plan was to repair to Chantebled in the first instance, in order that Ambroise and Denis might begin by talking to Gervais, who was of a gentler nature than Gregoire, and with whom they thought they might devise some means of conciliation. Then they intended to betake themselves to the mill, lecture Gregoire, and impose on him such peace conditions as they might have agreed upon. As they drew nearer and nearer to the farm, however, the difficulties of their undertaking appeared to them, and seemed to increase in magnitude. An arrangement would not be arrived at so easily as they had at first imagined. So they girded their loins in readiness for a hard battle.

"Suppose we begin by going to see mamma," Denis suggested. "We should see and embrace her, and that would give us some courage."

Ambroise deemed the idea an excellent one. "Yes, let us go by all means, particularly as mamma has always been a good counsellor. She must have some idea."

They climbed to the first floor of the house, to the spacious room where Marianne spent her days on a couch beside the window. And to their stupefaction they found her seated on that couch with Gregoire standing by her and holding both her hands, while on the other side were Gervais and Claire, laughing softly.

"Why! what is this?" exclaimed Ambroise in amazement. "The work is done!"

"And we who despaired of being able to accomplish it!" declared Denis, with a gesture of bewilderment.

Mathieu was equally stupefied and delighted, and on noticing the surprise occasioned by the arrival of the two big brothers from Paris, he proceeded to explain the position.

"I went to Paris this morning to fetch them," he said, "and I've brought them here to reconcile us all!"

A joyous peal of laughter resounded. The big brothers were too late! Neither their wisdom nor their diplomacy had been needed. They themselves made merry over it, feeling the while greatly relieved that the victory should have been won without any battle.

Marianne, whose eyes were moist, and who felt divinely happy, so happy that she seemed already well again, simply replied to Mathieu: "You see, my friend, it's done. But as yet I know nothing further. Gregoire came here and kissed me, and wished me to send for Gervais and Claire at once. Then, of his own accord, he told them that they were all three mad in causing me such grief, and that they ought to come to an understanding together. Thereupon they kissed one another. And now it's done; it's all over."

But Gregoire gayly intervened. "Wait a moment; just listen; I cut too fine a figure in the story as mamma relates it, and I must tell you the truth. I wasn't the first to desire the reconciliation; the first was my wife, Therese. She has a good sterling heart and the very brains of a mule, in such wise that whenever she is determined on anything

I always have to do it in the end. Well, yesterday evening we had a bit of a quarrel, for she had heard, I don't know how, that mamma was ill with grief. And this pained her, and she tried to prove to me how stupid the quarrel was, for we should all of us lose by it. This morning she began again, and of course she convinced me, more particularly as, with the thought of poor mamma lying ill through our fault, I had hardly slept all night. But father Lepailleur still had to be convinced, and Therese undertook to do that also. She even hit upon something extraordinary, so that the old man might imagine that he was the conqueror of conquerors. She persuaded him at last to sell you that terrible enclosure at such an insane price that he will be able to shout 'victory!' over all the house-tops."

Then turning to his brother and sister, Gregoire added, in a jocular tone; "My dear Gervais, my dear Claire, let yourselves be robbed, I beg of you. The peace of my home is at stake. Give my father-in-law the last joy of believing that he alone has always been in the right, and that we have never been anything but fools."

"Oh! as much money as he likes," replied Gervais, laughing. "Besides, that enclosure has always been a dishonor for the estate, streaking it with stones and brambles, like a nasty sore. We have long dreamt of seeing the property spotless, with its crops waving without a break under the sun. And Chantebled is rich enough to pay for its glory."

Thus the affair was settled. The wheat of the farm would return to the mill to be ground, and the mother would get well again. It was the force of life, the need of love, the union necessary for the whole family if it were to continue victorious, that had imposed true brotherliness on the sons, who for a moment had been foolish enough to destroy their power by assailing one another.

The delight of finding themselves once more together there, Denis, Ambroise, Gervais, Gregoire, the four big brothers, and Claire, the big sister, all reconciled and again invincible, increased when Charlotte arrived, bringing with her the other three daughters, Louise, Madeleine, and Marthe, who had married and settled in the district. Louise, having heard that her mother was ill, had gone to fetch her sisters, in order that they might repair to Chantebled together. And what a hearty laugh there was when the procession entered!

"Let them all come!" cried Ambroise, in a jocular way. "Let's have the family complete, a real meeting of the great privy council. You see, mamma, you must get well at once; the whole of your court is at your knees, and unanimously decides that it can no longer allow you to have even a headache."

Then, as Benjamin put in an appearance the very last, behind the three sisters, the laughter broke out afresh.

"And to think that we were forgetting Benjamin!" Mathieu exclaimed.

"Come, little one, come and kiss me in your turn," said Marianne affectionately, in a low voice. "The others jest because you are the last of the brood. But if I spoil you that only concerns ourselves, does it not? Tell them that you spent the morning with me, and that if you went out for a walk it was because I wished you to do so."

Benjamin smiled with a gentle and rather sad expression. "But I was downstairs, mamma; I saw them go up one after the other. I waited for them all to kiss, before coming up in my turn."

He was already one-and-twenty and extremely handsome, with a bright face, large brown eyes, long curly hair, and a frizzy, downy beard. Though he had never been ill, his mother would have it that he was weak, and insisted on coddling him. All of them, moreover, were very fond of him, both for his grace of person and the gentle charm of his disposition. He had grown up in a kind of dream, full of a desire which he could not put into words, ever seeking the unknown, something which he knew not, did not possess. And when his parents saw that he had no taste for any profession, and that even the idea of marrying did not appeal to him, they evinced no anger, but, on the contrary, they secretly plotted to keep this son, their last-born, life's final gift, to themselves. Had they not surrendered all the others? Would they not be forgiven for yielding to the egotism of love by reserving one for themselves, one who would be theirs entirely, who would never marry, or toil and moil, but would merely live beside them and love them, and be loved in return? This was the dream of their old age, the share which, in return for long fruitfulness, they would have liked to snatch from devouring life, which, though it gives one everything, yet takes everything away.

"Oh! just listen, Benjamin," Ambroise suddenly resumed, "you are interested in our brave Nicolas, I know. Would you like to have some news of him? I heard from him only the day before yesterday. And it's right that I should speak of him, since he's the only one of the brood, as mamma puts it, who cannot be here."

Benjamin at once became quite excited, asking, "Is it true? Has he written to you? What does he say? What is he doing?"

He could never think without emotion of Nicolas's departure for Senegal. He was twelve years old at that time, and nearly nine years had gone by since then, yet the scene, with that eternal farewell, that flight, as it were, into the infinite of time and hope, was ever present in his mind.

"You know that I have business relations with Nicolas," resumed Ambroise. "Oh! if we had but a few fellows as intelligent and courageous as he is in our colonies, we should soon rake in all the scattered wealth of those virgin lands. Well, Nicolas, as you are aware, went to Senegal with Lisbeth, who was the very companion and helpmate he needed. Thanks to the few thousand francs which they possessed between them, they soon established a prosperous business; but I divined that the field was still too small for them, and that they dreamt of clearing and conquering a larger expanse. And now, all at once, Nicolas writes to me that he is starting for the Soudan, the valley of the Niger, which has only lately been opened. He is taking his wife and his four children with him, and they are all going off to conquer as fortune may will it, like valiant pioneers beset by the idea of founding a new world. I confess that it amazes me, for it is a very hazardous enterprise. But all the same one must admit that our Nicolas is a very plucky fellow, and one can't help admiring his great energy and faith in thus setting out for an almost unknown region, fully convinced that he will subject and populate it."

Silence fell. A great gust seemed to have swept by, the gust of the infinite coming from the far away mysterious virgin plains. And the family could picture that young fellow, one of themselves, going off through the deserts, carrying the good seed of humanity under the spreading sky into unknown climes.

"Ah!" said Benjamin softly, his eyes dilating and gazing far, far away as if to the world's end; "ah! he's happy, for he sees other rivers, and other forests, and other suns than ours!"

But Marianne shuddered. "No, no, my boy," said she; "there are no other rivers than the Yeuse, no other forests but our woods of Lillebonne, no other sun but that of Chantebled. Come and kiss me again—let us all kiss once more, and I shall get well, and we shall never be parted again."

The laughter began afresh with the embraces. It was a great day, a day of victory, the most decisive victory which the family had ever won by refusing to let discord destroy it. Henceforth it would be invincible.

At twilight, on the evening of that day, Mathieu and Marianne again found themselves, as on the previous evening, hand in hand near the window whence they could see the estate stretching to the horizon; that horizon behind which arose the breath of Paris, the tawny cloud of its gigantic forge. But how little did that serene evening resemble the other, and how great was their present felicity, their trust in the goodness of their work.

"Do you feel better?" Mathieu asked his wife; "do you feel your strength returning; does your heart beat more freely?"

"Oh! my friend, I feel cured; I was only pining with grief. To-morrow I shall be strong."

Then Mathieu sank into a deep reverie, as he sat there face to face with his conquest—that estate which spread out under the setting sun. And again, as in the morning, did recollections crowd upon him; he remembered a morning more than forty years previously when he had left Marianne, with thirty sous in her purse, in the little tumbledown shooting-box on the verge of the woods. They lived there on next to nothing; they owed money, they typified gay improvidence with the four little mouths which they already had to feed, those children who had sprung from their love, their faith in life.

Then he recalled his return home at night time, the three hundred francs, a month's salary, which he had carried in his pocket, the calculations which he had made, the cowardly anxiety which he had felt, disturbed as he was by the poisonous egotism which he had encountered in Paris. There were the Beauchenes, with their factory, and their only son, Maurice, whom they were bringing up to be a future prince, the Beauchenes, who had prophesied to him that he and his wife and their troop of children could only expect a life of black misery, and death in a garret. There were also the Seguins, then his landlords, who had shown him their millions, and their magnificent mansion, full of treasures, crushing him the while, treating him with derisive pity because he did not behave sensibly like themselves, who were content with having but two children, a boy and a girl. And even those poor Moranges had talked to him of giving a royal dowry to their one daughter Reine, dreaming at that time of an appointment that would bring in twelve thousand francs a year, and full of contempt for the misery which a numerous family entails. And then the very Lepailleurs, the people of the mill, had evinced distrust because there were twelve francs owing to them for milk and eggs; for it had seemed to them doubtful whether a bourgeois, insane enough to have so many children, could possibly pay his debts. Ah! the views of the others had then appeared to be correct; he had repeated to himself that he would never have a factory, nor a mansion, nor even a mill, and that in all probability he would never earn twelve thousand francs a year. The others had everything and he nothing. The others, the rich, behaved sensibly, and did not burden themselves with offspring; whereas, he, the poor man, already had more children than he could provide for. What madness it had seemed to be!

But forty years had rolled away, and behold his madness was wisdom! He had conquered by his divine improvidence; the poor man had vanquished the wealthy. He had placed his trust in the future, and now the whole harvest was garnered. The Beauchene factory was his through his son Denis; the Seguins' mansion was his through his son Ambroise; the Lepailleurs' mill was his through his son Gregoire. Tragical, even excessive punishment, had blown those sorry Moranges away in a tempest of blood and insanity. And other social wastage had swept by and rolled into the gutter; Seraphine, the useless creature, had succumbed to her passions; the Moineauds had been dispersed, annihilated by their poisonous environment. And he, Mathieu, and Marianne alone remained erect, face to face with that estate of Chantebled, which they had conquered from the Seguins, and where their children, Gervais and Claire, at present reigned, prolonging the dynasty of their race. This was their kingdom; as far as the eye could see the fields spread out with wondrous fertility under the sun's farewell, proclaiming the battles, the heroic creative labor of their lives. There was their work, there was what they had produced, whether in the realm of animate or inanimate nature, thanks to the power of love within them, and their energy of will. By love, and resolution, and action, they had created a world.

"Look, look!" murmured Mathieu, waving his arm, "all that has sprung from us, and we must continue to love, we must continue to be happy, in order that it may all live."

"Ah!" Marianne gayly replied, "it will live forever now, since we have all become reconciled and united amid our victory."

Victory! yes, it was the natural, necessary victory that is reaped by the numerous family! Thanks to numbers they had ended by invading every sphere and possessing everything. Fruitfulness was the invincible, sovereign conqueress. Yet their conquest had not been meditated and planned; ever serenely loyal in their dealings with others, they owed it simply to the fulfilment of duty throughout their long years of toil. And they now stood before it hand in hand, like heroic figures, glorious because they had ever been good and strong, because they had created abundantly, because they had given abundance of joy, and health, and hope to the world amid all the everlasting struggles and the everlasting tears.

XXIII

A nd Mathieu and Marianne lived more than a score of years longer, and Mathieu was ninety years old and Marianne eighty-seven, when their three eldest sons, Denis, Ambroise, and Gervais, ever erect beside them, planned that they would celebrate their diamond wedding, the seventieth anniversary of their marriage, by a fete at which they would assemble all the members of the family at Chantebled.

It was no little affair. When they had drawn up a complete list, they found that one hundred and fifty-eight children, grandchildren, and great-grandchildren had sprung from Mathieu and Marianne, without counting a few little ones of a fourth generation. By adding to the above those who had married into the family as husbands and wives they would be three hundred in number. And where at the farm could they find a room large enough for the huge table of the patriarchal feast that they dreamt of? The anniversary fell on June 2, and the spring that year was one of incomparable mildness and beauty. So they decided that they would lunch out of doors, and place the tables in front of the old pavilion, on the large lawn, enclosed by curtains of superb elms and hornbeams, which gave the spot the aspect of a huge hall of verdure. There they would be at home, on the very breast of the beneficent earth, under the central and now gigantic oak, planted by the two ancestors, whose blessed fruitfulness the whole swarming progeny was about to celebrate.

Thus the festival was settled and organized amid a great impulse of love and joy. All were eager to take part in it, all hastened to the triumphal gathering, from the white-haired old men to the urchins who still sucked their thumbs. And the broad blue sky and the flaming sun were bent on participating in it also, as well as the whole estate, the streaming springs and the fields in flower, giving promise of bounteous harvests. Magnificent looked the huge horseshoe table set out amid the grass, with handsome china and snowy cloths which the sunbeams flecked athwart the foliage. The august pair, the father and mother, were to sit side by side, in the centre, under the oak tree. It was decided also that the other couples should not be separated, that it would be charming to place them side by side according to the generation they belonged to. But as for the young folks, the youths and maidens, the urchins and the little girls, they, it was thought, might well be left to seat themselves as their fancy listed.

Early in the morning those bidden to the feast began to arrive in bands; the dispersed family returned to the common nest, swooping down upon it from the four points of the compass. But alas! death's scythe had been at work, and there were many who could not come. Departed ones slept, each year more numerous, in the peaceful, flowery, Janville cemetery. Near Rose and Blaise, who had been the first to depart, others had gone thither to sleep the eternal sleep, each time carrying away a little more of the family's heart, and making of that sacred spot a place of worship and eternal souvenir. First Charlotte, after long illness, had joined Blaise, happy in leaving Berthe to replace her beside Mathieu and Marianne, who were heart-stricken by her death, as if indeed they were for the second time losing their dear son. Afterwards their daughter Claire had likewise departed from them, leaving the farm to her husband Frederic and her brother Gervais, who likewise had become a widower during the ensuing year. Then, too, Mathieu and Marianne had lost their son Gregoire, the master of the mill, whose widow Therese still ruled there amid a numerous progeny. And again they had to mourn another of their daughters, the kind-hearted Marguerite, Dr. Chambouvet's wife, who sickened and died, through having sheltered a poor workman's little children, who were affected with croup. And the other losses could no longer be counted among them were some who had married into the family, wives and husbands, and there were in particular many children, the tithe that death always exacts, those who are struck down by the storms which sweep over the human crop, all the dear little ones for whom the living weep, and who sanctify the ground in which they rest.

But if the dear departed yonder slept in deepest silence, how gay was the uproar and how great the victory of life that morning along the roads which led to Chantebled! The number of those who were born surpassed that of those who died. From each that departed, a whole florescence of living beings seemed to blossom forth. They sprang up in dozens from the ground where their forerunners had laid themselves to sleep when weary of their work. And they flocked to Chantebled from every side, even as swallows return at spring to revivify their old nests, filling the blue sky with the joy of their return. Outside the farm, vehicles were ever setting down fresh families with troops of children, whose sea of fair heads was always expanding. Great-grandfathers with snowy hair came leading little ones who could scarcely toddle. There were very nice-looking old ladies whom young girls of dazzling freshness assisted to alight. There were mothers expecting the arrival of other babes, and fathers to whom the charming idea had occurred of inviting their daughters' affianced lovers. And they were all related, they had all sprung from a common ancestry, they were all mingled in an inextricable tangle, fathers, mothers, brothers, sisters, fathers-in-law, mothers-in-law, brothers-in-law, sisters-in-law, sons, daughters, uncles, aunts, and cousins, of every possible degree, down to the fourth generation. And they were all one family; one sole little nation, assembling in joy and pride to celebrate that diamond wedding, the rare prodigious nuptials of two heroic creatures whom life had glorified and from whom all had sprung! And what an epic, what a Biblical numbering of that people suggested itself! How even name all those who entered the farm, how simply set forth their names, their ages, their degree of relationship, the health, the strength, and the hope that they had brought into the world!

Before everybody else there were those of the farm itself, all those who had been born and who had grown up there. Gervais, now sixty-two, was helped by his two eldest sons, Leon and Henri, who between them had ten children; while his three daughters, Mathilde, Leontine, and Julienne, who were married in the district, in like way numbered between them twelve. Then Frederic, Claire's husband, who was five years older than Gervais, had surrendered his post as a faithful lieutenant to his son Joseph, while his daughters Angele and Lucille, as well as a second son Jules, also helped on the farm, the four supplying a troop of fifteen children, some of them boys and some girls.

Then, of all those who came from without, the mill claimed the first place. Therese, Gregoire's widow, arrived with her offspring, her son Robert, who now managed the mill under her control, and her three daughters, Genevieve, Aline, and Natalie, followed by quite a train of children, ten belonging to the daughters and four to Robert. Next came Louise, notary Mazaud's wife, and Madeleine, architect Herbette's wife, followed by Dr. Chambouvet, who had lost his wife, the good Marguerite. And here again were three valiant companies; in the first, four daughters, of whom Colette was the eldest; in the second, five sons with Hilary at the head of them; and in the third, a son and daughter only, Sebastien and Christine; the whole, however, forming quite an army, for there were twenty of Mathieu's great-grandchildren in the rear.

But Paris arrived on the scene with Denis and his wife Marthe, who headed a grand cortege. Denis, now nearly seventy, and a great-grandfather through his daughters Hortense and Marcelle, had enjoyed the happy rest which follows accomplished labor ever since he had handed his works over to his eldest sons Lucien and Paul, who were both men of more than forty, and whose own sons were already on the road to every sort of fortune. And what with the mother and father, the four children, the fifteen grandchildren, and the three great-grandchildren, two of whom were yet in swaddling clothes, this was really an invading tribe packed into five vehicles.

Then the final entry was that of the little nation which had sprung from Ambroise, who to his great grief had early lost his wife Andree. His was such a green old age that at sixty-seven he still directed his business, in which his sons Leonce and Charles remained simple *employes* like his sons-in-law—the husbands of his daughters, Pauline and Sophie—who trembled before him, uncontested king that he remained, obeyed by one and all, grandfather of seven big bearded young men and nine strong young women, through four of whom he had become a great-grandfather even before his elder, the wise Denis. For this troop six carriages were required. And the defile lasted two hours, and the farm was soon full of a happy, laughing throng, holiday-making in the bright June sunlight.

Mathieu and Marianne had not yet put in an appearance. Ambroise, who was the grand master of the ceremonies that day, had made them promise to remain in their room, like sovereigns hidden from their people, until he should go to fetch them. He desired that they should appear in all solemnity. And when he made up his mind to summon them, the whole nation being assembled together, he found his brother Benjamin on the threshold of the house defending the door like a bodyguard.

He, Benjamin, had remained the one idler, the one unfruitful scion of that swarming tribe, which had toiled and multiplied so prodigiously. Now three-and-forty years of age, without a wife and without children, he lived, it seemed, solely for the joy of the old home, as a companion to his father and a passionate worshipper of his mother, who with the egotism of love had set themselves upon keeping him for themselves alone. At first they had not been opposed to his marrying, but when they had seen him refuse one match after another, they had secretly felt great delight. Nevertheless, as years rolled by, some unacknowledged remorse had come to them amid their happiness at having him beside them like some hoarded treasure, the delight of an avaricious old age, following a life of prodigality. Did not their Benjamin suffer at having been thus monopolized, shut up for their sole pleasure within the four walls of their house? He had at all times displayed an anxious dreaminess, his eyes had ever sought far-away things, the unknown land where perfect satisfaction dwelt, yonder, behind the horizon. And now that age was stealing upon him his torment seemed to increase, as if he were in despair at finding himself unable to try the possibilities of the unknown, before he ended a useless life devoid of happiness.

However, Benjamin moved away from the door, Ambroise gave his orders, and Mathieu and Marianne appeared upon the verdant lawn in the sunlight. An acclamation, merry laughter, affectionate clapping of hands greeted them. The gay excited throng, the whole swarming family cried aloud: "Long live the Father! Long live the Mother! Long life, long life to the Father and the Mother!"

At ninety years of age Mathieu was still very upright and slim, closely buttoned in a black frock-coat like a young bridegroom. Over his bare head fell a snowy fleece, for after long wearing his hair cut short he had now in a final impulse of coquetry allowed it to grow, so that it seemed liked the *renouveau* of an old but vigorous tree. Age might have withered and worn and wrinkled his face, but he still retained the eyes of his young days, large lustrous eyes, at once smiling and pensive, which still bespoke a man of thought and action, one who was very simple, very gay, and very good-hearted. And Marianne at eighty-seven years of age also held herself very upright in her light bridal gown, still strong and still showing some of the healthy beauty of other days. With hair white like Mathieu's, and softened face, illumined as by a last glow under her silky tresses, she resembled one of those sacred marbles whose features time has ravined, without, however, being able to efface from them the tranquil splendor of life. She seemed, indeed, like some fruitful Cybele, retaining all firmness of contour, and living anew in the broad daylight with gentle good humor sparkling in her large black eyes.

Arm-in-arm close to one another, like a worthy couple who had come from afar, who had walked on side by side without ever parting for seventy long years, Mathieu and Marianne smiled with tears of joy in their eyes at the whole swarming family which had sprung from their love, and which still acclaimed them:

"Long live the Father! Long live the Mother! Long life, long life to the Father and the Mother!"

Then came the ceremony of reciting a compliment and offering a bouquet. A fair-haired little girl named Rose, five years of age, had been intrusted with this duty. She had been chosen because she was the eldest child of the fourth generation. She was the daughter of Angeline, who was the daughter of Berthe, who was the daughter of Charlotte, wife of Blaise. And when the two ancestors saw her approach them with her big bouquet, their emotion increased, happy tears again gathered in their eyes, and recollections faltered on their lips: "Oh! our little Rose! Our Blaise, our Charlotte!"

All the past revived before them. The name of Rose had been given to the child in memory of the other long-mourned Rose, who had been the first to leave them, and who slept yonder in the little cemetery. There in his turn had Blaise been laid, and thither Charlotte had followed them. Then Berthe, Blaise's daughter, who had married Philippe Havard, had given birth to Angeline. And, later, Angeline, having married Georges Delmas, had given birth to Rose. Berthe and Philippe Havard, Angeline and Georges Delmas stood behind the child. And she represented one and all, the dead, the living, the whole flourishing line, its many griefs, its many joys, all the valiant toil of creation, all the river of life that it typified, for everything ended in her, dear, frail, fair-haired angel, with eyes bright like the dawn, in whose depths the future sparkled.

"Oh! our Rose! our Rose!"

With a big bouquet between her little hands Rose had stepped forward. She had been learning a very fine compliment for a fortnight past, and that very morning she had recited it to her mother without making a single mistake. But when she found herself there among all these people she could not recollect a word of it. Still that did not trouble her, she was already a very bold little damsel, and she frankly dropped her bouquet and sprang at the necks of Mathieu and Marianne, exclaiming in her shrill, flute-like voice: "Grandpapa, grandmamma, it's your fete, and I kiss you with all my heart!"

And that suited everybody remarkably well. They even found it far better than any compliment. Laughter and clapping of hands and acclamations again arose. Then they forthwith began to take their seats at table.

This, however, was quite an affair, so large was the horse-shoe table spread out under the oak on the short, freshly cut grass. First Mathieu and Marianne, still arm in arm, went ceremoniously to seat themselves in the centre with their backs towards the trunk of the great tree. On Mathieu's left, Marthe and Denis, Louise and her husband, notary Mazaud, took their places, since it had been fittingly decided that the husbands and wives should not be separated. On the right of Marianne came Ambroise, Therese, Gervais, Dr. Chambouvet, three widowers and a widow, then another married couple, Madeleine and her husband, architect Herbette, and then Benjamin alone. The other married folks afterwards installed themselves according to the generation they belonged to; and then, as had been decided, youth and childhood, the whole troop of young people and little ones took seats as they pleased amid no little turbulence.

What a moment of sovereign glory it was for Mathieu and Marianne! They found themselves there in a triumph of which they would never have dared to dream. Life, as if to reward them for having shown faith in her, for having increased her sway with all bravery, seemed to have taken pleasure in prolonging their existences beyond the usual limits so that their eyes might behold the marvellous blossoming of their work. The whole of their dear Chantebled, everything good and beautiful that they had there begotten and established, participated in the festival. From the cultivated fields that they had set in the place of marshes came the broad quiver of great coming harvests; from the pasture lands amid the distant woods came the warm breath of cattle and innumerable flocks which ever increased the ark of life; and they heard, too, the loud babble of the captured springs with which they had fertilized the now fruitful moorlands, the flow of that water which is like the very blood of our mother earth. The social task was accomplished, bread was won, subsistence had been created, drawn from the nothingness of barren soil.

And on what a lovely and well-loved spot did their happy, grateful race offer them that festival! Those elms and hornbeams, which made the lawn a great hall of greenery, had been planted by themselves; they had seen them growing day by day like the most peaceable and most sturdy of their children. And in particular that oak, now so gigantic, thanks to the clear waters of the adjoining basin through which one of the sources ever streamed, was their own big son, one that dated from the day when they had founded Chantebled, he, Mathieu, digging the hole and she, Marianne, holding the sapling erect. And now, as that tree stood there, shading them with its expanse of verdure, was it not like some royal symbol of the whole family? Like that oak the family had grown and multiplied, ever throwing out fresh branches which spread far over the ground; and like that oak it now formed by itself a perfect forest sprung from a single trunk, vivified by the same sap, strong in the same health, and full of song, and breeziness, and sunlight.

Leaning against that giant tree Mathieu and Marianne became merged in its sovereign glory and majesty, and was not their royalty akin to its own? Had they not begotten as many beings as the tree had begotten branches? Did they not reign there over a nation of their children, who lived by them, even as the leaves above lived by the tree? The three hundred big and little ones seated around them were but a prolongation of themselves; they belonged to the same tree of life, they had sprung from their love and still clung to them by every fibre. Mathieu and Marianne divined how joyous they all were at glorifying themselves in making much of them; how moved the elder ones, how turbulently merry the younger felt. They could hear their own hearts beating in the breasts of the fair-haired urchins who already laughed with ecstasy at the sight of the cakes and pastry on the table. And their work of human creation was assembled in front of them and within them, in the same way as the oak's huge dome spread out above it; and all around they were likewise encompassed by the fruitfulness of their other work, the fertility and growth of nature which had increased even as they themselves multiplied.

Then was the true beauty which had its abode in Mathieu and Marianne made manifest, that beauty of having loved one another for seventy years and of still worshipping one another now even as on the first day. For seventy years had they trod life's pathway side by side and arm in arm, without a quarrel, without ever a deed of unfaithfulness. They could certainly recall great sorrows, but these had always come from without. And if they had sometimes sobbed they had consoled one another by mingling their tears. Under their white locks they had retained the faith of their early days, their hearts remained blended, merged one into the other, even as on the morrow of their marriage, each having then been freely given and never taken back. In them the power of love, the will of action, the divine desire whose flame creates worlds, had happily met and united. He, adoring his wife, had known no other joy than the passion of creation, looking on the work that had to be performed and the work that was accomplished as the sole why and wherefore of his being, his duty and his reward. She, adoring her husband, had simply striven to be a true companion, spouse, mother, and good counsellor, one who was endowed with delicacy of judgment and helped to overcome all difficulties. Between them they were reason, and health, and strength. If, too, they had always triumphed athwart obstacles and tears, it was only by reason of their long agreement, their common fealty amid an eternal renewal of their love, whose armor rendered them invincible. They could not be conquered, they had conquered by the very power of their union without designing it. And they ended heroically, as conquerors of happiness, hand in hand, pure as crystal is, very great, very handsome, the more so from their extreme age, their long, long life, which one love had entirely filled. And the sole strength of their innumerable offspring now gathered there, the conquering tribe that had sprung from their loins, was the strength of union inherited from them: the loyal love transmitted from ancestors to children, the mutual affection which impelled them to help one another and ever fight for a better life in all brotherliness.

But mirthful sounds arose, the banquet was at last being served. All the servants of the farm had gathered to discharge this duty—they would not allow a single person from without to help them. Nearly all had grown up on the estate, and belonged, as it were, to the family. By and by they would have a table for themselves, and in their turn celebrate the diamond wedding. And it was amid exclamations and merry laughter that they brought the first dishes.

All at once, however, the serving ceased, silence fell, an unexpected incident attracted all attention. A young man, whom none apparently could recognize, was stepping across the lawn, between the arms of the horse-shoe table. He smiled gayly as he walked on, only stopping when he was face to face with Mathieu and Marianne. Then in a loud voice he said: "Good day, grandfather! good day, grandmother! You must have another cover laid, for I have come to celebrate the day with you."

The onlookers remained silent, in great astonishment. Who was this young man whom none had ever seen before? Assuredly he could not belong to the family, for they would have known his name, have recognized his face? Why, then, did he address the ancestors by the venerated names of grandfather and grandmother? And the stupefaction was the greater by reason of his extraordinary resemblance to Mathieu. Assuredly, he was a Froment, he had the bright eyes and the lofty tower-like forehead of the race. Mathieu lived again in him, such as he appeared in a piously-preserved portrait representing him at the age of seven-and-twenty when he had begun the conquest of Chantebled.

Mathieu, for his part, rose, trembling, while Marianne smiled divinely, for she understood the truth before all the others.

"Who are you, my child?" asked Mathieu, "you, who call me grandfather, and who resemble me as if you were my brother?"

"I am Dominique, the eldest son of your son Nicolas, who lives with my mother, Lisbeth, in the vast free country yonder, the other France!"

"And how old are you?"

"I shall be seven-and-twenty next August, when, yonder, the waters of the Niger, the good giant, come back to fertilize our spreading fields."

"And tell us, are you married, have you any children?"

"I have taken for my wife a French woman, born in Senegal, and in the brick house which I have built, four children are already growing up under the flaming sun of the Soudan."

"And tell us also, have you any brothers, any sisters?"

"My father, Nicolas, and Lisbeth, my mother, have had eighteen children, two of whom are dead. We are sixteen, nine boys and seven girls."

At this Mathieu laughed gayly, as if to say that his son Nicolas at fifty years of age had already proved a more valiant artisan of life than himself.

"Well then, my boy," he said, "since you are the son of my son Nicolas, come and embrace us to celebrate our wedding. And a cover shall be placed for you; you are at home here."

In four strides Dominique made the round of the tables, then cast his strong arms about the old people and embraced them—they the while feeling faint with happy emotion, so delightful was that surprise, yet another child falling among them, and on that day, as from some distant sky, and telling them of the other family, the other nation which had sprung from them, and which was swarming yonder with increase of fruitfulness amid the fiery glow of the tropics.

That surprise was due to the sly craft of Ambroise, who merrily explained how he had prepared it like a masterly coup de theatre. For a week past he had been lodging and hiding Dominique in his house in Paris; the young man having been sent from the Soudan by his father to negotiate certain business matters, and in particular to order of Denis a quantity of special agricultural machinery adapted to the soil of that far-away region. Thus Denis alone had been taken into the other's confidence.

When all those seated at the table saw Dominique in the old people's arms, and learnt the whole story, there came an extraordinary outburst of delight; deafening acclamations arose once more; and what with their enthusiastic greetings and embraces they almost stifled the messenger from the sister family, that prince of the second dynasty of the Froments which ruled in the land of the future France.

Mathieu gayly gave his orders: "There, place his cover in front of us! He alone will be in front of us like the ambassador of some powerful empire. Remember that, apart from his father and mother, he represents nine brothers and seven sisters, without counting the four children that he already has himself. There, my boy, sit down; and now let the service continue."

The feast proved a mirthful one under the big oak tree whose shade was spangled by the sunbeams. Delicious freshness arose from the grass, friendly nature seemed to contribute its share of caresses. The laughter never ceased, old folks became playful children once more in presence of the ninety and the eighty-seven years of the bridegroom and the bride. Faces beamed softly under white and dark and sunny hair; the whole assembly was joyful, beautiful with a healthy rapturous beauty; the children radiant, the youths superb, the maidens adorable, the married folk united, side by side. And what good appetites there were! What a gay tumult greeted the advent of each fresh dish! And how the good wine was honored to celebrate the goodness of life which had granted the two patriarchs the supreme grace of assembling them all at their table on such a glorious occasion! At dessert came toasts and health-drinking and fresh acclamations. But, amid all the chatter which flew from one to the other end of the table, the conversation invariably reverted to the surprise at the outset: that triumphal entry of the brotherly ambassador. It was he, his unexpected presence, all that he had not yet said, all the adventurous romance which he surely personated, that fanned the growing fever, the excitement of the family, intoxicated by that open-air gala. And as soon as the coffee was served no end of questions arose on every side, and he had to speak out.

"Well, what can I say?" he replied, laughing, to a question put to him by Ambroise, who wished to know what he thought of Chantebled, where he had taken him for a stroll during the morning. "I'm afraid that if I speak in all frankness, you won't think me very complimentary. Cultivation, no doubt, is quite an art here, a splendid effort of will and science and organization, as is needed to draw from this old soil such crops as it can still produce. You toil a great deal, and you effect prodigies. But, good heavens! how small your kingdom is! How can you live here without hurting yourselves by ever rubbing against other people's elbows? You are all heaped up to such a degree that you no longer have the amount of air needful for a man's lungs. Your largest stretches of land, what you call your big estates, are mere clods of soil where the few cattle that one sees look to me like lost ants. But ah! the immensity of our Niger; the immensity of the plains it waters; the immensity of our fields, whose only limit is the distant horizon!"

Benjamin had listened, quivering. Ever since that son of the great river had arrived, he had continued gazing at him, with passion rising in his dreamy eyes. And on hearing him speak in this fashion he could no longer restrain himself, but rose, went round the table, and sat down beside him.

"The Niger—the immense plains—tell us all about them," he said.

"The Niger, the good giant, the father of us all over yonder!" responded Dominique. "I was barely eight years old when my parents quitted Senegal, yielding to an impulse of reckless bravery and wild hope, possessed by a craving to plunge into the Soudan and conquer as chance might will it. There are many days' march among rocks and scrub and rivers from St. Louis to our present farm, far beyond Djenny. And I no longer remember the first journey. It seems to me as if I sprang from good father Niger himself, from the wondrous fertility of his waters. He is gentle but immense, rolling countless waves like the sea, and so broad, so vast, that no bridge can span him as he flows from horizon to horizon. He carries archipelagoes on his breast, and stretches out arms covered with herbage like pasture land. And there are the depths where flotillas of huge fishes roam at their ease. Father Niger has his tempests, too, and his days of fire, when his waters beget life in the burning clasp of the sun. And he has his delightful nights, his soft and rosy nights, when peace descends on earth from the stars. . . He is the ancestor, the founder, the fertilizer of the Western Soudan, which he has dowered with incalculable wealth, wresting it from the invasion of neighboring Saharas, building it up of his own fertile ooze. It is he who every year at regular seasons floods the valley like an ocean and leaves it rich, pregnant, as it were, with amazing vegetation. Even like the Nile, he has vanquished the sands; he is the father of untold generations, the creative deity of a world as yet unknown, which in later times will enrich old Europe. . . And the valley of the Niger, the good giant's colossal daughter. Ah! what pure immensity is hers; what a flight, so to say, into the infinite! The plain opens and expands, unbroken and limitless. Ever and ever comes the plain, fields are succeeded by other fields stretching out of sight, whose end a plough would only reach in months and months. All the food needed for a great nation will be reaped there when cultivation is practised with a little courage and a little science, for it is still a virgin kingdom such as the good river created it, thousands of years ago. To-morrow this kingdom will belong to the workers who are bold enough to take it, each carving for himself a domain as large as his strength of toil can dream of; not an estate of acres, but leagues and leagues of ploughland wavy with eternal crops. . . And what breadth of atmosphere there is in that immensity! What delight it is to inhale all the air of that space at one breath, and how healthy and strong the life, for one is no longer piled one upon the other, but one feels free and powerful, master of that part of the earth which one has desired under the sun which shines for all."

Benjamin listened and questioned, never satisfied. "How are you installed there?" he asked. "How do you live? What are your habits? What is your work?"

Dominique began to laugh again, conscious as he was that he was astonishing, upsetting all these unknown relatives who pressed so close to him, aglow with increasing curiosity. Women and old men had in turn left their places to draw near to him; even children had gathered around, as if to listen to a fine story.

"Oh! we live in republican fashion," said he; "every member of our community has to help in the common fraternal task. The family counts more or less expert artisans of all kinds for the rough work. My father in particular has revealed himself to be a very skilful mason, for he had to build a place for us when we arrived. He even made his own bricks, thanks to some deposits of clayey soil which exist near Djenny. So our farm is now a little village: each married couple will have its own house. Then, too, we are not only agriculturists, we are fishermen and hunters also. We have our boats; the Niger abounds in fish to an extraordinary degree, and there are wonderful hauls at times. And even the shooting and hunting would suffice to feed us; game is plentiful, there are partridges and wild guinea-fowl, not to mention the flamingoes, the pelicans, the egrets, the thousands of creatures who do not prey on one another. Black lions visit us at times: eagles fly slowly over our heads; at dusk hippopotami come in parties of three and four to gambol in the river with the clumsy grace of negro children bathing. But, after all, we are more particularly cultivators, kings of the plain, especially when the waters of the Niger withdraw after fertilizing our fields. Our estate has no limits; it stretches as far as we can labor. And ah! if you could only see the natives, who do not even plough, but have few if any appliances beyond sticks, with which they just scratch the soil before confiding the seed to it! There is no trouble, no worry; the earth is rich, the sun ardent, and thus the crop will always be a fine one. When we ourselves employ the plough, when we bestow a little care on the soil which teems with life, what prodigious crops there are, an abundance of grain such as your barns could never hold! As soon as we possess the agricultural machinery, which I have come to order here in France, we shall need flotillas of boats in order to send you the overplus of our granaries. . . When the river subsides, when its waters fall, the crop we more particularly grow is rice; there are, indeed, plains of rice, which occasionally yield two crops. Then come millet and ground-beans, and by and by will come corn, when we can grow it on a large scale. Vast cotton fields follow one after the other, and we also grow manioc and indigo, while in our kitchen gardens we have onions and pimentoes, and gourds and cucumbers. And I don't mention the natural vegetation, the precious gum-trees, of which we possess quite a forest; the butter-trees, the flour-trees, the silk-trees, which grow on our ground like briers alongside your roads. . . Finally, we are shepherds; we own ever-increasing flocks, whose numbers we don't even know. Our goats, our bearded sheep may be counted by the thousand; our horses scamper freely through paddocks as large as cities, and when our hunch-backed cattle come down to the Niger to drink at that hour of serene splendor the sunset, they cover a league of the river banks. . . And, above everything else, we are free men and joyous men, working for the delight of living without restraint, and our reward is the thought that our work is very great and good and beautiful, since it is the creation of another France, the sovereign France of to-morrow."

From that moment Dominique paused no more. There was no longer any need to question him, he poured forth all the beauty and grandeur in his mind. He spoke of Djenny, the ancient queen city, whose people and whose monuments came from Egypt, the city which even yet reigns over the valley. He spoke of four other centres, Bamakoo, Niamina, Segu, and Sansandig, big villages which would some day be great towns. And he spoke particularly of Timbuctoo the glorious, so long unknown, with a veil of legends cast over it as if it were some forbidden paradise, with its gold, its ivory, its beautiful women, all rising like a mirage of inaccessible delight beyond the devouring sands. He spoke of Timbuctoo, the gate of the Sahara and the Western Soudan, the frontier town where life ended and met and mingled, whither the camel of the desert brought the weapons and merchandise of Europe as well as salt, that indispensable commodity, and where the pirogues of the Niger landed the precious ivory, the surface gold, the ostrich feathers, the gum, the crops, all the wealth of the fruitful valley. He spoke of Timbuctoo the store-place, the metropolis and market of Central Africa, with its piles of ivory, its piles of virgin gold, its sacks of rice, millet, and ground-nuts, its cakes of indigo, its tufts of ostrich plumes, its metals, its dates, its stuffs, its iron-ware, and particularly its slabs of rock salt, brought on the backs of beasts of burden from Taudeni, the frightful Saharian city of salt, whose soil is salt for leagues around, an infernal mine of that salt which is so precious in the Soudan that it serves as a medium of exchange, as money more precious even than gold. And finally, he spoke of Timbuctoo impoverished, fallen from its high estate, the opulent and resplendent city of former times now almost in ruins, hiding remnants of its treasures behind cracked walls in fear of the robbers of the desert; but withal apt to become once more a city of glory and fortune, royally seated as it is between the Soudan, that granary of abundance, and the Sahara, the road to Europe, as soon as France shall have opened that road, have connected the provinces of her new empire, and have founded that huge new France of which the ancient fatherland will be but the directing mind.

"That is the dream!" cried Dominique, "that is the gigantic work which the future will achieve! Algeria, connected with Timbuctoo by the Sahara railway line, over which electric engines will carry the whole of old Europe through the far expanse of sand! Timbuctoo connected with Senegal by flotillas of steam vessels and yet other railways, all intersecting the vast empire on every side! New France connected with mother France, the old land, by a wondrous development of the means of communication, and founded, and got ready for the hundred millions of inhabitants who will some day spring up there! . . . Doubtless these things cannot be done in a night. The trans-Saharian railway is not yet laid down; there are two thousand five hundred kilometres* of bare desert to be crossed which can hardly tempt railway companies; and a certain amount of prosperity must be developed by starting cultivation, seeking and working mines, and increasing exportations before a pecuniary

---

* About 1,553 English miles.

effort can be possible on the part of the motherland. Moreover, there is the question of the natives, mostly of gentle race, though some are ferocious bandits, whose savagery is increased by religious fanaticism, thus rendering the difficulties of our conquest all the greater. Until the terrible problem of Islamism is solved we shall always be coming in conflict with it. And only life, long years of life, can create a new nation, adapt it to the new land, blend diverse elements together, and yield normal existence, homogeneous strength, and genius proper to the clime. But no matter! From this day a new France is born yonder, a huge empire; and it needs our blood—and some must be given it, in order that it may be peopled and be able to draw its incalculable wealth from the soil, and become the greatest, the strongest, and the mightiest in the world!"

Transported with enthusiasm, quivering at the thought of the distant ideal at last revealed to him, Benjamin sat there with tears in his eyes. Ah! the healthy life! the noble life! the other life! the whole mission and work of which he had as yet but confusedly dreamt! Again he asked a question: "And are there many French families there, colonizing like yours?"

Dominique burst into a loud laugh. "Oh, no," said he, "there are certainly a few colonists in our old possessions of Senegal, but yonder in the Niger valley, beyond Djenny, there are, I think, only ourselves. We are the pioneers, the vanguard, the riskers full of faith and hope. And there is some merit in it, for to sensible stay-at-home folks it all seems like defying common sense. Can you picture it? A French family installed among savages, and unprotected, save for the vicinity of a little fort, where a French officer commands a dozen native soldiers—a French family, which is sometimes called upon to fight in person, and which establishes a farm in a land where the fanaticism of some head tribesman may any day stir up trouble. It seems so insane that folks get angry at the mere thought of it, yet it enraptures us and gives us gayety and health, and the courage to achieve victory. We are opening the road, we are giving the example, we are carrying our dear old France yonder, taking to ourselves a huge expanse of virgin land, which will become a province. We have already founded a village which in a hundred years will be a great town. In the colonies no race is more fruitful than the French, though it seems to become barren on its own ancient soil. Thus we shall swarm and swarm, and fill the world! So come then, come then, all of you; since here you are set too closely, since you lack air in your little fields and your overheated, pestilence-breeding towns. There is room for everybody yonder; there are new lands, there is open air that none has breathed, and there is a task to be accomplished which will make all of you heroes, strong, sturdy men, well pleased to live! Come with me. I will take the men, I will take all the women who are willing, and you will carve for yourselves other provinces and found other cities for the future glory and power of the great new France."

He laughed so gayly, he was so handsome, so spirited, so robust, that once again the whole table acclaimed him. They would certainly not follow him yonder, for all those married couples already had their own nests; and all those young folks were already too strongly rooted to the old land by the ties of their race—a race which after displaying such adventurous instincts has now fallen asleep, as it were, at its own fireside. But what a marvellous story it all was—a story to which big and little alike, had listened in rapture, and which to-morrow would, doubtless, arouse within them a passion for glorious enterprise far away! The seed of the unknown was sown, and would grow into a crop of fabulous magnitude.

For the moment Benjamin was the only one who cried amid the enthusiasm which drowned his words: "Yes, yes, I want to live. Take me, take me with you!"

But Dominique resumed, by way of conclusion: "And there is one thing, grandfather, which I have not yet told you. My father has given the name of Chantebled to our farm yonder. He often tells us how you founded your estate here, in an impulse of far-seeing audacity, although everybody jeered and shrugged their shoulders and declared that you must be mad. And, yonder, my father has to put up with the same derision, the same contemptuous pity, for people declare that the good Niger will some day sweep away our village, even if a band of prowling natives does not kill and eat us! But I'm easy in mind about all that, we shall conquer as you conquered, for what seems to be the folly of action is really divine wisdom. There will be another kingdom of the Froments yonder, another huge Chantebled, of which you and my grandmother will be the ancestors, the distant patriarchs, worshipped like deities. . . And I drink to your health, grandfather, and I drink to yours, grandmother, on behalf of your other future people, who will grow up full of spirit under the burning sun of the tropics!"

Then with great emotion Mathieu, who had risen, replied in a powerful voice: "To your health! my boy. To the health of my son

Nicolas, his wife, Lisbeth, and all who have been born from them! And to the health of all who will follow, from generation to generation!"

And Marianne, who had likewise risen, in her turn said: "To the health of your wives, and your daughters, your spouses and your mothers! To the health of those who will love and produce the greatest sum of life, in order that the greatest possible sum of happiness may follow!"

Then, the banquet ended, they quitted the table and spread freely over the lawn. There was a last ovation around Mathieu and Marianne, who were encompassed by their eager offspring. At one and the same time a score of arms were outstretched, carrying children, whose fair or dark heads they were asked to kiss. Aged as they were, returning to a divine state of childhood, they did not always recognize those little lads and lasses. They made mistakes, used wrong names, fancied that one child was another. Laughter thereupon arose, the mistakes were rectified, and appeals were made to the old people's memory. They likewise laughed, the errors were amusing, but it mattered little if they no longer remembered a name, the child at any rate belonged to the harvest that had sprung from them.

Then there were certain granddaughters and great-granddaughters whom they themselves summoned and kissed by way of bringing good luck to the babes that were expected, the children of their children's children, the race which would ever spread and perpetuate them through the far-off ages. And there were mothers, also, who were nursing, mothers whose little ones, after sleeping quietly during the feast, had now awakened, shrieking their hunger aloud. These had to be fed, and the mothers merrily seated themselves together under the trees and gave them the breast in all serenity. Therein lay the royal beauty of woman, wife and mother; fruitful maternity triumphed over virginity by which life is slain. Ah! might manners and customs change, might the idea of morality and the idea of beauty be altered, and the world recast, based on the triumphant beauty of the mother suckling her babe in all the majesty of her symbolism! From fresh sowings there ever came fresh harvests, the sun ever rose anew above the horizon, and milk streamed forth endlessly like the eternal sap of living humanity. And that river of milk carried life through the veins of the world, and expanded and overflowed for the centuries of the future.

The greatest possible sum of life in order that the greatest possible happiness might result: that was the act of faith in life, the act of hope in the justice and goodness of life's work. Victorious fruitfulness remained the one true force, the sovereign power which alone moulded the future. She was the great revolutionary, the incessant artisan of progress, the mother of every civilization, ever re-creating her army of innumerable fighters, throwing through the centuries millions after millions of poor and hungry and rebellious beings into the fight for truth and justice. Not a single forward step in history has ever been taken without numerousness having urged humanity forward. To-morrow, like yesterday, will be won by the swarming of the multitude whose quest is happiness. And to-morrow will give the benefits which our age has awaited; economic equality obtained even as political equality has been obtained; a just apportionment of wealth rendered easy; and compulsory work re-established as the one glorious and essential need.

It is not true that labor has been imposed on mankind as punishment for sin, it is on the contrary an honor, a mark of nobility, the most precious of boons, the joy, the health, the strength, the very soul of the world, which itself labors incessantly, ever creating the future. And misery, the great, abominable social crime, will disappear amid the glorification of labor, the distribution of the universal task among one and all, each accepting his legitimate share of duties and rights. And may children come, they will simply be instruments of wealth, they will but increase the human capital, the free happiness of a life in which the children of some will no longer be beasts of burden, or food for slaughter or for vice, to serve the egotism of the children of others. And life will then again prove the conqueror; there will come the renascence of life, honored and worshipped, the religion of life so long crushed beneath the hateful nightmare of Roman Catholicism, from which on divers occasions the nations have sought to free themselves by violence, and which they will drive away at last on the now near day when cult and power, and sovereign beauty shall be vested in the fruitful earth and the fruitful spouse.

In that last resplendent hour of eventide, Mathieu and Marianne reigned by virtue of their numerous race. They ended as heroes of life, because of the great creative work which they had accomplished amid battle and toil and grief. Often had they sobbed, but with extreme old age had come peace, deep smiling peace, made up of the good labor performed and the certainty of approaching rest while their children and their children's children resumed the fight, labored and suffered, lived in their own turn. And a part of Mathieu and Marianne's heroic grandeur sprang from the divine desire with which they had glowed, the desire which moulds and regulates the world. They were like a sacred temple in which the god had fixed his abode, they were animated by the inextinguishable fire with which the universe ever burns for the work of continual creation. Their radiant beauty under their white hair came from the light which yet filled their eyes, the light of love's power, which age had been unable to extinguish. Doubtless, as they themselves jestingly remarked at times, they had been prodigals, their family had been such a large one. But, after all, had they not been right? Their children had diminished no other's share, each had come with his or her own means of subsistence. And, besides, 'tis good to garner in excess when the granaries of a country are empty. Many such improvidents are needed to combat the egotism of others at times of great dearth. Amid all the frightful loss and wastage, the race is strengthened, the country is made afresh, a good civic example is given by such healthy prodigality as Mathieu and Marianne had shown.

But a last act of heroism was required of them. A month after the festival, when Dominique was on the point of returning to the Soudan, Benjamin one evening told them of his passion, of the irresistible summons from the unknown distant plains, which he could but obey.

"Dear father, darling mother, let me go with Dominique! I have struggled, I feel horrified with myself at quitting you thus, at your great age. But I suffer too dreadfully; my soul is full of yearnings, and seems ready to burst; and I shall die of shameful sloth, if I do not go."

They listened with breaking hearts. Their son's words did not surprise them; they had heard them coming ever since their diamond wedding. And they trembled, and felt that they could not refuse; for they knew that they were guilty in having kept their last-born in the family nest after surrendering to life all the others. Ah! how insatiable life was—it would not so much as suffer that tardy avarice of theirs; it demanded even the precious, discreetly hidden treasure from which, with jealous egotism, they had dreamt of parting only when they might find themselves upon the threshold of the grave.

Deep silence reigned; but at last Mathieu slowly answered: "I cannot keep you back, my son; go whither life calls you. . . If I knew, however, that I should die to-night, I would ask you to wait till to-morrow."

In her turn Marianne gently said: "Why cannot we die at once? We should then escape this last great pang, and you would only carry our memory away with you."

Once again did the cemetery of Janville appear, the field of peace, where dear ones already slept, and where they would soon join them. No sadness tinged that thought, however; they hoped that they would lie down there together on the same day, for they could not imagine life, one without the other. And, besides, would they not forever live in their children; forever be united, immortal, in their race?

"Dear father, darling mother," Benjamin repeated; "it is I who will be dead to-morrow if I do not go. To wait for your death—good God! would not that be to desire it? You must still live long years, and I wish to live like you."

There came another pause, then Mathieu and Marianne replied together: "Go then, my boy. You are right, one must live."

But on the day of farewell, what a wrench, what a final pang there was when they had to tear themselves from that flesh of their flesh, all that remained to them, in order to hand over to life the supreme gift it demanded! The departure of Nicolas seemed to begin afresh; again came the "never more" of the migratory child taking wing, given to the passing wind for the sowing of unknown distant lands, far beyond the frontiers.

"Never more!" cried Mathieu in tears.

And Marianne repeated in a great sob which rose from the very depths of her being: "Never more! Never more!"

There was now no longer any mere question of increasing a family, of building up the country afresh, of re-peopling France for the struggles of the future, the question was one of the expansion of humanity, of the reclaiming of deserts, of the peopling of the entire earth. After one's country came the earth; after one's family, one's nation, and then mankind. And what an invading flight, what a sudden outlook upon the world's immensity! All the freshness of the oceans, all the perfumes of virgin continents, blended in a mighty gust like a breeze from the offing. Scarcely fifteen hundred million souls are to-day scattered through the few cultivated patches of the globe, and is that not indeed paltry, when the globe, ploughed from end to end, might nourish ten times that number? What narrowness of mind there is in seeking to limit mankind to its present figure, in admitting simply the continuance of exchanges among nations, and of capitals dying where they stand—as Babylon, Nineveh, and Memphis died—while other queens of the earth arise, inherit, and flourish amid fresh forms of civilization, and this without population ever more increasing! Such a theory is deadly, for nothing remains stationary: whatever ceases to increase decreases and disappears. Life is the rising tide whose waves daily continue the work of creation, and perfect the work of awaited happiness, which shall come when the times are accomplished. The flux and reflux of nations are but periods of the forward march: the great centuries of light, which dark ages at times replace, simply mark the phases of that march. Another step forward is ever taken, a little more of the earth is conquered, a little more life is brought into play. The law seems to lie in a double phenomenon; fruitfulness creating civilization, and civilization restraining fruitfulness. And equilibrium will come from it all on the day when the earth, being entirely inhabited, cleared, and utilized, shall at last have accomplished its destiny. And the divine dream, the generous utopian thought soars into the heavens; families blended into nations, nations blended into mankind, one sole brotherly people making of the world one sole city of peace and truth and justice! Ah! may eternal fruitfulness ever expand, may the seed of humanity be carried over the frontiers, peopling the untilled deserts afar, and increasing mankind through the coming centuries until dawns the reign of sovereign life, mistress at last both of time and of space!

And after the departure of Benjamin, whom Dominique took with him, Mathieu and Marianne recovered the joyful serenity and peace born of the work which they had so prodigally accomplished. Nothing more was theirs; nothing save the happiness of having given all to life. The "Never more" of separation became the "Still more" of life—life incessantly increasing, expanding beyond the limitless horizon. Candid and smiling, those all but centenarian heroes triumphed in the overflowing florescence of their race. The milk had streamed even athwart the seas—from the old land of France to the immensity of virgin Africa, the young and giant France of to-morrow. After the foundation of Chantebled, on a disdained, neglected spot of the national patrimony, another Chantebled was rising and becoming a kingdom in the vast deserted tracts which life yet had to fertilize. And this was the exodus, human expansion throughout the world, mankind upon the march towards the Infinite.

ÉMILE ZOLA

A Note About the Author

Émile Zola (1840–1902) was a French novelist, journalist, and playwright. Born in Paris to a French mother and Italian father, Zola was raised in Aix-en-Provence. At 18, Zola moved back to Paris, where he befriended Paul Cézanne and began his writing career. During this early period, Zola worked as a clerk for a publisher while writing literary and art reviews as well as political journalism for local newspapers. Following the success of his novel *Thérèse Raquin* (1867), Zola began a series of twenty novels known as *Les Rougon-Macquart*, a sprawling collection following the fates of a single family living under the Second Empire of Napoleon III. Zola's work earned him a reputation as a leading figure in literary naturalism, a style noted for its rejection of Romanticism in favor of detachment, rationalism, and social commentary. Following the infamous Dreyfus affair of 1894, in which a French-Jewish artillery officer was falsely convicted of spying for the German Embassy, Zola wrote a scathing open letter to French President Félix Faure accusing the government and military of antisemitism and obstruction of justice. Having sacrificed his reputation as a writer and intellectual, Zola helped reverse public opinion on the affair, placing pressure on the government that led to Dreyfus' full exoneration in 1906. Nominated for the Nobel Prize in Literature in 1901 and 1902, Zola is considered one of the most influential and talented writers in French history.

A Note from the Publisher

Spanning many genres, from non-fiction essays to literature classics to children's books and lyric poetry, Mint Edition books showcase the master works of our time in a modern new package. The text is freshly typeset, is clean and easy to read, and features a new note about the author in each volume. Many books also include exclusive new introductory material. Every book boasts a striking new cover, which makes it as appropriate for collecting as it is for gift giving. Mint Edition books are only printed when a reader orders them, so natural resources are not wasted. We're proud that our books are never manufactured in excess and exist only in the exact quantity they need to be read and enjoyed.

Discover more of your favorite classics with Bookfinity™.

- Track your reading with custom book lists.
- Get great book recommendations for your personalized Reader Type.
- Add reviews for your favorite books.
- AND MUCH MORE!

Visit **bookfinity.com** and take the fun Reader Type quiz to get started.

Enjoy our classic and modern companion pairings!

Bookfinity is a registered trademark of Ingram Book Group LLC. © 2023 Bookfinity. All rights reserved.

Printed in the USA
CPSIA information can be obtained
at www.ICGtesting.com
JSHW022204140824
68134JS00018B/857

9 781513 281056